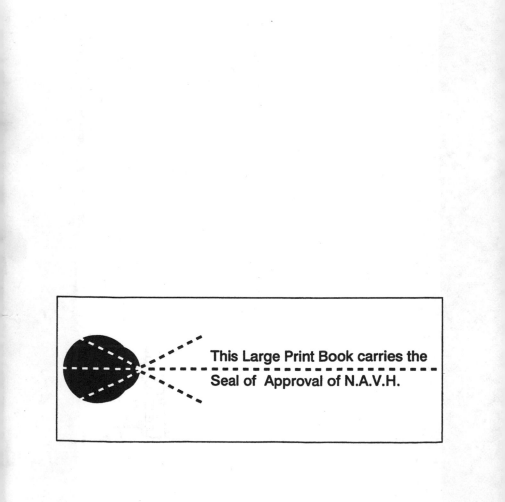

DOCTOR
ON
TRIAL

Henry Denker

Thorndike Press • Thorndike, Maine

Library of Congress Cataloging in Publication Data:

Denker, Henry.
  Doctor on trial / Henry Denker. — 1st ed.
    p. cm.
  ISBN 1-56054-603-4 (alk. paper : lg. print)
  1. Large type books. I. Title.
  [PS3507.E5475D6   1993]   92-38685
  813'.54—dc20   CIP

Thorndike Large Print® General Series edition published in 1993 by arrangement with William Morrow and Company, Inc.

Cover design by James B. Murray.

The tree indicium is a trademark of Thorndike Press.

This book is printed on acid-free, high opacity paper. ∞

To Edith, my wife

Chapter One

"Get Dr. Forrester!" the frantic call rang through the Emergency Service of City Hospital. "We got a gunshot wound here! A bleeder!"

Two orderlies rushed the gurney toward the Acute Care room at the end of the corridor. One of them calling again, "Dr. Forrester!"

In one of the examining rooms Dr. Kate Forrester turned from the patient she had been treating and said to the nurse, "Take over! Send this blood specimen to the lab. Call me the minute the results get back!"

Kate Forrester raced out of the room and along the corridor. The loose, untended condition of her blond hair, lack of makeup, wrinkled condition of her lab coat testified to the many hours of continuous service she had already put in on the Emergency Service. Saturday nights in Emergency in this large New York City hospital were always hectic. Tonight was even more so because the doctor scheduled to serve with Kate had come down with a bad case of the flu. Kate had been promised help, but as yet none had arrived. So she did what young resident doctors always do — the best they can, under seemingly impossible circumstances.

As she hurried past Examining Room C, Nurse Adelaide Cronin called, "Doctor, when you have a moment . . ." But Kate raced on toward Acute Care, where a young lad of fourteen lay bleeding from a gunshot wound to the arm suffered because he had unfortunately been caught in the line of fire between two competing drug dealers on a West Side street not far from where City Hospital stood.

Aware of the demands on Dr. Forrester's time on this night, Nurse Cronin turned back to the patient in Room C to begin taking a preliminary history. A competent nurse with more than sixteen years' experience, Cronin would have preferred to carry out this function without interference. But the mother of the patient persisted in hovering over her protectively.

"Tell me," Cronin addressed the patient, a dark-haired woman of nineteen, "what brought you here?"

Her mother interrupted. "I would like you to summon a doctor. My daughter is very sick. I want her to have the best medical attention."

"I've already notified Dr. Forrester," Cronin protested.

"I want the chief of service," the woman insisted. "We can afford the best."

8

"I'm afraid that at this hour on a Saturday night the chief would not be available," Cronin said, turning back to the patient. "Now, then, what brought you in?"

"She was suffering from nausea and vomiting . . ." her mother replied.

Aware of any mother's natural concern, Cronin took a moment to explain. "Mrs. . . . ."

"Stuyvesant," the women replied, "Mrs. *Claude* Stuyvesant."

The name was instantly recognizable to Cronin, but did not alter her routine or her attitude.

"Mrs. Stuyvesant, since this information must be entered on the patient's chart, as long as she is able to answer, it is best to have her symptoms in her own words. It makes for an accurate record. It helps the doctor to arrive at a diagnosis. So, please . . ."

"Sorry," the mother said, retreating a step from the examining table on which her daughter lay. From the manner in which the patient's dark hair was matted to her perspiring forehead, from the slightly spasmodic way in which she breathed, from the tension obvious in her body, Cronin could read some of the signs of the young woman's distress. She resumed her question, at the same time taking her pulse and her blood pressure.

"Now, tell me, what brought you in?"

9

In a voice shaded by pain, the young woman replied, haltingly, "It started around six this morning . . ."

"What started?" Cronin asked.

"The pain. In my stomach. Then I . . . I began to get this nausea," the patient said, sounding lethargic.

"Vomit?" Cronin asked.

"Yes. Not much came up. That's when I . . . the, the sweating began."

"Claudia, darling, don't forget about your diarrhea," her mother reminded.

"I was getting to that, Mother. There's been . . . there was diarrhea."

"Severe?" Cronin asked.

Claudia Stuyvesant made an attempt to recall before she said, "Not really," and closed her eyes as if about to drift off to sleep.

By that time Cronin had determined that the patient had a pulse rate of 110. Tachycardia. Diaphoresis, heavy sweating. Blood pressure 100/60. Cronin slipped a fresh aseptic plastic sleeve over the digital thermometer.

"Under your tongue, please," she said, then reached to the wall-mounted cabinet to assemble the materials she would need for an intravenous infusion. The combination of diarrhea and rapid pulse indicated to Cronin that the young woman was likely suffering from dehydration.

10

The temperature reading of 100.2 served to reinforce that assumption. Once Cronin had affixed the I.V., Mrs. Stuyvesant asked, "Aren't you going to give her anything?"

"Only the doctor can prescribe," Cronin replied.

"Then, where is he?" the woman asked. "We've been here almost half an hour. First out at the Admitting Desk, then waiting for you —"

"Mrs. Stuyvesant, in Emergency we see each patient just as soon as we can. Now, Dr. Forrester will be in very soon." With that Cronin left the room.

"Well, I never —" the woman exclaimed.

Despite her discomfort, her daughter pleaded, "Mother, please . . . not one of your scenes, please?" She closed her eyes again.

"Believe me, if Dr. Eaves were in town, he'd have been at your apartment in a second. But of all times to get sick — a Saturday night."

"Mother, please?"

"I don't like to remind you, Claudia, but who was it who said a year ago, 'Mother, I'm eighteen, and able to take care of myself. I'm going out on my own.' Wasn't me, wasn't your father. Eighteen," she repeated sadly. "In our circle, when I was your age, a girl came out at eighteen. She was married to a nice young man by twenty or twenty-one. But these days . . . these days . . ."

At that moment, having clamped off the bleeding artery in the young gunshot victim and sent him up to Surgery, Kate Forrester was ready to join Nurse Cronin, who awaited her outside Room C. Cronin briefed the doctor on the case. They entered the room.

At a glance Kate took in the relationship. Nervous mother. Uncomfortable daughter. First, put them both at ease. Establish a personal relationship. Kate asked the patient, "Well, now, your name?"

Before the patient could respond, the mother replied, "She's already been questioned by one nurse. We want her to be seen by a doctor."

"I *am* a doctor," Kate Forrester replied.

The woman seemed about to dispute her until her eyes fixed on the plastic identification badge on the lapel of Kate's white lab coat: DR. K. FORRESTER.

"Oh!" Mrs. Stuyvesant said, in a single sound expressing her surprise and embarrassment. "I'm . . . I'm sure you'll do the best you can."

Half annoyed, half amused by the woman's reply, Kate was now free to turn her attention to the patient.

"Your name?"

"Claudia Stuyvesant," the patient said with a slight pain-induced gasp.

Kate observed the patient was lethargic as well, having difficulty focusing her eyes. She reached for the patient's pulse, not only to confirm Cronin's findings but to take the time to absorb the medical situation.

Young woman, nineteen, possibly twenty. Generalized symptoms. In pain, at the same time lethargic. Lethargic, yet under considerable emotional tension. Is she tense because of the presence of her worried mother or from fear of a serious ailment? Surely her mother's presence is not helping. How will they respond if I have to admit her and keep her overnight?

If Kate could persuade the girl to talk freely, she might, with a few target questions, put her at ease and possibly arrive at a reasonably accurate diagnosis.

"All right, now, Claudia, tell me why you're here."

"It should be obvious why she's here," her mother replied.

"Please, Mrs. . . ." Kate began.

"Mrs. Stuyvesant. Mrs. *Claude* Stuyvesant," the mother replied, expecting that Kate would respond with instant recognition.

But the importance of that name was of far less consequence to Kate than her patient's condition. So she suggested, "Mrs. Stuyvesant, there is a reception area out at the Admitting Desk. Why not wait out there?" When the woman gave no indication of moving, Kate asked, "Please?"

"It's . . . it's all right, Doctor," the young patient interceded.

To relieve the patient of both guilt and embarrassment, Kate said, "If you must remain, Mrs. Stuyvesant, please allow the patient to answer my questions." She turned back to her patient. "Now, Claudia, what brought you here?"

"Stomach pains."

"When did they start?"

"Early this morning."

"You told *me* they just started tonight," her mother intervened, but a look from Kate caused her to say, "Sorry."

"Claudia, have you had such stomach pains before?" Kate asked.

"No, not like this. This is different."

"Different. How?"

"Hurts more," was all Claudia could add.

Kate Forrester scanned the sheet on which Cronin had recorded her findings.

"It says here you complain of vomiting. How often? When?"

"Since this morning. Several times."

"Bad?" the doctor asked.

14

"I get nausea. I *feel* like vomiting. But . . . but . . ."

"But nothing comes up?" Kate suggested.

"Right. Nothing much."

"Claudia, when did you eat last?"

"Last night." She tried to recall, then added, "Afternoon . . . yesterday afternoon actually."

The doctor was trying to tie together a group of vaguely defined symptoms and signs to arrive at a tentative diagnosis.

This patient is too young for me to consider a diagnosis of a heart attack. The signs and symptoms she presents — slight fever, racing pulse, nausea, diarrhea, abdominal pain — would likely indicate a stomach virus or some kind of food poisoning. But they could also indicate appendicitis or dozens of other illnesses.

"Claudia, point out exactly where your pain started."

"Kind of like . . . like sort of all over."

"Show me," the doctor said.

The young woman traced her hand over her stomach in a generalized way.

"Not in the center of the stomach?" Claudia shook her head. "And it didn't move down to here?" Kate indicated the lower right quadrant of the stomach. Again Claudia shook her head. While that ruled out the likelihood of an inflamed appendix, it brought the doctor no closer to a diagnosis.

15

Claudia's rapid pulse was a disturbing factor — that plus her low grade fever, which could cause dehydration. Together they could be a sign of sepsis, infection, somewhere in her body. But dehydration could also result from diarrhea and lack of food.

With so little to go on, Kate turned to ask Nurse Cronin for a kit to take a blood sample. The nurse had anticipated her. Kate tightened the rubber tube around Claudia's arm above her elbow, causing a vein to protrude. She eased the hypodermic needle in carefully, drew up the plunger until the transparent plastic tube was filled with dark blood. She passed the tube to Cronin.

"Complete CBC and electrolytes. Tell the lab I want them stat! And let's send up a urine specimen. Meantime we'll keep her on the I.V. until the results come back."

Once Cronin hurried out with the blood sample, Kate said, "Claudia, while we're waiting, I'd like to ask you a few questions and do a physical. So let's get that shirt off. I want to go over your chest and back."

As Claudia started to unbutton her blouse, from down the corridor the distress call of a nurse could be heard.

"Dr. Forrester! Dr. Forrester!"

The urgency in that voice told Kate that her services were demanded in a life-threatening situation. With a hasty "I'll be back," Kate started for the door.

Mrs. Stuyvesant stood in the doorway, demanding, "Doctor! You're not leaving my sick daughter, are you?"

"They need me," Kate responded as she brushed by Mrs. Stuyvesant, barely touching her.

"Well, I never . . . deserting a sick patient," the woman complained.

"Mother, please?" Claudia Stuyvesant said weakly.

Kate Forrester raced down the hall toward the nurse who stood in the open doorway of one of the examining rooms. Kate entered to find a man, no more than thirty-three or thirty-four, she judged. Sensors for an electrocardiogram had been taped to his chest, arms, and legs by the nurse, who reported briskly, "Severe pain just below the breastbone. Profuse diaphoresis."

Dr. Forrester had already made those observations. The grimace on the man's unshaven face, the sweat that oozed from his brow had told her that. Both could be signs of a heart attack. The look in his eyes betrayed one thing more: Fear. Fear, too, could be a symptom in cases of severe heart attack. Somehow a patient often sensed when he was close to dying. This patient was exhibiting that high degree of fear.

Kate Forrester read the first cardiogram tape that revealed the patient's heart action. As the tape continued to flow from the machine, the gasping man's eyes pleaded, *Tell me, Doctor, am I going to die?*

Kate was relieved to say, "Your heart's doing fine. Just fine. You are not going to die."

"But the pain . . ." was all he was able to say through his spasmodic breathing.

"Your pain will go away very soon," Kate assured, then ordered the nurse, "Demerol. One hundred m.g.'s. And do a chest plate." She stethoscoped the patient's back and chest to rule out other possibilities. "Get a blood up to the lab. Stat. I want a reading on his bilirubin as soon as possible. If I'm right, he's passing a gallstone. Possibly lodged in the bile duct. Meantime get him into X ray. And call me when you get the plate."

She smiled at the patient to reassure him and she left.

Kate started back toward Room C, to discover Mrs. Stuyvesant staring at her from the doorway. When Kate reached her, the woman said, "I trust that now you will be able to give my daughter your undivided attention."

18

Kate did not dignify the remark with even a glance. She approached the examining table and her young patient.

"Now, Claudia, where were we?"

"You had just asked her to take off her blouse," the mother was quick to remind.

Kate's first impulse was to resent the reminder, but instead she said, "Thank you. Now, Claudia, let's do a thorough chest and back examination. Off with that blouse. And sit up, please."

Claudia finished unbuttoning her blouse and wriggled out of it, revealing her chest and her bare breasts.

In a young woman of nineteen, presenting such symptoms, Kate could not rule out pregnancy as a possible cause, so, while she asked, "Have you eaten anything unusual in the past twenty-four hours?" she tried to determine if the patient's breasts were even slightly engorged the way they might be if she were pregnant. They did not appear to be.

"No, I ate nothing unusual, not that . . . not that I can think of," Claudia Stuyvesant said.

"Did you feel feverish earlier today?" Kate asked as she began to stethoscope the patient's chest.

"No," Claudia said, stiffening to the feel of Kate's cold stethoscope.

19

"Anyone at home experiencing similar symptoms?"

"Isn't anyone at home. I mean I . . . I live alone."

"And you can see what comes of that," her mother was quick to add.

"Mother, please . . ."

"Have you ever had any previous stomach problems?" Kate asked.

"No. Nothing like this," Claudia responded.

"Gall bladder attack?"

"No."

Kate knew the lab reports would confirm or refute that. She tried to appear casual and routine as she asked a most significant question.

"Do you regularly use drugs of any kind? Prescribed, over the counter, or any other?"

There was a moment of hesitation before Claudia replied. "No. No drugs."

Kate Forrester was forced to evaluate. *Is she denying the use of drugs because her mother is in the room? Or because it is true? If true, why that slight hesitation? Or is her hesitation due to her lethargic condition?*

Rather than press the issue, Kate continued her physical examination in silence. She listened to the patient's lungs, seeking telltale sounds, sounds that resembled snores, which might indicate bronchitis. There were none.

Nor did she find rasping sounds like Velcro ripping apart, which would indicate pneumonia. She percussed the young woman's back and chest, evoking a drumlike sound, thus ruling out any possibility of fluid in the lungs.

Kate lowered the focus of her examination to direct several light blows to the young patient's back, to see if she flinched in pain. She did not, thereby ruling out the likelihood of a kidney condition. In fact Kate detected that, in her lethargic state, the patient hardly reacted at all.

Kate examined the young woman's abdomen. The skin was still lightly tanned, except where she had worn a bikini last summer. Her abdomen rose and fell not with uneventful regularity but with a slight jerkiness that reflected moderate stomach pain. There was a fading bruise on her right hip. But the more important discovery Kate made was the lack of any wounds or evidence of previous surgery. So there was no reason to consider an intestinal obstruction due to resulting adhesions.

Kate also observed that the patient moved her head freely and had not complained of headaches. So the possibility of nervous-system disorder could be ruled out for the moment.

Kate applied her stethoscope to the young

woman's abdomen, listening for normal stomach sounds. Considering the circumstances, they were not too diminished. She pressed gently along the lower left quadrant of Claudia's abdomen, the area of the descending colon, suspecting there might be some inflammation and tenderness there. Colitis could give rise to the patient's generalized symptoms. But colitis usually presented a history of continuous symptoms, and this patient said her pain was unprecedented. So that diagnosis seemed unlikely.

Yet her diarrhea must be accounted for. There could be any number of causes. Kate had seen cases of young women who, to combat headaches or menstrual pain, had overused such over-the-counter drugs as Advil or Motrin. Which led to inflammation of the stomach, in turn causing them to take large quantities of antacids, such as Maalox or Mylanta, the overuse of which could induce diarrhea.

With signs and symptoms so vague and nonspecific, Kate could not afford to overlook any possible cause. She used the next phase of her examination as a pretext to be free of the nervous mother as well.

"Mrs. Stuyvesant, I'm about to do a pelvic examination. I think the patient would appreciate privacy."

"I'm her mother. There is no need for privacy between us," Mrs. Stuyvesant replied as she remained unmoved.

Kate slipped on transparent plastic gloves and proceeded to perform a bimanual pelvic examination, at the same time asking a question she had previously delayed because of the mother's presence.

"Claudia, have you been sexually active?"

"No," the young woman replied, reinforcing that with, "No, I haven't."

As Kate continued her examination, she asked, "Your last menstrual period . . . on time?"

"Yes."

"When you do have your period, do you use tampons?" Kate asked, considering the possibility of toxic shock syndrome.

"No. No tampons."

Kate had completed her pelvic examination. The patient had evidenced no sign of pelvic pain. So PID, pelvic inflammatory disease, could be ruled out. While Claudia's uterus felt slightly enlarged, it was not sufficiently so as to indicate an existing pregnancy. In addition, there was no noticeable discoloration of the cervix. Nor had Kate discovered any marked swelling in the fallopian tubes, eliminating that area as the source of Claudia's symptoms.

In a compulsively protective need to ensure

her daughter's privacy, Mrs. Stuyvesant helped her pull her jeans back up.

One thing was apparent to Kate: Claudia Stuyvesant was not a surgical emergency. Kate Forrester decided that until the results came down from the lab, the most conservative course was to continue the patient on the I.V. to fight dehydration and await developments. As she was noting her findings and conclusions on the patient's chart, there was a loud call from the Admitting Desk, "Dr. Forrester! Dr. Forrester!"

Kate interrupted writing up the patient's chart and started for the door.

"You're not leaving my daughter *again,* are you?" Nora Stuyvesant demanded. "Without *doing* anything?"

"Mrs. Stuyvesant, until your daughter's results come down from the lab, there is nothing more to be done for her."

The woman followed Kate out into the corridor. "You could at least give her an antibiotic!"

"Mrs. Stuyvesant, I appreciate your motherly concern, but an antibiotic would not be effective against a stomach virus. Which is what I suspect right now. And it might also have side effects."

Kate started away.

"Doctor! I want you to know that my husband is very well connected with important members of the board of trustees of this hospital and . . ."

What had been intended as a warning, if not a threat, was lost on Dr. Kate Forrester, who had only one thought in mind. Get to that next patient.

Chapter Two

Kate Forrester raced down the corridor toward the room alongside the Admitting Desk. From the urgency of the call, she knew the patient would be in the treatment room fitted out with EKG equipment, oxygen, and the other paraphernalia necessary for immediate treatment of a heart attack victim.

Her instinct proved right. On the examining table lay a robust man who appeared to be in his late fifties, his sweaty face whiter than pale, his huge, hairy chest heaving spasmodically. The nurse had already affixed the EKG sensors to his chest, arms, and legs. Oxygen tubes had been inserted into his nostrils. The nurse and an attendant were at the table awaiting Kate's diagnosis and orders.

Forrester quickly undid the belt of the patient's trousers, unzipped them, pulled them down sufficiently to have access to his stomach. While he heaved in staccato breaths, the fear of death clear on his sweaty face, Kate pushed on his bulging belly to make sure it was not distended and hard. It was not.

He was clearly not an abdominal case. She used her stethoscope to listen to his chest and back, testing for fluid in his lungs. No sign of that either. All signs pointed to a cardiac infarct. A shot of nitroglycerine was indicated to increase blood flow to his heart and reduce his pain. But there were dangers, too, if his blood pressure was too low. Kate tested and found that his pressure was high enough.

"Nitro," she ordered the nurse, who had taken care of so many heart attack cases in E.R., she knew the dosage too well to need reminding.

Kate studied the results of the EKG as they rolled out of the machine. Their erratic pattern confirmed that this was indeed a cardiac infarct of life-threatening size. She had to consider administering streptokinase to reopen the clogged arteries to his heart. Given within six hours of the onset of an attack, that drug could prevent permanent and possibly fatal damage to the heart.

But she would have to ascertain certain information before she could safely prescribe it, or strepto might do more harm than the attack itself.

She stood over the man, whose terror-stricken eyes were pleading for reassurance.

"Ever had an ulcer?" she asked. The man did not seem to understand. "An ulcer," Kate repeated. "Have you ever had —" Kate sensed the trouble. She called out, "Find Juan Castillo!"

The call went down the corridor: "Juan!"

"Hey, Castillo, they need you in Cardiac!" a distant voice relayed the call.

"Juan Castillo! Juan!"

By the time the summons had been transmitted from voice to voice, a slim, dark-haired young man came bounding into the room.

"Yes, Doctor?" he asked, his words tinged with a Spanish flavor.

"Juan, ask him, has he ever had an ulcer problem?"

Juan translated. The man responded through spasmodic breathing, "No."

"Ever had a stroke? Or a history of small strokes?" the doctor asked.

Again Juan translated. Again the man responded, "No."

Kate considered his answers for a moment, then ordered the nurse, "Get a specimen and check his stool for blood. I want the results stat."

"Streptokinase?" the nurse anticipated.

"I'd better check his blood pressure again." Kate pumped up the pressure cuff, which had been attached to his arm from the time he had been brought in. She applied her stethoscope to his arm, listened, then said, "One-forty over ninety. Not high enough to contraindicate strepto. Let me know as soon as those stool results come back. Meantime give him a shot of morphine for his pain."

Even before Kate had completed her orders to the nurse, a voice sought her out from the Admitting Desk: "Dr. Forrester! Dr. Forrester!"

She started toward the door, only to collide with Mrs. Stuyvesant, who had come seeking her.

"Doctor, my daughter is growing very restless. I insist you come look at her at once!"

"Mrs. Stuyvesant, there is nothing more we can do without those lab results," the doctor replied.

"How long will they take?" the woman demanded.

"Doctor!" came the urgent call from the front desk.

"I have to go," Kate Forrester said, seeking to slip by the woman, who blocked her way.

"My daughter needs your attention as much as anyone. And she needs it now!" Mrs. Stuyvesant insisted.

Nevertheless Kate reached out to edge the woman gently aside and, with a soft "I'm sorry," she started down the corridor.

Mrs. Stuyvesant glared after her, saying under her breath, "No one, not even a doctor, treats a Stuyvesant this way!"

As Dr. Kate Forrester reached the Admitting Desk, she was confronted by an old man who breathed in a spasmodic, painful manner similar to the cardiac patient she had just left. He appeared to be in his seventies. The grizzled white stubble on his sunken cheeks indicated that he had not shaved in three days or more. His face was so ruddy, the blue veins stood out, testifying to prolonged exposure to the outdoors.

His watery brown eyes blinked erratically. His forehead was damp. His thin lips dry, his lower lip was cracked in two places. His clothes were old, badly worn, the collar of his shirt frayed and dirty. When Kate took his hand to find his pulse, she noticed that the cuff of his old tweed jacket was frayed beyond mending.

His pulse was slow but regular; still, he complained, "The pain, Doctor. It's the pain brought me. I need something for pain."

She started to open his coat and shirt to test his chest and his stomach in an effort to localize his pain. His clothes were so old and dirty that she had to force herself to do it. Gingerly she parted his coat, then unbuttoned the remaining two buttons on his shirt. She applied her stethoscope. She listened while he continued to repeat, "The pain, it's the pain."

"Where?" she asked.

"All over. And it's bad. Very bad."

In her earliest course on basic diagnosis in medical school, the maxim had been drilled into her, Pain everywhere is pain nowhere. From what she observed, that could well be the case with this old man. But she had also been warned of the folly of jumping to the first and easiest diagnosis.

She tested his back and chest. Found no signs of fluid. She concentrated on his heart action. It was regular, steady, slow. She pressed her fingers into his stomach. Listened to his stomach sounds. Aside from indications of lack of a recent meal, she found nothing disturbing. She had barely completed her examination when she noticed Clara Beathard, one of the older nurses, standing not far from the table. Signaling with a slight movement of her head that, accompanied by a look in her eyes, warned, *Doctor, I need a word with you.*

Kate slipped away from the table.

"Doctor, you're wasting your time," Beathard whispered. "I've seen him before. More than once. Always the same symptoms. Always on rainy nights."

"Rainy . . ." Kate started to ask, until it dawned on her, and Beathard confirmed.

"You've been on duty so long, you don't know. Been raining since early this morning.

Whenever we get a long, steady rain, this old bird comes in with his phony symptoms. Don't waste your time, Dr. Forrester. Get rid of him."

"I suspected he was faking."

"With no other doctor on duty," the nurse said, "you've got your hands full as it is. I'll get rid of him for you."

"Right," Kate agreed. As the nurse started toward the old man, Kate said, "Hold it." She gestured Beathard back, then whispered, "Before you send him out, give him some hot coffee and a sandwich if you can find one."

"We only encourage him when we do," Beathard warned.

"I'll take that risk," Kate said. "After all, it's raining out and cold."

She started back to her last patient.

Chapter Three

In the Cardiac room Kate Forrester found her patient less stressed than he had been. Morphine had eased his pain. He no longer seemed so fearful of dying. He did not realize that was still an imminent threat.

Kate examined the EKG readings produced in the last few minutes. There was no question of a coronary infarct.

"When the lab reports and that blood stool come down," she ordered, "rush him up to Cardiac ICU with orders to put him on streptokinase if the results permit."

She reached the patient's side. "You're going to be okay. Just . . . just relax," she said. Even though he did not understand her words, she intended to reassure him by her attitude.

She started out of the cardiac treatment room only to be alerted by the shrill cry of a woman emanating from the Admissions area.

"Somebody! *Por favor! Mi niña!* My baby!" the woman cried out.

As Kate Forrester turned in the direction of the outcry, she could see, down the corridor, standing at the open door of Emergency

Room C, Mrs. Claude Stuyvesant, glaring in her direction. The woman obviously refused to accept the fact that without the lab results any treatment of her daughter might not only be useless but could prove dangerous.

Since the outcry from the Admissions area was a sound of true alarm, Kate ignored Mrs. Stuyvesant as she raced on the way to the Admitting Desk. There she found a young woman of obvious Hispanic origin, clutching to her breast a child of three or four, who appeared not to be asleep but yet whose eyes were lightly closed.

Kate eased open the child's eyelids to test for reflexive responses to a flashlight. The child's eyes did not respond in normal fashion.

"Doctor? Doctor?" the mother begged, as she twisted a rosary in her nervous fingers. "*Por favor,* Doctor, what is?"

Kate started to remove the child's clothes to make a cursory examination, asking, "Tell me what happened."

"Nothing happen . . ." the mother protested. "Maria she sleepin' and I see she is not breathin' too good. So I listen. Then I think better to see the doctor. I bring her here."

By that time Kate had completed a hurried examination of the child's arms, legs, and torso. Sadly she discovered what she had sus-

34

pected, a variety of black-and-blue hematomas, two other signs that appeared to be healed burns. Kate suspected a healed fracture in one leg and a swelling in the other.

"Did you ever hit Maria?" Kate asked.

"*Nada! Nunca!* Never hit!" the woman protested.

"Did *anyone* ever hit her?"

"No. *Nadie.* Nobody," the woman insisted. "But Maria she fall. She hurt herself."

Kate carried out several basic neurological tests and was sufficiently disturbed by her findings to decide that a complete set of X rays of the child's body was mandatory before referring her to the Department of Pediatric Neurology for further evaluation. If her suspicions were confirmed, the neurologist should also do an electroencephalogram and order a CAT scan of the child's brain.

"You have to leave her overnight."

"No, no! No can leave her," the mother protested.

"If you want her to live, you'd better leave her!" Kate Forrester ordered.

At that the woman began to weep. She tried to take the child in her arms, but Kate forbade it. "Don't! Now, go to the desk and give the clerk all the information. I will take care of Maria."

"No . . . no . . . I no can leave. . . .

No. . . ." the woman protested, weeping more freely and far more fearful and disturbed now.

At that moment from the entrance to Emergency was heard the angry, hoarse voice of a man insisting, "Felicia! *Dónde estás?* Where are you? I know you here! Felicia!"

The woman's reaction to that voice, the fit of trembling that seized her, told Kate Forrester that the angry man was either the woman's intimidating husband or her live-in male companion.

"Please, I got to take Maria . . . I got to. He will be very bad with me. . . ."

By that time the man had found them. He came charging toward them. He was short, but broad and powerful of build. His eyes, black and piercing, were hostile and enraged, like a man betrayed.

"Felicia!" he commanded. "Pick Maria up!"

The woman was torn between obeying her man and Kate Forrester's firm, forbidding shake of the head.

"I say, pick her up. Take her. We go home!" The mother hesitated. He shouted *"Rápido!"*

The woman was frozen with fear. But his glare proved more domineering than his words, for it carried a threat that Kate could well surmise. The woman yielded. She moved to sweep up the child in her arms. But Kate

Forrester intervened physically, placing herself between the mother and the gurney on which the child lay.

The man gestured the doctor away from the child. "*Quítate!* Doctor! *Quítate!* Move!"

"Maria stays here. She is very sick," Kate declared.

"I am the father," the man replied. "I decide if she is sick!" He approached the gurney expecting the doctor would give way. Kate did not. He reached out to shove her aside. She resisted, not giving an inch.

"If you move her, she may die," Kate warned.

The man placed his huge, powerful hands on Kate's shoulders, to push her aside.

"The father have the right over his child, always," he said, as they struggled.

"I don't give a damn about your rights. I care about the child's rights!" Kate Forrester protested, calling out, "Security!"

"Shut up! *Silencio!*"

"Security!" Kate called out even more loudly.

In his anger the man shoved Kate back so fiercely that she was hurled up against the wall, her head striking it sharply. Under other circumstances she might have slumped to the floor from such a blow, but she was determined to keep this child out of hands that would surely end her life. She lunged at the man, causing him to turn from the child to fight her off. Once more, he shoved her aside, and this time was able to sweep the child off the table and into his arms. By this time, uniformed security guard George Tolson, who had observed the attack on Kate, came racing toward them.

"You!" he commanded the man. "Put that child down!"

"She is mine. I have the right!" the man insisted.

"Doctor?" the guard invited her order.

"This child has been abused. She stays here tonight. And for as long as we decide is necessary. Use force if you have to," she ordered.

"Okay, Mister. Put her down!" Tolson commanded. "I said put . . . her . . . down!" His hand went to his holster. It was no idle gesture. The father knew it, for slowly he put the child down on the stretcher. "Now, stand back!"

The swarthy man moved back from the table, glared at his woman, and watched.

Dr. Kate Forrester approached little Maria, completed her examination. While she was doing so, the man grumbled, "She fell. She always fallin'. Something wrong with a child to be always fallin' . . ."

"We'll have her X-rayed, complete body

X rays, especially the long bones. That's where abuse shows up most often. Then a brain scan."

"What means that?" the frightened mother asked.

"There could be trouble up here." Kate pointed to the child's head.

The woman crossed herself and mumbled, *"Hombre malo . . . malo . . ."* She dared to look at her husband.

He tried to glare her to silence, but in the presence of the doctor and the security guard she found the courage she evidently lacked at home, for she refused to be silenced.

Kate took the woman aside. "Do you want to tell me now?" When the woman did not respond, Kate warned, "You'll have to tell the authorities later."

The woman began to weep once more. It was answer enough for Kate. She called, "Beathard!" When the nurse appeared, Kate instructed, "Take Maria to X ray. Complete body films of a child who appears to be four years old."

"Six," the mother corrected.

It was no surprise to Kate Forrester or Nurse Beathard. Abused children often were stunted, appearing far younger than they actually were. Kate added to her instructions, "Also I want an immediate EEG and a brain scan. Ask Dr. Golding to take personal charge of this case. I'm afraid we have a very sick, abused child on our hands."

Beathard started to wheel the gurney toward the double doors that led to the main hospital complex where the Pediatric Service was located.

Throughout, the father stood silent, glaring. Only the presence of armed guard Tolson prevented him from physically interfering. Once the gurney disappeared through the swinging double doors, Kate Forrester said to the woman, "Your child is in good hands. Dr. Golding is one of the best." She turned to the father. "You will leave now. And you will hear from the authorities. Very soon."

The man started away, calling back to his woman, "Felicia! *Ven aquí!*"

Reluctantly the woman started to follow.

"You don't have to go," Kate said. Felicia turned to her, eyes filling with tears. Kate took the woman's hand to reassure her. "If you want to stay, we can help you."

"Felicia!" the man called angrily.

"Help?" the woman asked. "He can no hit me anymore?"

"I'll call our Social Services people. They'll take you to a center where you will be safe. No one will hit you anymore."

The woman considered Kate's offer, while her man continued to insist, "Felicia, *ven aquí!*"

Torn, the woman's eyes appealed to Kate.

"You will be safe, I promise," Kate reassured.

"I . . . I stay . . ." the woman finally decided.

Kate turned to the security guard. "George, take her up to Social Services."

"Yes, Doctor. You sure you're okay?" he asked.

"I'm fine," Kate insisted.

"You sure you don't want someone to take a look at you?"

"No, I'm okay," Kate replied, though her head throbbed.

"You don't mind my saying so, Doctor, you take too many chances. You could have got hurt real bad."

"He would have had to kill me to take that child back. But thanks for caring, George. Now, get this woman to Social Services," Kate said before starting back to E.R.C. to discover if those lab results on Claudia Stuyvesant had come back.

On the way she heard one of the nurses call, "Dr. Forrester! Telephone. Man insists it's urgent."

Testily Kate called back, "Urgent? Tell him to call nine-one-one!"

"He's very insistent," the nurse informed her.

Kate raced to the nurses' station to take the call. Frustrated and harried, she snapped, "Hello! Who is this? And what's so urgent — ?"

"Honey, it's me," the man's voice said.

Kate lowered her voice to an impatient, angry whisper. "For God's sake, Walter, calling me here? At this hour? It's almost one in the morning."

"With you on emergency duty, where do you expect me to call you?" Walter Palmer demanded.

"The last time we talked, I made it clear that I don't expect you to call . . ." Kate started to say.

"You can't end things between us. Not like this. Not after the last two years," he protested.

"Walt, I have no time to talk now. And if I did, it still wouldn't change things between us," Kate declared. "Now, I have to go to . . ."

"Kate! Listen to me! I know you're exhausted right now. And you've got more to handle than you can. All I'm asking is let's discuss this when you're rested and calm."

"Yes, I'm exhausted. I just hope I can make it till six o'clock in the morning without cracking up. But that doesn't change how I feel about you. Now, I must go! And don't ever call me like this again!"

She slammed down the phone and turned away only to discover Mrs. Stuyvesant glaring at her.

"Doctor, I insist you take a look at Claudia at once. She's become so restless, she's pulled that intravenous out of her arm."

Without another word Kate Forrester started toward Room C with a new and added concern. A patient who seemed lethargic earlier and now suddenly had become overactive might be reflecting the emotional lability associated with the use of barbiturates. Added to that, the fading hematoma on her right hip, which might be the result of a fall, now caused Kate to suspect Claudia Stuyvesant had been lying when she denied using drugs.

When Kate reached the door of E.R.C., she found an orderly waiting with reports that had just come down from the lab on Patient Stuyvesant, Claudia. Kate studied them at once.

Unfortunately the findings were not particularly revealing. A hematocrit of 33 indicated slight anemia. A white count of 14,000 was on the high side, but neither alarming nor indicative of a serious infection. The urinalysis revealed no trace of blood, no indi-

43

cation of kidney stones.

In the face of such findings the only intelligent and professional course to follow was to keep the patient in the hospital to be further rehydrated, continue to check her vital signs, and do another CBC to see if there was any change for better or worse. Kate reinserted and taped the I.V. to Claudia's arm.

Throughout, Mrs. Stuyvesant stood beside her daughter, silently demanding of Kate disclosure of the lab report. When none was forthcoming, the woman left her daughter's side, took the doctor by the arm to guide her to a corner of the room.

"I know it's bad . . ." the woman began.

Kate Forrester interrupted. "Mrs. Stuyvesant, before you make any assumptions, the lab reports are not definitive. Surely not a sufficient basis on which to institute a course of treatment that may be unnecessary or even detrimental."

"I want a consultation with an older doctor. When my daughter's life is involved, I want the best!"

"At this hour, in this Emergency Room, in this hospital, I am the best," Kate replied.

"Then at least . . ." Mrs. Stuyvesant started to say.

"I know," Kate anticipated her, " 'Doctor, don't just stand there. *Do* something!' "

44

"Exactly!" Mrs. Stuyvesant said.

"Mrs. Stuyvesant, believe me, I know how you feel as a worried mother. But until your daughter's symptoms and lab results make it possible for me to arrive at a definitive diagnosis, it is better, safer medicine to stand there and do *nothing*."

"Well, I intend to see if Dr. Eaves's service can reach him, wherever he is!"

"You can use the pay phone at the end of the corridor," Kate said.

"Never mind. We have a phone in the limousine!" Mrs. Stuyvesant said, starting toward the street, where her car waited.

Anticipating that, freed from her mother's surveillance, Claudia might speak more openly, Kate went back into the room.

To make her questions appear casual, Kate completed her entries in the Stuyvesant chart while asking, "Claudia, I want a few answers from you, and I promise that whatever you tell me will be confidential and will not be revealed to your mother."

Claudia nodded slightly, but seemed no more at ease than she had been.

"First, *have* you been sexually active recently?"

This time in her more active state, Claudia's denial was instantaneous. "No, I told you before, no."

"And your periods?"

"Regular," Claudia affirmed.

"Now, about drugs, any kind of drugs, legal, illegal, prescribed or over-the-counter. Do you use any of them regularly?"

"No," the young patient insisted.

"Claudia, I have to warn you, withholding the truth can be dangerous. It can affect our diagnosis. And without a correct diagnosis we can't treat you in a way that will help."

Claudia appeared to consider Kate's grave warning. Kate assumed the truth would be forthcoming now.

"I . . . I . . . when I get my period, the cramps and all, I take Midol most times."

"That's all?" Kate persisted.

"That's all. And I don't always take that."

Kate would have persisted in her efforts, but a desperate cry for help summoned her from the Admitting Desk, "Doctor! Doctor Forrester!"

Kate recognized the voice of Sara Melendez, the woman who presided over night admissions to Emergency. Sara had held that post for some years, had seen every type of emergency case during that time, the sick, the desperately sick, and those who only thought they were sick. If Sara called for assistance with such alarm, there must be one of the most critically sick out there.

With a hasty "I'll be back" to Claudia, Kate started out of the room.

Chapter Four

Kate Forrester hurried down the corridor to meet a stretcher that two uniformed Emergency Medical Services officers were wheeling toward her with a briskness that bespoke urgent need for medical intervention. Behind them trailed a woman who could not keep pace with them. Kate flagged the EMS men to the one examining room that was empty. As they reached her, she asked, "What?"

"Overdose. Intentional, we figure," one of the officers informed her.

Once they transferred the patient to the examining table, they departed, leaving Kate with her new patient and the young woman. Kate began to examine him to determine if he was still aware or alert. At the same time she asked, "What happened?"

The young woman did not reply but held out a small, empty pill bottle. As Kate took it, she noticed the wedding ring on the young woman's left hand. Kate examined the bottle. Seconal. Fifty capsules, the prescription specified.

"Did he take them all?" Kate asked.

"All that were left," the young wife said, trying to stifle her impulse to give way to tears.

"How long since you found him this way?" Kate asked.

"When I came home," the young woman started to say.

"How long ago?" Kate insisted. "Hours?"

"Almost two hours now."

"And how long since you left the house?"

"Oh, that was hours before. I work nights."

Kate considered that fact, then asked, "What time did he expect you home?"

"Right after midnight," she said. "Why?"

Kate did not respond but did some crucial mathematics. Possibly as many as fifty capsules of Seconal. Possible elapsed time somewhere between three and four hours, if they were lucky. It might still be possible to avert the lethal effect. She pushed back the patient's eyelids, shined her pocket flashlight into his eyes. His pupils hardly reacted.

Kate asked, "His name?"

"Karl. Karl Christie."

Kate leaned close to the patient, spoke directly into his ear, "Karl. Karl, can you hear me? Karl!!"

His eyes moved slowly in her direction. Barely alert, still he was aware of her. Alert enough for her to institute the first requisite procedure. She called for Nurse Beathard to assist her.

"Tube. Saline solution. Suction syringe," Kate ordered. With the equipment in hand, Kate forced the patient's mouth open, inserted the tube, eased it down his throat and into his stomach. Beathard handed her a stainless steel pitcher full of saline solution. Kate started to pour some of it into the funnel at the head of the tube.

Once she had emptied half the pitcher into the tube and given it a chance to fill his stomach, she reached for the syringe and used it to suction out the saline wash. She expelled the recovered fluid into the steel basin, searching for the remnants of the capsules. On the third try she discovered some. She continued the procedure, washing the patient's stomach, slowly withdrawing all she could of the remnants of the drug. She felt she had managed to diminish part of the danger.

"I.V. and EKG," Kate ordered. While Beathard affixed an intravenous saline drip to overcome dehydration and began to set in place the sensors for the electrocardiogram to monitor heart action, Kate continued to study his heart rhythm, pulse rate, chest sounds.

Satisfied that the patient could abide it, Kate lifted him to a sitting position. Then she forced him to drink a solution of activated charcoal. Though the patient resisted, coughed some of it back up, Kate persisted. It might not only prevent the remains of the drug from being absorbed into his system, but could even recapture some that had already been absorbed.

Once more Kate checked his vital signs. She examined his eyes, his reflexes. She continued to speak to him until he responded — vaguely, and in a whisper, but he responded. He seemed conscious enough that Kate decided to take some time to more fully interrogate his wife.

"This the first time?" Kate asked.

The young wife would have liked to say it was, but she was forced to shake her head.

"Once before," the wife admitted. "You have to understand. He's very sensitive. And all the months of rejection . . . he's such a fine musician . . . but no one cares. No one cares." She gave way to tears. "Don't blame him. It's not his fault. Just save him, that's all I want. Save him."

"We're trying to do that. And I think he's out of danger. Although if you hadn't gotten back when you did . . ." Kate did not dwell on those consequences. "Tell me, did he know when you were due back?"

"Since I've been on nights — I'm a cashier in a restaurant — since I've been on nights, I usually get home around midnight."

"And he knew that?" Kate asked.

"Yes. That used to bug him. Me working

51

and him not. When I was switched to nights, he felt it even more. Most nights he'd come by to take me home, New York being what it is these days. Tonight, when he didn't come by, I was worried."

"Why? Were you expecting something like this?" Kate asked.

"I don't know. Just, I was . . . worried. He'd been more depressed than usual the past week. So I rushed home. Even took a cab, expensive as it is. But as I said, I was worried. Now what's going to happen to him?"

"I'll have Beathard stay with him to make sure his breathing remains stable. We'll check him out for any neurological damage. Then I'll have the psychiatrist come by to talk to him."

"Psychiatrist?"

"The psychiatrist will determine whether this was a true attempt at suicide or a call for help. Myself, I think it was a call for help. He wanted you to find him and save him. And you did. Now it's our job to get him help. We will."

"Thank you, Doctor, thank you very much," the young wife said, then had to force herself to ask, "The . . . there won't be any . . . police?"

"That's an old-fashioned notion. We're not here to punish people who do this," Kate assured her. "We're going to help him, not blame him."

Impulsively the young woman seized Kate's hand and kissed it. Embarrassed, Kate said, "Please don't. I'm glad we could help."

Kate gave instructions to Beathard and started back to check on other patients she had in various stages of recovery or diagnosis.

Kate Forrester had checked on Claudia Stuyvesant, whose symptoms and lab reports had not changed sufficiently to lead to a diagnosis. She had received, diagnosed, and treated a number of cases of run-of-the-mill stomach upsets, including two of salmonella infection. A serious flu that verged on fatal pneumonia. One miscarriage. Two victims of muggings, neither one badly enough injured to be referred to a Trauma Center. One kidney infection, which she referred for possible surgery.

She checked back on Claudia Stuyvesant and found her once more lethargic and half asleep. But her mother was no less anxious and by sheer look alone was more demanding.

Kate took advantage of a momentary lull to bring some of her charts up-to-date. That lull did not last longer than several minutes when once more came the alarm from the Admitting area: "Doctor! Dr. Forrester!"

As Kate hurried toward the Admitting Desk, she could see, even from afar, another team of EMS personnel pushing a stretcher toward her. On the stretcher lay a young woman. Hurrying alongside her, holding her hand, was a man who appeared to be in his mid-twenties.

They drew close enough so that Kate could hear him say, "It's going to be okay, honey. Honest. We're here. They called the doctor. You're going to be fine. Fine!"

Kate beckoned the EMS officers toward a freshly vacated examining room. When the stretcher was alongside the examining table, the young man and one officer assisted the patient up onto it. From the way she reacted, it was obvious that the woman was in too much pain and far too weak to have accomplished it on her own.

"Okay," Kate said to her. "Now, tell me."

At the same time she made a swift appraisal. The woman was sweating profusely. Her face was pale, lips colorless. She breathed with great difficulty and she was obviously in severe pain.

"Tell me what's wrong. What happened? When did this start?"

"I . . . I don't . . . I can't . . . I . . ." She struggled to explain but finally turned her head away, unable to complete the thought.

Disoriented as well, Kate realized. She addressed the young man. "How long has she been this way? How did it start?" At the same time Kate pushed back the sleeve of the patient's raincoat, the sleeve of her robe, and of her nightgown to take her blood pressure.

Meantime the man explained, "She was doing all right. I mean, she was feeling good until early this morning. Then around noon she started feeling . . . I don't know . . . sort of strange. I mean, she's been sickly before. Lots of times. Even before we got married. But lately she was feeling pretty good until this morning."

By that time Kate had taken the patient's blood pressure. Ninety over fifty. Significantly low. By itself not a definitive sign of her problem. Kate slipped a fresh plastic cover over the electronic thermometer and eased it into the patient's mouth.

"Under your tongue, please," Kate said. She watched the temperature register on the dial. One hundred point two. Low-grade fever. "Sit up, please." Her husband started to assist her, but Kate countermanded, "No! Let her do it by herself."

The young man shrank back guiltily as if caught in a crime. His wife started to raise herself. Kate observed that she evidenced signs of lower back pain. She had barely attained a sitting position when she slumped back, exhausted from effort and pain.

"I . . . couldn't . . ." The young patient shook her head hopelessly.

Both to explain and to apologize, her husband said, "She's been that way most of the day. Every time I get her to sit up, to take some hot soup, she says she can't. Then when she finally does, she gets nauseous and dizzy. Doctor, please? Do something?"

From the manner in which he pleaded, Kate knew he was not only very much in love with his wife but was terrified of losing her. And with good reason, Kate thought.

While the signs and symptoms the patient presented were not definitive, they were ominous and demanded immediate attention. She drew a sample of blood and called toward the corridor, "Juan! Juan Castillo! Room A. Stat!"

The orderly came racing into the room. "Yes, Dr. Forrester?" he asked, breathless.

"Rush this sample to the lab. I want a CBC. With electrolytes. And wait for the results!"

"Yes, Doctor," Juan said, taking the sealed test tube and starting on his way.

"Doctor?" the husband pleaded for some indication of his wife's condition.

Kate turned back to the patient to resume her physical examination. While she used her stethoscope to determine the condition of the patient's lungs, heart, and chest, she spoke to the husband, who clung to his wife's hand, more to reassure himself than to comfort her, for she appeared to have fallen asleep.

"You said before —" Kate started to say.

He interrupted to affirm, "Yes, she was feeling pretty good this morning."

"I didn't mean that," Kate replied. "You said that she has been sickly before. You used that word, *sickly*. And you said, 'Lots of times.' What did you mean?"

"Oh, that. She was that way since before we got married."

"What way?" Kate asked.

"She got these attacks."

"Attacks? What kind?"

"She had trouble breathing. But not like this. This is different."

Kate turned from the patient to her husband. "Tell me, this difficulty she had in breathing, what did the doctors call it? Asthma?"

"Yes. Asthma."

Now the signs and symptoms were beginning to take on the semblance of a syndrome. However, there were other facts to determine.

"Did her doctor ever prescribe any medication for her asthma?" Kate asked.

"Oh, yes," the husband assured her. "And it worked fine. Like I said, she was feeling real good. I can't understand what happened. And so suddenly."

"What kind of medication was she taking? Could it have been steroids?"

"Yes. That's right. That's what the pharmacist called it."

"You said, 'It *worked* fine.' Does that mean she isn't taking them anymore?"

"She was feeling so good, didn't have an attack for weeks. So we called the doctor and asked him if she could stop taking the stuff. And he said okay."

"And did she stop taking it all at once?" Kate asked.

"Well, when the doctor said she could stop, she just stopped," the young husband replied.

At once Kate reached out to take the woman's hand from the tender embrace of her husband. Carefully Kate examined the hand. Every finger, every fold of skin between the fingers. There she discovered what she suspected. Discoloration. Though she had never seen such a case before, she had heard it so accurately described by her professor of internal medicine and in her textbooks that she could fit the signs and symptoms together. Low blood pressure. Low-grade fever. Dizziness. Lethargy. Severe pain in lower back and legs. Disorientation. And now the final clue, darkening folds of the skin.

A full-blown case of Addisonian crisis, undoubtedly brought on by sudden cessation of the cortisone she had been taking for her asthma, followed by failure of her own adrenal glands to respond by producing its normal supply of cortisol and corticosterone.

Kate could already anticipate what the lab results would show. High potassium, low sodium, low bicarbonate. No time to await results. To avoid the risk of total vascular collapse, two things must be done at once: Restore fluids, supply steroids.

Once she had affixed the proper I.V.'s to correct both conditions, Kate turned the patient over to the nurse with instructions to observe her until the labs came back.

"And when they do, call me," Kate said, and resumed her rounds of patients already under her care.

As she strode down the corridor, she was reminded of what an older physician had once said to her: "Forrester, you will get more experience and a greater variety of cases in one week on Emergency than in a year of practice. And you will have to call on everything you've ever read or studied or witnessed to handle them properly."

After this night she was more than ready to agree.

Chapter Five

Two hours later. Two hours past midnight. Dr. Kate Forrester was becoming more than aware of her own fatigue. Still another cup of black coffee, hot and strong, had not given her the renewed energy she had hoped. In the last hour she had seen eight cases, treated them and dispatched them to the care of others, and sent seven more home after palliative treatment and much reassurance.

There was still the baffling case of Claudia Stuyvesant in Room C. The last two times Kate had looked in, Claudia's pain had appeared somewhat worse. But the second set of lab reports Kate had ordered to monitor any changes had not come down, so as yet no further treatment was indicated. At this hour of the early morning, lab reports took longer. There were fewer technicians on duty, and those who were took lengthier breaks for a meal or for coffee.

Since the diagnosis still eluded her, she decided to summon the surgical resident for a second opinion.

She picked up the phone. "Page Dr. Briscoe. Ask him to come to Room C in

Emergency. Stat!"

As she hung up, she caught the patient's mother staring at her with a look that seemed to say, *About time, young woman, about time.*

Minutes later Eric Briscoe entered Room C, asking, "Kate? You sent for me?"

"Yes." She gestured him to join her out of hearing of Mrs. Stuyvesant. She acquainted him with her findings, showed him the lab reports.

With Mrs. Stuyvesant hovering close by, Dr. Briscoe performed an abdominal examination on her daughter and a pelvic as well. Ignoring the woman's inquiring stare, he reported to Kate. "Stomach sensitive but not sufficient to indicate specific treatment."

"Uterus?" Kate asked.

"Very slightly enlarged, no marked discoloration of the cervix."

"Any cause for surgical intervention?"

"Not at this time," Briscoe said. "Repeat the labs and let me know —"

Before Kate could explain she had already done so, Mrs. Stuyvesant interrupted. "Repeat the labs, repeat the labs. Don't you doctors know anything else?" When the young surgeon turned to her, she said accusingly, "I was expecting an older man. Someone with more experience."

Ignoring her remark, Briscoe said quietly,

"Dr. Forrester, when the next set of reports comes down, let me know."

By three o'clock in the morning Dr. Kate Forrester had seen twenty-six new patients, sent four to Cardiac Intensive Care, sent two up to surgery, one for an appendectomy, one for possible emergency removal of her gall bladder, had seven under observation, and had released almost a dozen who had presented minor or false signs and symptoms.

Always on her mind, if sometimes subliminally, was that nagging case in Room C, Patient Claudia Stuyvesant. Six hours after admission to Emergency her case was still unresolved. Kate was on her way to look in on her again. That third set of labs should be back by now.

When she entered the room, Mrs. Stuyvesant was quick to say, "The lab results have been back for almost half an hour!"

"I've had other patients, Mrs. Stuyvesant." With that Kate scanned the results.

This time there had been changes, marked changes. Claudia's white count, high before, had risen to 21,000. Her red count, her hematocrit, had fallen to 19. While rehydration due to I.V.'s would normally lower the red cell count, this was a sharper drop than could be accounted for by such a simple answer.

To further confuse Kate, the patient seemed less agitated by her pain and more lethargic. Was that due to a change in her condition or simply to the lateness of the hour?

Kate decided to perform another abdominal examination. This time she discovered Claudia Stuyvesant's abdomen was palpably distended, somewhat tense. Her bowel sounds were diminished. Taken together these signs presented indications of a possible serious infection somewhere in the abdomen. With a sense of alarm that she was not quite able to conceal from the watchful eye of Mrs. Stuyvesant, Kate repeated her abdominal examination seeking some clue as to the focus of the possible infection.

A fleeting suspicion crossed her mind. Despite the mother's presence, the doctor leaned close to the girl and repeated several questions she had asked when taking her history.

"Claudia, I want you to be very honest with me. It's important. *Have* you been sexually active in the past few months?"

"No, really no."

"Did you miss your last period?"

"Regular. I've been very regular," Claudia insisted, unable totally to ignore her mother's gaze.

"She is not pregnant, if that's what you're getting at," Mrs. Stuyvesant said.

Aware that in the presence of her mother Claudia might avoid telling the truth, Kate decided to elicit the vital information that would either corroborate or dispel her suspicion that any infection might be related to a pregnancy, possibly even an ectopic pregnancy.

Impatient with the time it might take to coax a urine sample from the patient, Kate resorted to swifter action. "Scissors," she ordered Cronin.

Cronin presented a pair of round-ended surgical scissors. Kate proceeded to cut away the leg of Claudia Stuyvesant's jeans.

"What in the world are you doing?" Nora Stuyvesant demanded.

"Trying in the quickest way to secure a urine sample," Kate responded. By that time she had slit the jeans up to the crotch, cut through the patient's underpants. Cronin was ready with a catheter, which Kate inserted. Carefully she drew some urine into the test tube Cronin handed her.

"Assay kit!" Kate Forrester requested. Anticipating the doctor's demand, Cronin had already opened the kit, reached in for a clear plastic pipette and a round plastic tube. As Cronin was about to remove the rest of the contents and discard the carton, Kate said, "Expiration date?"

Cronin read off the label, "December thirtieth, 1993."

Assured the contents were fresh, Kate dipped the pipette into the test tube deeply enough to pick up drops of urine. She pressed her thumb over the top of the pipette to hold the urine in place until she could transfer it to the round plastic tube. She removed her thumb, permitting the drops to settle onto the membrane stretched across the open end of the round tube, one-half inch below its top.

Mrs. Stuyvesant, who had watched the procedure anxiously, asked, "Doctor, may I ask what you are doing?"

"Making an immuno-enzymetric assay for the semiquantitative detection of hCG in your daughter's urine."

As Kate had intended, the woman remained completely puzzled. Cronin was not. She knew that, with reason to doubt the patient's answers, Dr. Forrester was performing a pregnancy test in the quickest way possible.

"That immuno thing . . . hCG . . . what is that for?" the suspicious mother asked.

"hCG is human chorionic gonadotropin, a hormone produced as soon as fertilization takes place. This test will discover if there is any present in your daughter's urine sample," Kate explained.

"And if it is present, does that tell you what

my daughter is suffering from?"

Cronin glanced at the doctor, wondering what her response would be. Kate Forrester did not hesitate. "No. But it will tell me if she's pregnant."

"My daughter already told you she has not been sexually active!" Nora Stuyvesant protested.

Kate added to the specimen a few drops of the liquid contained in a small vial marked *Reagent A.*

"What are you doing?" the mother demanded.

"This test is very simple, very quick, and usually correct. Using this reagent, I immobilize any hCG present in Claudia's urine."

"But we've already told you . . ."

"Then there's no harm in verifying it," Kate said as she added a few drops of Reagent B to eliminate any loose hCG molecules from the urine sample, leaving only the hCG that was to be tested by the final application of Reagent C. Confident the result would corroborate her suspicion, Kate carefully added droplets of Reagent C to the hCG in the urine sample. She awaited the result. If her suspicion was correct, the mixture would turn blue, indicating a concentration of hCG in the patient's urine.

Kate studied the contents of the plastic tube,

waiting for the mixture to turn color. It did not turn intense blue. There was not even a trace of blue.

"Well?" Mrs. Stuyvesant asked, sensing that she had been vindicated.

"There are no signs of pregnancy," Kate Forrester was forced to concede, "which eliminates one possible diagnosis."

"Instead of pursuing farfetched theories, Doctor, *do* something!"

"Yes, yes, of course, Mrs. Stuyvesant."

But do what? Kate asked herself.

Something about this case did not ring true. It revived her suspicion that, despite any previous answer, perhaps young Claudia actually was on drugs. Many drugs could be masking or diminishing her pain, concealing from both the patient and the doctor the seriousness of the situation.

Kate considered ordering a toxic screen to discover if there were traces in her blood of morphine, heroin, Valium, or cocaine. Morphine could account for her vomiting, could also make her woozy, vague, hence unable to describe her pain too clearly. A toxic screen, which took at least twenty-four hours, would be of no help in making an immediate diagnosis, but might prove valuable in the patient's subsequent treatment.

Kate drew another blood sample and dispatched it to the lab for a complete toxic screen, an analysis for every likely drug a young woman in New York City might take if she were into the drug scene.

Despite the negative result of the urine pregnancy test, the suspicion continued to nag at Kate's professional intuition. "Claudia, from my own examination I know that you have been sexually active in the past. When you were, did you ever use an IUD or intrauterine contraceptive device?"

Before responding, Claudia hesitated, then, "Some time ago . . . yes, yes, I did." She glanced hastily and guiltily at her mother, adding defensively, "Dr. Eaves himself recommended it."

Whatever the tension between mother and daughter, Kate decided to pursue her suspicion. She picked up the wall phone and punched in a three-digit extension.

"Radiology? Dr. Forrester. I need a sonogram on a patient to run down the possibility of an ectopic pregnancy."

"You've already determined that she's not pregnant," Mrs. Stuyvesant protested.

Kate ignored the interruption to hear the X-ray technician say, "Dr. Forrester, I hope this can wait until tomorrow afternoon."

"Why tomorrow afternoon?" Kate demanded.

"You know sonograms are pretty tricky when it comes to ectopics, so only Dr. Gladwin does those. And she's not on until tomorrow afternoon. If you want a reliable result . . ." The technician's voice trailed off.

Aware that even if done under the best of circumstances and by the most experienced professional, sonogram findings were not perfect, Kate hung up. But only for a moment. She punched in another extension.

"Lab?" Kate asked. "This is Dr. Forrester in Emergency. I just sent a blood specimen down to you for a toxic screen. In addition I want a blood serum pregnancy test."

"I hope you don't want those results stat," the lab technician replied.

"I know the screen will take twenty-four hours or more. It's the blood serum pregnancy I'm most anxious about."

"That's what I meant," the technician explained. "Since serum pregnancies take special equipment and a special technician, we save them up and do them all every few days. If I had to guess, I'd say you won't be getting those results for at least a day and a half."

"Well," Kate considered, then decided, "Put it through for a blood serum pregnancy anyhow. The results might be helpful."

Having tried to order all the indicated tests, Kate decided to repeat the abdominal exam.

To her surprise and alarm, she discovered Claudia's abdomen was now distended to the point of being virtually rigid. At once Kate returned to the phone, but then decided to make this particular call from the nurses' station. No need to add to Mrs. Stuyvesant's mounting anxiety.

"Find Dr. Briscoe! Stat! Urgent he come to Room C in Emergency at once. Repeat! At once!"

Chapter Six

Kate Forrester waited outside Room C to intercept Briscoe and privately inform him of her latest findings. In less than five minutes she was relieved to see him come barging through the swinging doors that separated Emergency from the main hospital complex.

Briscoe absorbed her reports, then said, "A long surgical needle! I'll go in and see if there is any internal bleeding."

They entered the room to find Cronin taking the patient's blood pressure, now a continuing process.

Aware of the patient's nervous mother, Cronin reported softly, "Pressure's dropping."

"Add another I.V. Then get a long needle for Dr. Briscoe," Kate said as she took over monitoring the blood pressure.

At the mention of the word *needle* Mrs. Stuyvesant asked, "What are you going to do?"

"Madam, please leave!" Briscoe said. The woman's look defied him. "Please, leave!"

Finally Nora Stuyvesant relented, almost colliding with Cronin, who had returned with the long surgical needle and a hypo. While

71

Cronin assumed blood pressure monitoring, Kate Forrester watched Briscoe prepare to insert the needle through the patient's vagina to draw any free blood that would have accumulated in her stomach, if indeed there were any occult internal bleeding.

Just as he began the insertion, Cronin called suddenly, in an agitated whisper, "No pulse! She has no pulse!"

At once Kate Forrester and Eric Briscoe lifted the patient from the table to a gurney that had been standing against the wall.

"CPR!" Kate ordered. Cronin was quick to comply. With Cronin trailing alongside continuing to administer CPR, Kate Forrester and Eric Briscoe hurried the gurney out of the room, past the patient's startled mother, down the corridor to the Acute Care room, where emergency equipment was available. Mrs. Stuyvesant trailed behind, pleading, "What's wrong? What happened to my daughter?"

No one could stop to inform her. At the door to the Acute Care room, despite Mrs. Stuyvesant's plea, Kate prevented her from entering.

"She's my daughter. I have a right . . ."

"You'd only be in the way," Kate said, and swiftly shut the door.

Inside Acute Care the team of two physicians and three nurses went to work simultaneously. Kate ordered, "I.V.'s. Three. Large infusions of saline and Ringer's lactate, to replace her electrolytes. Cronin, continue CPR." Kate turned to the Acute Care nurse. "EKG leads!" As the nurse began to affix the sensors to the patient's chest so that they could follow her heart action on the screen, Kate ordered, "One ampule epinephrine!" The second Acute Care nurse provided the ampule and the hypodermic.

Kate swiftly tied a rubber tube around the patient's forearm, found the vein, and injected the epinephrine to stimulate heart action.

Meantime Briscoe reached for a long plastic tube, held open the patient's mouth, eased the tube carefully past her vocal cords, down her throat, and into her trachea. He affixed a pressure bag and ordered the second nurse, "Force air!" The nurse took the pressure bag in both her hands to drive air into the patient's lungs, careful to do so in coordination with Cronin, who was still administering CPR, so that they did not defeat each other's efforts by forcing in air while Cronin was exerting CPR pressure on the patient's chest.

Briscoe turned to the door, called out, "Castillo! Juan Castillo!"

From down the corridor came a reply, "Coming, Doctor!"

"Juan! Type-O blood! Four pints! Stat!"

Briscoe ordered.

At the mention of blood for transfusion, Mrs. Stuyvesant fell back against the wall for support. She was now too frightened to ask or protest.

Inside the room Briscoe joined Kate as she frantically took the patient's blood pressure. They both continued to watch for signs of heart action on the monitor. Soon it became obvious that despite obvious signs of heart action, all the added fluids and medications had failed to restore the patient's pulse or blood pressure.

"EMD," Kate was finally forced to admit in a grim whisper.

EMD — electromechanical dissociation — when the heart reflexively continues to pump but there is no pulse since there is no longer sufficient blood in the arterial system due to internal hemorrhaging.

"Where the hell is that blood?" Briscoe called.

Moments later Juan arrived with four pints of Type-O blood. At once Kate found a fresh vein in the patient's arm and proceeded to set up the transfusion, forcing the life-giving blood into Claudia before her system collapsed completely.

"If we can just revive her enough, I could rush her up to surgery," Briscoe said.

But after the infusion of three pints of blood, there was still no pulse. No pressure. It was obvious that the fresh blood could not replace the blood that she was still losing.

"I'm going in," Briscoe said. "Got to find that hemorrhage and tie it off."

He turned to the cabinet that held the minimal number of surgical instruments needed in Acute Care. He pulled on a pair of rubber gloves, selected a scalpel. While Kate continued to infuse blood and with one nurse forcing air into the patient's lungs and Cronin still applying CPR, Briscoe made a large exploratory incision across the patient's abdomen.

A torrent of fresh, bright red blood erupted from the incision. Instinctively, buttressed by his surgeon's habits, Briscoe ordered, "Suction!" to clear away the blood and give him access to the source of the bleeding. But he realized at once, as did Kate and the nurses, that in Acute Care there was no suction equipment available. He would have to work by feel. As he inserted his gloved hands into the wound, searching for the source of the hemorrhage, he called, "Clamp!" At the same time Kate, Cronin, and one Acute Care nurse continued with their duties.

Briscoe felt around in a sea of blood. The new blood having failed to replace the blood that was lost, Kate could not detect any pulse.

The Acute Care nurse continued to force air into the patient's lungs.

After many minutes of such combined but futile activity, Kate was forced to admit, "No pulse. She still has no pulse." Nevertheless she continued to feed blood, while Cronin continued CPR and the Acute Care nurse continued to force air.

It was Cronin who finally said what both doctors had refused to admit. "Gone. She's gone."

"She can't be gone!" Kate protested. "Just keep going. We'll get her back. We'll get her back!"

Briscoe drew away from the table, withdrawing his blood-drenched gloved hands from the open wound. "Forget it, Kate. There's no hope."

As both nurses ceased their ministrations, Kate took over the CPR action from Cronin, who pleaded, "Doctor, no, it won't do any good."

Sweat dripping from her forehead, blond hair straggling down the sides of her face, Kate Forrester continued to press down on the patient's chest in a desperate, if futile, effort to restore her to life. Kate Forrester, the physician, knew there was no hope. Kate Forrester, the woman, refused to give up.

"Kate! Dr. Forrester!" Briscoe ordered

firmly. "The patient is gone! There is no chance of reviving her. So stop! I said, stop!"

But he had to strip off his bloody gloves and take Kate in his arms to force her away from the table. Once the professional part of her mind took over, she asked, "Did you discover the cause?"

"I couldn't even find the source of the bleeding," Briscoe admitted. "But does it matter now?"

"No, no. I . . . I guess not," Kate agreed.

Nine hours after she had been admitted to Emergency in City Hospital, forty-five minutes after her pulse had failed, and despite all the furious modalities instituted to revive her, Claudia Stuyvesant, age nineteen, was dead.

Dead. From causes unknown. But which would become known once the mandatory autopsy was performed. By New York State law, in every case in which a patient is brought into the Emergency Service of any hospital and dies within twenty-four hours, an autopsy is required.

"I'd better go out and tell her mother," Briscoe said.

"No. That's my job," Kate Forrester said.

"It won't be easy," he warned.

"It's still my responsibility." Kate started for the door, then looked back at her young patient, from whom the nurses were now removing tubes, sensors, and all the other medical devices that had proved so futile. Cronin covered Claudia Stuyvesant's naked body with a plain green sheet.

Outside the door it was not necessary for Kate to speak the words. The distraught mother read it in her eyes.

"Killed her! You people killed her!"

"Mrs. Stuyvesant, we did all we could."

"I could have helped her. But you kept me out. I would have saved her!" the woman screamed. Nurses and patients came bolting out of examining rooms to stare down the corridor at the hysterical woman and the young woman doctor who tried to calm her.

"We did everything we could, everything," Kate tried to reassure her.

"Everything? 'Repeat the labs, repeat the labs.' You call that treatment? Examinations, I.V.'s — is that treatment?" the distraught mother said accusingly. "I bring in a healthy nineteen-year-old with a simple stomach upset, and in hours, just hours, you kill her. Nineteen years old. With her whole life ahead of her. Nineteen years of love and caring and hope for the future, gone, gone in a handful of hours. My child, my only child . . . Claudie . . . poor, poor Claudie . . . her whole life ahead of her. . . ."

"Please, Mrs. Stuyvesant," Kate tried to say, reaching out to comfort her.

"Don't you touch me, 'Doctor'! And don't think you'll get away with this! There are laws . . . laws to punish doctors like you!"

Despite the woman's accusations and threats, Kate felt great compassion for her.

"Mrs. Stuyvesant, is there anyone you wish to call? Or whom I can call for you?"

The woman glared at her through her tears, her eyes accusing and full of hate. It was Dr. Briscoe who finally led the distraught woman down the corridor toward the large bright red neon sign that announced EMERGENCY. Mrs. Stuyvesant went, weeping and moaning, "He'll blame me . . . he'll blame me. . . ."

As they passed the Admitting Desk, the nurse in charge rose from her chair to stare at them until they were gone. She started back along the corridor toward Kate.

"Dr. Forrester, do you know who that was?"

"Mrs. Stuyvesant," Kate replied, her eyes still on the exit door.

"Doctor, that wasn't just 'Mrs. Stuyvesant.' She is Mrs. *Claude* Stuyvesant," the nurse informed.

"So she said more than once," Kate replied, realizing, "He's big in real estate, isn't he?"

"In New York he *is* real estate," the nurse said. "Plus half a dozen other industries and a power at City Hall and Albany."

"But where was he when his daughter needed him?" Kate asked, without waiting for an answer.

Numb, exhausted, Kate Forrester went back into the Acute Care room. The nurses were just restoring the room to its normal condition. On the gurney lay the body of young Claudia Stuyvesant, draped in a green sheet. Kate could not resist lifting it to stare down at the pale face, the closed eyes, the untidy, damp dark hair of the dead patient. *Her* patient.

She had failed. The patient had been under her care for nine hours. She had available to her the resources of a large, well-equipped modern hospital. Yet she had lost a nineteen-year-old young woman who had everything to live for.

Had she been deluding herself all these years as to her abilities? Had she been misled, and misled others, by those excellent grades she had achieved in med school? Could one be an exceptional scholar in the classroom yet less than capable in applying all that knowledge when a human life hung in the balance? There had been students in med school who had fallen out along the way, interns and residents who had been defeated by the awesome responsibility of making decisions on which the lives of others depended. She even knew one intern who had such doubts that in his second year he had taken his own life.

Perhaps, she thought, that was what internship and residency were all about, weeding out those unable to face up to the realities of applied medical practice.

It came down to the final accusation: *Was there something that I, Kate Forrester, should have done, could have done, something I missed, something that would have been obvious to another doctor?*

Eric Briscoe returned from escorting Mrs. Stuyvesant to her limousine. He read the defeat and self-reproach in Kate's eyes.

"Katie, we all lose some. This one wasn't for lack of trying," he said consolingly.

She shook her head. Briscoe signaled Cronin to fetch him a pill. She returned shortly with a yellow pill and a cup of water. He forced Kate to swallow it.

He could not resist thinking, *If she's taking this so badly now, it's a good thing she didn't hear all the threats that hysterical mother made before I could get her into her limo. Poor Kate. I don't think she's heard the last of this case.*

At dawn, once Dr. Kate Forrester had completed the chart of the Stuyvesant case and signed the Certificate of Death, she was free to leave for the day.

Chapter Seven

Usually, when drained and exhausted from such a long, unbroken tour of Emergency duty, Kate Forrester would have been relieved if not delighted to return to her modest apartment. Every tired fiber of her body cried out for her comfortable bed and for ten, eleven, or even more hours of undisturbed sleep.

Not so at six o'clock on this particular morning. The death of Claudia Stuyvesant weighed too heavily on her. There was another case that made persistent demands on her professional conscience. She passed through the double doors into the main building of the hospital complex and took the elevator up to the third floor and the Pediatric wing. She sought out Dr. Harve Golding and found him in his darkened office studying a series of X rays of the entire body of a small child.

"Harve?" Kate asked.

Without turning from the viewing wall on which the X-ray films were mounted, Golding recognized her voice. "Kate? Come have a look."

She drew close to the backlighted glass wall

on which the films were mounted for best visibility.

"Lady, were you right!" Golding exclaimed. "Look at those two healed fractures on her left leg. One of the femur. One of the tibia."

"This one, on her right leg, is that the fresh one that I suspected?" Kate asked.

"That's it," Golding confirmed. "I'm almost afraid to see the results of her brain scan."

"You expect it'll be that bad?" Kate asked.

"I'm waiting for Sperber to come in. We need a full neurological evaluation to find out how much permanent damage there is, if any."

"Poor little Maria," Kate said. "God, how can people do this to little children?"

"Imagine what would have happened if you'd let them take her back," Golding said. "You can be proud of yourself, Kate. You saved a life tonight."

Saved one, lost one, Kate thought. *It may balance out mathematically, but it doesn't feel that way. Doesn't feel that way at all.*

"So go home, Katie, get some well-earned sleep," Golding urged cheerfully. "You've earned it." Expecting some rejoinder from her, he turned to ask, "Katie? Kate, something wrong?"

"Just a bad night, a bad night," Kate said as she left.

★ ★ ★

84

Most early mornings when Kate Forrester came off overnight Emergency duty she hailed a cab, was relieved to sink into the backseat and be driven home to the apartment she shared with Rosalind Chung in an apartment house the hospital had taken over to provide decent living conditions for its young residents and interns at prices they could afford in a city with the highest rents in the nation.

This morning, exhausted though she was, Kate chose to walk. The streets of the West Side of Manhattan were still wet from the overnight rain. The air smelled fresh, the rain having washed out most of the soot and contaminants. From across the Hudson a wave of cool early-morning air rode in on a strong breeze. It failed to be as invigorating for Kate as it normally would have.

Along Ninth Avenue the trucks were making early-morning deliveries to the small neighborhood grocery stores, modest little restaurants, meat markets, vegetable markets, all stocking up for their day's business. The West Side of New York was waking up to another day.

Kate made her way among trucks being unloaded by truckers and helpers. They greeted her with stares of admiration and occasional exclamations of seemingly sexual proposals, all intended to be amusing breaks in the humdrum routine of their daily chores.

Coming from a small farm in Illinois, having lived most of her life there, Kate had never quite got used to this form of good-natured banter that passed among truckmen, taxi drivers, and construction workers in New York. At first she had been offended. Later she became amused. Today she was aware only of the death of Claudia Stuyvesant.

She arrived at her front door, unlocked both locks, and let herself in, calling, "Rosie?"

There was no response. Kate remembered, Rosie was on Clinic duty and wouldn't be home till afternoon. Kate went into her own room, started slipping out of her clothes, realized that she had not yet run her tub. She turned on the steaming water, finished undressing, and was about to step into the tub when the phone rang. Her immediate reaction was *God, I hope it isn't Walter. This morning of all mornings I'm too tired to contend with personal problems.* But she had never developed the ability to ignore a ringing phone, particularly one that rang so persistently. By the ninth ring she decided, *No matter how I feel about Walter, or how firm I am that our relationship is over, the least I can do is answer. I owe him that much.*

"Hello?" she began.

"Kate . . ." It *was* Walter. "Sorry about calling you at the hospital. A foolish impulse. But we have to meet. I have to talk to you."

"Walt, I've told you, it wouldn't do any good."

"After all we've been to each other, the plans we've made . . ."

"Walter, those were plans that *you* made. I've got plans too. It'll take three or four more years before I find my niche in medicine. I can't think about marriage until I find it."

"You could if you loved me enough," Walter challenged.

Very slowly, very carefully Kate replied, "Walter, dear Walter, without knowing it, you and I have arrived at the same conclusion. Yes, I could *if* I loved you enough."

"Look, honey, if we could meet just once more . . ." he insisted.

"Walt, being in love isn't something you can convince someone about. Either I am or I'm not. Like you, yes. Love you, the way you deserve to be loved, I'm afraid not. Now, please, Walt, I'm beat, out of it. I've just had the most exhausting tour of duty I've had in the two years I've been at the hospital. I need a hot tub. I need sleep. Most of all, I think, I need to be left alone. So, please . . ."

Because he detected in her voice a state of more than mere exhaustion, Walter Palmer said, "Sure. Okay. But I'll call you soon. You need time. Time to think. Time to see things my way."

He hung up. As Kate reached out to return the phone to its cradle, she became aware that she was weeping. She brushed back the tears, wondering, *Am I so emotional about breaking up with Walter? After all, there was a time when I did think I was in love with him. Is that why I'm crying? Or is it the memory of Claudia Stuyvesant, her pale face, her black hair matted to her forehead in her final death sweat?*

She knew at once. It was the memory of nineteen-year-old Claudia.

She determined to put it behind her. These things happen in medicine. No doctor saves all his cases. A hot tub to relax her, a long, long sleep, and by evening she would be fresh and relaxed once more.

But once in bed, tired though she was, Kate could not fall asleep. The more determined she was to catch up on the sleep she desperately needed, the more awake she became. Despite her efforts to blot out the disastrous case of Claudia Stuyvesant, she began to relive every moment of it. She reviewed her initial interview, Claudia's responses, so generalized and eventually misleading. If she was in such desperate straits, why did she not feel more pain? Kate reviewed every procedure, the

I.V.'s, the lab results, not once but three times, that pregnancy test that was clearly negative. She had tried to secure a sonogram to corroborate her findings, but no expert technician was available. That was one of the risks of the Emergency Service. Doctors didn't always have available to them every form of assistance they might feel called upon to use.

Subtly her mind had turned from reviewing the events to explaining, arguing, justifying. Back in medical school no professor had ever taught that medicine was an exact science. That if you did all the indicated things, employed the correct modalities, the right medications, every patient would recover. But that was small solace in a case where an apparently healthy nineteen-year-old young woman with minor symptoms had died.

But then, part of Kate's troubled mind argued, *if she had been as healthy as first appeared, she would not have died. That violent hemorrhaging, why? Why did it remain so occult, so hidden from detection, until it had become impossible to contain?*

Briscoe had been there. He had concurred with Kate's observations and conclusions. Or was it more correct to say, lack of conclusions, inability to reach a diagnosis, a diagnosis of a treatable condition?

No, she was forced to admit, it did not relieve the ache to try to put the blame, or even part of it, onto Briscoe. Claudia Stuyvesant had been *her* patient from the outset. If anything went wrong, it was a failure on the part of Dr. Kate Forrester.

Kate Forrester, who from her earliest days in grade school had been a star pupil. Always first in her class. Always first to raise her hand and wave it in the teacher's face when volunteers were called for. Kate Forrester, who had gone on from the local high school, with honors, to the University of Illinois, where she accelerated her four-year course into three in order to gain swifter admittance into the University of Iowa Medical School. During her high school days, even before qualified by age to be a regular volunteer worker at the local hospital, she had been accepted. Of all volunteers the most curious, the most eager, was Kate Forrester. When she applied to the medical school, along with her application went the recommendations of three physicians, all chiefs of various services at the hospital.

Medical school had proved tougher than she had anticipated. That only meant that she worked even harder, always looking forward to the time when she would begin to put into use all her accumulated knowledge and experience, first as an intern, later as a resident. She had deliberately chosen a big city hospital, one of the biggest and best of big city hospitals. City Hospital. She wanted to learn from the best physicians and surgeons, compete against the best and brightest of young physicians and surgeons of the future generation. It was almost as if she were back in school waving an eager hand in the face of the teacher, begging, *Acknowledge me, call on me, test me. I know the answer!*

Except that this morning, tormented and unable to sleep, Kate Forrester had to admit to herself, *No, I don't know all the answers. I didn't know them last night and in the early hours of this day, when for some undetermined reason a young life slipped through my hands.*

A sharp stab of doubt caused Kate Forrester to ask herself, *Has it all been a mistake, my ambition, my devotion to medicine? When this case in Emergency, which at first appeared to be a simple stomach upset, turned into a true emergency crisis, did I fail?*

Did I fail?

Kate tried to console herself. *I'm too tired even to think straight, too guilt-ridden to be logical. Sleep. I need sleep.*

One persistent question refused to permit it: *Did I do everything I recalled having done? It is one thing to look back, explain, justify now, or am I explaining too much, justifying my conduct too much?*

The more Kate questioned, the more awake she became. Until she threw back the covers, dressed hastily, determined to go back to the hospital and check out Claudia Stuyvesant's chart to see exactly what she had written there.

She entered the E.R. from the street side. She was uncomfortably aware, or did she only imagine, that the staff, nurses, resident, intern, security, orderlies, were all staring at her. She ignored them. She headed straight for the central desk, began searching the charts.

The Stuyvesant chart was not there. Strange.

Charts only went with the patient when that patient was removed to another service. Intensive Care. Or Surgery. Or Cardiac ICU. But the Stuyvesant girl had been removed to the medical examiner's office, as required by law. The chart would not have gone with her body.

Reluctant to inquire about it, Kate had no choice. When she asked, the charge nurse explained, "Oh, that chart. Dr. Cummins sent for it early this morning."

Dr. Cummins? Kate considered. *Why would the administrator of the entire City Hospital complex take the time to look into that particular chart? Cummins is always so involved in money-*

raising efforts, fighting for city, state, and federal funding, that even the chiefs of the various services have trouble getting enough of his time to air their demands. I've heard them complain about that more than once. Why would Cummins send for that one chart? But if he's the man who has it, he's the man I am determined to see, busy as he is.

When she arrived at Cummins's office, contrary to her expectations, she had the uncomfortable feeling that somehow her arrival had been expected. She was immediately shown into the administrator's impressive office, a room of paneled walls, bookshelves filled with medical tomes. She found him poring over the chart and making notes. Without looking up, he said, "Sit down, Dr. Forrester. Please sit down."

Cummins continued his study, making notes, while Kate waited uncomfortably, straining to glance across the desk at the chart, yet trying to pretend that she did not.

When Cummins had finished, he spoke, as if only to himself, and with some relief. "Good." He turned his attention to her. "Now, then, Forrester —" It was his standard opening to every speech he delivered to subordinates, especially young residents and interns.

"Your notes in this chart seem quite adequate in the situation. Thorough, in fact. Of course, there is one thing. From what appears here, there is also no reason for the patient to have died. But I'm sure that will be cleared up when we receive the medical examiner's report. I'll call you the moment I hear."

"May I see that chart?" Kate asked.

"Of course. But I can't allow it to leave my office. If you would like to peruse it out in the waiting room . . ." He held out the chart to her. Before he released it, he said, "A very well-written chart, which may be helpful under the circumstances."

While Cummins's words were phrased in complimentary fashion, the look in his eyes hinted at possible trouble. Kate took the chart in hand and started for the door. There she stopped long enough to ask, "Dr. Cummins, may I ask why you called for this chart?"

"Oh," Cummins replied, "didn't I tell you? I received a call very early this morning. At home in fact."

"Call?"

"From Claude Stuyvesant."

Kate was now doubly anxious to read the chart.

She reviewed every entry in the chart. Every lab report. She studied them a second time. They recalled to her not only what she had done, based on the patient's condition and the results of the lab reports, but also her reason for each modality she had adopted. And even though it proved negative, she felt justified in performing that pregnancy test. In fact, the only report missing was the toxic screen. But that would be along later.

She now had in mind a clear picture of the case and how it had developed. She could even recall some of the interruptions in treatment forced on her by the demands of other cases.

She came away from Cummins's office greatly reassured. She could explain and defend her every action in the case of Claudia Stuyvesant.

She stopped by the Pediatric wing to see how little Maria was doing. Golding had gone off duty. But Mike Sperber, the staff pediatric neurologist, was expected on duty. He would take over the evaluation of the little girl to determine if there were signs of permanent neurological damage.

Kate looked in on the small room where the child had been installed. Maria was asleep, peacefully asleep, as if she knew she was now safe.

Chapter Eight

At the moment that Kate Forrester was leaving little Maria's room, several floors above, Hospital Administrator Dr. Cummins, having braced himself for the ordeal, ordered his secretary to get Claude Stuyvesant on the phone.

Once his secretary buzzed back, Cummins was truly sympathetic when he said, "Mr. Stuyvesant, I can't tell you how sorry I am, how sorry we all are, here at City Hospital, about the tragedy that struck your daughter."

"I should think you would be," came Stuyvesant's flat, curt response. "But I didn't call you early this morning seeking sympathy. I want to know, and I want it straight, what went wrong last night? Why did my daughter die?"

The sharpness, the directness of Stuyvesant's words confirmed Cummins's worst fears. One of the most influential businessmen and behind-the-scenes political powers in New York City, Claude Stuyvesant was notoriously at his most vindictive when he adopted that cold, flat tone.

Damage control, Cummins cautioned himself, *Damage control.* He proceeded to respond

96

in his most ingratiating professional manner, the one he usually employed when making appeals for huge contributions from the wealthy of the city.

"Mr. Stuyvesant, your early-morning call so distressed me that I decided I could not rest until I got to the bottom of this myself. I have spent the past few hours meticulously studying every single detail of your daughter's case. Every entry in her chart, every test that was done, every lab result. Everything that the doctor who had charge of her case did and ordered to be done. In fact I have the chart of her case in my hands as I speak to you now."

"Never mind all that, Cummins! I want to know one thing, and one thing only. *Who killed my daughter?*"

"Mr. Stuyvesant, I am trying to explain. No one killed your daughter. At this moment we don't even know why she died, aside from a hemorrhage of undetermined origin."

"Cummins, what the hell kind of hospital are you running? A patient bleeds to death and nobody knows why!" Stuyvesant said accusingly.

"I'm trying to explain, sir. According to your daughter's chart, Dr. Forrester did everything indicated —"

Again Stuyvesant interrupted. "Who the

hell is Dr. Forrester?"

"Dr. Forrester handled your daughter's case," Cummins explained. "When your daughter was brought in, she was in charge in Emergency."

"Oh yes, my wife told me about your 'Doctor Forrester.' She's a woman, isn't she?" Stuyvesant demanded.

"Yes," Cummins replied.

"And I suppose she is on your staff so that you can comply with all those goddamned federal and state regulations that say you've got to have so many women on your staff so many blacks, so many Hispanics. What the hell ever happened to the days when a person's *ability* counted for something in this country? I wouldn't let a woman doctor touch any member of my family with a ten-foot pole! And now you know why!"

Harvey Cummins felt sufficiently provoked to dispute Stuyvesant directly. "Mr. Stuyvesant, I want you to know that Katherine Forrester is one of the best-trained young doctors we have on our staff. If you saw her college and medical-school records, you would feel as I do. We were lucky to get her to come to City Hospital. It isn't easy these days, when lucrative private partnerships are being dangled in front of the brightest young physicians."

"I wish to hell someone had dangled such a partnership in front of her before she killed my daughter!" Stuyvesant bellowed.

"Mr. Stuyvesant, I'm trying to tell you, nothing that Dr. Forrester did caused your daughter's death."

"Cummins, *I* know that you have to defend your staff, no matter how negligent they are. But as *you* damn well know, I am very close with several members on your board of trustees. You haven't heard the last of this. Nor has your Dr. Forrester!"

Before Cummins could reply, Stuyvesant hung up. After a moment of indecision Cummins ordered, "Miss Hopkins, please get Judge Trumbull for me."

Out of deference to his age and his past service on the bench everyone addressed Lionel Trumbull as Judge, but he was actually the senior partner of the eminent Wall Street law firm of Trumbull, Drummond & Baines and was regarded as one of the shrewdest and least emotional lawyers in the profession.

After he had heard Cummins's report of his conversation with Claude Stuyvesant, Trumbull said, "Get that young woman in. Soon as possible. A man like Claude Stuyvesant, all his power, all the legal talent he has at his command, we've got to be very, very careful. We can be facing a malpractice action that

99

could cost millions. Millions!"

"Lionel, I assure you, I went over the entire chart. There was no malpractice. . . ." Cummins tried to explain.

"With juries these days," Trumbull interrupted, "*everything* is malpractice. Every cough, every sneeze, is the basis of a costly lawsuit. And when the death of a *young* woman is involved, millions! To say nothing of the damage Stuyvesant can do to the hospital and its reputation. I want to see that young woman!"

At two o'clock precisely as ordered, Kate Forrester presented herself at Dr. Cummins's office, to find the administrator not behind his ornate antique desk but seated at the head of the long conference table that occupied one corner of the large room. She was surprised to find, as well, another man, long past middle age, bald except for a fringe of graying hair. His face, though ruddy, was dour as if in judgment.

"Forrester, this is Judge Trumbull. Counsel to the hospital."

Mention of the word *counsel* made Kate aware that the purpose of this meeting was different from the medical consultation she had anticipated.

Suddenly Mrs. Stuyvesant's threats of two

nights ago became more real.

"Sit down, Forrester, please sit down," Cummins urged pleasantly.

"This has to do with the Stuyvesant case, doesn't it?" Kate asked, but remained standing.

Trumbull's eyes confirmed her suspicions, which made her feel even more anxious.

"Sit down, Doctor," Cummins repeated.

Kate slipped into a chair across the table from Trumbull.

"Yes," Cummins admitted sadly. "This has to do with the Stuyvesant case."

"Everything about the case is in her chart. As you know, I went over my notes very carefully. That chart is complete and accurate," Kate explained.

Not Cummins but Trumbull responded. "Dr. Forrester, you say you went over your notes very carefully?"

"Yes," Kate affirmed.

"Why?" Trumbull asked.

"Why?" Kate repeated, trying to understand the purpose of a question the answer to which she considered obvious. "Well — a case like this, so puzzling, and with such an unfortunate outcome, every conscientious doctor would be curious."

"Curious?" Trumbull asked. "About what?"

"Why it happened, of course," Kate replied. "I'm anxiously awaiting the medical examiner's report."

"So are we all," Cummins commented.

"Cummins, I think you ought to acquaint Dr. Forrester with the seriousness of the situation. She might want to take steps."

"Take steps?" Kate asked, puzzled. "What kind of 'steps'?"

"Please understand, Doctor," Trumbull replied, "as counsel to the hospital, my firm will undertake your defense. But in a situation like this some doctors like to retain their own counsel."

"Defense? Against what?" Kate demanded.

Trumbull looked to Cummins, assigning him the uncomfortable chore of explaining.

"Dr. Forrester, since you're from the Midwest, the name Stuyvesant may have no particular significance for you," Cummins said.

"I know he's big in real estate," Kate replied.

" 'Big in real estate' is a very modest way of putting it. The man owns gambling casinos in Atlantic City and Las Vegas, hotels in a dozen cities, enough office buildings here to comprise his own city."

"What's that to do with me?" Kate asked.

"The man has power," Cummins said. "The man *is* power. Financial. Social. Especially po-

102

litical. It's been said no man can be elected mayor of this city without the financial and verbal backing of Claude Stuyvesant. If he feels his daughter's case was mishandled, he might retaliate in some way."

Trumbull intervened to add, "My firm's had dealings with him in the past. Knowing him, I'm sure he'll retaliate. A malpractice suit is a certainty. So we have to be prepared."

"I did everything I could for his daughter," Kate protested.

"I believe that. Dr. Cummins believes that," Trumbull said. "But, if called upon, we have to be prepared to prove it to a jury."

"And we will prove it!" Kate stated indignantly.

"A good reason to consider what I said. While Trumbull, Drummond & Baines stands ready to defend you, you may wish to employ counsel of your own."

"Lawyers cost money," Kate replied. "And I'm still in debt after paying for my med-school education."

"Then depend on my firm," Trumbull said reassuringly. "Meantime a word of advice. Do not mention to anyone that you went back to review that Stuyvesant chart."

"But I did!" Kate insisted.

"Yes, of course. However, that leaves your action open to several possible interpretations," Trumbull pointed out.

"I was puzzled by the case. Professionally curious. So naturally I went back to review my handling of it," Kate said, trying to explain.

"Doctor, isn't it a fact that you were unsure of how you handled the case, that you might have made some mistake, and that *that* is the reason you went back to review your notes in the chart?"

"No, of course not!" Kate replied at once.

A moment of pointed silence from both men gave her time to realize this was precisely the kind of incriminating questions a hostile lawyer might ask her one day. Questions that had no basis in fact but that were accusatory and to which she could never adequately respond.

"I see what you mean," Kate said.

"My advice to you, young woman: Do not discuss this case with anyone except the man or woman I appoint to be your lawyer. You never know when you are making some perfectly innocent statement that may one day be used against you."

She repeated the phrase: " 'Used against me.' Suddenly I'm a defendant. My whole career, my years at college, at medical school — my plans for my life . . ."

In a show of support for her, Cummins said gently, "We'll do our best to protect you, my dear. But if Stuyvesant wins his malpractice suit . . ."

"Are you sure there'll be a malpractice suit?"

"These days," Trumbull said grimly, "with such enormous jury verdicts, even the wealthy are tempted. And the type of man Stuyvesant is, we have to be prepared for the worst."

"I did nothing wrong!" Kate declared. "And I can prove it. When do I see that lawyer?"

"My secretary will call you this afternoon to set a time," Trumbull said.

Kate Forrester came away from the interview angry, but also shaken by the threat that Trumbull had made so plain. All the way back to her apartment her resentment continued to grow. It wasn't fair. Not after all her sacrifices, after how hard she had worked, her years of study. It wasn't fair that some man, of whose existence she had hardly been aware, could suddenly loom up in her life and threaten her. She sought to console herself: If he is a man of such power and wealth, what could it benefit him to sue? Money, even millions, could not bring his daughter back.

Perhaps, Kate thought, perhaps if it were explained to him how his daughter was brought in, how nonspecific her symptoms were, that the lab reports only reflected certain aspects of her condition but not enough to permit a doctor to make a definitive diagnosis, if someone explained all that to him, surely he would understand. She must discuss it with that lawyer when they met.

She thrust open the door to the apartment to hear Rosalind call from the shower, "That you, Kate?"

"Yes, Rosie," she replied in a voice so desultory that her roommate came out of the shower drying her long black hair.

"What did Cummins want?"

"They're giving me a lawyer," Kate said, trying to sound more affirmative and less threatened than she actually felt.

"Lawyer? Why do you need a lawyer?" Rosie asked, growing resentful on Kate's behalf.

"They seem sure there'll be a malpractice suit."

"Malpractice?" Rosie echoed angrily. Despite her usual calm, reserved Oriental manner, Rosalind Chung was a young woman with a temper that, when aroused by injustice, came flaring to the surface. "The hours we work! The conditions! *We* should be the ones suing!"

Realizing that solace and encouragement, not anger, would serve Kate best, she embraced her. "Don't look so down, sweetie.

There isn't a resident or a doctor on that staff who won't go to bat for you. We'd love to air our gripes in a courtroom. And about time! I just made a fresh batch of coffee. Like some?"

Kate nodded vaguely. What her roommate had intended as encouragement had become an added burden. Kate did not want her situation to become a cause. She would much prefer the whole thing to blow over quietly so that she could get on with her career, which she had always envisioned as helping sick and needy people, not fighting for causes.

As Rosie handed her a steaming cup, Kate said, "I keep thinking . . ."

"Stop thinking," Rosie advised. "There isn't a doctor alive who hasn't had a case like this. More than one. Patients will die. Dying is the price of living. It happens to all of us sooner or later. And the way it happens doesn't always make scientific sense the way it does in our medical textbooks."

"When Briscoe led her mother out, the last thing she said was, 'He'll blame me, he'll blame me.' "

"What does that mean?" Rosie asked.

"Shocked and sad as she was about her daughter's sudden death, she was even more afraid of someone else."

"Who?"

"Claude Stuyvesant, I assume."

"Then I hope they give you a very good lawyer," Rosie said. "Because any man who could instill such fear in his own wife is not the kind of enemy to have."

Kate nodded vaguely. She tried to sip her coffee but instead shook her head slowly. "I have to call home and tell them."

"Can't it wait until things become clarified?" Rosie suggested.

"Do you mean clarified, or worse?" Kate responded. "No. I'll call. Dad has a right to know. After all he's done for me."

"Don't pile that guilt on top of what you're already feeling. We're all indebted to our parents," Rosie said. "Not because *we* wanted it that way but *they* wanted it. Do you think *I* wanted my father to drain the money out of his little restaurant to pay my tuition? He could have used it to enlarge the place. Double his business. But he kept saying, 'Too much work to run such a large place.' Not true. He could have done it, and done it well. Maybe even be retired by now. But no, his little Rosie was going to be what she always wanted to be, a doctor. So I can work endless hours. Put up with tyrannical department heads; arrogant, demanding patients; and live in a city where my life is in danger every time I step outside this house!"

Rosie realized her complaint had added to Kate's depressed mood, so she tried to joke. "Well, now that I got my gripes off my chest, it's your turn."

"I — I'd better call. Dad'll be coming in from the fields about now. For his dinner. At home dinner is always midday. Big dinners. For Dad; my brother, Clint; and four farmhands. Used to be seven. But Dad sold off part of his acreage. Same reason as your father, I guess. Though Dad's excuse was carrying that loan at the bank in times of unsettled interest rates made farming a losing proposition. It seems dads always have reasonable explanations for doing unreasonable things for their kids."

Rosie laughed. "I can tell you one thing. I'll never do *anything* for my kids. I don't want them to feel guilty or beholden. Let 'em fend for themselves, I say. But then, I've never been a mother. Not yet, that is. But someday — someday I guess I'll have *my* turn to make all those parental mistakes."

Kate moved to the phone, near the end of the couch. She glanced at her watch. She could picture the scene at home right now. Dad at the head of the table flanked on each side by his farmhands and her brother, Clint. Mom bringing to the table steaming bowls of stew or soup or vegetables. And two loaves of her own baked bread. Dad always maintained that store-bought stuff wasn't bread. To prove it, he would wad up a handful of the soft insides until it was a ball of gummy stuff not fit to eat. So, Mom baked her own. All that was going on right now in the Forrester kitchen back in southern Illinois, where the farm seemed a million miles away from cities like New York and Chicago.

Kate punched in the phone number. She heard the ring. Twice, three times, four. For a moment she felt a pang of fear. If no one answered at home at dinnertime, something must be wrong. But the sixth ring was interrupted.

"Hello?" she heard her mother say.

"Ma, it's me."

"Katie!" Her mother was delighted to recognize her voice, but was cautious as well. "Anything wrong, darling?"

"Nothing. Nothing's wrong," Kate said in denial. She would have preferred not to start the conversation on this note.

"You, calling long-distance when telephone rates are high, and nothing's wrong?" her mother asked. "If it was just a hello and how are things, you'da called at night."

"Is Dad there? Can I talk to him?" Kate asked.

Now her mother knew there was trouble.

It showed in her voice. "Yes, darling. I'll put him right on."

Kate waited a moment, heard her dad clear his throat.

"Dad?"

"Yes, sweetheart, nice to hear your voice again. Since you got on that damn Emergency Service, you don't call often as you should."

He's making talk, Kate realized, *trying to sound relaxed, easygoing, for my sake. But he senses it's serious. I'd better tell him. Now. Straight out.*

She did. A brief description of the situation. A layman's explanation of what she had done. And also the unfortunate outcome. Throughout her report of the events her father continued to make sounds of assent, indicating his comprehension. "Uh-huh." "Yeah, I can see that." "Of course, natural thing to do." In the background Kate could hear her mother, "What is it, Ben? What's Katie saying?" She could picture her mother standing beside Dad, just about reaching up to his shoulder when she was on tiptoe. Kate had inherited her own small frame from her mother. Dad's blond hair and Mom's tiny frame, the best of both they used to say when she was a little girl. She could picture them now.

When Kate had finished her brief recounting of the situation, the first thing Ben Forrester said was, "Maybe better if we get you a lawyer of your own choosing. Someone like George Keepworth. I'd trust him more than some stranger."

"No need, Dad. The hospital is obligated to pay for it," Kate replied.

"Would it help if I come east?" he asked.

"No, Dad, no need. We're not even sure yet that anything's going to happen. I was just calling to let you know. Before you might hear it from some other source," Kate explained.

"What do you mean, from some other source?" he asked, on edge now.

"This Claude Stuyvesant, he's a very important man in New York. Anything he's involved in has a way of getting into the news. Papers. Television."

"Well, you tell that 'important' sonofabitch he does anything to my little girl, I'll come east and put a notch or two in his 'important' ass!"

Dad must be extremely angry. However rough his language with other people, he would never use such words in the hearing of his wife or daughter.

"Nothing's going to happen to me," Kate promised, to forestall the possibility Dad might indeed chuck everything, pile into the car, and drive to New York. Her mother would be with him, of course, cautioning him to drive carefully every mile of the way. Kate had not intended to alarm him, but obviously she had.

"Just relax, Dad, and I'll keep you informed."

"You do that," he said. Then added, "You know, I think about it often — what in the world are you doing in a place like New York anyhow? People hereabout could use a good doctor. And they'd appreciate her a lot more than those savages. Think about coming home, settling down here among your own people."

Kate realized Dad was already preparing a fall-back position for her, even though at the moment legal proceedings were only a hypothetical threat.

"I'm not planning on coming home, Dad," Kate said. "I'm staying and fighting!"

"You're forgetting how people around here think of you, Katie. After all, smartest in your high school class. Smarter even than all the boys. They still talk about you, ask about you. Can't go into town without someone stopping to ask, 'And how's our Kate doing?' It's like you belong to the whole town. When I told them you'd been accepted into that City Hospital, they weren't surprised. They just took it naturally that you'd be accepted into the biggest and the best. After all, 'our Kate.' If you have to, you face up to that bastard Stuyvesant, let him have both barrels, you hear?"

"Yes, Dad, I hear," Kate said.

Kate hung up even more depressed than she had been. In his effort to encourage her, Dad had only laid on her the added burden of living up to the opinion of her friends and neighbors back home.

That lawyer, got to see that lawyer.

Chapter Nine

Accustomed as she was to large universities, medical schools, and hospitals, Kate Forrester had never before entered offices as imposing as those of the law firm of Trumbull, Drummond & Baines. The reception room was on the sixth of the eleven floors the firm occupied. Kate asked for Scott Van Cleve, the name she had been given by Judge Trumbull's secretary. The receptionist summoned a page, who led Kate from the sixth floor down to the second floor, past a number of large, well-furnished partners' suites, to a group of smaller, less-imposing offices, until they reached the end of the long, carpeted hallway. There the page stepped aside to gesture Kate in.

She entered a small office that was in such haphazard condition, she felt sure no one with a sane, orderly mind inhabited it. There were law books scattered across the desk as well as piled on the floor. Some were opened, some were closed with yellow slips protruding from them to denote relevant cases. There was not one but three yellow legal pads on the desk, each with notes scrawled on them. On one corner of the desk was a half-eaten sandwich, rewrapped in its plastic, and a cup half full of coffee that had obviously gone cold.

Kate suspected now that, as her father feared, it had been decided that her case be handed to one of the less able, if not the least able, lawyers in Trumbull's firm. If her career, and the sixteen years of study she had devoted to it, were to depend on this person, whoever he might be, then perhaps a very able single practitioner from back home, someone like George Keepworth, actually would be the better, safer choice.

She was debating leaving, when suddenly into the room burst a tall young man, who was obviously surprised to find her.

"Oh!" he blurted out, with some annoyance, as if she had intruded on his train of thought. "You're . . . uh . . ." He tried to recall. "That young woman that — are you the doctor person?"

Stifling the quick and angry retort she was on the verge of making, Kate replied, "Yes. Are you the lawyer 'person' I was supposed to see?"

He stared at her, then his harried frown relaxed into a smile. "Sorry. But these days when women don't want to be called girls or ladies, I find I'm always struggling for the right word."

"Person," she repeated.

"Seems natural enough," he said. "I'm Scott Van Cleve," he started to say, but realized "— but then you know my name. Else you wouldn't have asked for me. And yours is —"

Kate realized, *He doesn't even know my name, that's how unfamiliar he is with my situation. I ought to leave. Right now! George Keepworth must know a good lawyer in New York to recommend.*

She decided to at least hear what this harried young man had to say. At the same time she made her physician's diagnosis of him. He was lean, in apparently good health. There was no sign of eyeglasses, either on his desk or on him. His eating habits were bad, as witness that half-eaten sandwich, but that could also mean that he was extremely conscientious about his profession. He was very tall. His hair was dark, not quite black. At only two thirty in the afternoon he already needed a shave, which meant he had shaved many hours ago. So he must be an early riser. Perhaps he rose early to get in a morning run. That would account for his lean, healthy-appearing physique.

She was in the midst of her diagnosis when he caught her off guard with a brisk, "Okay! Let's get started!" He cleared all books and pads to one side of his desk, opened a drawer to take out a fresh legal pad. He fumbled for her name once more. "Miss . . . It is *miss,* isn't it? Or do you prefer *ms.?*"

"Personally I prefer 'Doctor,' " Kate informed him. "Dr. Forrester."

"Okay, Dr. Forrester, let's get started."

Assuming that to be a request to recite the events in her treatment of Claudia Stuyvesant, Kate began: "The patient was brought into Emergency about nine thirty at night, presenting vague symptoms —"

Van Cleve interrupted. "Doctor, when I said let's get started, I meant *I* will get started."

"I should think that if you're going to be my attorney, you'd want to hear my side of things," Kate replied, exhibiting a slight edge of testiness.

"I will, in time. First I feel it is my duty to explain your legal situation."

"As far as I know, I have no 'legal situation.' "

"Not yet. But try to think of it this way. We are engaged in preventive medicine of a legal nature. Because in the normal course of these things we must expect that there will be a malpractice action against the hospital. And against you, personally."

"I thought the hospital's insurance covered all doctors," Kate replied. "That's one of the reasons for being on staff at a large hospital. The doctor is protected."

"Protected, yes," Van Cleve said. "Immune, no."

The frown of concern on her face made the young attorney realize that insofar as her legal situation was concerned, Kate Forrester was a complete novice.

"Doctor, the reason that an individual attorney has been assigned to you is this: If there is a malpractice suit, as we expect, the hospital will be named as a defendant, you will be named, and that other doctor — what's his name?"

"Briscoe? Eric Briscoe?" Kate asked.

"Right. Briscoe. When attorneys sue for malpractice, they sue everybody in sight. Anyone in any way connected with the case. The reason for that is they don't know how the jury will react. They may hold the hospital liable because of hospital rules and practice. Or they hold the doctors personally liable —"

"That's the second time you've said that, Mr. Van Cleve," Kate interrupted. "What good is malpractice insurance if it doesn't protect the doctor?"

"It does protect the doctor. Within limits. It provides your legal defense. And pays any verdict for damages within limits. But if the amount of the jury's verdict exceeds the policy coverage, then the hospital and the doctors become liable for the difference. And the way juries have been acting in recent years, well, I don't have to tell you."

"You mean I could be personally liable, that for the rest of my career . . ." Kate tried to comprehend.

"I thought you should know the potential danger you face in this situation," Van Cleve said, as gently as he could.

"Yes . . ." Kate said in a soft voice. "Yes, of course I understand."

"Now that you do, I would like to hear your version of what happened."

"My first contact with the patient was at about nine thirty Saturday night. . . . " Kate began to recount in sequence everything she could recall without having the patient's chart in front of her.

Van Cleve listened, from time to time scribbling a note or two on his yellow pad. Each time Kate paused to ask herself, *What did I just say that he picked up on? Why is that important? Did I say something that hurts my case?*

Though he knew what was going through her mind, each time he urged, "Continue, Doctor, continue."

Once she had completed her recitation of the events, Claudia's symptoms, the signs that Kate had discovered, the lab results, the patient's reactions, Van Cleve continued to nod reflectively.

"Mr. Van Cleve?" Kate prodded him.

"I will go into things more deeply after I've had time to do my own research. But briefly, until the patient's collapse, what had been your own best diagnosis?"

"Those generalized symptoms are most indicative of a stomach virus," Kate replied.

"If I questioned six doctors, presented them with the same set of symptoms —"

"And signs," Kate corrected.

"Symptoms . . . signs . . . what's the difference?"

"Symptoms are what the patient describes. Signs are what the doctor discovers and observes. Then she puts the two together to arrive at a diagnosis," Kate complained.

"Thank you, Doctor." Kate did not know whether the young attorney was being appreciative or sarcastic. "Now, let me repeat: If I examined six doctors under oath, presented to them the same symptoms and *signs* as you described, what would their opinion be?"

"The same, I'm sure. Viral stomach disorder," Kate said.

Van Cleve made another note on his yellow pad, asking, "All six?"

"If not all six, at least five out of six," Kate confirmed.

"Viral stomach disorder," Van Cleve repeated thoughtfully, making another note. "Briscoe concurred?"

"Not in so many words," Kate said. "But he didn't find any other cause."

"Such as?" Van Cleve asked.

"Those symptoms — nausea, vomiting, diarrhea, stomach pain — could signify many conditions. Inflamed appendix. A vaginal inflammation. Pregnancy. Ulcers. Half a hundred conditions. The process of diagnosis in a case like this is to test for and exclude each of the possibilities until you arrive at the right one," Kate said.

"Which unfortunately you obviously never did," Van Cleve pointed out.

"Medicine is not an exact science!" Kate shot back defensively. "It becomes more so with each passing year, each new discovery, but it is not yet perfect! Probably never will be!"

"Which is going to be our problem," Van Cleve said grimly. "Patients — and juries consist of patients — assume that medicine *is* perfect. That if something goes wrong, if the patient dies, it must be the fault of the physician. We start there and try to fight it. We don't always win. And when we lose, the verdicts are tremendous. I just thought you ought to know."

Kate nodded gravely.

"That will be all for our first meeting, Doctor."

Kate Forrester sat fixed in her chair, unable to respond to the attorney's words.

"I'll call you as soon as we're served with papers. But I can tell you now, there'll be no surprises. You *will* be named as one of the codefendants. Be ready," Van Cleve warned.

Kate rose and turned to the door.

"Oh," Van Cleve called, "one further word of warning. This will not be the usual case involving malpractice or negligence. We are dealing here with the S-factor."

"The S-factor?" Kate asked, puzzled.

"The Stuyvesant factor. He will not only have the best negligence lawyers prosecuting his case, he will also have the sympathetic ear of every judge and every other city or state official who might be helpful. Very few people in this city or this state can say no to Claude Stuyvesant."

"That may be. But I still believe that the truth is my best defense," Kate insisted.

"Right now, young woman, your best defense is that City Hospital, their insurance company, and our law firm are all involved in this case. They'll spend lots of money to defend themselves, which means that at the same time they'll be defending you. On your own such a defense would put you in debt for the rest of your life. You'll hear from me, Doctor."

Later that day, after Scott Van Cleve had reported on the initial conference with his new client, Dr. Katherine Forrester, Judge Trumbull placed a call to the hospital administrator, Cummins.

"Harvey," the aging lawyer began, "just to keep you up-to-date, one of our junior associates, Van Cleve, met with your Dr. Forrester. The first become-familiar go-round. Nothing unusual turned up."

"Which doesn't surprise me," Cummins said.

"However," Trumbull was quick to warn, "this has given me cause to do some further thinking about this situation."

Uneasy with Trumbull's prologue, since a lawyer as busy and important as Trumbull did not usually make phone calls to report on routine matters, Cummins asked, " 'Further thinking'? Such as?"

"In line with your own policy of damage control, to which I heartily subscribe, and to be prepared for any future developments — after all, we *are* dealing with Claude Stuyvesant — it might just be a good idea, for the present, to limit Dr. Forrester's activities."

" 'Limit her activities'?" Cummins considered. "She is a well-qualified resident in general medicine, and we can use all the staff we have. . . ."

"Harvey, we might at some future time have to justify the hospital's conduct. . . ."

Cummins interrupted to protest, "There was nothing wrong with this hospital's conduct. Or with Dr. Forrester's, as far as we know."

"Exactly, Harvey. 'As far as we know,' " Trumbull pointed out.

"I have every confidence in her," Cummins declared.

"Of course," Trumbull was quick to agree. "Believe me, no one values loyalty to staff more than I do. However, lawyers have to take all possibilities into consideration before giving advice. Especially in cases where millions of dollars may be at stake. So I suggest, no, I urge, that you limit Dr. Forrester's activities. Especially as it relates to treating patients."

"Well, I don't know . . ." Cummins protested.

"Harvey, as counsel to the hospital it is my duty to warn you that in this situation loyalty may be a luxury you cannot afford."

"I wouldn't want to take any step that might reflect on Dr. Forrester's professional competence," Cummins insisted.

"I'm not advising anything like that. Just remove her from patient contact for the present time. But whatever you do, do it quietly. The one thing we can't risk right now is bad publicity."

Chapter Ten

Kate Forrester rose earlier than necessary the next morning. For she planned to arrive at the hospital before her scheduled time to report for her new assignment. The sight of little Maria Sanchez, half conscious, bearing the bruised evidence of her suffering, had made a lasting impression on Kate. She would stop by and see if the child was making any progress or was in an even worse state than she had been when first admitted. Some abused children were beyond saving. They just withered and died. Kate hoped this little one was not in that pitiful condition.

She discovered that Maria had already been consigned to the care of Dr. Mike Sperber, a specialist in neonatal and pediatric neurological problems.

Though Kate had had no previous contact with him, Sperber had obviously heard of her, for when she appeared in the doorway of Maria's room during his examination, he greeted her with what seemed a taunt but was actually his way of bestowing praise.

"Do I have the honor of meeting the new lightweight champ of the hospital world?"

Sperber asked. "Next time pick on a guy your own size."

"I don't understand."

"Golding told me about your standing up to this poor kid's old man. Good thing. She's on the borderline. One more episode and I wouldn't give you a dime for her chances."

"And now?" Kate asked, staring at Maria, who seemed only a little more aware than she had been when Kate had first seen her.

Sperber beckoned Kate into the room. As she drew close to the bed, he took Kate's hand and pressed it against the child's face. The child drew back, seeming to shrivel. But slowly she reacted to Kate's soft, warm hand by reaching out to grip her forefinger. Though not physically strong, there was a sense of desperate need in the child's grip.

"Forrester, do something for me?"

"I don't have much time. I have to report for my new assignment."

"Just pick her up. And for as long a time as you have, hold her in your arms. That's all. Just hold her. We've got to start teaching her that not all adults are dangerous. That it is safe to trust. Unfortunately, staff is too overworked to have time to do that. So just hold her."

Kate settled onto the bed. She tried to lift the child into her arms. Little Maria resisted, then gradually gave herself to Kate's embrace and after a time seemed content to rest against her breast.

"Good," Sperber said. "Now, every day, several times a day, even if it's only for a few minutes at a time, do that. Maybe in time we can win her back to a normal life."

"Her neurological condition?" Kate asked.

"Still in the evaluation process. I see signs of hope. But only signs," Sperber said.

Kate Forrester was a little late when she consulted the assignment list on the medical-staff bulletin board. She did not find her name among those residents assigned to one of the clinics or to other patient duties. Instead she had to consult the second page to discover that alongside her name — Forrester, K. — appeared the words *Dept. Clinical Effectiveness. Dr. Nicholas Troy, Room B-22.*

Troy? Dr. Troy? Kate pondered. The name was vaguely familiar, but she could not connect it with any specific medical service. As for the Department of Clinical Effectiveness, she had never even heard it referred to before. She knew that Room B-22 must be in the basement, somewhere among the many subterranean tunnels that connected the various buildings of the hospital complex.

Puzzled as she was, Kate had no choice but

to comply with her assignment.

Though Troy's office was spacious, it impressed Kate as cramped due to its large, old-fashioned computers and the number of open floor-to-ceiling filing cabinets. Troy himself, who seemed in his late sixties or older, was studying an endless computer printout that started on the far side of his desk, straddled the desk, and hung down in his lap. His hair was white, wispy, and in disarray from his habit of scratching his pink scalp with his forefinger whenever he was puzzled and frustrated. He was evidently frustrated as he spoke to Kate without looking up from the printout.

"Yes?" he asked impatiently.

"I'm Dr. Katherine Forrester."

"That's nice," Troy replied in an irritated manner. "What am I supposed to do about it?"

"I'm assigned to your department for the present."

"I never asked for you," he said brusquely, then muttered to himself, "Damn these figures!" Until he suddenly recalled a telephone conversation of yesterday to which he had paid scant attention at the time since it had interrupted his concentration. "Aha!" he exclaimed in recognition. "You're the one! Yes! Cummins spoke to me about you. My God, young woman, what horrible crime did you commit that they assigned you to Siberia? For a young doctor who must be itching to go out and heal the whole world, this department of mine, concerned with mere dry facts and figures, must be exile."

He finally looked up from his printout to study Kate. "Hmmm," he exclaimed, greatly impressed. "If I had met a doctor like you in my youth, I would not now be a crusty old bachelor. Someday, when I know you better, I may tell you of my blighted romance with an O.R. nurse. But first, let's face a few facts. You don't want to be here. And to be honest, I don't particularly want you here. Reason? You will undoubtedly be unhappy not treating patients because you will think that what I do here is not practicing medicine."

He turned from his desk and with a wide sweep of his hand encompassed the room, the files, the computers. "You see all this? Because of it all those other doctors are afraid of me. With my computers and my printouts I discover the errors of their ways. How the myths that medicine has held dear for years turn out to be untrue. Unintentional frauds, if you wish to be polite.

"Young doctors are always being educated by the men who precede them. The beliefs and convictions of the older generation are passed on to the younger. So that actually medicine is usually a generation behind. Thus most doctors go on piling up mistakes until change takes place."

Troy gestured Kate to be seated, and realized there was no empty chair for her. He cleared one by lifting a pile of printouts off the chair and unceremoniously dropping them on the floor. Kate sank into the chair prepared to endure Troy's lecture, for it was clear to her that he had few opportunities to justify his work, so he made the most of each.

"For instance, if we had done meticulous record keeping of cures eighty, ninety years ago, we would not have fooled ourselves and our patients into thinking that fresh air and sunshine could cure tuberculosis. And for years we ordered patients, 'Drink milk and cream. It will cure your ulcers.' Not only does it not cure ulcers, it can make them worse. To say nothing of raising the patient's cholesterol level.

"We should have been asking ourselves, these fairy tales of medicine, our deeply held, but possibly false beliefs, do they *really* cure? Let's find out from the cold, hard facts and figures. Does this or that course of treatment cure? How often? How many patients out of how many patients treated by it really benefit from it? Never mind what some revered professor *says,* what do the facts *prove?*

"In other words, I am a gadfly, an annoying curmudgeon, to all doctors. The conscience of the hospital. It is my job, after assembling and studying the facts and figures, to say, 'Ladies and gentlemen, we are practicing bad medicine. We have to abandon the old and seek the new. But, most of all, we must take nothing for granted. Question, question, question!' "

Troy seemed to have exhausted himself, for he asked, "What do you say to a cup of tea? I know I could use one."

Kate nodded.

While waiting for the water in the glass pot on his single-burner electric hot plate to come to a boil, he admitted, "Forrester, I have a confession to make."

"Yes, Dr. Troy?"

"Your name was not unfamiliar to me. I heard about your situation. Very unfortunate. Even more unfortunate, it will grow worse," Troy said. As he was dipping the tea bag into the steaming water, he continued: "You will become another victim of our times. These days, everything is money, money, money. Lawyers, seeking ways to make it, seize on every medical misfortune to cry, 'Malpractice!' Every family outraged at the injustice of losing a loved one, seeks to console itself with cold cash. And why not? After all, on television shows they see sudden cures, medical miracles performed every week. And all in only sixty minutes. Actors who can't even properly apply a Band-Aid become heroes when they play doctors. So the public has come to expect that if an actor can do that, surely a real doctor can do it. You may well become a victim of that system. That's why you are here. Because you might be tainted, they don't want you upstairs in Emergency or in Clinic or on the wards. After all, if you were to suffer another accident, the insurance company would blame the hospital for keeping you on."

"Then why don't they let me go?" Kate asked.

"Aha! There you have put your finger on the insanity of our system," Troy exclaimed. "If they let you go now, that *would* be a public admission that you were incompetent. Which could mean they were at fault for hiring you in the first place. So they can't let you go. But neither can they risk exposing patients to your care."

"I'll quit!" Kate threatened, half rising from her chair.

Troy reached out to raise her face with a gentle finger under her strong chin. "That really would be an admission of guilt. And you don't look to me like a woman who got this far by quitting. Stay and fight, knowing there is a chance you may lose. The important thing: Assert your conviction in your treatment of that Stuyvesant girl. As I understand it, you took all the correct and indicated steps. If the outcome was tragic, it was not your fault."

He stared at her for a moment. "You *did* perform all the correct and indicated procedures, didn't you?"

"Yes, yes, I did. My entries on the patient's chart prove that," Kate insisted.

"Entries . . . In my day I have seen doctors make entries that were lies, complete lies, made up and written in the chart hours, and sometimes days, after the patient had died," Troy scoffed.

"My entries are accurate, and truthful, and were made the same night," Kate declared.

"I will make it a point to get a look at them," Troy said. "Just to satisfy my own mind. Meantime work here. You may be surprised at what you will discover. You might even come to realize that I am not some old nut who is hiding out in a basement office because he dreads the idea of retiring."

To make her choice seem less onerous, Troy smiled. "Look, my dear, what is one week or one month out of your young life? Just think what it will mean to an old man. For there is a relativity to these things. You, with so many years ahead of you, what is a month to you? But I, with so few years ahead of me, to me a month is like a lifetime. What harm could it do if every morning I am eager to come in here to see your lovely face? Now, finish your tea and let's get to work!"

Chapter Eleven

News of the death of the only child of a man so much in the public eye as Claude Stuyvesant had been picked up by all the wire services and featured by all the New York City newspapers. It had been an item on all the local television news programs. For two days the switchboard of City Hospital had been flooded with calls from the media, which Administrator Cummins had referred to Claire Hockaday, his public information officer. Ms. Hockaday responded to all questions with only a single, terse, prepared statement: "This past Saturday night patient Claudia Stuyvesant was brought to the Emergency Service of this hospital with an undiagnosed illness. She later died early Sunday morning from causes unknown at this time."

Pursuant to strict legal advice, Ms. Hockaday did not respond to any questions, nor did she release any further information. Left to their own imaginative devices, each local television news department had played the story from a different angle. One channel hinted that Claudia Stuyvesant's sudden death was due to a drug overdose. Another suggested it was suicide. By the third day, under the relentless torrent of sordid news, of rapes, muggings, and murder that is daily fare on New York City television, most stations dropped the Stuyvesant story.

Only at Channel 3, Hank Daniels, editor of the six-o'clock evening news, continued to regard it with more than passing interest. For some days Daniels and his investigative reporter, Ramón Gallante, had been accumulating a revealing series of interviews on health care in the New York area.

Gallante had taped conversations with a score of disappointed patients, surviving relatives, and a number of disgruntled employees in city hospitals. He had prodded them to reveal the faults, shortcomings, high costs, and wasteful practices in various health institutions. But neither Gallante nor Daniels was yet satisfied that any of those interviews was a strong enough grabber to catch and hold an audience for a week-long series.

Two days before, while having his morning coffee, Hank Daniels first saw and heard the Stuyvesant item. By the time he reached the studios of Channel 3, he had decided. He left word for Ramón Gallante to see him the moment he arrived.

"Ray," Daniels said as he broached the subject to Gallante, "do you think you could wangle an interview with Claude Stuyvesant?"

"He's a tough interview, unless he's got one of his blockbuster deals to announce. Then *he* sends for *you.*"

"What if we can make *sure* he'll send for you?" Daniels asked, smiling.

"Hank, you got an angle?" Gallante asked, tempted.

"Did you watch Channel Two this morning? And Channel Four?"

"Vaguely. I was getting dressed. What about Two and Four?"

"Two labeled Claudia Stuyvesant's death 'due to suspicious circumstances.' Which could mean suicide. And Four called her death 'sudden and due to circumstances as yet unexplained, and which are awaiting further testing.' Which hints that she O.D.'d on cocaine, heroin, or some other drug."

"Gotcha, Hank." Gallante smiled. "I call Stuyvesant to give him a chance to refute the slanders being cast upon his innocent daughter, who is now unable to defend her reputation."

"We are serving the highest cause of good journalism by helping to set the record straight," Daniels agreed, also smiling.

"I'll get on it right away," Gallante promised.

"Get that and I've got a great follow-up."

"Such as?"

"Nothing like a little controversy to draw a crowd and raise our ratings. Once we have Stuyvesant on tape, I call City Hospital and . . ."

"Give them equal time," Gallante supplied, smiling broadly now. "Hank, in my book you'll always be the best TV newsman in this town! What a kickoff to the series!"

Ramón Gallante spent twenty frustrating minutes on the phone. First with Claude Stuyvesant's secretary, then with Stuyvesant's executive secretary, before he finally played his trump card.

"Ms. Parker, do you realize the position in which you put Channel Three?"

With practiced poise, Florence Parker replied, "Mr. Stuyvesant is still in shock over this entire tragic event and is unable to comment at this time."

"I understand and, believe me, I sympathize. But Ms. Parker, put yourself in the place of an honest news reporter. At six o'clock tomorrow evening I will have to report that when I asked if Claude Stuyvesant's daughter committed suicide, as one channel hinted, or died of an overdose, as another channel hinted, Mr. Stuyvesant refused to refute either allegation. I would hate to have to say that, Ms. Parker. But you see my predicament."

Florence Parker had dealt with too many brash, intrusive newspeople not to recognize insidious blackmail when she heard it.

"Just a moment, Mr. Gallante. I'll get back to you."

Gallante was delighted to hold on in anticipation of Ms. Parker's response. In moments she was on the line.

"Mr. Gallante, exactly what did you have in mind?"

"Mr. Stuyvesant won't have to leave his office. I'll come up with a small camera crew. I'll take no more than fifteen minutes of his valuable time. And that'll be it. He can say anything he wants. We won't censor him. All I'll do is cut for time."

"Fifteen minutes?" Ms. Parker tried to pin him down.

"Fifteen minutes. Give you my word," Gallante promised.

"When?"

"Name it. I'm at your service."

"Will three o'clock this afternoon be convenient?"

"Three o'clock. I'll be there!"

Gallante hung up the phone with great anticipation.

* * *

By quarter after four that afternoon Ramón Gallante and his crew had returned from Claude Stuyvesant's office to the studios of Channel 3.

"How'd it go, Ray?" Daniels asked.

"Controversy, Hank? Did you say controversy? Well, I've got it. In the can. Very hot. So hot that on the way back I stopped at City Hospital and shot some exterior footage. When I get this all cut together, it'll be one hell of a lead to the series."

"Can I call City Hospital and invite them to set the record straight?"

"Call them, call them," Gallante said. "Now I've got to edit this stuff together."

From the excitement in Gallante's eyes and voice, Hank Daniels knew that the interview with Stuyvesant had more than justified his original hunch. With considerable satisfaction he lifted the receiver of his phone.

"Maggie, get me . . . what's his name . . . the doctor who is administrator of City Hospital."

"Dr. Cummins."

"Right. Get him!"

"Dr. Cummins," Hank Daniels began, "in pursuance of our fairness policy here at Channel Three, I feel compelled to tell you that tomorrow evening at six o'clock we are starting a new series titled *It's Your Life: What Are Your Chances of Survival in a New York City Hospital?* Our kickoff story is an interview with Claude Stuyvesant concerning the death of his daughter at City Hospital several nights ago. Mr. Stuyvesant makes some startling charges."

"Charges? What did he say?" Cummins asked anxiously.

"He said many things, Doctor. But we can't use them all. So the best way is for you to watch our six-o'clock news tomorrow evening and prepare your reply accordingly."

"Reply?" Cummins asked gingerly.

"Yes, sir. I am inviting you to reply the following evening at six. Either live or on tape, whichever you prefer. We'll allot you three minutes. Can I count on you making such a reply?"

"I'll . . . I'll have to get back to you," Cummins said. He hung up the phone and immediately called Judge Trumbull.

The next morning Dr. Kate Forrester reported to the basement office of Dr. Troy. She found him in his usual condition, desk piled high with computer printouts, wispy hair in disarray. He was scratching his pink scalp with the forefinger of his right hand in an elegant manner that endowed that mundane

143

act with a certain flair.

Without turning from his work, he tossed a casual greeting in her direction.

"Ah, good morning, Forrester."

"Good morning, Doctor."

The weariness in her voice made him glance at her over the rims of his Ben Franklin reading glasses.

"Had a bad night, did we?"

"No, not really," Kate said in an attempt at denial.

"Insufficient sleep, eh?" Another look and he changed his diagnosis. "No sleep at all. Don't deny it, my dear. Tossing, turning, wondering what they are going to decide at the meeting this morning. Frankly, I don't blame —"

Kate interrupted him. "Meeting? This morning? What meeting?"

"Oh," Troy replied, flustered. "I thought you knew."

"What did you think I knew that is being kept from me?" Kate asked.

"The way gossip floats around this hospital, I just assumed you knew," Troy said, obviously distressed that he had broached the subject.

"Dr. Troy, please! Tell me!"

"There is . . . this morning they are holding a special meeting of the medical board of the hospital. A very special meeting."

"To discuss my case?" Kate asked.

He shrugged sadly, forced to agree.

"Without my having a chance to defend myself?" she demanded.

"From what I heard, it didn't have to do with accusing or defending you, but with television," Troy said.

"Television? About me?" Kate asked, more puzzled than she had been. "We'll see about that!" she declared as she started out the door.

Around the conference table Dr. Harvey Cummins had assembled the chiefs of each department of the medical staff for an emergency meeting. Aware that their decision might involve legal consequences, he had also invited Lionel Trumbull as counsel to the hospital.

With a grave air, Cummins opened the meeting: "Gentlemen, and ladies, what I hoped might be contained as an in-house embarrassment threatens now to break out into a public scandal."

"Public scandal?" one of the chiefs asked in dismay. "That's all we need!"

"Channel Three is starting a series called *It's Your Life: What Are Your Chances of Survival in a New York City Hospital?*"

Dr. Eleanor Knolte, chief of pediatrics, remarked acerbically, "What they like to call

145

investigative reporting. I wish, for a change, someone would do some investigative reporting of the media! So they've latched onto the case of the Stuyvesant girl, have they?"

"Worse," Cummins said.

"What can be worse?" Knolte asked.

"The reason for this emergency meeting: Yesterday I received a call from the producer. He claims Ramón Gallante has taped a long interview with Claude Stuyvesant about his daughter's case. Gallante plans to start his series with that interview this evening."

"We've got to stop him!" Knolte protested.

"Too late," Cummins informed her. "The interview will air this evening on the six-o'clock news. Gallante's producer only called to find out if we wished to respond. That, ladies and gentlemen, is the decision to be made at this meeting. Does City Hospital respond, and if so, what stand do we take?"

There was an immediate outpouring of opinions for and against responding to Gallante and to whatever charges Stuyvesant might make. Once Cummins restored order, more considered opinions began to emerge.

Dr. Solomon Freund, a neurologist of some note, who had once been chief of neurology and was now professor emeritus, waited for all other opinions to subside before he spoke, softly and slowly.

"Ladies and gentlemen, let me point out that before we make any decision, we should discover the cause of the Stuyvesant girl's death. As far as I've heard, there's been no autopsy report as yet, has there?"

A number of no's went around the table.

"In that case," Freund continued, "I think it would be ill advised to say anything to anybody until we know the facts in the case."

"You mean," Harold Wildman, newly appointed chief of thoracic surgery, asked, "you would let some television scandalmonger slander this hospital and do nothing? Let a powerful man like Claude Stuyvesant accuse this hospital of whatever he likes and we don't even refute him?"

"I mean," Freund replied, "that until we know the facts, we ought not to embarrass ourselves by making statements that might turn out to be untrue. We'd only look like criminals trying to cover up a crime. We've committed no crime. We have no need to cover up. I say, make no response."

"Ordinarily, Sol, I would agree," Cummins said. "But in this case we have to be concerned with public reaction. We have beds to fill in order to get money from the government. Because without government funding we would have to close our doors. With such bad publicity, patients will be reluctant to come here.

147

We have to make some response."

"Yes, but what?" Freund demanded.

Lionel Trumbull felt forced to present his opinion.

"Doctors, in my vast legal experience I have found that sometimes it does more harm than good to reply to charges of this nature. Replies call forth refutations. Then possibly more charges. Endless bad publicity. The best thing is not to get into a head-to-head confrontation with a powerful man like Stuyvesant. I suggest we watch Stuyvesant's interview. Then if we do decide to reply, someone, either Dr. Cummins or Ms. Hockaday, your public information officer, goes on television and in very dignified fashion reports to the people of this city. Informs them of the number of cases we treat each year in Emergency, the number of patients who go home cured or helped. So that we present to the television audience a record of good, effective emergency health care delivered to all those who come to our doors seeking help. Succinct. Specific. Factual."

Trumbull's advice appeared to go down well with all those around the table.

"Then I take it," Cummins said, "the sense of this meeting is, if we respond it will be a dignified, fact-filled reply, making no attempt to get into a dogfight with Stuyvesant.

I shall have Dr. Troy assemble the statistics."

"Do I also take it," Dr. Freund asked, "that you plan no defense of Dr. Forrester at this time?"

"In the interest of caution," Trumbull advised, "and with a view to a very likely malpractice suit, I say we avoid that issue at this time."

"Won't that look like we're abandoning her?" Freund asked.

Cummins replied at once and sharply, "This hospital stands behind its staff! And it will do so in Dr. Forrester's case."

"In fact," Trumbull added, "we have evidenced our willingness to defend her to the hilt. She has already met with the attorney in my office who is preparing her defense."

"As long as she is being protected," Freund appeared relieved to say, "I agree with the consensus here."

"Good!" Cummins said. "I shall get Troy cracking on those figures. And I assume that we shall all be watching Channel Three with considerable interest this evening."

By the time Kate Forrester arrived at Cummins's waiting room, the meeting had broken up. When she asked to see the administrator, she was shown in at once. She found Cummins quite affable as he said, "I

149

assume you're here to ask to be transferred back to your usual duties. I thought you might enjoy working with Troy. It's a fascinating approach to medicine."

"Dr. Cummins, did that meeting you just held have to do with me?"

"In a small way, yes," Cummins said.

"Then I'd like to know what was decided," Kate said. "It's the least I'm entitled to."

"You are also entitled to know that this evening at six o'clock on Channel Three Claude Stuyvesant will be interviewed about his daughter's death."

"Stuyvesant intends to make a public issue of this?" Kate said, realizing the implications.

"A man with his prestige and power, Mr. New York, you didn't think he'd keep quiet about it, did you? Why, I remember once he wanted to get tax concessions on a piece of property. The city refused. He went on television and accused the mayor of depriving this city of three thousand new jobs. Eventually even the mayor had to cave in to him. For a man who keeps insisting he likes his privacy, Stuyvesant knows how to use the media when he wants to."

"Do you know if he'll attack me?" Kate asked.

"We have no idea what he'll say. But we'll all be a lot smarter after six tonight."

Kate nodded thoughtfully, though inside she felt a stab of pain in her stomach. Then she asked, "Is that why you have assigned me to Dr. Troy?"

"A precautionary measure. Trumbull's legal advice. Keep a low profile. Just in case it becomes important once the papers are filed in the malpractice case."

"Why is everyone so sure there's going to be a case?" Kate asked. "With all his millions, billions I've heard, why would Stuyvesant want to go through a painful trial only to get more money?"

"Stuyvesant is a vindictive man. He's been known to spend more on legal fees than he wins in court, just to make a point. So we have to be guided by our lawyers' advice. I understand you've already met with one."

"Yes. A young man named Van Cleve."

"And how did you find him?"

"He seems quite intelligent. Very serious about his work. I think he may do," Kate said.

"Good! As long as you know that this hospital is giving you all the protection you will require."

"I just wish I didn't require it."

"We'll know later this evening. Meantime get back to Dr. Troy. He'll need plenty of help to accumulate the statistics I'll need if we agree to reply."

Chapter Twelve

Dr. Kate Forrester sat alone before the television set in the apartment she shared with Rosalind Chung. She watched with impatient anxiety as she endured the bits and snatches of national and local news before the segment the anchor woman had headlined at the top of the program as: "Share a father's grim first-hand experience with medical care in New York City. The opening segment of Ramón Gallante's newest investigative series — about hospitals, doctors, and your chances of receiving decent health care in our largest and supposedly best medical institutions."

There followed more news, two more commercial breaks, which meant eight commercials squeezed into three minutes, followed by a weatherman who made bad jokes, and a sports reporter who made even worse ones.

To Kate it all appeared calculated to add to her torment; she shouted at the screen, "Get on with it!"

Finally the anchor woman announced, "And now, *It's Your Life,* with our own investigative reporter, Ramón Gallante, on one father's very sad experience. Ramón!"

From a close-up of the anchor woman, the camera cut to the tape of Ramón Gallante, microphone in hand, standing before City Hospital. In the background, nurses and other hospital personnel were leaving and arriving. Some of them stopped to gape at Gallante.

"I am standing outside an institution well known to most New Yorkers — City Hospital. Regarded by many as one of the most prestigious providers of health care in the metropolitan area. It contains the best, latest, and certainly the most expensive of equipment, plus a staff carefully selected and supposedly one of the finest available anywhere. And yet, how good is it, really? Good enough for you to entrust *your* life to? Or your child's life?"

In her modest living room Kate Forrester felt the burning acid of anger rise into her throat.

In the office of Hospital Administrator Harvey Cummins, he and members of his staff watched with controlled hostility.

In one of the offices at Trumbull, Drummond & Baines, Scott Van Cleve and Lionel Trumbull both watched. Scott had his eyes trained on the tube. Trumbull divided his attention between the tube and Scott's reaction, which was becoming more apparent from the angry flush on his craggy face.

While Gallante's voice continued, the TV picture dissolved from the view of City Hospital to Stuyvesant Tower on Wall Street. The camera moved in on Gallante, who stood before that building.

"Now, from footage shot earlier, I stand before another edifice in the Manhattan skyline, mighty Stuyvesant Tower. A landmark in the financial capital of the world. Not many of you will ever enter this enclave of the rich and powerful. I do so now only to meet the man whose name graces this monument of glass and steel."

As Gallante turned to pretend to enter the building, the picture cut to a richly paneled oak door on which the name CLAUDE J. STUYVESANT appeared in bold letters carved out of stainless steel. On cue the door opened, and the camera moved through, as Gallante spoke. "Now, to meet, face-to-face, the legend who goes with the impressive name, Claude J. Stuyvesant. And to hear the tragic story of one father's experience with City Hospital."

The picture dissolved to Claude Stuyvesant seated behind his huge desk on which the most prominent article was a photograph of his daughter. A muscular man of tall frame, with a strong jaw, his ruddy complexion testified to many hours spent on the open sea pursuing his hobby, which was commanding his large sailing vessel in transoceanic races. Behind him was an entire wall of glass beyond which stretched the vast harbor of New York City as it might be seen from a helicopter. Together Stuyvesant's appearance and his vast surroundings gave great impact to his presence.

"Mr. Stuyvesant," Gallante began, "your daughter, Claudia, was not exactly the typical patient who is brought into the Emergency Service of a city hospital, was she?"

"I suppose people expect that when a Stuyvesant becomes ill, a whole retinue of expensive doctors is available day and night. It just so happens that our family physician was out of town at some medical convention on the night in question. Which is no excuse for what happened to my only daughter." Stuyvesant now spoke with great emotion. "You bring up a child for nineteen years and in one night, less than one night, just hours, they kill her. Murder, it was no less than murder!"

"When you say that, Mr. Stuyvesant, surely you don't mean that the staff of City Hospital conspired to kill your daughter, do you?"

"Conspired? No. But I do hold them responsible. They put my daughter into the hands of a woman doctor . . . a woman named

Forrester. I think her first name was . . ."
He made a pretense at groping for it, then
seemed to remember. "Oh, yes, Katherine
Forrester. If I seem to forget her name, it is
because I would like to blot it out of my memory for all time."

Claude Stuyvesant's angular face, his tightly
muscled jaw, his vengeful gray eyes, his very
posture projected the hatred he felt.

Alone in her living room, hearing this man
denounce her in such vehement terms, Kate
Forrester rose from her chair, enraged, but
at the same time hurt almost to the point of
tears. She turned to the phone and consulted
the slip on which Scott Van Cleve had written
his number. She started to punch it in, but
was interrupted by another outburst from
Stuyvesant.

"If my daughter received such treatment at
City Hospital, imagine what the rest of the
people of this city can expect," Stuyvesant said
accusingly.

"Mr. Stuyvesant, have they yet determined
the nature of your daughter's death?" Gallante
asked.

"No. That must await the autopsy,"
Stuyvesant replied. "You have no idea, Mr.
Gallante, the pain, the grief, of a father when
he has in his mind this image of his innocent
young daughter, lying naked and dead, in a

vault at the medical examiner's office, waiting to be cut open, invaded by strange hands, to find the cause of her death. As if dying weren't enough. And to think it could all have been avoided by proper medical treatment."

"Do you think it's fair to make such a statement, sir, without knowing more about the case?" Gallante prodded, at the same time trying to give every impression of pursuing the truth.

"Fair?" Stuyvesant countered. "Fair? In this case the facts are apparent. A young woman of nineteen, with a simple pain in the stomach, is treated in a city hospital and dies within a matter of hours. Only this morning my lawyers pointed out to me that there is a Latin phrase in the law, *res ipsa loquitur*, meaning the thing speaks for itself, no more proof is needed. They said this is one malpractice case in which that might well apply."

"Then I take it, sir, you are planning to sue for malpractice?"

"That's the only way to get the hospitals in this city to toe the mark! Sue them. Let them know there is a price for negligence. And for arrogance. That young woman, she was arrogant as well as negligent," Stuyvesant said accusingly.

"Then I assume you will be suing her as well?" Gallante asked.

"Suing her will be the least of what I do to her," Stuyvesant said.

"Sir, may I ask what else you can do that would be worse?" Gallante asked.

"A malpractice suit can take years in the courts. I want results much quicker than that!"

"Results, sir?" Gallante asked.

"I want that woman forbidden to practice medicine in this city, in this state, anywhere, ever again!" Stuyvesant declared.

"And just how does one do that?" Gallante asked.

"First thing I asked my lawyers. What's the procedure to remove an incompetent, dangerous doctor from the ranks of practicing physicians? They told me there is such a procedure. Make a complaint to the state health commissioner. Have the whole case reviewed by the Office of Professional Medical Conduct. Once the facts are presented to them, I promise you they will remove that woman's license to practice."

Hoping to draw an even more newsworthy bit from him, Gallante asked, "Mr. Stuyvesant, if your accusation were to be declared unfounded, couldn't there be repercussions? Legal repercussions?"

"You mean a lawsuit?" Stuyvesant asked.

"Against you. For damage to that doctor's reputation. With your notorious wealth, that might result in a judgment of millions."

Stuyvesant snorted. "She'd dare sue me? Let her! My lawyers'll keep her tied up in the courts for the rest of her life. I'll teach her to treat my daughter as she did, to ignore my wife as she did!"

"Thank you, sir," Gallante said, confident he had a number of quotes that would be picked up by his rivals on the other TV channels, all of whom would have to credit him.

The moment the interview was over, Kate punched in Scott Van Cleve's phone number.

Pondering the effect of the interview, Van Cleve sounded detached as he said, "Hello? Who is — ?"

"It's me, Dr. Kate Forrester. Who goes around killing patients."

"Oh, you just saw it," Van Cleve said.

"Yes, I saw it. What are we going to do about it?"

"Exactly nothing."

"Are you advising me to let Stuyvesant get away with such outrageous accusations?"

"For the time being, yes," he confirmed.

"If I don't refute his charges at once, isn't that an admission of guilt?" Kate asked. "I'm going to call that TV station right now and explain what really happened Saturday night —"

Van Cleve interrupted. "Doctor! Now you listen to me. Very carefully. You will do no such thing."

"I can't let him get away with those lies," Kate protested.

"For the time being, you will."

"I thought it was your job to protect me," Kate rebuked.

"It is. That's why, as your lawyer, I forbid you to get into a public brawl with a man as powerful as C. J. Stuyvesant."

"Still, to let such lies go unchallenged —"

"Doctor . . . listen to me, please? Nothing you say will convince the public. They're in a state of war against *all* doctors. Medical expenses are running too high. Health care is out of reach of the people who need it most. The climate for doctors is bad right now, very bad. So even if Gallante comes after you, you are 'unavailable for comment,' as the phrase goes."

"But the public should know the truth," Kate replied. "I want to tell them."

"*You* are the last person in the world to tell them."

"I'm the only one who knows what happened," she protested. "After all, I was the doctor involved."

"Exactly! And, because you were, you're too emotional about it." Then he pointed out,

160

"To television reporters controversy is merchandise they sell for profit. Gallante is only trying to stir things up for his own professional advantage. He's liable to trap you into blurting out something that hurts our case, or worse, something that slanders Stuyvesant. Then Stuyvesant turns around and sues you. To him that would be an amusing hobby, which would cripple you financially for the rest of your life."

In her highly emotional state Kate had not considered such consequences.

"Some of the worst legal blunders occur when an outraged person goes seeking justice," Van Cleve cautioned.

"But if his charges —" she started to say.

"We will refute his charges in the only two places that count: in a courtroom if there's a malpractice trial; and, if you do have a hearing, before the state board. Meantime let's wait for that autopsy report."

"All right, then. I'll do it your way," Kate conceded reluctantly.

Kate had no sooner hung up than the phone rang while her hand was still on the receiver. She lifted it once more to answer.

"Hello . . ."

"Kate . . . Katie . . ."

"Walter?" she responded, startled. "Walter, I've already told you my decision. Besides,

161

I have other problems right now. Important problems."

"That's why I'm calling," Walter said.

"You saw it, you heard Stuyvesant?"

"Half the city must have heard him," Walter replied. "Look, I'm coming up there. You need help. I'm going to help you. First thing we'll go see Tom Brady, my lawyer. Don't worry. I'll pay for it. We'll find out how we get that bastard Stuyvesant to retract every lie he told about you. . . ."

"Walter . . . Walter . . ." Kate kept trying to interrupt. Finally she declared, "Walter! Stop it! Right now!"

"Kate, we can't let him get away with this," Walter protested.

"Walter, for weeks now I've been trying to tell you, it's no longer 'we' and 'us.' That's over. We live different lives. Have different aims and ambitions. We'd never make a go of it. You're a great success at what you do, making money. But that isn't enough for me."

"No," Walter seemed to agree, then said sarcastically, "You have to serve humanity. Very noble. Now you see what it gets you. One mistake and you're being attacked on television, threatened with a malpractice lawsuit, with having your license revoked. What you need is a man, a husband, to protect you from your own unselfish impulses. So that if you *do* make a mistake, your whole world doesn't collapse. After all, you're only human. . . ."

"What does that mean?" Kate interrupted.

"What does *what* mean?" Walter replied.

" 'After all, you're only human,' " Kate repeated his words to him.

"None of us is perfect," Walter said, trying to ameliorate what he suddenly realized had sounded like an accusation.

"I'm not talking about 'none of us,' " Kate responded angrily. "I'm talking about *me*. You're implying Stuyvesant turned a healthy young daughter over to me and, because I'm 'only human' due to something I did or didn't do, she was dead hours later."

"I never said . . ." Walter tried to explain.

Kate would not permit him. "First, Claudia Stuyvesant wasn't anyone's 'healthy young daughter.' If she were, her mother wouldn't have brought her into Emergency late at night. She was sick. And in a condition we're not even sure of yet. She was treated in the best way we know, based on the information I was able to ascertain. She was not neglected or mistreated and certainly not murdered! So he won't get away with it!"

"That's what I'm trying to say," Walter protested. "I want to help. I want to provide you with a lawyer."

"Walter, I appreciate what you're offering. Because you want to revive what we were to each other. And this is one way you can do it. But no, thanks."

"Maybe . . ." Walter started to say, then seemed to reconsider, but finally admitted, "Maybe it's that. But maybe it's something else."

"Like what?" Kate asked, puzzled.

"Guilt," Walter admitted.

"Guilt?" Kate repeated, more than puzzled now.

"I . . . I just hope I wasn't the cause of all this trouble," Walter confessed.

"You?"

"Saturday night. I called you in Emergency. Don't you remember?"

"Of course I remember. What about it?" Kate asked.

"There you were racing from patient to patient, in addition to the Stuyvesant girl, and I insisted they drag you to the phone. Remember you said, 'I just hope I can make it until six o'clock'?"

"Of course. I was exhausted."

"Then you said, 'If I can just get through the night without cracking up, I'll be lucky.'"

"Every intern, every resident on E.R. duty feels that way. A long night, followed by a long day, followed by another long night, how would you expect us to feel?"

"That's my point. While you had patients who were sick, in pain, even dying, I was like a spoiled child insisting on your attention. Listening to Stuyvesant accuse you made me feel guilty. I blame myself too."

"Too?" Kate asked. "What do you mean, 'too'?"

"I mean . . . I mean, whatever blame . . ." Once he realized what he had said, Walter stopped abruptly.

"Walter, if you blame yourself, *too,* that means you blame me."

"Of course not!"

"You're saying I was too tired, too hassled, too beat to perform like a good, competent doctor. I blew the case. I did kill that girl!"

"I never said . . ." Walter said in an effort at refutation.

"Then why volunteer to share the blame? Why offer to get me a lawyer and pay for it? If *you* feel that I'm guilty, what must the rest of this city think by now?"

Kate heard the front door being unlocked and heard Rosie Chung call, "Kate? You here?"

Kate called back, "Yes, I'm here." Then she returned to the phone. "Walter, thank you for your offer. Whether it was made out of consideration for me or to appease your own guilt, the answer is still no. And one thing more — please, don't call again. You won't change my feeling about us."

Before Walter could respond, Kate hung up. She realized there was a film of sweat on the telephone where her hand had gripped it.

By then Rosie had hung up her coat and was into the living room. "He's a very persistent cuss."

"He was only calling to help," Kate explained.

"You're going to need it," Rosie said. Kate glanced at her questioningly. "I saw the whole thing on TV. Then got right into a cab and came home. I knew you'd need someone to talk to after Stuyvesant's vicious accusations. Believe me, Katie, I know how you must feel, because I know how I feel. And nobody's accused me."

She embraced Kate. "Don't you worry, sweetie. You've got friends. Lots of friends. The whole staff is outraged. Stuyvesant might as well have accused us all. So if he's looking for a fight, he's going to get one. There's talk among the residents of chipping in to hire you a lawyer."

"I already have a lawyer," Kate pointed out.

"I mean a lawyer that you pay, who's responsible to you alone," Rosie said. "We have it all figured out. Bert Hoffman said, from what he knows about the law, you can sue Stuyvesant for slander and libel."

"Sure, I sue Stuyvesant. As he said, it takes years for the case to come to court. But what happens to me during those years? No amount of money in this world is going to buy back those years of my life. Something's got to be done. Now. And I've got to do it. By myself. For myself. I don't want anyone else fighting my war."

"Do what, Katie?"

"Tell them what really happened," Kate said with determination.

"Tell who? How?" Rosie asked.

"Tell the whole city. On television!" Kate replied.

"I think you ought to talk to that lawyer first," Rosie advised.

"I already did."

"What did he say?" Rosie asked.

"He told me to do nothing," Kate admitted.

"Then maybe that's what you ought to do," Rosie cautioned.

"Oh, sure," Kate scoffed. "It's very easy for him to give *me* that advice. It's not *his* reputation, not *his* career, not *his* life that's on the line. It's mine! If even Walter can suspect me, then Stuyvesant's accusations must have poisoned the minds of most of the people of this city. They should know the truth. And

I'm the only one who can tell them."

Kate started looking up the number in the phone book, while Rosie cautioned, "Katie, you might only be making matters worse."

But Kate was already punching in the number. In moments an operator responded. "Station WNYO — Channel Three."

"Ramón Gallante, please!"

"Mr. Gallante does not take calls."

"Then let me talk to the producer of the six-o'clock news."

"One moment, please," the operator said politely. In moments a harried, irritable voice came on the line. "Daniels. Who is this and what do you want?"

"I'm Katherine Forrester."

"Yeah? So?" Daniels responded impatiently.

Kate had expected that he would recognize her name instantly. "I'm *Doctor* Katherine Forrester."

"Look, Doctor, if you're calling to complain about the Stuyvesant interview, we do not *make* the news. We only report it. The man had a legitimate gripe about a subject on which Gallante is currently doing an investigative series. We thought the interview was pertinent, so we used it. That's it. Period! Now, I'm reviewing tape for tomorrow evening, so I've got to go."

"You mean you won't give me a chance to explain the doctor's side of things?" Kate asked.

Daniels's voice changed from harried and aggressive to interested and alert. "You mean come on camera and explain?"

"Yes!"

"Let me have your number. I'll have Gallante get back to you."

It didn't take more than three minutes for Kate's phone to ring.

"Dr. Forrester? Gallante here. I understand you'd like to refute the accusations Stuyvesant made against City Hospital and, more specifically, against yourself."

"Yes, I would."

Hank Daniels leaned across Gallante's desk, anticipating the outcome of the conversation. As Gallante nodded to signify Kate's agreement, Daniels whispered, "Get her in her normal hospital background. Good color."

"Doctor, in all fairness," Gallante continued, "we would like to present you, as we did Mr. Stuyvesant, in your normal working background. At the hospital. In Emergency, preferably."

"Thanks to your interview with Mr. Stuyvesant, I have a feeling the hospital won't allow that."

Gallante shook off Daniels's inquisitive

stare. "Outside the hospital, then," the producer whispered.

"What about outside the hospital? I can have a remote truck and crew there."

"Live, live," Daniels whispered urgently.

Gallante nodded. "Doctor, what if, in the interest of getting your response unedited or cut, we do it live? Tomorrow evening?"

"As long as I have a chance to respond to that totally unwarranted and poisonous attack on my reputation," Kate agreed.

"Good! That's our policy. Fairness. Equal time. See you outside City Hospital. Quarter to six. That'll give us a chance to spitball a few questions and answers before we go on the air."

"I'll be there," Kate assured him.

As Gallante hung up the phone, Hank Daniels said, "This could be even better than having the hospital respond. More human interest."

As Kate hung up the phone, Rosie said, "God, Katie, I hope this isn't a mistake."

"Somebody has to stop this poison from spreading," she said, as she looked up the phone number of the medical examiner's office.

Though it was evening, because of the number of murders, suicides, drug O.D.'s, and accidental deaths in New York City,

170

the medical examiner's office was a twenty-four-hour operation.

One of the examiner's assistant pathologists was in charge for the night. From the impatient tone of his voice Kate knew he was a man overtaxed by people making the same kind of request she was about to make.

"Dr. Kennedy, this is Dr. Kate Forrester, City Hospital."

"I know, I know," Kennedy said, to forestall her request. "The Stuyvesant cadaver. This is only the fourth call today. Doctor, with the district attorney bugging me for results in eight different killings so that he can get to the grand jury in time, the Stuyvesant case is tenth in line. Dr. Schwartzman will get to it as soon as he can."

"But this case is extremely important," Kate started to say.

"Don't I know," the harried forensic pathologist replied. "After all, pressure from the real estate king."

"Has Stuyvesant been pressuring the medical examiner?" Kate asked.

"Doctor, when we get three calls from the mayor's office about one particular autopsy result, we don't have to be told there's a lot of political muscle behind it. Now, I'll tell you what I told the mayor's secretary. Dr. Schwartzman will get around to the Stuyvesant case as soon as he can!"

The slow, thoughtful manner in which Kate returned the phone to its cradle caused Rosie to ask, "Katie? Something wrong?"

"Ever have the feeling that you're getting a deliberate runaround?"

Chapter Thirteen

Several times during the following day Channel 3 exploited Kate's appearance to the full. It ran teaser promo announcements promising a surprise guest on Ramón Gallante's series on health care in New York City. As the afternoon wore on, the promos became more specific and tantalizing. Starting at five o'clock the promos promised "a live interview with the doctor whom Claude Stuyvesant has accused of killing his daughter."

Word filtered through City Hospital even more quickly than the usual gossip. Before six o'clock it had reached the office of Administrator Cummins. Immediately he had his secretary page Kate Forrester to caution her against her appearance. But she had already left the hospital. Cummins was forced to watch her interview on television.

In other parts of the hospital those people not actively engaged in patient care were staring down from the windows at Gallante's remote crew, which was setting up across the street. Gallante himself directed the two cameras about the angles he wanted.

"We'll open with the hospital full on camera

173

one. Then move in until you get me in frame. Then cut to camera two for my close-up. I'll do my intro and the lead-in. Then pull back enough to include that woman doctor. It'll be two-shots the rest of the way until I do my sign-off solo."

He turned away from the cameramen so quickly that he collided with Kate. Pulling back, he called to his crew, "For Christ's sake, guys, keep the area clear!" Then to Kate he said, "Look, lady, we're doing a TV remote here, so, please, move it!"

"Mr. Gallante?"

"Yes, yes, no time for autographs now."

"I'm Dr. Forrester," Kate said.

"You? You are the 'infamous' Dr. Forrester? I thought lady doctors looked this pretty and this blond only on TV soap operas. Pleased to meet you." He looked her over, shook his head in smiling disbelief. "Let's go over a few questions so you can be prepared with your answers."

"Right!" Kate said.

"You're aware that this is part of my series, *It's Your Life: What Are Your Chances of Survival in a New York City Hospital?*"

"Nobody is more aware," Kate snapped back.

"Mr. Stuyvesant came on to complain about his daughter's treatment at this hospital, which

174

resulted in her death. That's the first thing I'll say. Then you are free to respond. After that I have a few more questions about the state of health care in Emergency Rooms in this hospital and others around the city. You can comment on that in any way you like. This is a freewheeling interview. But keep talking. One thing we have no time for on TV news is pauses. Only presidents of the United States are allowed to pause on TV news."

"I do not intend to pause," Kate said, determined to make use of every second of air time Gallante would grant her, and more.

"Okay. Stand by for the news from the studio, then we'll get our cue and we'll be on!"

Gallante watched the top of the news on the monitor in the back of the truck before he came out to join Kate. He posed her against the background of the hospital. Microphone in hand, he stood braced for his cue. The woman who worked camera one threw him a signal. Gallante was on.

"Ramón Gallante here. And here, as you can see, behind me is City Hospital, as we continue our investigative series, *It's Your Life*. Your health care, is it enough, is it good enough? With me this evening is Dr. Kate Forrester."

With his free hand he reached to draw Kate

close and into the picture.

"Those of you who were with us last evening know that Dr. Forrester is the woman whom Claude Stuyvesant accused of responsibility for the death of his nineteen-year-old daughter, Claudia, in the Emergency Room of this very hospital. This evening Dr. Forrester is here to respond to Mr. Stuyvesant's charges against her. Doctor?"

"Mr. Stuyvesant's charges against me and this hospital are totally false and groundless. Everything that could be done for his daughter was done. In accord with the best medical practice."

"But she did die, didn't she, Doctor?"

"Yes. But no one knows why."

"She was here, in this modern hospital, for nine hours, surrounded by the best medical equipment, treated with the latest medical techniques, but she died and no one knows why?" Gallante asked, making a comment more than seeking information.

"Claudia Stuyvesant did not present sufficient signs and symptoms to enable a physician to make a definitive diagnosis," Kate explained.

"In this whole large hospital, not a single doctor was able to make a diagnosis?" Gallante asked.

"*I* was in charge. *I* was not able to make

a diagnosis. And I doubt any other doctor could have done so under the same circumstances," Kate replied.

"You didn't call in any other, more experienced, doctor for consultation?" Gallante asked. "You just handled the case on your own?"

"I did call in another doctor. A surgeon."

"And his name?"

"Dr. Briscoe. Dr. Eric Briscoe."

"And what did Dr. Briscoe say?" Gallante asked.

"He had no more basis on which to make a diagnosis than I did. There simply weren't enough facts and definitive lab findings."

"Yet Claudia Stuyvesant was so sick that within hours she died." Gallante was working Kate over like a picador in a bullring, with those tiny telling stabs that prepare the bull for the final fatal thrust.

"The patient's pulse was elevated, and there was distension of her stomach," Kate explained, "but that did not indicate her true condition."

"Pain? Was there pain?" Gallante asked.

"Yes, but not sufficient pain to reveal the seriousness of her situation."

"Doctor, exactly what do you call 'sufficient pain' to indicate that a young woman of nineteen in good health this morning is going to die tonight?" Gallante asked. "How do you determine that? I'm sure our viewers would like to know. Especially those now suffering pain and trying to decide where to go for help."

Fully aware that Gallante was attempting to ridicule her, Kate determined not to permit it.

"Mr. Gallante, this is not the place, nor do you have time enough for me to explain the medical ramifications involved."

"As you say, Doctor." Gallante seemed about to terminate the interview, then pretended to be seized by a sudden thought. "Doctor, you made a most interesting statement a few moments ago. You said you couldn't make a diagnosis on the Stuyvesant girl, yet you treated her with the latest medical techniques —"

Kate interjected, "You said that, I did not!"

"Are you telling our viewers that you didn't even treat her?" Gallante asked.

"We did treat her!" Kate insisted.

"How do you treat an undiagnosed illness? Is there some magic pill that you doctors at City Hospital use in all mystifying cases?" Gallante asked, casting a faint but superior smile in the direction of the camera.

"Until you can make a diagnosis, all you do is try to reduce the patient's fever, feed intravenous fluids to avoid dehydration. And do all the lab tests that you think will help you arrive at a correct diagnosis," Kate explained firmly.

"Reduce the fever. And feed fluids intravenously," Gallante repeated. "That doesn't sound much better than 'take two aspirin and call me in the morning.' But unfortunately by morning Claudia Stuyvesant was dead."

"We monitored her vital signs continuously," Kate protested. "There was no indication —"

"Are you telling my viewers that though the patient was so close to death, she gave no indication?" Gallante asked.

"You have to understand the situation . . ."

"I'm trying, Doctor, believe me, I'm trying," Gallante taunted.

"A doctor has two things to work with: what she herself observes and what the patient tells her. Sometimes what the patient tells her may not be true," Kate pointed out.

"You mean a patient seeking help would lie to the doctor who might help her?"

"Patients have frequently been known to lie to doctors. About their sexual habits and practices. About drug use. If a patient is a drug abuser, her symptoms and signs may be masked or distorted. Her pain may appear less intense and her condition less threatening

179

than it actually is."

"Doctor, are you telling my audience that Claudia Stuyvesant was a drug-addicted, sexually loose young woman?"

"Mr. Gallante, don't twist my words! I am saying there are many possibilities that must be explored, and I expect the autopsy will reveal that," Kate corrected.

Knowing that he had evoked some provocative quotes that would be repeated on other late-night news shows, Gallante was ready to move in for the kill.

"Doctor, since we are running out of time, let me sum up for our viewers. This young woman of nineteen, Claudia Stuyvesant, was brought to the Emergency Service of this hospital, placed in your care. You treated her for nine hours —"

"Along with treating a great number of other patients," Kate interjected.

"Yes, of course. Along with a great number of other patients. But you treated her for nine hours. Never made a diagnosis. Applied a few superficial modalities, which evidently proved no more effective than chicken soup, because at the end of that time Claudia Stuyvesant was dead!"

"Everything medically possible under the circumstances was done for her!" Kate protested.

"Then why did she die?" Gallante challenged.

"Unfortunately nobody knows. But, as I said, the medical examiner will discover why."

"Doctor, do you do that often?" Gallante asked.

"Do what often?" Kate asked, puzzled, as Gallante had intended she be.

"Depend on the medical examiner to make your definitive diagnosis for you?" Gallante asked, casting half a glance into camera. Before Kate could respond, he continued: "This is Ramón Gallante reporting from City Hospital and returning you to the studio."

"Embarrassed?" Dr. Cummins shouted into his telephone. "Humiliated! She has placed this hospital in a highly vulnerable situation. God, I wish I could have stopped her!"

On the other end of the line, in the offices of Trumbull, Drummond & Baines, senior partner Lionel Trumbull sat behind his huge desk shaking his head disapprovingly toward his young associate Scott Van Cleve while waiting for an opportunity to break into what had been an endless tirade from the excitable hospital administrator. Finally Trumbull found an opening in Cummins's lament.

"Harvey . . . Harvey . . . I hope you're not contemplating taking any rash action,"

Trumbull cautioned.

"Why did Forrester do it? Why did she give that leering journalistic scavenger the chance to point up that it was at *this* hospital the Stuyvesant girl died? If Forrester chose to take such a risk personally, she should have considered what it would do to us!"

"Harvey, I'm sure if someone threatened to destroy your career, you would fight back too," Trumbull replied.

"Of course! But did she have to choose that way to fight?" Cummins asked. "This can be a disaster, Lionel. A total disaster for this hospital!"

"Not necessarily," Trumbull pointed out.

"No?" the administrator asked, surprised.

"What impression did she make on the TV audience? One doctor may have mishandled one case. Not your hospital. Not your entire staff. One doctor. A female doctor at that. From a purely public relations point of view that might not be as damaging as you think," Trumbull consoled him.

Somewhat mollified, Cummins relented. "I'll keep after Troy for those performance figures on our Emergency Service. If they show what I expect, then *I* should go on television. From right here in my office. The same dignified way as Stuyvesant. I will make a calm, reasoned, well-documented presentation of our achievements."

"And give that — what did you call him? — leering journalistic scavenger — more ammunition for his series?" Trumbull countered. "No. If you want to fight Stuyvesant, save it for the courtroom, where it will count. Though, frankly, I am looking forward to his lawyers meeting with our insurance company. I'll feel a whole lot better if they can settle this matter even before the complaint is drawn."

"Sure," Cummins agreed dolefully, "they'll settle and then raise our malpractice premiums sky-high!"

"It would be worth it. Consider the damage side of such a case, Harvey! Nineteen-year-old victim. Deprived of a useful lifetime of sixty, seventy years. If we are forced to go to court, a jury could have a picnic with that. Settle now, if we can."

"And what about Forrester?" Cummins asked.

"Do nothing except continue to restrict her duties. If I have to, I want to be able to take the legal position that as soon as you had a hint of even the possibility her capabilities were limited, in order to ensure the safety of all patients, you immediately relieved her of any clinical duties."

Having given the harried administrator that

soothing advice, Trumbull hung up and turned to Scott Van Cleve, who had been privy to the entire conversation on the extension telephone.

Now giving vent to his genuine concerns, Trumbull thundered, "I thought you told that young woman to keep her mouth shut!"

"I did. But evidently being accused of murder was too much for her to swallow without a reply."

"Van Cleve, maybe you young men can accept it, but frankly I will never believe that women have the emotional toughness to succeed in a man's world."

Diplomatically Scott Van Cleve pointed out, "I've assisted Mary Lawler in court. She's a tiger. And very sharp."

"Well," Trumbull conceded, "Lawler's an exception. That's why I selected her to head up our Litigation Department. But other women . . ." He shook his head sadly. But on further consideration he felt forced to admit, "There are one or two other damned capable women in this firm, but as a general rule —"

Before Trumbull could expand on his chauvinistic prejudices, Scott said, "I'll talk to Dr. Forrester. At once."

The phone was ringing when Kate Forrester

unlocked the door to the apartment. She rushed to answer it, prepared to defend herself against a tirade from Administrator Cummins or anyone else who might feel compelled to criticize her interview.

"Doctor," she heard a newly familiar voice, which she identified as Attorney Scott Van Cleve, "I have just seen your interview on television and —"

"And you don't approve," Kate anticipated him.

Rather than confront that head on, Van Cleve asked, "Doctor, may I ask what you do when a patient refuses to follow your advice?"

"There are some patients who refuse to stay in the hospital. We make them sign a release. We call it 'signing out against advice.' "

"We have a similar procedure in the law. But it is the *lawyer* who can sign out."

"Are you saying you want to quit my defense?" Kate asked.

"I am saying, if you refuse to follow my advice, I can serve no useful purpose. You would be better off with some lawyer whose advice you *do* respect," Van Cleve said.

"My decision had nothing to do with you. It had to do with me. I refuse to stand mute in the face of false accusations by any man simply because he happens to be Claude

Stuyvesant. Call it pride. Call it a sense of personal worth and dignity. I will not stand for it!" Kate declared.

Van Cleve knew that to argue with such an angry, principled young woman was futile. So he asked, "Doctor, are there times when the doctor tells the patient, for the next twenty-four hours or several days, to avoid certain foods? Or, don't have any breakfast before we take a blood or urine sample?"

"Of course," Kate agreed.

"What I am saying is no different. Until we get a clear view of what Stuyvesant is going to do legally, do not make any public statements. Repeat, make no public statements."

"You mean I have to just take it?" Kate demanded.

"No. Resent him. Hate him. Curse him. Write his name a thousand times and burn the paper. Make voodoo dolls of him and stick pins in them. But do not —"

Kate said it for him: "I get the idea. Not a word about him in public."

"Yes, Doctor. That is the idea. Now, let's try to get along as attorney and client. Okay?"

After a long moment of silence Kate conceded, "Okay."

Chapter Fourteen

In the wake of Kate Forrester's appearance on television, Cummins called another meeting of the chiefs of service and invited Lionel Trumbull to attend as well.

As soon as opinions were requested, Dr. Harold Wildman, chief of thoracic surgery, was first to respond.

"Mind you, I was all for defending Forrester when this first came up. But by going on television she's taken a single unfortunate case and made it seem as if this hospital is a collection of ill-trained, fumbling doctors."

"I thought she comported herself very well under the circumstances," another chief pointed out. "It was that vulture Gallante who did the damage."

"But she gave him the opportunity," Wildman retorted. "Suppose she did mishandle the Stuyvesant case, she should have let it just blow over. It would have been forgotten soon enough."

"I wouldn't be too sanguine about that. Not with Claude Stuyvesant involved," Eleanor Knolte, chief of pediatrics, replied. "You don't make friends trying to justify your mistakes. Not in this profession. The best rule, which I hope Forrester will learn one day, is, The less said the better. Right now, her mistake in judgment does call for steps to minimize the damage."

Professor Emeritus Sol Freund, who had already signified his intention to retire, took a different approach. "Ladies and gentlemen, we keep talking about 'her' and 'her possible mistake.' I say, we are talking about *us*. From what I can make out, presented with the same patient, what happened to Forrester could have happened to any of us. We must continue to defend her, and by defending her defend all conscientious doctors. We are only human. We make mistakes. Should we be burned at the stake for that?"

"Sol, it's all very well for you to be so understanding," Wildman countered. "But those of us facing years of practice burdened by outrageous malpractice premiums have to think of the future. This kind of bad publicity can make our premiums go only one way. Up! So, when you are basking in the Florida sun in blissful retirement, with no premiums to pay, I, and a lot of others around this table, will be paying through the nose for what Forrester did! I say we take the position that what happened to the Stuyvesant girl was not the fault of this hospital or its staff. It was the result of one doctor being unable to deal with the pressures she encountered in Emergency."

Freund stared across the wide conference table at his younger colleague. "Are you suggesting we throw her to the wolves?"

"I am only saying we consider dissociating ourselves."

"In my dictionary *dissociate* and *throw her to the wolves* are synonymous. Especially under the new system, this nationwide computer network, where, if a doctor is disciplined or terminated for some cause in one state, it becomes known in every other state almost overnight. It is equivalent to barring her from ever again working in any decent hospital. I cannot bring myself to endorse any such action against Dr. Forrester. But then, I guess I was brought up in a different era of medicine. When I was an intern, I worked under a neurosurgeon named Kessler, who had studied under Cushing up in Boston. Kessler used to say, 'These interns, these kids who come to us fresh out of medical school, they are our children. We have to help them grow up to take our places. From the first time they have trouble finding a vein to draw blood until they are able to approach the surgeon's table with confidence, we have to be patient with their mistakes, understanding, kind, compassionate. It is the solemn duty of older physicians to the young.' "

"Cushing, and your Dr. Kessler, didn't have to pay outrageous malpractice premiums!" Wildman shot back.

"Is that all you can think about? What about a little loyalty to our young doctors?" Freund demanded.

"There are times when we have to choose *between* loyalties," Wildman shot back. "Loyalty to Forrester? Or loyalty to this hospital? I say we owe our loyalty to the greater cause, this hospital! And no old man with antiquated notions about loyalty is going to change my mind!"

Before the meeting could evolve into a bitter personal battle between Freund and Wildman, between the older generation and the new, Cummins intervened.

"Gentlemen, gentlemen, we have more to consider here than malpractice premiums. We have beds to fill. Because if we don't, we will have to close our doors. With the kind of bad publicity we've already had, patients will be reluctant to come to us," Cummins warned dourly.

Wallace Simons, chief of obstetrics and gynecology, spoke up: "I'm afraid I'm forced to agree. Our chief responsibility is to this hospital. Among the four hundred and sixty-three doctors, men and women, on staff and attending, only one doctor stands accused. The rest of us are good, competent physicians and surgeons, the equal of any in this city, in this country. If we have one bad apple, let's terminate her and state the reasons why. Then no patient need fear to come to us for treatment. And that will be the end of it!"

From the faces around the table, most of the men and women appeared compelled to agree, until attorney Trumbull said softly, but with concern, "Not quite!"

"And why not?" Simons demanded.

"What would happen if Forrester has a hearing before the State Board of Professional Medical Conduct and they exonerate her?" Trumbull asked. "She can turn around and sue us for having damaged her reputation. Derogatory statements or actions reflecting on a person's professional ability, if untrue, are slander or libel per se. And if she is exonerated by the state board, that is prima facie evidence that those statements are untrue. Doctors, you are staring at a multimillion-dollar lawsuit. Both against this hospital and against each of you personally."

"Then how *do* we dissociate ourselves without running that risk?" Wildman asked.

"Let Claude Stuyvesant condemn her. Let *him* risk a costly suit for libel and slander,"

Trumbull advised. "We condemn no one."

"We have to do *something* about that young woman!" Simons insisted.

"After the state board makes its determination, if they find her guilty of unprofessional conduct, you can get rid of her without fear of reprisals or lawsuits," Trumbull advised.

"And in the meantime?" Simons asked.

"I think Dr. Cummins has provided the ideal solution." Trumbull said. "Keep her isolated from treating patients, which reduces our risk."

"In other words," Sol Freund interjected from his side of the table, "we will keep this young woman in professional solitary confinement before we have the public hanging. And then we are going to do it in a nice, safe, surgical, and legally antiseptic manner. So nobody gets sued."

Trumbull's face flushed in anger. Cummins intervened to respond, "I would not classify taking action against a physician that the state board finds incompetent 'a public hanging.' "

"Of course not," Freund replied. "We mustn't use dirty words that can later be turned against us if there is a lawsuit. Gentlemen, I say, under the circumstances it is cowardly to abandon a bright young physician in order to save our skins."

From the faces around the table it was clear

that very few agreed with him.

The next afternoon Kate Forrester appeared on the Neurology floor of the Pediatric wing. Despite her personal professional problems she had made it a practice to follow up on little Maria Sanchez. Once Maria had recovered sufficiently to be more alert and responsive, Kate made it a habit on each visit to bring a small, inexpensive gift, a rag doll, a picture book for coloring. When Maria had remarked on how sweet Kate smelled, she brought the child a small sample vial of perfume she had received as a party favor months ago when she had gone to a stock-exchange dinner with Walter.

As she always did, Kate went to the door of Maria's room, peeked in to make sure the child was neither asleep nor being tested by one of the residents. Today Maria was awake, alone, and seemed rather despondent.

"Maria?" Kate called softly.

At once the child turned toward the door and sat up in bed, great expectations brightening her black eyes. The gift hidden behind her back, Kate slipped into the room. With a flourish she presented the brightly wrapped package. The child reached for it, eagerly tore off the red and gold paper and uncovered a book. This time not a coloring book but a book that Kate had brought to teach Maria to read.

The bright color of the cover was exciting enough to make the child throw her arms around Kate. They were embracing when Dr. Harve Golding came into the room quite hurriedly. He was visibly embarrassed. "Kate, can I talk to you?"

"Of course."

She gently disengaged herself from Maria's embrace and joined him at the door. She feared an unfortunate development in Maria's prognosis. Perhaps some new test had revealed neurological deficiencies from abuse, deficiencies that had not been detected heretofore.

Harve gestured Kate out into the corridor. At once she asked, in a voice so soft the child could not hear, "Harve, have they decided what they will be doing with Maria?"

"I'm fighting to keep her here. The city wants to put her into foster care until the court case comes up. And she's not ready for that."

"I suppose foster care is cheaper than hospitalization," Kate admitted. "These days everything comes down to dollars. Too bad. She seems to be thriving here. Gets better every time I see her."

"Gets better every time *because* you see her," Harve corrected. "Though with all your other worries, you really shouldn't bother."

"It's no bother. I find her delightful. She needs someone to love her. Maybe I need someone to love."

"Well, actually," Harve Golding started to say, then changed his mind.

"Okay, Harve, what is it?" Kate asked bluntly.

"Cummins has issued an order that you are not to appear in any area of the hospital where patients are involved."

"I'm not treating anyone. I'm just visiting a lonely child. What harm can that do?" Kate protested.

"He's extremely sensitive to the kind of gossip that your presence might stir up. I'm sorry, Kate. It's a lousy thing to do, but I have no choice."

"Of course, I understand," Kate said. "I'll just go in and say good-bye."

She went back in to find Maria rubbing her small hands over the glossy cover of the book. Maria smiled up at Kate. She opened the book, inviting Kate to read to her.

"Maria, this is a special kind of present. It's what grown-ups call a going-away present."

"Going . . . a . . . way. . . ." the child repeated. "I going away now?"

"No, Maria. I am going away."

Tears flooded the child's black eyes. "You go away?" she asked, and there was pain in the asking.

The look on Maria's pinched face, her beseeching eyes, caused Kate to decide. "No, no, I am *not* going away." She sat on the side of the bed, took the child in her arm, opened the book, and began to instruct: "Maria, this is an *A*. Say it. *A*."

The child complied.

They had reached the letter *E* when Kate heard the sound of steps behind her. She turned to find Harve Golding in the doorway. She braced for a reprimand.

"Katie, at least have the good sense to close the door," Golding said. He smiled, drew back, closing the door behind him. Kate turned back to Maria and said, *"E*. This letter is *E*."

At the time Kate Forrester was encouraging little Maria to show off her newly gained knowledge, one of the confidential phones on the desk of the mayor's executive secretary was ringing with a persistence that demanded a response.

"Mayor's office. Madelaine speaking," she said softly, in full knowledge that only very few selected people had access to this private unlisted number.

"I have to talk to him," a masculine voice insisted.

196

"Dr. Schwartzman?" Madeleine Corman said, identifying the voice.

"Yes," the medical examiner replied.

"I'll put him right on."

In a few moments, for only as long as it took the mayor to clear visitors from his office, Schwartzman heard his voice. "Ab?"

"Look, holding up the Stuyvesant autopsy report until after the funeral is one thing. That I can do. But I can't change the results," Schwartzman explained.

"Messy?" The mayor asked.

"Stuyvesant won't like my findings," the medical examiner warned. "Cause of death can't be toned down."

"What was it?"

"Massive hemorrhage. Due to a ruptured ectopic pregnancy," Schwartzman stated.

"You're right. Stuyvesant won't like that."

"I can't fake it; that would be a crime," Schwartzman pointed out.

The mayor considered the situation for a moment, then said, "Ab, when you have to release your findings to the media, simply state, 'Death was due to massive internal hemorrhage.' "

"And if the press gets nosy, as they will, this being a Stuyvesant, what then?" Schwartzman asked.

"I can say to Stuyvesant that we did our

197

best to keep it out of the news. After all, we'll be hitting him up for a bigger-than-usual contribution at the Party's dinner next month."

"Right. In the publicity release I confine the cause to 'massive internal hemorrhage' period!" Schwartzman agreed, but added as an afterthought, "Oh, by the way, when you talk to Stuyvesant, suggest that he have the body cremated."

"Cremated? Why?" the mayor asked.

"If there are any legal proceedings, he won't want the body exhumed and tested," Schwartzman advised.

"Why? What else did you find?" the mayor asked.

"Nothing. But to make sure, I didn't look."

Chapter Fifteen

A small detachment of uniformed police had been ordered by the mayor to assure that the funeral of Claudia Stuyvesant was carried out with a minimum of interference from the news and television media and the curious crowds which were expected to throng around St. Thomas's Church on Fifth Avenue.

A half hour before the assigned time of ten o'clock in the morning, notables began to arrive and take their places in the pews as assigned by the church ushers.

The mayor of the city was among the first. Men and women listed in the *Fortune* Five Hundred list of the largest companies in the country were well represented among the mourners. But the main group consisted of employees of Stuyvesant's own companies and the many civic and charitable organizations that were beholden to him for donations.

Once most pews were occupied and all invited mourners were seated, the church was open to any of the public who wished to attend. Among the curious were older men and women, drawn by the desire to mingle with the mighty. There were young people as well, men and women in their early twenties or late teens, some of whom had been classmates or friends of Claudia Stuyvesant in life.

Among the crowd was also Dr. Kate Forrester. She climbed the worn brown sandstone steps and, along with others, entered the lofty church. She stared up at the ornate carved altar, before which rested the simple coffin of plain polished dark wood. It was closed.

With the choir humming softly in the background, there was a buzz of subdued conversation until the minister, in his vestments, entered from a door to the side of the altar. With that as prologue, from the door on the opposite side an usher preceded the mother and the father of Claudia Stuyvesant. Nora Stuyvesant was dressed in black, a veil obscuring her face. Attired in a black frock coat and striped trousers, a white shirt with a stiff wing collar and striped gray cravat, Claude Stuyvesant was an imposing figure. Tall, rugged, tanned from the sun and the wind, he was in all respects a man of power, physical as well as economic and political.

When his wife seemed to falter, Stuyvesant assisted her to the front pew. Once they were seated, the choir lifted their voices in a hymn. During this Kate Forrester glanced guardedly at the people around her. She recognized many as typical residents and habitués of Greenwich Village, where Claudia Stuyvesant had lived the last year of her life. As Kate's eyes drifted aimlessly over the crowd, she caught sight of one face that startled her.

Scott Van Cleve, her assigned attorney, sat in the aisle seat some rows ahead of her. Her first thought: *What is he doing here? He's no friend of the Stuyvesants. Or is he?* Her thoughts were interrupted when the hymn came to an end and the minister assumed his place in the pulpit to deliver his eulogy.

He was profuse in his condolences to the Stuyvesants, praising them for their devoted parenthood. For lack of specific accomplishments upon which to enlarge, he dealt briefly with the life of Claudia Stuyvesant and only in the most general of terms. He spent much more time on his vision of what Claudia might have accomplished if only she had lived out a normal life span.

Kate took that particular portion of the eulogy to be an accusation against her. She clasped her hands tightly in her lap, determined to fend off any feelings of guilt. The minister's words spoken, the choir's voices rose in another hymn. Thereafter, the mayor spoke briefly, as did two of Claudia's friends who had been her classmates at private school. They added their grieving sentiments, one in the form of a poem.

The minister announced that the interment would be private, limited to only the immediate family. By inference all others, especially the media, were being ordered not to attend. The honorary pallbearers, each of whom had been personally selected by Claude Stuyvesant, lifted the coffin and started up the aisle toward the huge front doors. Behind the coffin followed Stuyvesant and his wife. They had taken only a dozen steps when Nora Stuyvesant started to totter. Before she could collapse, Stuyvesant caught her by one arm, and from the other side of the aisle Scott Van Cleve leaped forward to seize her other arm. Between them the two men prevented her falling. Thus assisted, Nora Stuyvesant made her way up the aisle.

As they approached the pew in which Kate Forrester stood in respect, along with the others, Stuyvesant's sorrowful look suddenly changed to one of anger. Kate realized he had obviously recognized her from her television interview of several days ago. She had the feeling that even in these surroundings and at this solemn moment he might lash out at her with another of his vitriolic accusations. She stared back at him with the conviction of the innocent.

On the other side of Stuyvesant, Scott Van

Cleve stared at her with a look of angry rebuke.

To escape Scott's reproving stare, Kate averted her eyes from him to stare across the aisle at the mourners in the opposite pews. One face she found there intrigued her. A young man whose eyes were fixed on the coffin, which started moving out of their line of sight. He was cadaverously thin, in his early twenties, with longish brown hair pulled back in an untidy ponytail. He wore a faded blue shirt, collar open, and a Western-type denim jacket. Hardly fit attire for such a solemn occasion, Kate thought. However, it was his eyes and the strange manner in which they fixed on the coffin of Claudia Stuyvesant that made a lasting impression on Kate.

Scott Van Cleve, Claude Stuyvesant, and his wife reached the doors to the street. Kate heard a shout go up from the television crews, reporters, and curious bystanders outside. "Here they come! Start rolling!"

Kate pushed through the mourners to reach the doors in time to see Ramón Gallante hold up a microphone to Claude Stuyvesant. She could not hear what Gallante asked, but she was chilled to hear Stuyvesant's loud, angry reply, "I have already started proceedings against her."

While the coffin was being slid into the

hearse, Stuyvesant's chauffeur helped him assist his wife into their black stretch limousine. Kate stood on the third step of the church watching as the hearse pulled away, followed only by the Stuyvesant limousine. Burial would indeed be private.

As they disappeared from sight, Kate saw Scott Van Cleve push his way through the crowd in great haste to seize the arm of one of the pallbearers. He exchanged some brief words with the man, who appeared annoyed as well as puzzled. But evidently Van Cleve had discovered what he wanted to know, for he turned back to mingle with the departing crowd. He pushed his way through in such determined fashion that Kate herself resented him.

She watched Van Cleve reach the side of the young woman who had read the poem in tribute to Claudia. He started to question her. But she brushed by him without responding and hurried down the steps. Van Cleve pursued her. As he did, he passed a young man in his early twenties, with a dark complexion and long hair tied back in a ponytail. Kate recognized him as the same man who stood across the aisle from her in the opposite pew, who had stared so intently as the coffin of Claudia Stuyvesant passed by. Now he looked around furtively, as if hoping not to be noticed, started quickly down the church steps and along the avenue to lose himself in the street crowd. He had not spoken to any of the other young people among the mourners, a number of whom were gathered in small groups on the church steps and on the street. He appeared isolated and cut off even from his contemporaries.

Kate was marking his strange conduct when she was turned about by Scott Van Cleve asking, "And what are *you* doing here?"

"I could ask you the same thing." Kate said in confrontation.

"I'm here on business. Legal business," he explained.

"I'm here out of —" She could not find a proper reason. "Just say, I was curious. I had to be here."

"I'm glad Gallante didn't spot you. You can be sure he'd comment. 'Aha! Criminal drawn back to witness the result of her crime.' I don't put anything past that bastard."

"You didn't answer *my* question," Kate pointed out.

"I told you, legal business," Van Cleve said. "At crucial and emotional occasions like this, you never know what you will discover."

"And *did* you discover anything?"

"Yes."

"Such as?" Kate asked.

"Well, the coffin, for one thing."

"What about it?" Kate asked. "Polished wood. In simple good taste."

"Exactly," Van Cleve said.

"What's wrong with simple good taste?" Kate asked.

"For a Stuyvesant, no metal casket — of permanence, resistant to eternal deterioration? Besides, it was sealed. There had been no chance to view the body, either at the church or for the usual viewing the day before at some upscale funeral chapel. That's what started me thinking. But I was troubled even more by the way those pallbearers carried that coffin."

"Is that why you collared one of them?" Kate asked.

"He thought I was crazy when I asked him if the coffin was heavy."

"What did he say?"

"Interesting reply. 'How would I know? I've never been a pallbearer before. But it was a lot less than I expected.' Get that? A lot less than he expected."

"Mr. Van Cleve, what's the significance of all this?"

"Precisely what *I* wanted to know," he said. "Especially when the funeral was suddenly scheduled for today. That means Claudia's body has been returned to the family, which in turn means the autopsy is over. Have *you* heard anything about a medical examiner's report?"

"No," Kate said.

"Neither have I," Van Cleve said. "And why was the body never available for viewing by any mourners?"

"Sometimes, when death results from a bad accident, or there's been a disfiguring autopsy, the family refuses to allow the body to be viewed," Kate said.

"Was that the case with Claudia Stuyvesant?" he asked.

"No," Kate replied.

"You know what I suspect?" Van Cleve said. "There was no body in that coffin."

"No body?" Kate asked, startled. "Then why this funeral?"

"That's what I want to know. If no body, what *was* in that coffin? Only the ashes left after cremation?" Van Cleve suggested. "What's Stuyvesant covering up?"

"Drugs?" Kate suggested.

"You told me you ordered a toxic screen that night."

"I did," Kate confirmed.

"What was the report?" he asked.

"I've never seen it. It wasn't in her chart the last time I examined it."

"Then let's get hold of it. Now!" Van Cleve said.

Though Dr. Cummins was reluctant to allow anyone except Lionel Trumbull to examine the chart of patient Stuyvesant, Claudia, he finally yielded.

Eagerly Kate Forrester and Scott Van Cleve leafed through it page by page, but in the end could find no toxicological report.

"Strange," Kate said. She lifted the phone and asked the operator, "Page Dr. Briscoe, please!" It took almost ten minutes before the phone rang back. "Eric? Kate. Eric, since the Stuyvesant case, have you seen a tox report on her?"

"I didn't look," Briscoe replied. "Why? What's up?"

"That's what we'd like to know."

" 'We'?"

"My attorney and I," Kate said.

"Attorney? You have a personal attorney?" Briscoe asked, suddenly taking on a more cautious tone. "Why?"

"With the possibility of Stuyvesant taking legal steps against me, they thought I needed my own lawyer."

"I guess," Briscoe replied. "But I never saw any tox report."

Kate's only other recourse was to find the technician who had worked on the last blood sample she had sent down to the lab on Saturday night, a woman named Carmelita Espinosa. When Kate found her, Mrs. Espinosa was engaged in feeding another blood sample into the computerized scanner, which would yield readings on a new patient.

She met Kate's questions with brief replies. Did Mrs. Espinosa recall doing the Stuyvesant screen? She never recalled specimens and results by patients' names. Did she recall the night of the Stuyvesant case? Yes. Did she do any toxic screens that night? Yes. She did three. All three came up positive.

"All three came up positive?" Kate asked again, to make absolutely sure.

"Yes," Mrs. Espinosa said.

"The printout from the computer, did you send that up to Emergency?"

"Wherever a request comes from, that's where I direct the printout," Mrs. Espinosa confirmed.

Kate and Van Cleve glanced at each other. With the same thought: *That tox report should be in Claudia's chart. But it is not. Where is it?*

Chapter Sixteen

Dr. Kate Forrester was relieved to be summoned from her work in Dr. Troy's basement office by a call from Dr. Cummins's secretary. Kate had developed an affection for old Troy and an admiration for his devotion to his work. But for herself she had not been able to accept statistical studies of the effectiveness of medicine as a substitute for directly ministering to human beings and their ailments. She hoped this call to Cummins's office meant that, with the Stuyvesant funeral behind them and the furor over her television interview having subsided, the administrator was ready to reinstate her to her rightful function as a resident in general medicine.

When she was shown into his private office, Cummins was on his feet, awaiting her arrival.

"Dr. Cummins . . ."

He did not reply, greeting her only with a look of suppressed fury. He held in his hand a thin sheaf of papers. One glimpse and Kate was able to recognize the seal of the Office of the Medical Examiner of New York County.

"You might want to sit down before you

read this," Cummins warned.

Kate reached for the report, took it in hand cautiously. She sat down, began to read. She had not gone beyond the first paragraph when she felt forced to stare up at Cummins. He pointed down at the report, ordering Kate to continue reading.

". . . ectopic pregnancy," Kate read in disbelief, "causing rupture of her left fallopian tube . . ."

"Resulting in severe internal hemorrhaging . . . and death," Cummins finished the sentence. "When you go back and check your notes in her chart, her signs and symptoms, you will find they are consistent with such a condition."

"Her signs and symptoms were also consistent with dozens of other conditions as well," Kate pointed out. "Besides, I did do a pelvic on her."

"And obviously you missed it," Cummins pointed out angrily.

"Briscoe did a pelvic, too, and found nothing," Kate replied.

"Nevertheless this was a diagnosis you could have made. If you had, and if you had immediately instituted the proper surgical intervention, that girl would be alive today. Unfortunately, in the public mind, this will give credence to the words of that media vulture Gallante when he said, 'If the rich can't expect good medical treatment, what chance does the average citizen have?' "

"Twice, twice she denied having had sexual relations. . . ." Kate tried to explain.

"You should have suspected she was lying."

"I did. That's why I performed a urine pregnancy test. It came up negative!"

"Based on this report it is obvious that you came up with a wrong result," Cummins replied. "If ever we had any hope of avoiding a malpractice suit, this document destroys it. It will be a key piece of evidence in the trial. To say nothing of your hearing before the State Board as well."

Kate fingered the report, then vaguely handed it back, protesting, "I've done that pregnancy test dozens of times."

"Forrester, I'm sorry about this turn of events. Of course we'll continue to do our best for you," Cummins said. But his attitude was so forlorn that Kate was reminded of a college professor who had once told her, "A man only says he'll do his best when he expects to fail."

Tormented by the medical examiner's findings, instead of returning to her basement office, Kate hurried through the underground tunnels of the hospital complex back to the Emergency Service.

There she sought out Room C, where she had treated Claudia Stuyvesant. She approached the same cabinet from which Nurse Cronin had produced the pregnancy-test kit she had used that night on Claudia Stuyvesant. Kate took out several similar kits. She examined each carton to study the expiration date.

To be used before December 30, 1993.

There was still more than a year of viability left. There was no reason to suspect the materials contained in those kits. Yet the medical examiner's report proved beyond doubt that the test she had performed had yielded a false and misleading result. A fatal and misleading result. Had she made some mistake? Or was she a victim of that small percentage of false negatives that will occur? Still puzzled, Kate returned to her basement office. There she found a note alongside the printout on her worktable. Troy had left it before he went off to lunch.

Call your lawyer. Urgent.

Kate was greeted with a harried, "Van Cleve here." Evidently he was deeply involved in some legal document. But at the sound of her voice he took command of the conversation. "Doctor, we have to meet. Tonight. And be prepared for a long session. Because I have just seen a copy of the medical examiner's report."

"So have I," she replied.

"Then you know that I need some answers from you. Some very convincing answers. I hate to trouble you to come all the way down to Wall Street, especially at night. But it is important I see you in my office no later than six this evening."

Feeling challenged by Van Cleve's brisk attitude, Kate responded in kind. "Six o'clock, Mr. Van Cleve. I'll be there!"

Before Scott Van Cleve began his interrogation, he made sure Kate was comfortably seated in the chair across from his desk. He offered her some hot coffee, which she refused. But she suspected he thought she might need something to see her through the ordeal she was facing.

"Okay!" Van Cleve declared as he sank into his desk chair. That simple, overused word suddenly sounded like the opening shot proclaiming the battle was about to begin. "Doctor, we know what the medical examiner found."

"And we also have a hunch as to why someone prevailed on him not to announce his findings before Claudia Stuyvesant's funeral," Kate pointed out.

"Less scandal that way. But everybody who knows Stuyvesant also knows one other thing:

Now there definitely *will* be a lawsuit. And there *will* be charges against you before the State Board. To his egocentric mind you not only killed his daughter —"

Kate anticipated his next words: "I have also caused the name of Stuyvesant to be held up to public shame."

"So we have to be prepared for the worst," Van Cleve warned. "Now, Doctor, we know we can't disprove what the medical examiner found. That puts the onus on us to explain why *you* didn't find that condition."

"Ectopics are not always easy to detect," Kate protested.

Van Cleve brushed aside her interruption to continue: "Easy to detect or not, we have to prove to the satisfaction of the medical world, and to the public as well, that everything you did was in accord with good medical practice. That's the legal test. In the courtroom and in the hearing room."

"And it was!" Kate insisted.

"Then why didn't you detect her condition?" Van Cleve shot back.

"Eric Briscoe didn't detect it either," Kate countered.

"That's no excuse. Besides, Stuyvesant hasn't charged Briscoe with anything. Stuyvesant is focusing on *you*. What *you* did. What *you* found. And *didn't* find. So I have to know exactly what you did and why. Including all thoughts that went through your mind while you treated Claudia Stuyvesant."

"I don't even know where to start."

"Start at the beginning. From the moment you first saw her."

"Actually I saw her mother before I even saw her."

"We'll get to her mother later," Van Cleve said. "Start with your first look at your patient. Don't omit anything. Let me be the judge of what's important and what's not."

Kate proceeded to recite in as much detail as she could recall the medical history she took of Claudia Stuyvesant. The blood tests she ordered. The signs she observed. Twice she interrupted herself to ask, "Am I making this too detailed and complicated?"

"No. Just go on," he urged, making a note or two from time to time.

Kate resumed each time, again in detail. Again commenting, "All this is in the patient's chart. I made a note of everything."

"Doctor, during a trial or a hearing they are not going to allow you to just read the patient's chart. You will have to testify in your own words. So continue."

When Kate finished relating all the events of that night, Van Cleve remarked, "At the outset you said that you saw Mrs. Stuyvesant before you saw her daughter."

"Yes."

"And that seemed to be especially significant to you. Why?"

"It was obvious there was friction between them. Tension of some kind, which I didn't understand until later. Too late."

"And what was that?" Van Cleve asked.

"When it was all over, after Claudia had expired, several people heard her mother say, 'He'll blame me . . . He'll blame me. . . .' "

"What did you take that to mean?" Van Cleve asked.

"At the time I thought it was strange of her to say that at such a tragic moment. But from what I've since learned about Stuyvesant, I realize now how deeply afraid of him his wife must be."

"She was fearful he would blame her for his daughter's death?"

"Which could also account for her concern when I first saw her," Kate explained. "Her daughter had moved out, was living on her own, most likely in defiance of her father's wishes."

"So Stuyvesant was blaming his wife for failing to control their daughter," Van Cleve surmised.

"I sensed that conflict prevented Claudia

217

Stuyvesant from feeling completely free to talk."

"If she had felt free, what might she have told you different from what she did?" he asked.

"That she had been sexually active. That would surely have affected my diagnosis. And that she used drugs."

"For the moment let's accept that she lied to you about drugs. To defend you properly, I must know specifically how that could have affected the outcome of her case."

"Depends on what she was on," Kate said. "Cocaine, angel dust, crack, perc . . ."

"Perc?" Van Cleve asked.

"Percodan," Kate explained. "Each drug produces a different effect. Cocaine, in fact, can have different effects on different people, all the way from a slight high to stopping all heart action cold. Instant death."

"And the effect of drugs on an ectopic pregnancy?" Van Cleve asked. "How could that have misled you?"

"This is going to require understanding the difference between a normal pregnancy and an ectopic."

"Take your time. Explain. It's important I understand," Van Cleve insisted.

"An ectopic does not present in the same way as a normal pregnancy. For example, in a normal pregnancy the uterus is palpably enlarged, but in the case of an ectopic not nearly so much. In a normal pregnancy the cervix is discolored — not necessarily so in an ectopic. The cervix may be tender, but that could be due to a number of other causes as well. And a tender mass may be detected."

"*May* be detected. . . ." Van Cleve pointed out. "Why *may?*"

"It isn't always possible to feel it," Kate explained. "In this case it was not apparent to me or to Briscoe."

Van Cleve began to assemble some of the facts. "So, if you were dealing with a young woman who denied being sexually active —"

"And who denied missing any periods," Kate added.

"And if no mass was apparent to the doctor's touch, the uterus was only minimally enlarged — cervix not discolored — her pain was being masked or diminished by drug use — altogether that could present a very misleading picture," Van Cleve realized.

"With all symptoms and signs pointing to a viral stomach infection and nothing more revealing, I don't think any doctor would have diagnosed a pregnancy, let alone an ectopic."

"Yet it was there, it was there," Van Cleve realized grimly. "Drugs," he said suddenly. "Any other effects of drugs on this case?"

"Might have made her lethargic and dull at one time, affecting her responses to my questions, yet overactive later. Could also have induced her nausea."

"Her nausea could have been caused by narcotics?"

"Or by something she ate, which was in line with her first complaint. Nausea, vomiting, diarrhea," Kate pointed out.

"So that nausea, too, was not a clear symptom of any specific condition?"

"Exactly."

"Every sign she presented was a little off, but none so alarming as to ring any specific bells. Still, she died of massive internal hemorrhaging. Wouldn't that have presented some important signs?"

"Her hematocrit could have been one sign," Kate said.

"Hematocrit? What's that?"

"Part of every CBC, complete blood count, it indicates the level of red blood cells," Kate explained.

"How's it work?"

"The lab spins off the red cells from the plasma in the blood. Then they place the resulting column of red cells against the column of remaining plasma to determine the percentage of red cells in the blood. Normal for a woman is between thirty and thirty-five percent."

"And Claudia's hematocrit that night?" Van Cleve asked.

"Thirty-one, as I remember."

"Then she was certainly within the range of normal," Van Cleve concluded.

"Which proved to be very misleading," Kate pointed out.

"How?" Van Cleve demanded, becoming a bit frustrated.

"Put the whole case together," Kate explained. "She came in complaining of nausea, vomiting, and diarrhea. Which means she was likely dehydrated. So, Cronin put her on an I.V."

"Wasn't that the right thing to do?" Van Cleve asked. Kate nodded. "Then what went wrong?"

"When a patient is dehydrated, her red cell count appears higher than it actually is."

Truly confused now, Van Cleve asked, "Doctor, what are you trying to tell me?"

"Dehydration robs the blood of moisture content. That reduces the amount of plasma, which by comparison makes the red cell count appear higher than it is."

Beginning to understand, Van Cleve added, "So that her red cell count, which would have been low due to her hemorrhaging, actually appeared normal due to her dehydration."

"Go to the head of the class," Kate replied tartly.

"Man, this is one giant medical jigsaw puzzle. And a person can't get the whole picture if any of the pieces are missing or off kilter," Van Cleve realized.

"Just as the doctor can't make an accurate diagnosis without all the facts," Kate added.

Van Cleve pushed aside his yellow legal pad and started to pace in the confined space of his small office. Suddenly he turned to Kate.

"There was one fact that could have put all the others into focus. Might even have made some of the missing information unnecessary. That pregnancy test."

"Yes," Kate agreed somberly. "That pregnancy test."

"How come your result was negative, yet the medical examiner found actual physical evidence of a pregnancy?" Van Cleve asked.

"No medical test is one hundred percent perfect," Kate explained.

Van Cleve began thinking aloud now. "So, soon I may have to go to court or before the hearing committee of the State Board and argue, 'My client, Dr. Forrester, did everything correctly, but she was misled by a false test result because no medical test is one hundred percent perfect.' Not a very strong argument."

"I tried to get a sonogram to confirm the result," Kate protested, "but no qualified technician was available. You have to realize the conditions under which we work in Emergency. Long, long stretches without a break. Crowded quarters. Shortage of examining rooms. Sometimes we have to treat patients on stretchers in the corridors. And there are always more patients than the doctor has time for. We give every patient the best care we can."

"Dr. Forrester, do you realize what you have just admitted?" Van Cleve asked with the accusing attitude of an opposing attorney.

"Admitted?" Kate asked, puzzled.

"You have virtually said that, due to conditions, you did *not* give Claudia Stuyvesant good medical care."

"I did give her good medical care!" Kate protested.

"You gave her 'the best care' that you could," Van Cleve pointed out. "Which is the same as saying, not perfect care, not even good care. Just the best you could do under difficult circumstances. 'Difficult circumstances' is no excuse for an unnecessary death. Doctor, you can thank your lucky stars that you've got an insurance company defending you on the malpractice end of this."

"And what about that hearing and my career? Mr. Van Cleve, I have spent eight years of study, two years of internship, preparing to practice medicine. It's all I've ever wanted to do. Since I was a kid in high school, volunteering to help out in our local hospital, that's all I dreamed of, being a doctor, treating people, healing them. It can't just . . . I mean, they can't just . . ." Then with more resolve, Kate said, "I won't let them take that away from me!"

"I'll do my best to help you," Van Cleve assured her. Honesty made him add, "But I can make no promises, Doctor."

Kate Forrester had come to the offices of Trumbull, Drummond & Baines anticipating protection from a state proceeding that endangered her brief career. She left feeling far more threatened than when she had arrived.

Scott Van Cleve watched her go, feeling even more deeply disturbed than he had admitted to her. More so than the first time he had seen her, he was aware of her strong face, which reflected her determination to devote her life to the practice of medicine. But her very determination only served to compound his fears.

I can't let this go to court, he realized. *I certainly can't let it get as far as a hearing. There must be some way I can manage this to prevent both eventualities from coming to pass. There must be some way,* he argued. But finally had to settle for, *There may be some way. If we are lucky.*

Finally he had to admit to himself, *Luck is a very fragile and tricky gambit on which to rely in a case with such drastic possible consequences.*

He left his office much later that night, still racking his brain for some solution.

He knew one thing. He would surely have wanted to meet a young woman as attractive and with such convictions as Kate Forrester, in any way except this.

Scott Van Cleve lived in a small flat on the third floor of a brownstone house in the East Sixties. The cab had just pulled up in front of the place when Scott called to the driver, "City Hospital."

"City Hospital?" The driver turned to dispute him. "That's clear through the park on the West Side."

"I know. City Hospital!"

"Hey, Mac, you suddenly sick or something?" the driver asked. "There's hospitals lots closer."

"No. Not sick. Curious."

" 'Not sick. Curious,' " the driver repeated, annoyed more than concerned. "Okay, Mister Curious. The rider is always right. He may be crazy, but he's always right. City Hospital."

Ten minutes later the cab pulled up at the Emergency Entrance to City Hospital.

"If you wait, I'll only be a few minutes," Scott said.

"Listen, Mr. Curious, better pay me now. If you go in there, you may not come out alive. Specially if you get into the hands of that lady doctor I heard about."

Scott's first reaction was to respond sharply, but he said nothing, merely paid the driver, adding a smaller tip than he had planned. He started into Emergency.

He waited near the entrance until the Admitting nurse was involved with a hysterical mother and a sick child. Then he slipped past her and started down the corridor. He discovered two patients on gurneys along the wall. One with an intravenous on a pole alongside the stretcher. The other twisted in pain and moaning, which added to the cacophony of sounds that included children crying, parents bickering in several languages, shouted orders, demands for equipment from nurses, attendants, and the two doctors on duty this night.

He eased past the open doors of the examining and treatment rooms. Each was occupied. Some patients waited for attention, some were receiving it. Nurses went from room to room looking in, checking the patient's condition, moving on to the next room.

By the time he had been confronted by Security Guard Tolson and forcefully told to get out, Scott Van Cleve had confirmed what his client had told him. Emergency in the late-night hours was bedlam, organized bedlam. That most patients did receive good care, did benefit from it and were sent home or on to other services in safe condition seemed a miracle.

Dr. Kate Forrester had not exaggerated the facts in defense of her own conduct. However, this assurance did not bring Scott Van Cleve any closer to a legal strategy for avoiding the lawsuit or the hearing to remove her license to practice.

Chapter Seventeen

The release of the medical examiner's report on the case of Claudia Stuyvesant caused repercussions in other quarters as well.

By the following morning there was a full-scale meeting in the conference room at Trumbull, Drummond & Baines. So crucial was this meeting deemed that all three senior partners were in attendance, along with Dr. Cummins and Marcus Naughton, president of the board of trustees of City Hospital. Scott Van Cleve had also been requested to attend.

Lionel Trumbull opened the meeting with a simple, bald, not particularly legalistic statement: "Gentlemen, we are up to our ass in trouble."

"Don't I know," Hospital Board Chairman Naughton agreed grimly. "That medical examiner's report is the kiss of death. No pun intended. It leaves us defenseless, utterly defenseless."

"Not only that," Trumbull warned, "but public news that when she died, his daughter was pregnant out of wedlock is the kind of disgrace that a man like Stuyvesant won't take easily. He'll sue now out of sheer spite. Of course, he'll ask for the moon!"

"And get it," Cummins agreed dolefully.

"Has anyone heard from the insurance company? Since the autopsy was made public?" Drummond asked.

"Not a word," Trumbull said, "which is what troubles me most. Just picture their law library right this minute. A dozen young lawyers hunting down every possible decision that will allow them to get out from under liability on this damn thing."

"Let's not panic, Lionel," Drummond cautioned. "I think, with the right approach, Stuyvesant could be induced to settle this thing in a quiet manner. With a few million thrown in, of course."

"Only a few million?" Cummins asked. "The insurance company might possibly go for that."

"How much *will* they go for? That's the first thing we have to find out," Trumbull declared.

"And the second thing?" Cummins asked.

"Who makes the approach to Stuyvesant," Trumbull replied. He turned to Board Chairman Naughton. "Marc, Stuyvesant is a member of your golf club, isn't he?"

"Yes, but I can't say I really know him," Naughton begged off. "I've been in a foursome with him a few times. That's not the same as knowing him. Besides, golf isn't really his thing. Yachting is."

"Well, do we know anyone who's close to him in that area?" Trumbull asked. "Somebody who can man-to-man it with him?"

"We have a man on the hospital board who's quite a yachtsman — Harry Lindsay," Naughton suggested.

"Contact Lindsay. Find out if he'll talk to Stuyvesant," Trumbull said. "Meantime we have to concoct a scenario that the bastard'll buy. I'm open to ideas." He looked around the table, inviting suggestions. There were none.

Scott Van Cleve took advantage of the silence to interject, "To a man like Stuyvesant a couple of million dollars is no real incentive."

"We already know that," Trumbull said. He made no secret of his annoyance at young Van Cleve's statement of the obvious.

Nevertheless Van Cleve pressed on: "I was about to say he's a man who is very sensitive about his public image. Vanity is the button we should push."

"He's an outraged, publicly disgraced father, with no patience for vanity," Cummins protested.

"Unless we use that to our advantage," Van Cleve said.

Because no one else had anything to suggest,

Trumbull turned back to young Van Cleve, prepared to disparage any suggestion he might offer. "Yes, Van Cleve?"

"When Lindsay goes to see him, he should of course commiserate with him. It was a terrible tragedy, what happened to his daughter. Everyone empathizes with his shock and sorrow. But a great man — and here's where Lindsay has to make his point — turns adversity to a benefit —"

"How the hell can a man's losing his daughter be turned into a benefit?" Hospital Administrator Cummins demanded.

"Dr. Cummins, I've heard quite a lot about your Emergency Service."

"You have? From whom?"

"My client," Van Cleve said.

"At this point I wouldn't exactly consider Dr. Forrester an unbiased source of information," Cummins replied.

"Feeling the same way, I did my own investigation. With all due respect, Dr. Cummins, your Emergency Service is a pretty old, run-down, overtaxed place. People falling all over each other. Patients treated in the corridor because there aren't sufficient examining rooms."

"We do the best we can with the funds we have available!" Cummins protested.

"Exactly, Doctor." Van Cleve continued:

231

"Now, what if someone went to Claude Stuyvesant and said, 'C.J., you're a big man in this city. An important man. With your millions, money doesn't mean much to you. Let's turn this tragedy to some public good.' I'm sure he'll be curious. So our emissary Lindsay says, 'The way to honor your daughter's memory, and do a public good, is to take the two million dollars from the insurance company and donate it to the Claudia Stuyvesant Memorial Emergency Service at City Hospital.' "

The men around the table looked to Van Cleve with fresh interest. He continued:

"Maybe even have Lindsay take Stuyvesant there one of those busy nights. Let him see for himself. The sick; their families; the tired, unruly little kids who can't be left at home though they should be in bed and asleep. I'm sure even a tough man like Stuyvesant would be moved. And of course Lindsay should subtly point out the acclaim Stuyvesant would receive for such a great public service."

"Not bad, Van Cleve, not bad," Trumbull granted.

"Naturally," Van Cleve concluded, "as part of the settlement he drops all charges against the hospital and everybody involved."

"Naturally," Trumbull agreed. "That's what this meeting is all about."

Van Cleve leaned back in his chair, confident he had launched a strategy that would also free his client from the threat of having her license revoked by the state of New York.

Trumbull addressed Hospital Board Chairman Naughton. "Marc, I'm sure you'll waste no time getting in touch with Lindsay. Brief him on exactly what we'd like him to do."

"The moment I get back to my office," Naughton assured him.

His strategy approved, Scott Van Cleve was impatient to get to a phone. He located Kate Forrester in Troy's basement office.

"Doctor, I think your nightmare may be over."

"How?" Kate asked, hardly daring to breathe. He could picture her lovely face lighting up, her blue eyes bright and happy, finally.

"I have worked out a way to settle this whole thing, get everyone off the hook, you included, and even get a new and improved Emergency Service for City Hospital."

"That sounds terrific," Kate said enthusiastically.

"Of course Stuyvesant has to buy it. I think he will. And so do the others."

"Maybe, just maybe, I'll get a decent night's sleep now," Kate said.

"It's been rough, hasn't it?" he asked.

Since the night Claudia Stuyvesant had died, Kate had not confessed her fears to anyone, not even someone she knew as well as she knew Rosie Chung. With this sudden promise of exoneration, the words tumbled out of her in a flood.

"It's been hell," she admitted. "I lie in bed sleepless. Then I finally drift off, only to be shocked awake minutes later with the fear of what may happen. Drift off again, wake with a start again. I relive that whole night, that case, try to fall asleep, doze off, then another shock."

"It sure sounds like hell," Van Cleve commiserated. "Well, if this works, that'll all be over."

"Thanks. Thanks very much, Mr. Van Cleve."

When Harry Lindsay called to ask for a meeting with Claude Stuyvesant, the financier assumed this was another move toward forming a syndicate to build a new yacht to defend against the Australians for the America's Cup. So he invited Lindsay to lunch as his guest at the Yacht Club uptown on Forty-fourth Street.

Over drinks the conversation proceeded in the vein Stuyvesant had expected. Later, over lunch, it became even more detailed about the possibilities of building a yacht that would meet all the conventions and still defeat the Australians. It was finally over coffee that Lindsay broached his real mission.

"C.J., out of respect for your feelings I have refrained from dwelling on the painful loss you have suffered," Lindsay began. "Yet there are times when out of tragedy can come some good. Some great public good."

"You tell me how a man losing his only child can be a public good, and I'll tell you you're crazy!" was Stuyvesant's first and bitter reaction.

"C.J., you have every right to tell me to butt out. Every right to get up and walk away from this table. But I would consider it a personal favor if you would at least listen."

"Nobody has ever accused me of being an unreasonable man!" Stuyvesant protested in a loud and unreasonable tone of voice.

Not encouraged, but at least given the opportunity he had sought, Lindsay continued: "What if there were a way to make people remember the name Claudia Stuyvesant? And bless it as well?"

Stuyvesant glared across the table, dubious and only slightly less angry than he had been. But it was a look that invited further detail.

"Would you wish on any other father what happened to you?" Stuyvesant treated it as the rhetorical question Lindsay intended. "Well, there is a way for you to help prevent that."

"How?" Stuyvesant asked, grudgingly exhibiting genuine curiosity.

"Have you ever been inside the Emergency Service of City Hospital?"

"Of course not!"

"You ought to go there one night. See how crowded it is, how overworked the personnel, how old and run-down the physical plant. Then imagine what a new Emergency Service could do for the poor of this city and for the other people who depend on it."

"Harry, if you're trying to hit me up for a donation, you can have a check in the morning. Just state a figure."

Lindsay paused a moment, then said softly, "Two million dollars."

"Two million —" Stuyvesant repeated, stunned. "When you hinted at a contribution, I thought the usual — a hundred thousand. But two million —"

"What if it didn't cost you a dime?" Lindsay asked.

"What do you mean?"

"C.J., we have word from the insurance company that they are willing to settle your lawsuit for two million. If you contribute that money to City Hospital for a Claudia Stuyves-

236

ant Memorial Emergency Service, your daughter's name would be in people's memories forever. And the whole thing wouldn't cost you a dime out of your own pocket. It becomes a bookkeeping transaction. And, while I haven't investigated it yet, there may even be a good-sized tax benefit in it for you as well."

"Claudia Stuyvesant Memorial . . ." Stuyvesant pondered quietly.

"C.J.?"

"The last few years, I don't know what came over that girl. Rebellious! Maybe my wife's fault, not keeping a close rein on her, and me being so busy with things," he said softly. "Harry, there's no right way to bring up a child in these times. You give them everything, and it doesn't seem to work. Nothing seems to work these days, nothing."

Stuyvesant started to pour himself another cup of coffee, but realized it was only a ruse to avoid making a painful admission. He set down the silver coffeepot, glanced at Lindsay.

"Harry, you know why Claudia died?"

"I've heard."

"By this time a lot of people have heard. Ectopic pregnancy that ruptured and caused a hemorrhage." It was the most painful admission of a proud man's life. "I would have given anything, done anything. . . . But she

237

never even came to me — never."

"C.J., I'm suggesting you put this whole sad chapter of your life in the past. Let people remember only that Claudia's death resulted in a fine charitable act that benefited this city."

Stuyvesant drummed his fingers on the stiff white linen tablecloth, finally nodded. "You've got a deal, Harry."

"Then you'll settle with the insurance company and take no further legal steps against anyone?" Lindsay asked, trying to confirm an agreement.

"Yes, I will drop the lawsuit."

"Good!" Lindsay said, feeling his mission had been accomplished.

"But that woman doctor . . ." Stuyvesant said.

"She's also covered by the insurance company under the hospital policy. They won't settle just half a claim."

"I don't mean that. Hell, a malpractice award against her isn't worth the paper it's written on. I want her conduct of my daughter's case judged by a jury of her peers!" Stuyvesant declared.

"You mean before the state board?"

"My lawyers have already filed my complaint. I want her before the state board, where she won't be protected by any insurance company or any hospital. By God, I'll make sure

238

she never practices medicine again!"

"C.J., I don't know how the hospital will react to that. They'd like to get this whole thing behind them."

"Either they leave that woman to me or there's no Claudia Stuyvesant Memorial wing!"

Around a small conference table in Trumbull's office, Dr. Cummins, Scott Van Cleve, and the attorney for the insurance company were receiving Harry Lindsay's report on his meeting with Claude Stuyvesant.

"So, gentlemen, that's the deal. Two million to City Hospital for a Claudia Stuyvesant Memorial Emergency Service."

"Harry, you did damn well," Trumbull said. He turned to the insurance company lawyer. "How does that set with your people?"

"Two million, plus a complete release from all malpractice claims?"

"Right," Lindsay said.

"We're lucky to get out from under with that figure," the insurance company attorney confessed. "I'll draw the papers."

Scott Van Cleve interjected, "That covers Dr. Forrester, too, doesn't it?"

"Of course," Lindsay replied. Then admitted, "Insofar as the malpractice suit is concerned."

"Exactly what does that mean?" Van Cleve persisted.

"Stuyvesant reserves his right to press for a hearing before the state board," Lindsay informed. "In fact he's already filed his complaint."

"He can't settle on one hand and still continue to pursue his vendetta on the other," Van Cleve protested. "That's not what I proposed at our last meeting. It was for *everyone* to be free and clear!"

Trumbull felt compelled to take charge of the meeting. "Van Cleve, let's not permit our personal feelings to run away with us. After all, we are attorneys. Legally all that our client, City Hospital, owes Dr. Forrester is to defend her against any malpractice suit. Which we have done."

"To cut Dr. Forrester adrift to defend herself against unjustified charges before a board that is being urged by a man of no small political power in this city and this state, is that fair?" Van Cleve challenged.

"However you phrase it, the hospital, the insurance company, and this law firm have done all we are legally obligated to do on behalf of Dr. Forrester," Trumbull declared with finality.

"Exactly," Cummins confirmed. "We are willing to allow Forrester to serve out the term

240

of her contract, which I believe is another ten months, unless the state board decides she is guilty. In which event her contract will automatically terminate. And we will be finished with this whole distasteful affair."

"Don't you feel any obligation to her? She is a loyal, devoted, highly capable young doctor who would be a credit to your profession," Van Cleve insisted.

"I would hardly say she has been a credit to our hospital in this case," Cummins countered.

"So isolate her, quarantine her, say she's not part of us. We are perfect and she has stained our excellent record!" Van Cleve accused angrily. " 'Let him who is without sin cast the first stone,' Doctor."

A flush of anger rose into Cummins's face. Trumbull came to his aid. "Van Cleve, you don't have to run a huge institution like City Hospital. Dr. Cummins does. So we shall abide by his judgment in this matter. Gentlemen, I think Harry Lindsay has done an excellent job and deserves our gratitude. Now, let's get the paperwork done on that settlement before Stuyvesant has a change of heart."

After congratulatory handshakes with Lindsay, the meeting ended. The men withdrew from Trumbull's office. As Van Cleve started out, Trumbull called to him: "Van Cleve, a moment, please?"

"Yes, sir?" Van Cleve asked, returning to the conference table.

"It is obvious to me that you've become very emotional about this Forrester matter. It could be because you're so devoted to pro bono work, fighting for the underdog. *Or . . .*" and he paused before continuing: "*Or,* could it be because of your personal interest, not in Dr. Forrester's *cause,* but the doctor *herself?* Understandable. She is a very attractive young woman."

Van Cleve's impulse was to deny it. But there was sufficient truth in Trumbull's observation so that he could not deny it, even to himself.

"Now, son, your private life is yours. But I want to talk to you on another level. When I first recruited you for this firm, I listened to your lofty ambitions about doing pro bono work. And I said to myself, 'He's one of the new breed, full of the lofty, idealistic aspirations of the young crusader for justice.' Now, mind you, I think that's fine. For a *very young* lawyer. But, I also thought, 'Once he's been around this firm for a while and sees other young men devoting themselves to corporate law, earning three, four, and five times what he makes, he'll change.' They all do. But you're one who hasn't. I can't tell you how many times in the partners' meetings I have to defend you."

"I've lived up to my end of our agreement," Van Cleve pointed out.

"No one says you haven't. But we expected that you would mellow. Time. Circumstances. Competitiveness. All would make you change as the others have. But in your case . . ." Trumbull shook his head in futility. "That's why, in this Forrester matter I feel I have to draw the line."

"Draw the line?" Van Cleve asked, puzzled.

"As soon as the Stuyvesant settlement goes through, that ends our responsibility to Dr. Forrester."

"Meaning?"

"Her hearing before the State Board of Professional Medical Conduct is a purely personal matter. She must make arrangements to defend herself."

"Are you saying I'm off the case?" Van Cleve asked.

"I am saying Trumbull, Drummond & Baines is no longer obligated to defend her."

"And if I insist on continuing?" Van Cleve asked.

"Not as a member of this firm," Trumbull said firmly.

"I see."

"Personally I would hate to lose a bright

young lawyer in whom I see great potential. But don't force my hand."

Van Cleve did not respond, merely nodded his head gravely and departed.

Scott Van Cleve returned to his small, cluttered office to ponder the choice Trumbull had posed. Give up the Forrester hearing or resign from the firm.

He reached for his phone. He punched in the number. He heard her voice.

"Dr. Forrester?"

"Yes."

"Doctor — we have to meet."

"Why? Did something happen?" Kate asked.

"I'll explain when we meet."

"When?"

"As soon as possible," he said.

"Okay," she agreed. "Tonight."

"This afternoon if possible."

"This afternoon? What's so urgent? What happened?" Kate asked, alarmed by his insistence.

"Not something I can discuss on the phone. I'll pick you up at the hospital at three."

Chapter Eighteen

Even though she had cut short her visit with little Maria, Kate was late coming out of the hospital. Scott Van Cleve paced across the street, rehearsing in his mind the least painful way to break the news to her. He was sure that despite her initial shock she would understand what happened and how he had tried to solve her problem. It might take her a longer time to understand why he had to take the course he had chosen. He was prepared for that.

He caught sight of her now. Determined, almost defiant, she emerged from City Hospital. She spied him, raced swiftly across the street against the light. When she reached him, his first sudden and unexpected impulse was to kiss her. But that would defeat what he had come to do.

"What happened?" Kate asked directly.

"Let's go someplace where we can talk quietly," he suggested.

"There's a little coffee house down the street."

A small place did not seem appropriate to him; he would feel confined, imprisoned. This was not a bold, brave thing he was about to do.

"It's a nice day. Central Park isn't too far," he said.

They were into the park, away from the sounds of automobile horns, away from the occasional screech of tires brought to a sudden stop, away from the inevitable shouts and epithets that usually followed. Deep enough into the park, one could almost forget the city around them.

He led her to a bench shaded from the glare of the setting sun by a large oak. When she was seated and attentive, he began simply, "It didn't work."

"What didn't work?" Kate asked.

He explained his carefully thought-out strategy to defuse Stuyvesant's hostility. How Lindsay met with Stuyvesant. How Stuyvesant responded and agreed to donate all monies received to a new Emergency Service.

"Then it worked very well," Kate said. "Why do you say it didn't?"

"The part that didn't work applies to you," Van Cleve admitted.

Kate did not seem to comprehend.

"Stuyvesant insists on demanding that hearing before the state board."

Kate listened. A moment later she nodded,

absorbing the unfortunate fact, then said, "Of course we'll have to fight him!"

"That's —" Scott Van Cleve started to say, then confessed, "You'd have been better off if I'd never suggested my plan."

"I'm no worse off now," she said, until it occurred to her, "Am I?"

"Yes."

"How?" she asked.

"Before there was a community of interest. The insurance company, the hospital, our law firm — all had as much at stake as you did. But now that they're off the hook . . ."

"We're on our own," Kate realized, aware of what that could mean.

"That's not the worst of it."

"What is?" she asked, staring into his eyes.

"Mr. Trumbull has given me an ultimatum," he started to explain. He didn't have to.

She said it: "Drop my defense or leave the firm."

He nodded. Her eyes filmed up. He thought, *No tears, please, don't cry. Please?*

"Is there," Kate asked, "is there another lawyer you might suggest?"

"I hadn't even thought about that yet."

"Then do think. And let me know."

"Look. I'm sorry," he blurted out. "My original plan provided that Stuyvesant drop all charges against you. I never expected it to boomerang."

"No need to explain," Kate said. "I'm sure you meant only the best for me. But after all, you have your career to protect too. No one knows what that means better than I."

"Look," Van Cleve pleaded, "I'll do everything I can. In an informal way of course. I can advise you, confer with any new lawyer you get, give him any ideas, any advice. It just can't be official, that's all."

Kate did not respond but rose and started away. Van Cleve followed. At the exit from the park Kate increased her pace to escape him.

"Can't I even walk you home?" he asked.

"I'd rather be alone. I've got a lot of thinking to do," she said.

"Wait, please!" he called out. She stopped, turned back to look at him. "It's not my fault," he started to protest. "No, it *is* my fault," he admitted. "If only we could be true to those lofty aims and ambitions we cherished when we were students. When I was in law school, I revered lawyers like Clarence Darrow. Who could defend a rich banker's son one week and a penniless labor leader for free the next."

The look of compassion in her blue eyes permitted him to continue.

"But men like Darrow are heroes, legends.

And I, unfortunately, am no hero, no legend. Just a young lawyer in a big city. With a big law firm. Which offers mighty tempting rewards for young men who play the game. All the firm's lip service about pro bono work is just so much bait they hold out to get you. After that, the rule is, play the game or get out."

Kate felt sorry enough for his dilemma to want to understand and forgive.

"I know what you mean," she said. "But my problem is quite different. I have no choices. No one has said to me, 'Play the game or else.' If I lose now, there *is* no game. Not for me. I'm sorry for you, Van Cleve. But I've got to do for myself now."

Kate turned away. As he watched her, he wondered, *Is this the last time I will ever see her?*

Kate walked away, stunned, surprised, deeply hurt and afraid, yet stolid, determined not to cry. She could feel sorry for Van Cleve. His look of embarrassment, of pain, as he admitted his weakness, was not the look of a man of courage or strength. Let him struggle with his own weakness; she had other problems to face now. Alone.

She opened the door to her apartment, calling, "Rosie?"

249

Rosalind Chung came out of her bedroom to greet her. "You're home early."

"I — I just had a meeting with my lawyer. My ex-lawyer actually."

"Katie, what happened?" Rosie asked, no longer casual, beckoning, come, sit down on the couch, tell me.

Kate related her meeting with Scott Van Cleve.

"What do you do now?" Rosie asked.

"I don't know. Maybe call home. Ask Dad's advice, and he'll ask George Keepworth. No, I don't want to upset Dad and Mom."

"I know," Rosalind said with sudden decision, "we'll raise a fund!"

" 'We'? Who?"

"The medical staff, at least all the residents and interns," Rosalind said. "I'll round up a group when I go on duty tonight."

"Don't get yourself into trouble," Kate warned.

"This time it's you, next time it could be me or any one of us," Rosalind said. "I can't tell you how many times since this happened to you that I've asked myself, 'Why do we keep knocking ourselves out?' We give up the best part of our lives, put off getting married, having children, and for what? Only to be persecuted in the end, like they're doing to you now. Well, that's going to stop! We've got to take a stand, and this is the time!"

"No, Rosie. This is my fight. I don't want anyone else getting into trouble on my account. I saw what almost happened to Van Cleve."

"If you change your mind . . ."

"I won't!" Kate said.

Rosie had gone off to fulfill her night assignment at the hospital. Kate Forrester was alone and had been for some hours. She had made herself a sandwich, but could not eat. She had brewed fresh coffee and had had too much. She paced their small living room until she felt she would wear out the carpet.

She had considered all her possible choices.

A new lawyer? Costly. Likely too costly. Can't let Dad know. Things on the farm are tough enough, with the drought last year and the low prices for soybeans and wheat this year. First thing he'd do is sell more acreage. But that's Clint's inheritance. Everything he's worked for. I received my share when Dad sold off acreage to pay for my college and part of my medical school. I have no right to ask for any more, or even put Dad in a position of offering.

Why do I need a lawyer? The fact that it's usually done that way doesn't mean it's the only way. I read in the papers from time to time about prisoners who write up their own appeals in long-

hand and win new trials, even from the Supreme Court. Why not me? Why not appear before that board myself? Tell them the truth. They'll believe me, they have to!

But in the end she realized, *If it were that simple, why did Scott Van Cleve, and evidently his law firm, think that it was such an involved and time-consuming procedure that he must drop my case?*

She knew one thing. She had better try to get some sleep. Lack of food, lack of sleep, could conspire to sap her health and her strength at a time when she needed them most.

Getting to bed was one thing, getting some sleep was another. She did doze off several times, but each time woke shortly thereafter to the grim realization of her situation.

The phone rang. In the darkness she groped for it. Found it.

"Hello?" she said, her voice hoarse from lack of use.

"Doctor? I've spent a great part of the night thinking over this afternoon . . ." Scott Van Cleve began.

"And you have the name of a good lawyer for me," Kate assumed.

"I do."

"Wait. I'll get a pencil and pad."

After a moment he asked, "Got one?"

"Yes."

"Then write this down carefully."

"Shoot!" she said.

"Scott — Van — Cleve," he said.

Kate was stunned for a moment, then reminded him, "Are you aware of what this means?"

"I am."

"This isn't fair to you," she said.

"I know. But in my career this will only be a blip, an interruption, like a skipped heartbeat on one of your EKG screens. But to you it can mean your lifetime, your career. So, if you'll retain me as your lawyer, I want to go to work. Right away. Right now in fact."

"Right now? It's past midnight!" Kate protested.

"I know. But if I want to get started on your case in the morning, I need to ask some questions now! Can I come up?"

"Why, yes, sure," she said.

"Be there in a minute," he said.

"All the way from the East Side?" she asked.

"East Side? I'm in the phone booth down on your corner," he explained.

"Phone booth?" Kate was startled. "Give me a minute to make myself presentable."

"Don't! I want to see how you look in the morning," he said, and hung up.

She sprang out of bed, went straight to the bathroom to study her face and her hair in the mirror over the washstand. No time to put on makeup. But she could make her hair look a bit neater. She started to comb it into some semblance of order, when the doorbell rang. One more run of the comb through her blond hair and she started for the door, until she became aware that she was dressed only in her nightgown. She reached for her robe and was still slipping into it when she opened the door.

There he stood, tall, rangy, craggy face, eyes fixed on her for a long moment before he said, "Do you always look this good in the morning?"

"Do I have to answer that?" she countered.

"As your lawyer I should know everything about you. I insist you answer."

"Come in and stop making a fool of yourself," she said, able at last to laugh. "Have you had supper? We always call it supper on the farm."

"Walking around almost all night? How could I?"

"Neither have I. I'll make us something," she said, heading for her small kitchen.

They talked while she brewed fresh coffee, scrambled eggs, fried bacon, toasted whole wheat bread. He sat on the utility stool, admiring every simple thing she did. Several times she caught him staring. He started to

254

remind her of Owen Lindquist, a boy in her high school senior class, who never did summon up the nerve to ask her for a date, but who stared at her in the same way.

Scott asked her to review the Stuyvesant case in specific detail, seeking some point at which to begin his own investigation, in order to confirm her actions through the testimony of other witnesses.

By the time they were through eating, finishing up with coffee in the living room, Van Cleve had decided that his best corroborating witness was Eric Briscoe. His next witness would be Nurse Adelaide Cronin. Then possibly the lab technician, or technicians, who had made the several blood studies on Claudia Stuyvesant.

But first, talk to Eric Briscoe. Also to Briscoe's lawyer, when he retained one.

It was past four o'clock in the morning when Scott left. Reluctantly. At the door he cautioned, "Now, lock up good. Both locks," he urged protectively.

"I always do," Kate said, as reluctant to see him go as he was to leave.

"Maybe you ought to install a third lock," he suggested. "In times like these you can't be too careful."

"We've thought about it," she said.

He was startled. " 'We'?"

"Rosie Chung and I. We share the place."

"Rosie?"

"Rosalind."

"Rosalind," he repeated, considerably relieved. "Nice name for a woman, Rosalind."

"Nice woman," Kate added. "She's on staff at the hospital too."

"Good, good," he said, starting toward the elevator.

She watched until he stepped into the car. She wondered, *Did he think some man and I were living here together? And if I were, he's my lawyer, not my keeper. With no right to dictate my lifestyle.*

But a moment later she thought, *It was nice to see him so concerned. Well, possibly not nice, but at least interesting.*

Despite the lateness of the hour, Scott Van Cleve walked back to his apartment across town on the East Side of Manhattan. He wanted time to think, to assess everything Kate had told him about her handling of the Claudia Stuyvesant case. He was analyzing not only what she said but the manner in which she said it. He wanted to satisfy himself as to how credible a witness she might prove to be.

She appeared truthful, eminently truthful. Allowing, of course, for details overlooked or remembered slightly differently than the record might reveal. But that was only natural. In fact the honest witness was more likely to make such mistakes than the prepared and lying witness, who had rehearsed and memorized every last detail.

So the first thing he must do was to make absolutely sure that her memory of events squared with the records. If it did, there might be a way to bring this entire situation to an end privately and without the attention a public hearing might attract.

So, before following up on any corroborating witnesses, he decided to try. However, after the dismal failure of his previous strategy, which only served to isolate Kate from the protection of his law firm, Scott decided to take this step without arousing in her any hopes that might prove to be false.

First, check those hospital records again.

This time when he requested the chart of Claudia Stuyvesant, he met no resistance from Administrator Cummins. Not only was it forthcoming at once, but the administrator was quite self-conscious as he volunteered, "I'm sure that as an attorney you understand that my obligation to the hospital supersedes all other considerations. If we can't assist Dr. Forrester, we surely wish her well."

Scott spent several hours with the complete case history. Aside from the missing tox report, everything in the file confirmed what Kate had told him. Convinced of her reliability as a witness, he was ready to take his next step.

Scott Van Cleve turned off Fifth Avenue and started down Fortieth Street toward Madison. It was a block of undistinguished office buildings, some new, some old, some more than thirty stories high, some only as tall as eight. The building Scott sought, in which the New York City branch of the Board of Professional Medical Conduct had offices, proved to be one of the older buildings.

He consulted the listings in the lobby. Under *State Office of Professional Medical Conduct* he found the name *Hoskins, Albert, Counsel.*

Though Hoskins was listed as counsel, Scott knew that if he were unsuccessful in preventing a hearing, the attorney would serve as prosecutor in the Forrester matter.

Scott made his way into the old, not too well lighted elevator, pressed the number of the floor. The ancient car started up with a slight jerky movement, stopped at the right floor, also with a jerky movement. Scott stepped out to find the receptionist at

258

a cluttered desk.

"Mr. Hoskins, please?" Scott asked.

The receptionist, who also served as a typist, seemed annoyed by the intrusion and, without interrupting her typing, replied, "He's in conference. Do you have an appointment?"

"No. But I'll wait," Scott said.

"Your name?"

"Scott Van Cleve."

"Would Mr. Hoskins know what this is about?"

"I'm an attorney."

"If it's about employment on the staff here, you don't see Mr. Hoskins. He's too busy. You see Mrs. Ross."

"I'm here about a matter before the board. The matter of my client, Dr. Katherine Forrester."

The young woman stopped typing at once. "Oh, *that* one." Unintentionally she informed him of the importance the entire office staff placed on Claude Stuyvesant's complaint. "Yes, I think you'd better wait, Mr. Van Cleve."

Minutes later the phone on the receptionist's desk rang. She answered. "Yes, sir, there is someone waiting. A Mr. Van Cleve. Says he represents Dr. Forrester. Yes, sir. Right away!"

She hung up the phone, at the same time

pointing down the hallway to her left, "Mr. Hoskins's office is at the end."

Scott entered the office of Albert Hoskins, chief attorney for the board. He found him sitting behind a large desk on which neat stacks of files testified to the great number of complaints leveled against physicians in the city of New York. A bulky man, Hoskins seemed to move with great effort as he rose to extend his hand slowly across the desk.

"Mr. Van Cleve, is it?" he asked, as he appraised his adversary smugly. "Well, sit down, sit down. Make yourself comfortable," Hoskins invited warmly.

A bit too warmly, Scott thought.

"Now, then, Van Cleve, you want to see me about the Forrester matter even before any notice to appear has been served?" Hoskins asked.

"I know that Claude Stuyvesant has filed a complaint against my client. I also know that in line with the board's established procedure, before there is any hearing, your first step is to form an investigative committee."

"For the protection of innocent physicians and their reputations the committee studies all medical records, documents, and follows up with consultations with medical experts. If they find no ground for the complaint, we put an end to the matter right then and there.

Quietly. Confidentially."

"Exactly why I am here," Scott Van Cleve replied. "I have gone over the Stuyvesant case in minute detail. Dr. Forrester has established to my satisfaction that every step she took was in keeping with the highest standards of medical practice. The lab tests will bear her out. I'm sure when I speak to Dr. Briscoe, he will corroborate everything Dr. Forrester has told me."

"Your point, Mr. Van Cleve?" Hoskins asked, becoming somewhat impatient.

"I want your word that when that happens, the matter will be closed, so that no further damage is done to Dr. Forrester's reputation and career."

"You want my word, do you?" Hoskins countered. "Well, Mr. Van Cleve, I am sorry to say that all the material, the patient's chart, the backup material, the opinions of several medical experts, has already been turned over to an investigating committee."

"That committee's been appointed?" Scott was surprised to hear the matter had already been acted upon.

"Oh, yes," Hoskins affirmed.

"Are you always so quick to act?" Scott demanded.

A slight flush rose into Hoskin's fleshy cheeks. "We treat all cases with great speed

261

and thoroughness."

"Even when the complainant is not Claude Stuyvesant?"

The flush in Hoskins's cheeks grew deeper, more florid, this time augmented by anger.

"Mr. Van Cleve, if you are accusing, or even hinting, that this office engages in favoritism or yields to political pressure, I may ask to have you barred from representing anyone before this board!"

"Thanks for confirming my suspicions," Scott replied. "As for barring me, I invite you to do that. So that I can go to the media and let the whole city know how this office is being manipulated by one very powerful man."

"Careful what you say, Van Cleve!"

"Hoskins, I know how appealing it must be, how tantalizing for a man like you, stuck in a civil service job, to look forward to a nice, fat partnership in one of the large law firms Stuyvesant retains. Is that what he promised you if you destroy Dr. Forrester's career?"

"That is a vicious, absolutely groundless accusation! I could complain against you to the bar association. Or even ask the appellate division to censure you for making such derogatory accusations against a fellow member of the bar!"

Scott knew it was useless to pursue the matter. "Since you seem so determined, I see we have nothing more to discuss."

"I quite agree," Hoskins said, "but as long as you're here, you might do something for me."

"I? What?" Scott asked, suspicious.

Hoskins held out a legal document. Scott hesitated, then took it. It was a Notice to Appear for a hearing before the State Board of Professional Medical Conduct, and it named Katherine Forrester as the respondent. Appended to it was a Statement of Charges.

"You can save me the trouble of serving this on your client," Hoskins said.

"Then the investigating committee has already arrived at its decision," Scott remarked. "Have you ever had any case that moved along so swiftly?"

"This is not our usual run of cases," Hoskins protested. "Usually they involve unnecessary surgery, or surgery done negligently, or doctors on drugs or alcohol. But for a doctor to miss such an obvious diagnosis and have it result in death, that is no 'usual' case, Mr. Van Cleve. The public must be protected. And that is my job! Mr. Stuyvesant has nothing to do with this!"

More disturbing than Hoskins's denials, which had made no impression on him, Scott discovered there was only a single respondent, Dr. Katherine Forrester.

The name Dr. Eric Briscoe did not appear at all.

Chapter Nineteen

Still nurturing the hope that he could bring his young protégé, Van Cleve, around to his way of practicing law, Lionel Trumbull had prevailed on his partners to permit Scott the continued use of his office during his defense of Kate Forrester.

However, that did not include the availability of other services, such as the firm's staff of investigators. Scott was thus forced to do his own legwork, digging into all aspects of the Stuyvesant death.

Time was an added pressure. The Notice to Appear demanded Kate Forrester's presence at the hearing within two weeks. So Scott had little time to consult documents and records, to interview potential witnesses, and to formulate his defense.

His first witness must, by any test, be Dr. Eric Briscoe, who had himself been a participant in the tragic events leading up to Claudia Stuyvesant's death.

Scott had been waiting almost an hour in Briscoe's office before the young surgeon raced in, apologizing, "Sorry, but I was assisting at a colon resection. The malignancy turned out to be more extensive than Dr. Goodrich expected."

As Scott rose to shake hands, Briscoe urged, "Please. At ease. No need to disturb yourself." He took his place behind his cluttered desk, unbuttoned his white lab coat, stretched to throw off the fatigue of the operating room, then said, "Well, Van Cleve, what can I do for you?"

"You realize this isn't for me," Scott said. "It's for Kate Forrester."

"Of course. That's what I meant. Whatever I can do for Kate I want to do. She's a terrific young woman. Bright, capable, energetic. Excellent doctor. I hate to see her in this kind of mess. The life of an intern or a resident is no fun. And doing time in Emergency those long hours, believe me, it's above and beyond the call of duty. But she did well, damn well. And now to be blamed for this. Shame. You know, this is the kind of thing that could have happened to any of us."

"I'm glad to hear you say that, Doctor. Because thus far that's the best defense theory I can come up with. It was an unfortunate situation in which the doctor did her best under impossible conditions. That any doctor, young or old, would have done exactly what Kate Forrester did."

Briscoe nodded firmly, but interposed,

266

"Van Cleve, I'm due to assist one of the attending surgeons on a complicated exenteration. Patient with extensive cancer spreading from the uterus into the abdominal cavity. So I hope this won't take too long."

"I just need a general idea of what you'll testify to at the hearing."

"Testify? You — you want me to testify?" Briscoe asked.

"Dr. Forrester's own version will naturally be considered prejudiced, so we'll need corroboration. Who better to give me that? You were there. You examined the patient. Saw all the lab reports."

Briscoe nodded, but noticeably more reserved this time.

"Dr. Briscoe, the crucial question is this: Presented with all the findings, the lab reports, the patient's symptoms and her signs as observed by Kate Forrester, would you say, in your professional opinion, that the treatment she followed was the proper course indicated in those circumstances?"

"In my professional opinion?" Briscoe questioned.

"As a trained surgeon, having witnessed a number of such cases, is it your opinion that Dr. Forrester handled that case competently?"

"She did a good job. I mean —" Briscoe appeared to be at a loss for words.

"Dr. Briscoe, let me put this another way. Was what Dr. Forrester did in accord with the standard of medicine as practiced in this community?"

"Standard of medicine as practiced —" Briscoe considered.

"That's legal language. Let me simplify it. Did Kate Forrester do a proper professional job in the circumstances?" When Briscoe hesitated, Scott persisted. "That shouldn't be too tough to answer. Of course, when I put you on the stand, the questions will be phrased more legalistically. Both Hoskins and I —"

"Hoskins?" Briscoe asked, startled. "Who's he?"

"Counsel for the Office of Professional Medical Conduct."

"What's *he* got to do with this?" Briscoe asked.

"He'll be serving as prosecutor at Dr. Forrester's hearing before the board."

"You mean he'll be asking questions too?" Briscoe considered.

"Of course. He has a right to cross-examine any witness I present."

"Van Cleve, when you called me, I thought you just wanted information. But being a witness — I've never been a witness before. In any kind of case."

Aware of Briscoe's growing reluctance,

Scott was forced to adopt a new approach. "For the moment let's forget testifying. Just answer some questions."

"You understand I want to help Kate in any way I can. I'm very fond of that girl. So I will do my best to answer any questions you have. Fire away."

"Good," Scott said, picking up his yellow pad. "Now, then, when, based on her findings, Dr. Forrester sent for you, did you consider that to be usual, reasonable, precautionary conduct on the part of a medical resident in Emergency under the circumstances?"

"Well — uh. Yes, I considered that routine, usual. Reasonable. She had a baffling case on her hands." But Briscoe went no farther.

"You were saying . . ." Scott prodded. When Briscoe did not continue, Scott coaxed, "She had a baffling case. . . . Then what were you going to say?"

"I guess, with those lab reports, the patient's vital signs, and unable to make a specific diagnosis, it would be — uh — usual to call in a surgeon to determine if there was need for surgical intervention," Briscoe agreed.

Scott Van Cleve realized that Briscoe was beginning to embroider his answers with too many conditions.

"To put it another way, Doctor, was it sound medical practice in a baffling case, presenting a fever, a high white cell count, and the other lab findings, to send for a surgeon to get his opinion?"

"Yes, yes, that would be sound," Briscoe was forced to admit.

"And what *was* your opinion?" Scott asked directly.

"Well, you have to understand that my opinion was in large measure conditioned by what Dr. Forrester had told me."

"Didn't you examine the patient?"

"Yes, of course I did."

"Did you agree with Dr. Forrester?" Scott pressed.

"As I said, my opinion was in large measure based on what she told me. She was the one who took the patient's history. I only got it secondhand. Hearsay, I think you lawyers call it. Well, when I am told that a patient is not sexually active, hasn't missed a period, I do not suspect an ectopic pregnancy, as the medical examiner's report found."

"What *do* you suspect under those circumstances?" Scott asked.

"Possibility of an infection, intestinal virus, pelvic inflammation condition. But no ruptured ectopic pregnancy."

Scott realized that Eric Briscoe was intent

not on cooperating in the defense of Kate Forrester but on insulating himself from any involvement. Scott pressed on in an effort to salvage what he could from this interview, which had turned out to be so disappointing.

"Doctor, you did perform an examination on Claudia Stuyvesant that night, didn't you? Including a pelvic."

"Yes," Briscoe replied sharply.

"During the course of that examination didn't you discover anything to indicate what that young woman's condition was?"

"I tried to tell you, I was making my examination under a given set of facts. I relied on Dr. Forrester's findings." He began to reiterate, "No sexual activity, no missed periods. . . ."

Scott interrupted. "Wasn't Dr. Forrester also acting under the same set of facts? So that her professional conclusions and yours were identical?"

Briscoe's concern came to the surface in a rush of color to his cheeks. "Look, Van Cleve, *I* am not charged with anything! And I don't intend to be! I am going to finish my residency at City Hospital, leave here with a good reputation, and go back to a partnership that's waiting for me in Colorado."

Scott studied Briscoe for a long moment, saw a gleam of sweat on the surgeon's flushed face. He could sympathize with Briscoe's determination not to become involved. But he had his own client to protect.

"Briscoe, just answer one more question: Did anyone warn, advise, or threaten you not to cooperate with my investigation in this case?"

Briscoe hesitated, then in a soft, self-conscious voice, "No. Nobody."

Scott knew Briscoe was lying. But to confront him would serve no worthwhile purpose. And to subpoena such a reluctant witness would prove a disaster. Worse, if Hoskins called him to testify, which now seemed possible, Briscoe would prove a difficult witness to attack. It might turn out to be the better part of legal judgment not to cross-examine him at all. Was it possible that in some way, by influence or by threat, Claude Stuyvesant had reached out to silence Briscoe too?

Scott Van Cleve slipped his yellow pad back into his briefcase, saying, "Thank you, Dr. Briscoe. For your time." He started for the door.

"Damn it, Van Cleve, I would expect you to understand!" Briscoe exploded.

Scott turned back to face him. "Understand? Sure. You want to go back to Colorado and practice surgery with a clear record, if not a clear conscience," he said accusingly.

"You have no idea the flak I took merely because Kate mentioned my name in that damned television interview."

"Scared the hell out of you, did it?" Scott asked. "Sure. So, save your own ass and to hell with anyone else!"

"If I could help Kate, that would be one thing. But nothing I can testify to will help her. I'd be taking an enormous risk for no good reason. I'm sorry for Kate. Because I like her, like her a lot. But there's nothing I can do. Nothing!"

Scott Van Cleve glared at him, making no secret of his contempt. Then he continued toward the door.

Briscoe shouted at him: "*I* didn't come up with that negative pregnancy result. *She* did! She misled both of us!"

Scott did not trouble to respond but continued out of the office, down the corridor, with Briscoe's last accusation echoing in his ears.

Chapter Twenty

The more involved and frustrated Scott Van Cleve became in the defense of Dr. Kate Forrester and the more closely he worked with her, the more aware he became that day by day his feelings were growing more personal as well. Which presented dangers of its own.

He recalled only too well the advice of his professor in Evidence and Trial Practice in his second year in law school. "Never become so personally involved with a case or a client that you lose your objectivity. Some of the most shocking disclosures a trial lawyer is confronted with in a courtroom will come from the mouth of his own client. So treat every client as a hostile witness. Question every statement he makes. Find corroboration, or be prepared to refuse to let him testify."

Failing to secure the cooperation and corroboration of Dr. Briscoe, and with the day of the hearing ever closer, Scott Van Cleve decided to apply the professor's test to Kate Forrester's version of what happened to Claudia Stuyvesant that night in Emergency.

To that end, he decided to consult several physicians who specialized in obstetrics and gynecology. Each woman or man he selected was an accredited, board-certified specialist. Each was attached to an institution other than City Hospital. He wanted no opinions that might be colored by the doctor's hospital affiliation.

In each instance, during the interview, Scott also assessed the physician's potential as a defense witness. Provided, of course, that the doctor proved amenable to testifying. With the hostility of juries toward physicians in recent years, doctors had come to look upon the legal system as an inquisition rather than as a fair judicial proceeding. Of course, there were those experts known to be professional witnesses whose opinions, pro or con, were for sale at a price and hence suspect as well as expensive.

But, Scott reasoned, there might be a doctor or two who, impelled solely by a sense of justice, would come to Kate's assistance. First, however, he needed to corroborate Kate's conduct of the Stuyvesant case.

The first doctor with whom he was able to secure an interview was ob-gyn specialist Stephen Willows. Scott felt ill at ease as he sat in Willows's waiting room. It was occupied entirely by women, some in the late stages of pregnancy, some in the early stages, some who appeared not pregnant at all but were probably awaiting routine checkups. He tried to conceal his embarrassment by flipping through a magazine in which he had absolutely no interest. He could not resist stealing an occasional glance to confirm that the women regarded him with great curiosity.

He almost felt called upon to explain his presence by declaring, "No, I am not a husband here to have his sperm tested. Or to secure advice on when and how to have intercourse so that I can impregnate my wife." Instead he dug deeper into the magazine until gradually the waiting room emptied and he was alone.

The receptionist announced, "Mr. Van Cleve, Dr. Willows will see you now."

He found Willows to be a man close to sixty, or possibly older, white-haired, bespectacled, with the air of an efficient and capable man.

An ideal witness, Scott decided.

Willows looked up from making a note in the chart of his last patient as he said, "Yes, young man? You're the lawyer who tried to get me on the phone yesterday?"

"Yes, Doctor."

"Well, get on with it, get on with it. I'm due to make my hospital rounds in half an hour," Willows said, not with annoyance but rather affably.

"Dr. Willows, this has to do with a hearing

before the Office of Professional Medical Conduct."

"Oh," Willows remarked, abandoning his affability, "one of those."

"Yes, sir, one of those. And in this case quite unjustified."

"That's what lawyers usually say," Willows then warned, "I am not a professional witness. In fact the only time I testified in a lawsuit was *against* a doctor."

"I would still like your opinion, sir."

"Fire away!" Willows said, resigned to hearing Scott's version of the case.

Once Scott had presented a summary of the events as he had learned them from Kate and from the chart of Claudia Stuyvesant, Willows appeared quite thoughtful before he said. "The patient denied she was sexually active?"

"Yes, sir."

"And that she had missed a period?"

"That's right, Doctor."

"And to make sure, the doctor did a urine pregnancy test?"

"Yes, sir. Which, unfortunately, turned out to be misleading when it came up negative," Scott admitted.

"Myself," Willows said, "I put more credence in a radio-immunoassay test than a urine test. But under the stress and time limits of an Emergency Service, your Dr. Forrester did the right thing. Too bad the result turned out wrong."

"Sir, if you were there that night, handling that same case, what would you conclude?"

Willows marshaled all the facts: "Patient presenting generalized symptoms, nausea, vomiting, diarrhea. And stomach pain. I might assume the young woman was telling the truth when she said she was celibate and had missed no period."

"As the doctor, what would you conclude?" Scott asked.

"I would diagnose it as run-of-the-mill viral stomach upset."

"Not an ectopic pregnancy?" Scott asked, tensely awaiting his response.

"Ectopics are tricky cases to diagnose. Very few of them present in the same way," Willows said. "I would stick with the viral stomach infection. Unless, of course, some later symptoms or signs appeared, or the lab results forced me to change my mind."

"So that, in your opinion, what my client did on that night would be considered good medical practice?" Scott said, trying to pinpoint a conclusion.

"Ah, there! Now you're talking like a lawyer trying to inveigle me into testifying," Willows warned. "I won't take the stand. And I won't testify. But, in my opinion, that doctor, whoever she is, did exactly what most good doctors would have done under the circumstances."

"If the patient were on drugs, cocaine, crack, or other drugs, would that have made a difference?"

"Oh, indeed!" Willows exclaimed. "It would certainly have disguised the degree and extent of her condition."

"Dr. Willows, aware of all this and knowing that a young doctor's career depends on it, would you reconsider testifying?" Scott asked.

"And risk having my malpractice insurance cancelled? In these times the less any doctor has to do with the law, the better. Sorry. Give the young woman my sincerest sympathy and best wishes that she emerge from this with her professional reputation intact."

Scott Van Cleve was no more successful in securing the cooperation of the other specialists he interviewed.

Of one thing he was now convinced. The answer to whether Claudia Stuyvesant was a drug user could prove critical to Kate Forrester's defense.

When Scott Van Cleve appeared in the reception room of the medical examiner's office announcing that he wished to see that city official about the Stuyvesant case, the receptionist mistook him for a reporter from one of those scandal sheets that are prominent at the checkout counters of supermarkets.

"Sorry, sir, but all information on the Stuyvesant case is strictly private and confidential. Dr. Schwartzman sees no one about that case."

Scott Van Cleve grew so insistent that the receptionist finally sent for one of the junior forensic pathologists, who proved to be even more obstructive. It was only after Scott threatened to resort to a court order for access to the detailed records of the Stuyvesant autopsy that he was admitted to see the chief.

Dr. Abner Schwartzman, chief medical examiner, was on the phone arguing with some persistent city official when Van Cleve was shown into his office. It gave the young attorney a chance to study the man. He found him to be short, stocky enough to fill his creaking swivel chair, and like some short men, aggressive and argumentative. At the moment he was responding quite vehemently to someone on the other end of the phone.

"Now, you listen to *me* for a change," Schwartzman bellowed as he motioned Scott to a chair. "You disagree with our findings? Call in your own pathologist!" He listened for a brief instant, then ended the conversation with a sharp, "Okay, we'll see you in court!"

He hung up, grumbling. "Everybody's a forensic expert!" He swung around his swivel chair to confront Scott Van Cleve. "So, young man? What's *your* complaint?"

"I'm an attorney and I am here to inquire about your findings in the Claudia Stuyvesant case."

"Our findings have already been made public," the medical examiner stated bluntly, as if that closed the matter.

"Your *complete* findings?" Scott asked in follow-up.

"Yes!" Schwartzman said, more vehemently than was necessary.

"I understand you performed that autopsy yourself," Scott said.

"I did. And everything I found is in my report, as is our usual practice," the man explained.

"There was nothing in the public release of your findings about the results of the toxic screen," Scott pointed out.

"Because no toxic screen was ever done."

"Why not?" Scott pressed.

"Young man — or shall I call you counselor? — I don't tell you how to try a case. Don't tell me how to conduct an autopsy."

"These days, with drugs rampant, I would think a toxic screen would be routine."

"Once I found the cause of death, there was no need to pursue the matter further," Schwartzman said.

"No need? Or against orders?" Scott asked.

"Look, kid, if you are confusing a courtesy toward Mr. Stuyvesant with a cover-up or some shenanigans, you are barking up the wrong tree."

"Exactly what do you call a 'courtesy,' Doctor?"

"The mayor asked, and I acceded, to Mr. Stuyvesant's request that the autopsy be done by me personally and the results not be made available until after the daughter's funeral. The family did not want to be besieged by the media on the day of the funeral. Not an unreasonable request, you must admit."

"Not a *usual* one either," Scott commented.

"It was a simple courtesy to grieving parents. And no harm was done."

"The facts, *all* the facts, may be vital in the defense of my client before the Office of Professional Medical Conduct."

"Oh, yes, I've heard some rumblings about that. Too bad," Schwartzman commiserated. "Sorry. But I can't help you."

"Can you at least tell me, as a pathologist, if the body were exhumed, could traces of drugs still be detected?" Scott asked.

"Not in this case," Schwartzman said.

"Because there were no drugs, or because we couldn't find any at this late stage?" Scott pursued.

"Because there is no body," the medical examiner said. "As soon as my autopsy was completed, the body was picked up by a hearse from a crematorium out on Long Island."

Scott was reminded of that pallbearer's statement when he questioned him about the coffin: "But it was a lot less than I expected."

"Think," Scott urged Kate Forrester. "Is there anything a doctor might observe that would be proof of drug abuse without having a tox report or some other laboratory confirmation?"

"Depends on the drug. Or drugs," Kate informed.

"Different drugs, different symptoms?" Scott asked. "For example?"

"Well, if it's alcohol, you get the well-known ones. Impaired coordination, flushing, vomiting, and nausea. . . ."

"She did complain of that." Scott seized on it.

"Yes, but cocaine might have induced nausea too," Kate pointed out.

"Go on, go on, more signs a doctor would observe that would lead to a diagnosis of drug abuse," Scott coaxed.

"I'm sure it wasn't alcohol in Claudia's case," Kate said.

"Then what?"

"Barbiturates are possible. Amobarbital. Pentobarbital. Phenobarb."

"And the detectable signs?" Scott persisted.

"Headache, confusion, ptosis. . . ."

"Ptosis?"

"Prolapse of an organ, such as a drooping upper eyelid."

"Did Claudia evidence that?"

"No."

"You said cocaine might have induced nausea," Scott said.

"And vomiting," Kate added. "Also stimulation followed by depression. Sweating. Anxiety."

"All of which Claudia presented," Scott reminded.

Kate smiled. " 'Presented'? You're beginning to talk like a doctor now."

"Before this is over, I'll have to learn to *think* like a doctor too," Scott said. "Now, could you testify that the signs and symptoms Claudia presented were those induced by using or abusing cocaine?"

Kate hesitated. Then shook her head. "Honestly? No."

"We need that testimony and we need it badly," Scott pointed out. "One half of our defense is that you were misled by a false pregnancy test. But the other half, the more important half, is that the patient, through her use of drugs of various kinds, made a proper diagnosis impossible. It clouded and distorted her symptoms, signs, and lab reports so that no doctor would have been able to say with any degree of certainty what her true condition was. Now, how do we get that?"

"Her own doctor would know," Kate said. "That Dr. Eaves that Mrs. Stuyvesant mentioned."

"Eaves," Scott considered.

"A very well-known internist. Very upper-class practice," Kate informed. "Of course, he might not want to talk."

"We'll see," Scott said, with a few thoughts of his own. "We'll see."

The office of Dr. Wilfred Eaves occupied the entire street floor of one of the most prestigious Park Avenue buildings, which happened to be owned by Claude Stuyvesant. Eaves's offices were run with very quiet efficiency by an office manager, who supervised a staff of four nurses, who saw to it that every patient was ensconced in a private examining room and ready for Eaves's examination so that not a minute of his precious time was wasted.

Eaves himself, who was always clothed in an immaculate white lab coat, which he changed four times every day, functioned with the precision of a highly polished machine. His diagnoses, almost always correct, were delivered in crisp but unmistakably clear language. His reputation was not only citywide but worldwide, so that many of his patients were of the ruling families of some Middle Eastern countries. If you had a sick child or other relative or feared for your own life, and if you could afford his high-priced services, Wilfred Eaves was the man to see after all other doctors had failed.

By the time Scott Van Cleve was admitted to Dr. Eaves's consultation room, he was duly impressed. Since many of Eaves's new patients were referrals, he immediately asked, "Did you bring any X rays, scans, or MRIs with you?"

"I'm not here as a patient."

"Good God, don't tell me that Ms. Berk allowed a drug company missionary man to slip by," Eaves said, visibly annoyed.

"No, sir. No drug company salesman. I'm an attorney."

Immediately Eaves pushed back from his desk and rose to his feet. "I do not talk to attorneys. If you have any complaints to make, or charges of malpractice, speak to my attorney. Get out!"

Scott remained seated. "Dr. Eaves, I am not here to complain or make charges or accusations. But only to elicit some information on behalf of a young doctor who must defend herself against charges before the State Board of Professional Medical Conduct."

"You are talking about Dr. Forrester, I presume."

"Yes."

"I'm afraid I can't help you. Good day, Mr. Van Cleve."

It did not escape Scott's notice that Eaves knew his name, though he had not mentioned it on entering. But he proceeded nevertheless. "Since you were the doctor of record for most of Claudia Stuyvesant's life, you would know. Was she addicted to or an habitual user of drugs of various kinds?"

"I cannot answer any questions that relate to any of my patients!" Eaves responded sharply.

"If I subpoena you, you will have to appear and testify."

"And if I do, I shall stand on a doctor's privilege not to reveal any confidential information about a patient," Eaves replied.

"The patient is dead. The defense of privilege may not pertain any longer," Scott said.

"I shall leave that decision to the chairman of the hearing," Eaves retorted.

"Even your refusal to testify may be of value, Doctor," Scott pointed out.

"Mr. Van Cleve, I'm a very busy man," Eaves said, eager to bring the interview to an end.

"Yes, of course," Scott said. "Thank you for your time."

The moment Scott Van Cleve left his office, Eaves picked up his phone.

"Ms. Berk, get me Claude Stuyvesant at once."

Very soon his phone rang back. Ms. Berk reported, "He's on the line, Doctor."

"Claude, he was here. That young lawyer, Van Cleve."

"And?" Stuyvesant asked.

"I told him nothing, as we agreed. But he strikes me as a digger."

"Don't worry, Wilfred, he'll get nowhere."

As Scott Van Cleve walked away from Dr. Eaves's Park Avenue offices, he was sure of one thing. Eaves had acted like a man with a guilty secret. There was no longer any doubt in his mind about Claudia Stuyvesant's drug habits. What he needed now was the proof.

Chapter Twenty-one

Dr. Eaves's aggressive reluctance to provide any information about Claudia's drug habits had served its purpose by confirming Scott's suspicion. If Eaves, who knew her habits and conditions best, refused to provide the information, perhaps those with whom she had spent her last few years might be more amenable. Armed with Claudia's most recent address as it appeared on her hospital chart, Scott Van Cleve searched out that house in the Greenwich Village section of lower Manhattan.

It was an old red-brick building below West Eighth Street, so old that one could assume it was built almost a century ago as a fine private residence for some wealthy family of merchants or traders.

In more recent years, with Manhattan rents climbing astronomically and with space becoming more precious, such old-time commodious one-family residences had been converted into single-room apartments for young struggling writers, actors, and others who came to New York with ambitions to conquer the world's greatest city.

In the small entryway Scott consulted the twelve names on the board, each with a bell button alongside. It would probably be futile to ring the bell designated STUYVESANT, C. But neither was there anything to be risked by doing so. He rang. To his surprise the buzzer responded, granting him entrance to the inner hall. He entered, started up the dark staircase. He had climbed two stories toward the skylight above, when he was confronted by a woman leaning over the rail to stare down at him.

Thin, in her late fifties, with dark but graying hair, the woman was obviously on guard and quite suspicious of anyone who would ring the bell of a dead tenant.

"Yes?" she asked in a tone that encompassed all her suspicions in a single demanding syllable.

"May I ask who you are?" Scott asked by way of initiating the conversation.

"It would seem that is more properly my question," the woman replied.

By that time Scott was on the third-floor landing and face-to-face with her. She was taller than he had expected, and thinner as well, but no less reserved and on guard.

"My name is Scott Van Cleve —" he began.

The woman interrupted. "I am Mrs. Benedick. This is my building. And frankly

I am getting fed up with ghouls like you who scan the obituary notices every day to find empty apartments. You should do what all the others have to do. Put your name on the list of a dozen buildings. And wait until your turn comes. But to come sniffing around like vultures at every death is . . . is . . ." She searched for the correct word, did not find it, but settled for "sacrilegious." And, because she was unsure, she insisted, "Yes, sacrilegious."

"I'm not here to inquire about the apartment," Scott informed her.

"You're not?" the woman asked, surprised.

"I'm an attorney and I represent —"

Even before he could pronounce the name of his client, the woman said in denial, "I don't know anything. About lawyers. Or about any possessions. I am inspecting the premises to see if her apartment only needs a thorough cleaning, or maybe a paint job, before I rent it out again."

"Would you mind if I just looked the place over?" Scott asked.

"What for?" the woman demanded.

"Just to look around. I promise I won't touch anything," Scott said.

"Well," the woman equivocated, "if all you do is look around — though there's nothing to look around at. . . ." She gave way to the open door behind her.

Her words took on more meaning as Scott stepped into the room. Aside from the flowered cretonne curtain that hung limply to one side of the doorless clothes closet, the room was completely empty. There was no piece of furniture, no mirror on the wall. There was no vestige of clothing in the empty closet. It was as if no one had lived here in a long time, no less a few weeks.

"Nothing, nothing at all," Scott observed softly.

"I told you, nothing to look around at," the woman reiterated.

"Usually when someone dies —" Scott started to say.

Once again the woman anticipated him. " 'Usually,' 'usually.' In this case nothing was usual. Poor girl died early Sunday morning. Monday afternoon, even before the news became public that she died, two moving men showed up. Had some legal-looking paper. They cleaned the place out. Lock, stock, and barrel. Everything. Including his clothes. . . ."

The woman stopped suddenly. "You said you're a lawyer. *His* lawyer?"

"No. But tell me, who is 'he'? Where is he?"

"He was living here. With her. It was two for the price of one. Though they never admitted it, fearing the rent would be raised. We get that here all the time. Men moving in with girls. Girls moving in with men. It's like musical chairs. Or musical beds is more like it."

"Do you know who he is? His name?"

"No. When they put a second name on the doorbell and on the mailbox, the rent goes up. So they don't use any names. Least, he didn't. But he sure raised hell when he found that they took all his things along with hers."

"Those two moving men, did they say who sent them and where they were taking the stuff?"

"No. Just showed me a legal paper. So I let them have the run of the place."

"This young man, do you know his name?"

"Only what I heard. She used to call him Rick."

"Rick," Scott repeated. "No last name?"

"Not that I ever heard," the woman said.

"Do you know anything at all about him? What he did for a living? What his habits were?"

"You ask me, he had only one 'habit.'" the woman replied with strange emphasis on the last word.

"Doing drugs?" Scott asked.

"I don't like to gossip, but I know the

signs," the woman declared.

"What about *her?*"

"What *about* her?" the woman countered, bristling.

"Was she on drugs too?"

"I told you, I don't like to gossip," she replied.

"But you 'know the signs,' " Scott reminded.

"I don't talk about tenants. Especially dead ones. Let them take their secrets to the grave, I always say," she replied with such finality that Scott knew he must forgo that line of questioning.

"This . . . this Rick . . . if you don't know his last name, or what he did for a living, can you at least give me a description?"

"Description . . . description . . ." the woman pondered. "Let me see. He's kind of dark-complexioned — not black, not even Hispanic — but dark. Like maybe Italian. And in his early twenties. Painfully thin. Of course, one thing about him I never liked. He wore his hair long, in a ponytail. I tell you, Sometimes from behind you could almost mistake him for a girl. Except he was tall. But I mean, from wearing his hair that way you could take him for a girl. These days, these days, especially in this neighborhood. . . ." she complained.

"And his name was Rick?"

"Rick," the woman repeated. "Does that help?"

"It's better than nothing. But not much better," Scott said thoughtfully. "I'll give you my card. If he should come back, ask him to call me."

"He won't come back," the woman said. "But if he does, I will."

"It's important. A doctor's career could depend on it," Scott informed.

"A doctor . . ." the woman recalled. "You mean that lady doctor that Stuyvesant was talking about on television? And then she went on and answered back? That doctor?"

"Yes."

"You ask me, she *needs* a lawyer," the woman said. "These days, hospitals, doctors, you can have 'em all! I get sick, I don't go to no hospital! Not these days."

"Just call me if you hear anything from him, or about him. Please?"

"Yeah. Sure. Okay."

He left the old rooming house thinking, *If that woman is typical of the kind of jury Kate would have faced in court, it's lucky that at least the malpractice issue has been settled.*

Chapter Twenty-two

In pursuit of clues to the lifestyle and habits of Claudia Stuyvesant in the year before her death, Scott Van Cleve resorted to the funeral program to track down the two classmates who had delivered brief remembrances of her on that day.

The young woman who had read the poem in Claudia's memory, and from whom Scott had failed to extract any information that day, was unavailable, since she had returned to Dallas, where she now lived. The other young woman, listed in the program as Shelley Monfort, still resided in the area. Scott discovered that she worked as a production assistant for a television talk show that originated in New York.

He had to wait impatiently until the show was off the air for the day before he could corner Shelley at her studio. From his first question Shelley Monfort proved evasive, and too quick with excuses.

"Look, Mr. Van Cleve, I really don't have the time. It's my job to line up the guests for the week, and we've already had a cancellation for tomorrow's show. So I've got to scrounge around and find some politician or some publicity-hungry novelist or some nut with a weird idea that will make good television. I should be on the phone right now."

"Ms. Monfort, this involves the career of a young woman, a doctor who —"

"Please, Mr. Van Cleve! I've troubles enough of my own. Besides, if it's not about television, there's really nothing I can do!" she snapped.

"But there is. You knew Claudia Stuyvesant," Scott said.

Shelley Monfort immediately became less frenetic but more attentive and reserved.

"What about Claudia?" she asked softly.

Scott explained the threat that confronted Kate Forrester. He pointed out how testimony about Claudia's conduct during the last year might help vindicate his client. "So all I will ask you to do is take an hour of your time and testify as to Claudia's habits in the past year or two."

"I really don't know —" she started to protest.

"But you do," Scott insisted. "The way you spoke at her funeral, you two were pretty close."

"*Used* to be," Shelley Monfort corrected.

"What happened?" Scott asked. "What changed?"

"Even when we were at school, she had this thing for the Village scene. Every time we had a break, a holiday, weekend off, she'd come down to the city, head straight for the Village. After a while she thought the rest of us were strange, odd, out of it because we couldn't get with it. She never realized, she was the one who was out of it."

"Drugs?" Scott asked. "Was she doing drugs even while she was in school?"

"I wouldn't know," Shelley Monfort said, not too skillful at carrying off her lie.

"Please. The truth can save a young woman's career, a good doctor's career," Scott urged.

"I wouldn't know," Shelley reiterated.

"I'm only asking you to tell the truth," Scott pointed out.

"Sorry. There is nothing I can add," the young production assistant said. "Now, I've got to go make my calls."

"Miss Monfort, if your career were about to be destroyed, wouldn't you want someone to take the time to help you?" Scott asked.

"Sorry," she persisted.

He realized it would be fruitless to pursue her with further questions. As Scott turned away, conscience, or guilt, caused the young woman to say, "You're asking me to help someone I don't even know. And to blacken the name of a girl I roomed with, loved, worried over. Hasn't enough damage been done to her reputation already? She's dead. Let her rest in peace."

Shelley Monfort was now on the verge of tears, so much so that Scott felt sorry for her despite her refusal to help.

"Whatever she was, whatever she did, I really don't know because we drifted apart, especially in the last year. That's what happens when people do drugs. They live in their own world. If you don't share drugs with them, it's like you don't exist. We tried, God knows we all tried to keep contact with her. She was the one who broke away, *she* deserted *us*. We could see it happening. There was nothing we could do, no one she would listen to. Except that stud she was living with."

"You mean Rick?" Scott asked.

"Oh," Shelley reacted, caught off guard, "you know about him?"

"Yes."

"Then I guess you know everything."

"Except where to find him," Scott said. "Do you know?"

"No. None of us do. All we knew, he was scrounging off Claudia."

"Did you ever meet him?"

"Not really," Shelley said.

"What does that mean?" Scott pressed.

Shelley hesitated, considering the advisability of admitting to any more than she already had.

"Please, Miss Monfort, it can't do Claudia any harm to tell me that much. Can it?"

"Well . . ." Shelley vacillated, until she admitted, "We didn't meet him but . . ."

"But saw him?" Scott concluded.

Shelley nodded. "Just about a year ago her mother called me. Said her father was becoming desperate about Claudia's way of life and was threatening to do something drastic. Her mother wanted us to make one last try to get her to move back home. So the two of us went to see her. As we were going up the stairs, a young man was coming down. We suspected it was the Rick she was living with. When we asked her, she didn't deny it."

"And that's the only time you ever saw him?" Scott asked.

"No. One other time," Shelley admitted.

"Her funeral?" Scott asked.

"Yes, how did you know?"

"Dr. Forrester spotted him too. She suspected who he was."

"Well, that was him. Ponytail and all," Shelley Monfort admitted. "That's all I know. Which I'm afraid isn't much help to you, is it?"

"Not unless you agree to testify," Scott said.

She shook her head in a firm manner that made him know she could not be convinced. "There is one thing more, if you know."

"What?"

"This Rick . . . Did she ever tell you his last name?"

Again Shelley hesitated. Then she admitted, "I guess that can't hurt her now. His name is Rick Thomas. The bastard!"

"Well, that's something to go on," Scott said. "Thanks."

As he started away, she called after him, "I'm sorry about your client. But I can't do anything to hurt Claudia. I'm sorry."

Chapter Twenty-three

Rosie Chung was getting dressed to go on night duty when Kate returned from her day's stint with Dr. Troy. She called from her bedroom. "Kate? Message. Your lawyer called."

Kate hurried to Rosie's door. "What did he say? Anything about seeing that friend of Claudia Stuyvesant?"

"All he said was to meet him down on Eighth Street and Fifth Avenue. At nine."

"Tonight?"

"Tonight," Rosie confirmed, adding, "He said wear warm clothes. And what he called 'good, serviceable shoes.' "

"I wonder what that means," Kate said.

"Me too," Rosie agreed, very carefully applying dark shadow to her almond-shaped eyes.

Which caused Kate to ask, "Mel on duty tonight?"

Rosie turned to her. "Why do you ask?"

"Every time he's the resident surgeon on night duty, you make up like you're going on a date, instead of unbroken hours of hell."

"I never want him to forget that I'm a woman as well as a doctor."

"No chance. He's crazy about you. Why else would he take you home to meet his folks?" Kate asked, still concerned by the message. "Warm clothes and serviceable shoes? Did Van Cleve say why he wanted me to meet him tonight?"

"No," Rosie replied. "I'll say one thing. He's got a very nice voice. Even when he's giving orders. Does he look like he sounds?"

"How does he sound?" Kate asked.

"Judging from his voice, I picture him to be a good, solid citizen. The Spencer Tracy type. Sturdy build. About five-ten . . ."

"Six-two," Kate interrupted to correct her.

"And blond. A typical American blond male."

"Brown," Kate said. "His hair is brown."

"Well," Rosie insisted, "with a voice like his he's got to be handsome. Sort of like Tom Cruise. Smooth. And cute."

"Craggy," Kate corrected once more.

"Craggy?" Rosie repeated in surprise. "I had this image of him with a dimple in his chin. A cleft. Like Kirk Douglas or Cary Grant in those films we see on late-night television when we're too tired to sleep."

"No cleft. Just a craggy face. Tall. Very lean. A runner's build. Only I don't think he runs. But he's nice. Very nice. And . . . well, devoted."

"Devoted?" Rosie turned from her mirror with newly aroused curiosity. "You mean there's something going on between you two aside from legal advice?"

"I mean devoted to his work. To my case."

"Oh." Rosie accepted this with obvious disappointment. "I thought, with Walter out of your life, you're finally able to consider other men."

Rosie was carefully slipping into one of the plain, dark dresses she usually wore under a lab coat when on Emergency duty, when Kate asked, "You never did like Walter, did you?"

"Oh, I liked Walter. I just didn't like him for you. You're entitled to more than a man whose sole ambition in life is making deals and money."

"You never said anything," Kate pointed out.

"I knew you'd arrive at the right answer in your own time. Besides, who am I to give advice to the lovelorn? I wish I were as smart about my own life," Rosie confessed.

"What's wrong with Mel?" Kate asked.

"My father. His mother. Poor sweet lady. The first time Mel brought me home, she was so nervous, all she could blurt out to make me feel comfortable was, 'We love Chinese food. Almost every Sunday we go to this lovely little Chinese restaurant in the neighborhood.'

Then, because she needed reinforcement, she turned to her husband, 'Don't we, Max?' So he did his best by adding, 'Except when there's a football game. Then we have Chinese sent in.' Nice people. But terribly nervous about the idea of their darling son marrying a Chinese girl."

"You mustn't be too hard on them," Kate advised.

"My father's no better. He'll never understand how a properly raised Chinese girl can cross the line and fall in love with an American man. Even though my father never said it, I know how he feels. He worked hard, sacrificed, scrimped, and saved to give his daughter the education she wanted. And what happens? I can hear him now, 'We lose our only daughter. To an outsider. What kind of grandchildren will I have? Will they look like our Rosie? Or will they look like him?' *Him*. That's what my father calls Mel. And the sad part? I know exactly how my father feels. He risked his life, all our lives, to escape from Communist China. He likes being an American. He feels very proud. Only he never expected his daughter to marry an American. So I'm sorry for my father. But I . . . I love Mel. What can I do?"

Before Kate could commiserate, Rosie said, "Got to rush. Mel and I are meeting for coffee before we go on duty. Some romance. A cup of coffee before going on duty. But we keep telling each other, one day, one day it's all going to be great."

She gave Kate a hug, saying, "Don't be late. Van Cleve said nine o'clock. Warm clothes. Serviceable shoes." She started for the front door, calling, "For God's sake, don't tell him how wrong I was about him."

Dressed in a warm suit, wearing a pair of sturdy brown walking shoes, Kate Forrester climbed to the street from the West Fourth Street station of the Independent subway. The streets were still damp from the spring rain that had fallen during early evening. She started down the dark street toward the appointed corner, feeling that subliminal sense of danger that most New Yorkers feel at night alone on an empty street. In addition she was consciously concerned. Why had Van Cleve called so suddenly, left such a cryptic message without explanation?

She spied him at the appointed corner, standing under the streetlight. Tall as he was, and lean, in a double-breasted trenchcoat, he was an intriguing figure, possibly out of some mystery novel or film. He caught sight of her.

As they met, he was so full of his plan that he assumed she knew more than she did.

"Rick. His name is Rick Thomas."

"Who?" Kate asked.

"The man Claudia lived with. The man you spotted at the funeral. Two people described him exactly as you did. Now the question is, if you saw him again, could you identify him?"

"I think so. *If* I saw him again. Can you arrange that?" Kate asked.

"That's what we'll try to do tonight. Let's go."

They started along the street as Kate pointed out, "Ponytail. Pale, thin face. Dark complexion. Wearing jeans. Those are hardly unusual clues to follow. Especially in this part of New York."

"I talked to Dan Farrell about that."

"Dan Farrell?"

"A retired police detective. He handles all investigations for the law firm. He couldn't actually do it for me but he did give me advice on how you track down a man with no known address, only a name and a general description."

"How?"

"No question that Claudia was on drugs. Which means he was too. In fact, Shelley Monfort thinks he's the one who got her on the stuff. Farrell said that if Rick is a druggie, then his lifeline — actually, the words Farrell used were 'his umbilical cord' — is some

307

dealer in the same neighborhood where they lived together."

"You can find a drug dealer on every corner down here. And uptown as well," Kate said. "Some nights or early mornings when I come out of the hospital, I see three or four of them, hanging out across the street, ready to deal. The police don't seem to scare them at all."

"Farrell says that on some corner close to where they lived is a dealer, or several dealers, who've been selling drugs to Rick Thomas and Claudia. With her gone, Rick's source of money is gone. He'll be hitting up the dealers who know him for credit. No strange dealer is going to carry him. Farrell said, 'Find that dealer and you'll find this Thomas guy.' "

"And did you?"

"I think so," Van Cleve said. "I questioned every dealer on every corner for a few blocks around. Of course they all denied knowing anyone named Rick or Thomas. They must have suspected I was a narc or a DEA officer. Except for one dealer. Oh, he denied it. But I could tell he was lying. He's the one we watch tonight. On the chance that Rick tries to make a buy tonight."

"And if he doesn't?"

"We come back tomorrow night. And the night after. And the night after that," Van Cleve said grimly.

"What if he never shows up?"

"That blows the strongest element in our defense," he admitted grimly.

They had arrived at the corner Van Cleve had staked out. He gestured Kate down three steps into the open basement area of a private house from which they could keep watch on a man who stood alone on the corner, under the light from the streetlamp. From time to time the man looked down the street in one direction, then in the other, as if suspicious of being observed. Yet when a police patrol car drove by slowly, it did not stop.

Several times thereafter expensive foreign and domestic sports cars drove up, stopped only long enough for the driver to pass some money to the dealer, receive several small envelopes, then drove off quickly. A number of times customers on foot approached, singly or in groups of two, to effect similar transactions.

Each time the customer was a sole young man, Van Cleve whispered urgently, "Is he the one?"

Each time Kate stared for as long as the young man was in the full light of the streetlamps, but each time she had to say, "No. Not him."

They settled down to watching again. After

a while Van Cleve whispered, "If, while I was in law school, someone had told me I'd wind up on a stakeout on a misty night in Greenwich Village, I would have said he was crazy. I should have stayed back in Shenandoah."

"Shenandoah?" Kate asked.

"Where I come from. Small town in Pennsylvania. Though my neighbors would never admit it was a small town. We were actually the big town among a lot of little really small ones. People came to Shenandoah to shop, to bank. But ever since I was a kid, I had this dream of becoming a big, important lawyer and going to New York. I guess most kids dream of coming to New York. Conquering the big city. We must get that dream from seeing too many movies or television shows. You, too, evidently."

"The best medicine in the world is practiced here," Kate said. "So I came to learn. And wound up —"

Before she could continue, Van Cleve gripped her arm, causing her to study another suspect. Kate watched until another young man was almost out of light range.

"No. Not him," she was forced to say. "Jeans. Ponytail. Sallow complexion. But not him."

They settled down to watch again.

"You said you came to learn and wound

up . . ." Van Cleve reminded her. "Wound up under attack? Wound up stripped of your medical status?"

"Wound up feeling betrayed, bruised, hurt," Kate admitted. "As if I had been professionally raped."

"I know how you feel," Van Cleve said.

"You can't. Nobody can, unless it happens to you," Kate replied.

"How do you think it feels to go to work for a big law firm under a specific promise that you'll be allowed to devote a part of your time to people who need and deserve your help but can't afford it? Then, because you live up to your part of the deal, the firm says in effect, you're fired?" Van Cleve asked. "Maybe we have more in common than either of us realizes."

Suddenly he gripped Kate's arm. Another suspect had appeared for her to identify. Kate stared hard, then had to admit softly, "No. Not him." That young man had disappeared into the darkness before Kate said, "I'm getting this terrible feeling that even if Rick Thomas did show up, I wouldn't know him."

"Don't be discouraged," Van Cleve urged. "I'm sure when you see him, you'll know it."

It started to rain lightly. A fine mist that one could only see by looking up into the light from the streetlamp.

Kate had worn a tweed coat but no raincoat. Van Cleve started to unbelt his double-breasted trenchcoat to offer it to her, but she refused.

"It's big enough for two," he said, opening the coat and surrounding her with its protective overlap. "Better?"

"Better," Kate said, though she felt uncomfortable in such close proximity to a man who, though he was her lawyer, was still a virtual stranger.

Another car drove up. Another transaction was made. The car was on its way. A young woman came from around the corner. She held out a small folded bill, received several small envelopes, clutched them in her fist, and hurried into the misty darkness. Another car pulled up, but before the driver could extend his hand to start the transaction, a police car came around the corner. The sports car took off with such sudden acceleration that it skidded on the damp street, almost sideswiping one of the parked cars. The police car took off in pursuit. The dealer stepped into the gutter to get a better view of the chase and its results. Then he stepped back into his accustomed place of business.

Kate and Scott Van Cleve resumed their watch.

"Do you think you could ever go back?" Kate asked.

"Back?" Van Cleve asked, taken unawares by her sudden question.

"Back home. That town in Pennsylvania."

"Shenandoah," Van Cleve reminded her. "I've thought about it. Especially the last two weeks. I wonder, could I live in a small town again? Practice law there? Little cases like the sale of a small house. The will of some man or woman who hasn't much to leave to anyone. Fights over the boundary between bickering neighbors. I don't know. Maybe I've been infected with the New York disease. If it isn't big, it isn't important. Even the causes I like to defend. They have to be big causes. I think New York changes a man's sense of values. I hope not. But I'm afraid that's true. You get that feeling too?"

"If we lose, my choice won't be going back or staying but finding some place in this country or some other country where they need a doctor so desperately they'll take the rejects."

"You are not a reject!" Scott Van Cleve insisted.

"I may be if we don't find Rick Thomas," Kate retorted.

"We'll find him," he said, and because he wasn't sure, he reiterated, "We'll find him."

★ ★ ★

They had waited and watched as customers arrived, on foot and by car, made their furtive purchases and had gone. Some of them resembled Rick Thomas but only in superficial ways, such as dress or hairstyle.

Kate reached out from the protection of Scott's trenchcoat to appraise the air.

"It's stopped raining," she said.

"Oh. Yeah," Van Cleve agreed, almost reluctantly. He opened his coat to allow Kate her freedom. He seemed uncomfortable, needed to talk to cover his embarrassment. "Your family . . . you mentioned your dad is a farmer. What's he raise?"

"Corn," Kate explained. "Soybeans. Some wheat. Mainly corn, though."

"Difficult way of life?"

"Not easy. But there's great satisfaction in it. Especially in the good years. To plow, plant, gamble on the weather and see a crop through to harvest, to stand in the middle of a cornfield with the stalks so high, they tower over you, that gives a man a real sense of accomplishment."

"You really love your father."

"Love. And admire," Kate confirmed. "He's a good man. A good father. A good husband. And he serves a purpose in this world. In our money-mad civilization, that counts with me."

"How do lawyers count with you?" he asked.

"I guess they're necessary," Kate admitted.

"Just 'necessary'? The picture of a lawyer standing in the middle of a law library with law books towering over him doesn't give you the same sense of satisfaction," Van Cleve concluded wryly.

"I didn't mean lawyers aren't of value. How could I, with my future, my career, depending on one now?" Kate apologized.

"Thanks. Thanks a lot," he said. "Makes my years in law school mean something finally."

She turned to look up into his craggy face, his gray eyes. The twinkle there confirmed her suspicion that he had been teasing her.

"Your father," Kate said. "You never said what he does."

"Did," he corrected.

"Oh. Sorry," Kate said. "I just assumed . . ."

"You had every right to assume," he said. "If I'm twenty-nine, my father would be fifty-five, sixty. Not a ripe old age in these times. He would have been fifty-eight."

"What happened?" Kate asked.

"He was a railroad engineer. On the run from the coal breakers around home to the steel mills outside of Pittsburgh. One night, rounding Horseshoe Curve, he derailed. Speeding, the railroad's experts said."

"Oh, too bad," Kate commiserated. "How old were you at the time?"

"Seven."

"Your mother was left a young widow with a child of seven. How did she make out, what did she do?"

"Thanks to the men on his crew there was his pension. Small, but better than nothing."

"Thanks to the men on his crew? You mean railroad men vote on who gets a pension?" Kate asked.

"They didn't vote. They just kept their mouths shut. He was drunk that night," Scott said, hesitating before he could admit, "He was drunk damn near every night. And when he was, he was mean and reckless. If that had come to light about that night, there might have been no pension."

"You were only seven and you knew," Kate commented sadly.

"I think I knew from the earliest time I could remember. The way he treated my mother. Shouting whenever she begged him to drink less. Not stop, mind you, just drink a little less. And once . . . well, twice . . . no, three times, he actually . . . yes, he hit her. When I tried to stop him, a little six-year-old kid, he whacked me so hard, I landed across the room against the wall, shaking every bit of my mother's favorite crockery in the old china closet she had inherited from her mother. When I came to, I was in her lap and she was on the floor cradling me, crying."

"What a tragic memory to have of one's own father," Kate said.

"For a long time, after I was grown up enough to think about such things, I considered going to a psychiatrist to clear up one thing that's troubled me from the day he died. Never did, though."

"It still torments you, doesn't it?" Kate asked.

"Yes, Doctor, it still torments me. The night he was killed, they came to tell my mother. She had to decide whether to wake me to tell me or let me sleep till morning. I woke on my own. I guess it was the stir in the house. All the activity. My mother crying. I ran to her. She took me in her arms, held me close, and said, 'You poor little boy, you poor little boy.' I was confused, frightened. I didn't know what she meant. Then she said, 'Van . . .' Everybody else called me Scotty, but she always called me Van. "Van, your father is never coming home again.' She broke into tears once more. But I didn't. I felt good, good, good! He's never coming

317

home again to curse her, to hit her, to beat me. Good! That's a pretty terrible way for a kid to feel."

"Or to talk about, even now," Kate said softly.

"Yes, especially to talk about for the first time —" But his words were cut off abruptly as he said, "Look!"

Kate stared across to where the dealer was being approached by another customer. A young man. Unnaturally thin. In jeans, Pony-tail. Darkish coloring.

"That him?" Van Cleve whispered.

"I think so," Kate whispered back.

At once he sprang from their hiding place and started across the damp gutter calling, "Rick! Rick Thomas!" The suspect wheeled around, caught sight of Van Cleve, and started down the street into the darkness. Van Cleve raced after him, with Kate following swiftly in those sturdy, dependable shoes. Down the street the fugitive fled, Van Cleve in pursuit, gaining slightly but not enough to seize him. Until the young man's foot caught in a pothole while attempting to cross the street. He tripped and went sprawling in the damp gut-ter, his precious glassine envelopes scattering. Before he could regain his feet, Van Cleve was on him, pinning him to the wet street, jacking up his arm behind his back.

"Hey, man, you crazy? I ain't no Rick Thomas. I never even heard of any Rick Thomas."

Van Cleve lifted him, dragged him into the light of the nearest streetlamp. He seized him by the hair, held his face up to the light so that Kate could get a good look at him. The suspect struggled. Van Cleve jerked his arm up higher behind his back, causing him to cry out in pain. But he held still.

"Okay, Doctor. Is this him?"

Kate stared into the face of the terrified young man. She would have wanted to end their search but was finally forced to admit, "No, no, he isn't."

Almost reluctantly Van Cleve released his grip on the man's arm and set him free, with a self-conscious and hardly adequate, "Sorry."

"Crazy. Man, you are one crazy bastard!" the young man spat out in anger and contempt. "Where are they? Where is my stuff?" He lunged forward into the gutter, down on all fours, to scour the gutter for the glassine envelopes of the drugs he craved so desperately.

Van Cleve stared at him, shaking his head. "The stuff's turned him into an animal. Look at him. God, it makes me sick!"

Kate refrained from commenting on the possible connection between his memories of his father and his intense revulsion toward anyone in the grip of an unconquerable habit.

Perhaps, she wondered, that is why he is so obsessed with tracking down proof of Claudia Stuyvesant's drug practices.

Disappointed, Van Cleve and Kate started back toward their point of vantage. Before they reached it, the dealer who had sole possession of the corner, interrupted them by blocking their path. Scott was prepared for a physical attack. Kate feared the man was armed and hoped that Scott would not resist.

"Hey, you," the dealer challenged, "you flipped your wig? Chasing a guy you don't even know. Down here you get blown away for less than that. Lucky the guy didn't have a piece on him. You ain't going to last long around here."

"Thanks for the warning," Van Cleve replied.

His sarcasm was not lost on the dealer.

"Now, sonny, you listen to me and listen real good. Chasing some crackhead down the street and raising a stink is stupid. But worse, you are interfering with my business. And that is a lot more dangerous. Do I make myself clear?"

"I know a warning when I hear one," Van Cleve admitted.

"Okay. Now we got what those diplomats call a frank exchange of views. So I'll tell you what. I don't know what this Rick Thomas is to you. And I don't care. I just don't want you hanging around ruining my business. Mainly I don't want anyone stirring up the boys in blue. They cruise by, I don't bother them, they don't bother me. They know if they run me in, I'm back out on this corner in a couple of hours. But if you are going to raise a lot of noise and trouble the cops can't ignore that. Specially when guys are being chased and knocked to the ground and roughed up. That's not good for my business. Now, this Rick Thomas, you want him?"

"We need him. Very much," Van Cleve said.

"Okay," the dealer replied. "He's one of my regulars. Or was. Till two weeks ago when he run out of money. If I put the word out that because of his being a longtime customer I am willing to carry him for a while, he'll be back here in a minute."

"You could deliver him to us?" Scott asked.

"Could. And would. But we got to make a deal. Once you got him, I never see either of you around here again. Okay?"

"Okay," Van Cleve was eager to agree.

"Tomorrow night. Like between nine and midnight. You be here."

"Don't worry. We'll be here."

Relieved, delighted, Van Cleve and Kate started down the street.

"How's that for loyalty to an old customer?" Kate remarked.

"I don't care how it's done, so long as we get Rick Thomas's testimony."

Chapter Twenty-four

The next night Kate Forrester and Scott Van Cleve arrived to take up their prearranged vigil. It was another damp and misty night. This time Kate was prepared, wearing a raincoat and rain hat. The brim of the hat was turned up at a jaunty angle, converting her neat and graceful features into such a pleasing sight that Scott resented that she was wearing her own raincoat. But he warned himself, *Never become too personally involved with a client. It can distort your professional perspective. Besides, if you lose her case, you will lose any chance at all with her.*

From Kate's point of view she found she no longer thought of him as Van Cleve but rather as Scott.

On this night they took up positions behind one of the cars parked across the narrow street from the dealer. They waited. They watched. During the minutes, then the hours, they talked. Of themselves. Of their ambitions. Of their views of the world and the nation, of which they discovered they had many thoughts in common.

They agreed that the world had grown too

complex to deal with the problems of ordinary people. That mankind — or, as Kate insisted on calling it, *humankind* — had learned little in the past century. Wars still went on. But they had become more destructive. Science advanced but only presented more challenges. There were still the poor and the hungry. In all nations. Children with bellies bulging from lack of food still existed. The most common diseases that had been wiped out by medical science in many countries still ravaged other countries.

"You don't have to go to other countries to see that kind of suffering," Kate observed. "Just spend a night in Emergency, you'll see enough."

"Oh, I've been there," Scott replied.

"You have? What was wrong with you?"

"Nothing. Just wanted to have a look around," he admitted.

After only an instant Kate realized, "You went there to check up on me."

"Only on what you'd told me. The bedlam. The number of cases. The constant hassle," Scott admitted, then explained, "A lawyer, a good lawyer, never takes anyone's word for anything. He has to know it himself. To prevent any surprises."

"Were you surprised?" Kate asked.

"Only by one thing."

"Oh? What?" she asked defensively.

"How you can keep your sanity in a place like that. Running from patient to patient, case to case, and no two alike," Scott said. "I gained a new respect for doctors, young doctors."

"Why, thank you," she replied acerbically.

He wondered, *Why isn't she pleased? I have just given her a compliment.*

To change the mood, he asked, "Is medicine all you thought it was going to be?"

"Pretty much. After doing volunteer work during high school I had a pretty good idea," Kate said. "Of course back home we didn't have the number of drug cases or abuse cases. Some but not nearly so many."

"Ever get the yen to go back and practice there?"

"Sometimes. But for me need is the deciding thing. Practice where the need is greatest," Kate said with a conviction that he admired.

"You'd settle for here? Live here? Marry here? Bring up your kids here?" he asked.

"I . . . I hadn't thought that far ahead," she admitted.

"You do intend to marry, don't you?"

"The right man, the right time, yes, someday. But first I have to become the doctor I know I can be."

"Ever think about that right man? What

he'd be like? What he'd . . ."

Before Scott could complete that thought, they both froze. From across the street the dealer had flagged them a signal. They watched. Into the light on the corner came a young man who wore worn jeans, had a ponytail, and was unnaturally thin.

"Him?" Scott whispered.

"I think so."

They bolted across the street just as the dealer was slipping an envelope to the young suspect.

"Rick! Rick Thomas!" Scott called.

The young man turned instinctively, then started away. Scott and Kate pursued him. Within half a block they had caught up with him. Scott threw his arms around him, pushed him up against the iron railing of one of the small private houses. He held him there despite his struggle to break free. Before long, from sheer physical weakness or lack of will, Rick Thomas ceased to resist. He breathed in short, quick breaths, trembling from cold or lack of drugs.

"Easy man, easy," Scott said. "We don't mean trouble. We're not police. We're not Drug Enforcement."

"How'd you know me? Who sent you? *Him?*"

"Nobody 'sent' us. I'm a lawyer. This is

my client. We need your help."

Rick Thomas stared into their eyes. "Someone needs my help? That's a kick. I'm the one needs help." He studied them both another moment, then concluded, "He didn't send you, did he?"

" 'He'?" Scott asked, puzzled.

"He. Him. Her father."

"Claude Stuyvesant?"

"Yeah. Him," Rick Thomas said with considerable vehemence. "Took my things. Everything I owned. Which was little enough. Just came in with some kind of legal paper and cleaned the place out. If I didn't have friends, I'd be sleeping out on the street."

"Rick, like some coffee, some food, a drink, maybe?"

"Haven't had anything since breakfast," he admitted.

At a small, inexpensive all-night restaurant on Sixth Avenue, over a little plastic-topped table, while Rick ate so voraciously that it was obvious that he had missed many meals in the last few days, Scott asked questions. Rick answered them, at times with his mouth full of food. At other times he gulped hot coffee before he could respond.

"Rick, the night that Claudia got sick, where were you?"

"Right there," he replied. "I wouldn't leave her when she needed me."

"But it was her mother who brought her to the hospital," Kate pointed out.

"Sure," Rick agreed. "She wanted her mother. I guess when someone gets real sick, first thing they think of is mother. Besides, she thought it was better, safer, if her mother brought her. Especially since her own doctor wasn't in town."

"So, when she left for the hospital, that was the last time you saw her?" Scott asked.

"Before she left," Rick corrected. "She didn't want me there when her mother arrived."

Scott signaled Kate that he wanted the next question to be his alone.

"Rick, that night, that afternoon, the night before, was Claudia *on* anything?"

"Christ! People think we go around like zombies all the time!" Rick exploded.

"Rick, I'm not asking about all the time," Scott said. "I'm only asking about that night, that afternoon, the night before. Was she on anything?"

Rick took a gulp of coffee before he admitted, "Yeah, we both were. You know, that's the way we met. At a party down here, where there was all kinds of stuff around."

"Like what?" Scott asked.

"Yellow jackets. Blues. Rainbows. Coke. Angel."

"She was into it pretty heavy, was she?" Scott asked.

"She always had a dozen prescriptions from different doctors. Valium. Darvon. Robaxen. Barbs. You name it. She had it. Which is also why she didn't want me to take her to the hospital."

"Why?"

"If they discovered she was on something, she didn't want me to get into trouble. She was very thoughtful that way. Really, she was a terrific girl, she was. And I loved her. I did," he insisted.

"Any other reason she didn't want you there?" Scott asked.

"She didn't want *him* to know I was there. For fear of what he'd do."

"Cut off her allowance," Scott assumed.

"Fear of what he'd do to *me*. Or have someone do to me," Rick added with pointed significance. "He was capable of anything where she was concerned."

"So I've heard," Scott agreed, then reflected, with a glance toward Kate, "So she was on drugs. And for quite some time."

"Even before she ever left his home," Rick added.

"Rick," Scott asked, "did you know — did

329

you know that she was pregnant?"

"That was something I heard later. Is it true? She was pregnant?"

"Yes," Kate said.

"All she told me, she was worried. I mean, she skipped her period. But only once. She was waiting to see what would happen the second month."

From the look in his eyes, both Kate and Scott knew the man was telling the truth.

"Look," Rick said suddenly, "how do I know he didn't send you? To blame me for what happened to Claudia."

"Rick, we're talking to you because this woman is the doctor who took care of Claudia on the night she died."

"You?" Rick asked, staring at Kate. "You're the lady doctor they were talking about on television?" He studied her face. "Yeah. I can see now. I saw you the time Ramón Gallante interviewed you. He was pretty rough on you. You're the one, all right. What do you want with me?"

Briefly Scott explained the charges Claude Stuyvesant had lodged against Kate. Thus the desperate need for his testimony on Claudia's drug use.

"All you would be required to do, Rick, is tell that committee the truth. As you told it to us now."

"He won't — he won't be able to do anything to me? Have me brought up on any criminal charges?" Rick asked.

"No," Scott assured him. "You will be in a hearing room. Not before a judge but before a committee. Who only want to hear the truth, as you know it."

"Stuyvesant . . . he's a powerful man. Got the best connections. Once when I refused to stop seeing Claudia, he had me hassled by the cops. Beat me up so bad they had to take me to Saint Vincent's Emergency."

"He won't be able to do anything to you now. Just tell the truth, knowing that you're doing it to save the career of the doctor who tried to save Claudia's life. And who could have done it if she'd been told the truth that night."

When Rick avoided answering, Scott persisted. "Don't worry about testifying. I'll spend a few hours with you beforehand preparing you on what you'll be asked by me and possibly by the other lawyer. Above all, I won't ask you to lie. The truth is all we're after. Okay?"

While Rick considered Scott's request, he said softly, "So she really was pregnant. I could have been a father."

"No, Rick," Kate said. "The kind of pregnancy Claudia had, the thing that killed her, would never have resulted in a baby being born."

"We used to talk about that. I mean, we talked about if she really got pregnant, we'd get married and leave this town. We'd give up this kind of life. Go somewhere they don't even know the name Stuyvesant. I'd get a regular job. I'm good with engines, cars. I'd be a helluva good mechanic once I put my mind to it. It's the drugs do it. I mean, when you're on 'em, you don't feel like doing anything. You got big dreams, but you're only fooling yourself. You don't do anything. But once you quit — and we were going to quit — we talked about quitting all the time, but . . . I guess that's all in the past now."

"The thing now, Rick, this doctor's career depends on you. You have to tell the truth."

"I will, I will! Anything to get back at that bastard Stuyvesant."

"Tell you what, Rick, since you don't have a room now, why not stay at my place until the hearing?" Scott offered. "That'll give me a chance to prepare you."

Rick considered Scott's offer, then said, "I'm crashing with a friend of mine. So I'm okay for the time being. But, look, Mr. Van Cleve, if you . . . I mean, I'm a little tapped out right now. When Claudia was alive, we had her allowance. But right now . . ."

"Sure. I understand," Scott replied, reaching into his pocket to produce two twenty-dollar bills. Before he handed them over, he said, "Tell me where you're staying and I'll pick you up on the morning I want you to testify. That should be early next week. The hearing starts on the Monday. It'll take a few days for the prosecution to put in their case. Then I'll need you to help us refute them."

"Early next week," Rick repeated to make sure to remember.

"Right. I'll pick you up at eight that morning. That'll give us time to go over the questions I'll be asking you. Meantime I'll check with you every day."

"Right," Rick confirmed.

"Where do I find you?"

"Ninety-seven Charles Street. The apartment is under the name of Lengel. Marty Lengel. Ring from down in the hallway. But ring four times. One, two, three short ones, then pause, then one long ring. That way I'll know it's you and not one of his gorillas."

"Ninety-seven Charles Street. Lengel. Eight o'clock," Scott said, making a note in his book. "Be there."

"Don't worry. Just the thought of getting back at the old bastard is all I need!"

After Scott had taken down Rick's new phone number, they watched him start out of the restaurant. At the door he looked back, made a *V* for victory sign toward them, and was gone.

As he turned the corner and disappeared from sight, Kate said, "I wish there were some way to make sure he'll show up."

"So do I," Scott said. "I considered subpoenaing him. But jumpy as he is now, I think a legal paper would scare him into skipping town. Besides, I think revenge is all the motivation he needs."

"You know what's going to happen to those two twenties, don't you?"

"I can guess," Scott agreed. "Another reason a subpoena wouldn't work. That's why I was willing to risk having him stay at my place. Since he refused, the best thing is for me to pick him up when we need him. But first, there's something we have to do."

As they made their way through the narrow streets of the Village until they found Charles Street, Kate explained those terms Rick had used and with which Scott Van Cleve was not familiar.

"The colors are the colors of the capsules the drugs are contained in. Yellow jackets are pentobarbital. Blues are amobarbital."

"And rainbows?" Scott asked.

"A combination of amobarbital and secobarbital," Kate explained.

"All prescription drugs," Scott concluded.

"Or black market. If there's a demand, you'll always find someone ready to clean up by making the stuff available."

They had reached Charles Street. They found Number 97. They climbed the half-dozen stone stairs, went into the dark entryway. Scott studied the names on the bell panel. He found the name LENGEL, M.

"That's a relief," Scott said. "I had to make sure there is such an address and such a person. Because I can admit to you now, without a witness to Claudia's drug habit, we wouldn't stand much chance."

Chapter Twenty-five

On the same day that Board Counsel Hoskins had handed Scott Van Cleve the Notice to Appear and Statement of Charges, the other mandatory step in the procedure had been initiated. The selection of the three members of the State Board of Professional Conduct who would sit in judgment on Dr. Katherine Forrester.

According to law, two of the members must be physicians or surgeons, chosen from the 131 professional members of the state board. The third committee member must be a layperson selected from the 37 lay members. All professional members had been chosen on recommendation from medical and surgical societies. But the lay members had been appointed with the approval of the governor, who used that power to reward political friends and supporters with a title of honor requiring little actual investment of time and no special aptitude.

One of the three members selected for the hearing committee would be designated chairman to preside.

The first professional member who had

336

been appointed was Dr. Maurice Truscott, a family practitioner from White Plains. Truscott had already reached the age when he was cutting down on accepting new patients. Thus he had more free time than most practicing doctors.

Due to the nature and the cause of Claudia Stuyvesant's death, the second professional member designated was a specialist in the field of obstetrics and gynecology, Dr. Gladys Ward. In her early forties, Dr. Ward had already established herself as one of the leading surgeons on female cancer problems in the metropolitan area.

When scanning the list of the thirty-seven lay members of the board to select the third and final member of the committee, the chairman of the state board had fixed on Clarence Mott. A retired businessman ever since he had sold out his real estate holdings to Claude Stuyvesant, Mott appealed to the board chairman as a fortuitous way of ingratiating himself with the real estate tycoon. The chairman had chosen to appoint Mott to preside over the Forrester hearing as well.

The final appointment to complete the required personnel for a proper and legally correct hearing was the appointment of an administrative officer. Since it was not expected that either the professional or the lay members of the committee would have the required legal knowledge to rule on questions of procedure, or the admissibility of evidence or testimony, it was the function of the administrative officer to serve in that capacity. Thus he had the powers of a judge, though he did not actually preside or vote. But in one sense his powers exceeded those of a judge. Procedure at a hearing being more flexible, it allowed the administrative officer to be more inventive and hence more biased if he were so inclined.

When word had reached the Albany office of the state Board of Health that such an appointment was about to be made, a call went out at once to the governor's office. A discreet question was asked. The answer came back in equally discreet terms: "The fact that Mr. Stuyvesant was a strong financial backer of the governor in the recent campaign should play no part in this selection."

Thus, by disclaiming in advance any hint of favoritism, it pointed out very clearly the governor's intention to reward political loyalty.

By the rules of procedure the administrative officer must be chosen from the legal staff of the state Department of Health, separate from the Board of Professional Medical Conduct, ostensibly to avoid any appearance of prejudice.

Once word had leaked out that there was to be an appointment to a hearing in which Claude Stuyvesant had such a consuming interest, State Senator Francis Cahill determined to intervene. Using his legislative influence, Cahill managed to have his nephew Kevin appointed.

Kevin Cahill, an attorney in his early thirties, had originally received his position on the legal staff of the state Board of Health through the intercession of his uncle. Kevin had served faithfully but with no particular distinction.

At times Uncle Francis felt he had wasted a bit of valuable political muscle in obtaining the job for his colorless nephew. For the senator had envisioned that, like many young lawyers who worked for governmental agencies, Kevin would accumulate sufficient experience, contacts, and favors to go out later into private practice and capitalize on them. The sale of such government experience had become commonplace in the state capital and in Washington as well.

To Uncle Francis's frustration young Kevin had exhibited no such ambitions. Thus, once the senator had managed to secure Kevin's appointment as administrative officer for the Forrester hearing, which in political circles by this time was referred to as the Stuyvesant hearing, the uncle invited his nephew to lunch.

"Kevin, I never said a word about this to your sainted mother when she was alive. But this is a time for plain talk between men. I am very disappointed in you."

"Sir?" the surprised Kevin replied.

"I thought by this time you would have been out of that state job and into private practice. I even spoke to Charlie Hagen of Hagen, Small and Levy about a job in their administrative law department, handling matters before state boards and eventually federal boards. But you haven't shown the kind of get-up-and-go I was hoping for."

"Uncle Francis, I like my work at the board," Kevin said in an effort to explain. "I feel I am helping protect the health of the people of the state of New York."

"Damn it, Kevin," the senator exploded. "No government job is an end in itself. It is only a stepping-stone to capitalizing on it in private practice!"

"I don't want to go into private practice," Kevin countered. "I want to stay where I am, do what I do, and eventually work up to become head of the legal staff of the board."

"Ridiculous!" his outraged uncle exclaimed. "Now, I used up a big political favor getting you this appointment to the Stuyvesant hearing. So don't blow it. Because I have word that Stuyvesant himself is determined to sit in on those hearings. In fact, I have word that if it were not for the old bastard, there'd be no hearing at all."

"I've already seen the report of the initial investigating committee," Kevin replied. "This hearing could go either way."

"It mustn't be *allowed* to go either way!" the senator declared. "Kevin, you listen to me! You want to become head of the legal staff one day? You want to repay your uncle for all he has done for you? Take my advice. Very sound advice. During that hearing every ruling you make must sound like it is a Supreme Court decision. Sound legal. Sound learned. But never, never rule against the interests of Claude Stuyvesant. I want him to take notice of you. Favorable notice. Because when the post of head of the legal staff becomes open, I want to be able to cash in on a favor that Claude Stuyvesant owes you. In a word, if you want that job, earn it. During the hearing. Clear?"

"Clear, Uncle Francis."

"When you go to New York to preside at that hearing, remember, it isn't only Dr. Forrester who is on trial. You are too!"

With the three members of the Committee

selected, and with the administrative officer designated, Albert Hoskins was ready to proceed to prosecute what had officially become titled *In the Matter of Katherine Forrester, M.D.*

Confronting the impending hearing and representing a client who had never before been involved in any judicial proceeding, Scott Van Cleve felt it vital to educate her in the legal aspects of the case, just as she had been educating him in its medical intricacies.

Now that they had found their crucial witness and had their evenings free, Scott used that time to prepare Kate for the procedure, the various strategies that would be at work, the personality conflicts that might arise.

To avoid the need for her to come down to the deserted Wall Street area at night, and in order not to impinge on Rosie Chung's erratic schedule, Scott scheduled his meeting with Kate at his apartment. He occupied the entire fourth floor of a private home in the east sixties. That he occupied the entire fourth floor sounded more impressive to Kate than it proved to be. She discovered that the white stone building was only twenty-one feet wide. And the entire floor consisted of a sitting room that faced a garden in the rear, a narrow kitchen, and one single small bedroom and bath.

Her first impression was of a modest bachelor's apartment, which, if it did not suffer from the overbearing touch of a professional decorator, could surely have benefited from a little feminine help.

To avoid taking up precious time going out to dinner, Scott had brought in sandwiches and made quite a ceremony of preparing coffee in an intricate foreign coffee maker.

They had settled down to work. Soon Scott abandoned eating and drinking, was on his feet, pacing, lecturing, while Kate listened.

"So forget everything you've ever seen on television or films about courtroom trials. A hearing is not like a trial. Lawyers? Yes. Witnesses? Yes. But in place of a judge, a committee chairman, who presides, and an administrative officer, who rules. And, of course, in place of a jury, a committee of three members, who will ultimately decide."

"I'm relieved that it's not a trial," Kate said. "That's good."

"No. That's bad," Scott corrected. "The rules of evidence are looser. Which means that unfavorable testimony that I might exclude during a trial can be admitted in a hearing. Instead of a jury of average citizens you will be judged by your peers. And right now your profession is under attack. I hear it everywhere. 'Doctors are overcharging, greedy

343

Scrooges.' 'Doctors don't think of their patient's health, only expensive foreign cars, tax-exempt meetings that are really vacations.' 'Doctors are milking Medicare.' "

"That's not true of most doctors!" Kate protested.

"The public thinks it is. Which means doctors feel they are all under attack. So, like the pioneers of old, doctors have drawn their wagons into a tight circle to defend their profession. Against the public. Against the media. *And* against any of their colleagues who draw fire on them. Which, unfortunately, now includes . . ."

"Me," Kate anticipated.

"Exactly."

Kate nodded, almost imperceptibly, thinking, *Is he preparing me to lose?*

"As we go along, you will have to teach me the detailed points of Claudia Stuyvesant's case. But first, have you and Rosie discovered anything about the background of the two medical committee members?"

"I consulted the *Medical Directory of New York State* and . . ."

"*Medical Directory?*" Scott asked.

"It lists every physician and surgeon in the state along with his curriculum vitae — which schools he attended, what his specialty is, which hospitals he's affiliated with, which boards he's been certified by, textbooks he's authored."

"His entire professional life," Scott realized. "What about Truscott?"

"City College. Cornell Medical School, interned at Bellevue Hospital. Residency at Lenox Hill Hospital. Private practice since 1953. No specialty. No board certification," Kate reported. "When I called his office, his nurse told me he was not taking on any new patients. He is semiretired."

"I don't like that," Scott said. "You know how older professionals are, always harking back to their early days. Always demeaning younger colleagues as upstarts. Telling them how tough it was for them in the old days and how easy it is for you now."

"On the other hand," Kate pointed out, "if we can judge from his attending City College, he came from modest beginnings. He might be very sympathetic to young doctors fighting their way up."

"Well," Scott conceded, "let's count him as neutral. Now, this Dr. Ward, what did you find out about her?"

"Harvard College, Yale Medical School. Board certified in Obstetrics and Gynecology. And also in oncological surgery," Kate reported. "Affiliated with Women's Hospital–Saint Luke's. And North Shore Hospital on

345

Long Island. She also has two textbooks and a number of papers to her credit. From what I've heard, very active in women's rights movements."

"Good, good," Scott said enthusiastically.

"I wouldn't be too sure about that," Kate warned.

"With her background, her experience, and her fight for women's rights, I'm sure she is not going to sit by and see a woman physician crucified for something she's not guilty of," Scott insisted.

Kate shook her head, stolidly.

"Kate?"

"Since Rosie is still considering ob-gyn as her specialty, she went to hear Ward lecture once. Addressing an audience of women medical students and interns, she made no bones about her loyalty to the women's cause. But also her demands of women. She demands more from them than she would from a man in a similar situation. In fact, Rosie heard her say, 'When a black fails, or a Jew fails, he fails for his entire group. I feel the same way about a woman who fails.' "

"Tough talk," Scott agreed.

"Tough woman," Kate responded.

Scott made a large question mark alongside her name.

After some further instructions to Kate on

346

how to act, what to say, what not to say during the course of the hearing, he put her in a cab and went back up to his apartment, free to make his own private assessment of the case.

He prepared himself some fresh coffee. With a coffee cup in one hand, he began to lay out all the papers and documents pertinent to the hearing in the order in which he expected Hoskins to introduce them:

Photocopies of Kate's notes in the chart of Claudia Stuyvesant. Copies of her entries in the order book noting each step and medication she had prescribed. Lab reports of the various blood tests she had ordered. Notes by Nurse Cronin when she took the final vital signs of the patient. The actions and medications used in trying to save Claudia Stuyvesant at the time her internal hemorrhage caused her death.

And finally, that autopsy report from the medical examiner that revealed the cause of Claudia Stuyvesant's death.

He also had a letter of general endorsement from Dr. Troy. While flattering, it was no more than a pat on the head to Kate Forrester and an expression of confidence and good wishes.

If only there were support from Kate's medical colleagues. Not from the interns and residents, who all supported her unequivocally, or from Nurses Cronin and Beathard, who could corroborate Kate's actions, but from older, more prestigious physicians, whose endorsement would carry weight with the committee. But none had consented to appear.

Scott recalled a saying that President John F. Kennedy had made popular after the failed invasion of Cuba: "Success has a thousand fathers, but failure is an orphan." Scott had never appreciated those words more than he did now.

As he surveyed the documents, he realized that his strongest piece of evidence was also his most vulnerable, the chart of Claudia Stuyvesant's case.

By the basic rules of evidence Kate would not be allowed simply to read the chart to the committee. She might be permitted to refer to it from time to time to refresh her recollection but she would have to testify in her own words. Whereas Hoskins, on cross-examination, would be free to read selected parts of the chart in order to challenge her testimony, question her medical decisions and the various modalities she had employed that night. It would not be difficult for a shrewd prosecutor to trip up an inexperienced witness. And Hoskins was a shrewd and experienced prosecutor in such cases, since it was the only practice he had been engaged in for the past eleven years. Goaded by the rewards Hoskins envisioned he would get if he succeeded in realizing Claude Stuyvesant's objectives, he would be doubly eager to destroy Kate Forrester.

The autopsy report was the single most damaging piece of evidence against Kate. Even if Scott had been able to convince several doctors to testify in her behalf, they could not explain away those findings. Or the fact that, had the ectopic pregnancy been diagnosed, surgery would almost surely have saved Claudia Stuyvesant's life.

He had one key weapon in his legal arsenal: Rick's testimony on Claudia's drug habit. Rick posed a double-barreled threat to Hoskins's case: He could testify to that; and his very appearance would startle and shock not only the prosecutor and the committee members but Claude Stuyvesant himself.

Scott made a note to call Rick again in the morning, as he had every morning since their meeting, to remind him about the date for the hearing. But, even more, to make sure that Rick was still where he was supposed to be, as ready and eager to testify as he had been.

Still, Scott could not ignore that nagging need to find some eminent corroborating physician to testify to the medical correctness of

Kate's actions on that night.

The only possible candidate he could find was Professor Emeritus Sol Freund. Kate had learned that Freund tried to defend her in the meeting of the chiefs of service several weeks before. Recently retired, Sol Freund had no further obligation or loyalty to either City Hospital or to Administrator Cummins. Nor was it likely that he would be beholden to Claude Stuyvesant.

The next day, when Scott found Sol Freund in his office at the hospital, the old man was just taking the last of his many diplomas and certifications off the walls, leaving twenty-six different discolored rectangles where such framed documents had hung for years.

Before Scott Van Cleve asked, the old man grumbled, "Emeritus emeritus . . . a fancy title but all it means is old man, get ready to get out! Well, I didn't have to be told. I knew when it was time."

He turned to take cognizance of Scott. "Well, young man, what can I do for you?"

"I'm an attorney," Scott began.

"Aha! The Angel of Death. What am I supposed to have done wrong? Some patient I took care of forty years ago now has a headache and I am being sued for malpractice?" Freund asked, stacking the last diploma alongside the others.

"I've come to ask your help in the case of Kate Forrester."

"My help? Mind you, I sympathize with that young lady. But what can I do?" Freund asked.

"I've had no success at all in finding any doctor in this hospital who would agree to testify on Dr. Forrester's behalf."

"Of course. Cummins. He has let it be known that any man or woman who tries to defend your client will not be around here very long. And yet who can blame him? He's got a hospital to protect. One of the reasons I have decided to retire. Medicine is no longer medicine. In my day you cared about the patients first, and business affairs second. Of course, in those days a man could retire and live the rest of his life on what a neurosurgeon now spends on malpractice insurance for only a year.

"Between insurance, Medicare, the government setting fees, medicine has become a business of dollars. Enough, I say! Enough!"

Scott listened respectfully to the old man's tirade.

"Doctor, what I need are several witnesses who can testify that what Kate Forrester did in the Stuyvesant case was neither negligent nor a departure from established medical treatment."

"You understand, I am a neurologist and far removed from the cases like that of the Stuyvesant girl."

"I've tried a number of specialists in ob-gyn and could get no help there," Scott confessed.

"No surprise. For a doctor to testify for your client is like saying, 'If I were there, I would have done exactly what she did.' Which means, if I did, the Stuyvesant girl would have died under my hand. No doctor is going to admit that."

"Still, it would help enormously if I had a respected doctor to testify."

Freund ignored Scott's plea. He started to take medical volumes off his bookshelves, glancing at the titles on the backbone, then separating them into different piles, one pile to ship to Florida, the rest to donate to the hospital's library. Scott realized his mission had been fruitless. He was on his way to the door.

"Hey, there, kid," Freund called. "This — this hearing — when does it take place?"

"Starts Monday," Scott said, hopeful for the moment.

"Monday . . ." Freund considered. "Ah, too bad."

"Sir?"

"Monday I will be on my way to frolicking

— isn't that the word they use in newspapers and magazines when they show people on the beach in Florida? — they are 'frolicking in the sun.' Well, on Monday Nettie and I will become two of the frolickers. We are leaving here Monday morning. Airline tickets, everything, all arranged."

He picked up another medical tome, glimpsed the title, put it on the smaller of the two stacks.

"You know, being the wife of a doctor is no fun," Freund said.

Puzzled by the seeming non sequitur, Scott listened nevertheless. The old man was obviously struggling with his professional conscience. Scott owed him the courtesy of hearing his self-justification.

"In the early years," Freund complained, "the wife, of course then she was only the fiancée, or the girlfriend. In my day we called them 'girlfriends.' Nowadays, who knows? Anyhow, in my day, when I was an intern, then a resident, my Nettie had to get used to waiting, to disappointments. My hours were outlandish. The emergencies never ended. I used to promise her, 'Nettie, darling, once I get into practice, things will be different.' And they were different. They were worse. To build up a practice, a young doctor had to be available at all hours of the day and night. Again, more broken promises, more disappointments.

"Then, when you finally become established and you are a professor of medicine, do things get better? No! You get calls from other doctors who are stumped by confusing cases, with patients' lives at stake. You have to be available for consultation. So I had to promise Nettie, 'Believe me, darling, once I retire . . .' She laughed and said to me, 'Sol, I'll believe it when we're on the plane and the stewardess is asking, "What would you like to drink?," and not a moment before.' Nettie got the tickets. Arranged for the limousine. For Monday morning. Besides, one truckload of our furniture and things is already on the way. We have to be there to receive them."

"I understand," Scott said sympathetically.

"You don't understand at all!" Freund exploded, then softened. "I don't even understand, so how can you? You think I like to say no to you, to Dr. Forrester? But I have no choice. I promised myself, this one time Nettie is not going to be disappointed. Besides, you know these legal proceedings. I've been a witness in more than one malpractice trial. You show up, there's a postponement. You show up again, another postponement. You can spend your life showing up only to be postponed. I'm sorry, young man."

The meeting was at an end, Scott realized. Though he left his phone number with Freund, once outside the doctor's office door he scratched the last possible name off his list of potential medical witnesses.

Having failed at that, Scott had only three things to depend on: Kate and how stalwart a witness she would be under cross-examination. His own skill in breaking down the witnesses whom Hoskins would present. And Rick Thomas.

His most immediate step was to begin the preparation of Kate Forrester for the fire she would face in the next few days.

Once Kate was comfortable in his apartment, Scott began: "Your function as a witness is to testify to facts. What happened. What you observed. What you did. That's all, and no more. Do not volunteer."

"I understand. Just answer the question. Don't volunteer."

"More than that," Scott warned. "No matter how Hoskins deliberately twists your answers, don't argue. Or you will wind up sounding like a shrill, emotional young woman instead of an intelligent, professional, controlled doctor."

Kate nodded.

"Now, let's have a trial run. That part of

355

the case where you called in Briscoe. 'Doctor, what made you do that?' "

Responding as a witness, Kate replied, "Since the patient's signs and symptoms were so imprecise, and her stomach pain could be indicative of an internal infection, I thought a surgeon's opinion was advisable to determine if an exploratory was necessary."

"What did you expect Dr. Briscoe would do?"

"Once I briefed him on the case, I expected he would make an examination of his own."

"Why?"

"Why?" Kate countered, puzzled by the question since the reason was obvious to her. "Why, to get another opinion."

"Meaning you were uncertain as to the validity of your own judgment, Doctor, is that right?" Scott asked, simulating the adversarial approach of a prosecutor.

"It wasn't a matter of the 'validity' of my opinion. The signs, the lab reports, did not add up to a definitive diagnosis. I wanted to make sure that I had not overlooked any possibilities," Kate protested.

Scott pounced on her unfortunate words. "So you admit you might have overlooked some possibilities in the case."

"I admit no such thing!" Kate insisted, her voice rising. "Confronted by a puzzling case,

I wanted another doctor's opinion. That is the usual practice in such situations."

Scott did not respond. After a moment of silence Kate said in a more chastened tone of voice, "I said too much, didn't I?"

"Yes," he pointed out. "The proper answer to 'Why did you call in Briscoe?' is simply, 'To get a second opinion.' That's all. A second opinion is a time-honored, accepted practice in medicine. Don't get involved in matters like overlooking any possibilities."

Kate nodded, resolving not to fall into that trap again.

"Now, let's continue," Scott said. "Doctor, once Dr. Briscoe arrived, what happened?"

"I reported to him the patient's vital signs. I showed him the lab results. Then he performed an examination. And he arrived at the same conclusion I did."

"Which was?"

"Until the patient's condition became more defined, there was nothing to do except continue I.V.'s, repeat the labs, and keep check on her vital signs," Kate responded.

"And after that?"

"After I sent another blood to the lab for a CBC, I had other cases to see," Kate said. "Besides —" She stopped abruptly. "I was about to volunteer, wasn't I?"

"Yes," Scott said. "A natural tendency.

Growing out of the naïve belief of most witnesses that the more of the truth you tell, the more likely they'll believe you. You must learn to overcome that.

"Now, let's go on," he continued. "Briscoe. Another blood specimen to the lab. You have other cases. Then Hoskins may ask, 'Doctor, how long between the time you sent that second blood down to the lab and the results came back?' "

"Two hours, a little more," Kate said.

"So that for two hours you did nothing for the patient?"

"I had other cases!" Kate protested. Then apologized. "Arguing again?"

"Arguing," Scott agreed. "The question was, 'So that for two hours you did nothing for the patient?' "

"Nurse Cronin continued to check her vital signs. And without a fresh lab report or a marked change in her vital signs, to administer any form of treatment would have been dangerous."

Scott interrupted by shaking his head.

"I know," Kate admitted. "The answer is, 'We did what was indicated for a patient in that condition. Continued the I.V. Continued to check her vital signs.' "

"That's it. Precise. Correct. Leaving Hoskins no chance targets to pounce on."

Kate nodded, smiled. "At least I'm learning."

"You are. And forgive me for being so tough on you. You'll appreciate that later," he was saying when his phone rang. Impatient with any interruption, Scott answered brusquely, "Van Cleve!"

"Hey, kid," the gentle voice of Dr. Freund rebuked, "no need to yell. Say hello in a nice, gentlemanly way."

"Hello, Doctor," Scott said, more gently now.

"Listen, I was talking to Nettie. Seems she has been following this Stuyvesant case on television. And she said, 'After fifty-one years we could spare another few days for such a nice young woman.' "

"What about your truckload of furniture?"

"Nettie's brother is smarter than I. He retired to Florida years ago. He'll be there to receive our stuff. Now, if you can guarantee me I will be done testifying on Monday, you got yourself a deal."

"Oh, terrific, Doctor! I can't thank you enough!"

"Don't thank me. Thank Nettie. And if you do, she'll say, 'Send a contribution to Cerebral Palsy.' That's her favorite charity. Just tell me when you want me. But first let me get a look at that Stuyvesant chart."

"Will do. And thanks again, Doctor." He hung up. "Freund. He's coming to testify."

Relieved and encouraged, Kate said, "Nice of him to do this for a woman who's a virtual stranger."

"I don't think he feels that any young doctor is a stranger," Scott said. "Well, let's push on. Monday isn't so far away."

Chapter Twenty-six

In the same old halting elevator that Scott had used once before but which was new to Kate Forrester, they ascended to the offices of the New York City branch of the Office of Professional Medical Conduct. As the elevator door opened, Albert Hoskins was passing by on his way to the hearing room.

"Ah, Van Cleve!" Hoskins said too effusively in greeting. "And is this Dr. Forrester?" He smiled at Kate while appraising her as a potential witness. He found her to be quite pretty. Which, however, did not enhance her status as a witness, since he also assumed that she was quite vulnerable. Her blue eyes seemed to tell him that. "Well, since the committee is assembled, I guess we're ready to begin."

With a gallant gesture he cleared the way for Kate to precede him toward the hearing room.

The room was different from what Kate had anticipated. She had expected it would resemble a courtroom, somewhat smaller but of the same general shape. This room was not only much smaller than a courtroom but the configuration of the tables and chairs created an oppressive and claustrophobic atmosphere. There were three long tables arranged so that they formed a U. The one table that served as the base had four chairs, three grouped together and one near the right end of the table. The other two tables formed the legs of the U and faced each other. In the center of the open area between the two tables was a single chair for witnesses. At the side near the wall a stenotypist was poised to record the proceedings.

Once Kate was seated, she realized that for as long as this hearing went on, she would be seated only ten feet from the committee that would judge her. And no more than a dozen feet across from this man Hoskins, who would prosecute her.

Scott detected her concern. He reached under the table to touch her hand. Cold. Icy cold. He gripped it to give her reassurance.

Once settled, if not at ease, Kate Forrester had the opportunity to study her judges. They were arranged so that Clarence Mott, the lay member, who had been appointed to preside, was in the center, flanked by Dr. Maurice Truscott on his left and Dr. Gladys Ward on his right. Kate was surprised to find her looking younger than her forty-two years. She was dark-haired, well groomed, and well tailored, in a black business-type suit brightened only by a touch of red from the collar of her silk blouse. Her features were small and precise, and she showed a minimum of makeup. But her black eyes were quite sharp, active, and penetrating. Kate could imagine those eyes peering over a surgical mask while she exercised control over an entire operating-room staff with hardly an unnecessary word. It was only when Chairman Mott exchanged a whispered comment with her that she smiled, suddenly betraying a softer side. But immediately thereafter she was once again the self-contained, serious doctor.

Kate passed over Chairman Mott to study Dr. Maurice Truscott. A man in his early sixties, he had a bushy head of silvery hair, an unusually large head, and a short, plump body. If he were a patient instead of a physician, some doctor would have put him on a diet at once. He wore rimless glasses, which he continued to adjust as they kept slipping down his broad nose. Though the hearing had not yet commenced, Truscott was already busy making notes. Kate could not even venture to guess why. He was obviously a studious type who perhaps had anticipatory observations to make about the process that was about to begin.

Lay member Clarence Mott sat back in his

chair impatiently awaiting the arrival of Administrative Officer Kevin Cahill. Mott consulted the gold watch he had laid out before him as if to remind both counsel that, in his mind, time was too important a commodity to be wasted.

Soon, carrying an overstuffed briefcase, Kevin Cahill came hurrying into the room, apologizing from the moment he crossed the threshold, "Sorry. But my plane from Albany was late. And traffic in from La Guardia at this hour is impossible."

Dryly Chairman Mott said reprovingly, "From Albany I always take the train."

Once Cahill was in his place at the end of the presiding table, Chairman Mott commenced. "I assume we all know why we're here, so there is no need for any introduction from me. Are you ready, Mr. Hoskins?"

Hoskins assumed a grave and ponderous attitude as he said, "Mr. Chairman, before I make my opening statement, I would like to introduce into the record several documents that are vital to my case."

As he laid out the documents, he identified them. "A complete copy of the chart and the excerpts from the order book in Emergency that pertain to the patient, Claudia Stuyvesant, deceased. The medical examiner's report as to the cause of her death. And the death certificate made out by and signed by Dr. Katherine Forrester." With a half turn toward Scott and Kate, he remarked genially, "I do not think Mr. Van Cleve will have any objection."

"Mr. Van Cleve?" Chairman Mott asked.

"No objection, sir."

"And now, Mr. Hoskins, your opening statement?"

"Chairman Mott, Dr. Ward, Dr. Truscott, Administrator Cahill, the matter before us is of great moment in the life of this respondent. And I have enormous sympathy for her during this difficult time. But I trust the members of this committee will keep in mind that our purpose here is not to protect doctors but to protect the people of this state. To protect them from physicians who, by lack of training, lack of ability, or due to personality weaknesses are unqualified to deliver safe health care and thus constitute a danger to the public at large."

Personality weaknesses, Kate pondered. *What in the world is he hinting at? Is he going to attack my character, my mental state of health? Is this one of the tactics that Scott tried to warn me against?*

Hoskins continued: "The testimony we will present will prove that this woman, Dr. Katherine Forrester, is unfortunately such a person and that this committee should recommend to the state board that her license to practice be revoked."

Kate had not wanted to betray her concern by glancing at Scott, but could not resist. However, he deliberately avoided eye contact with her and addressed the chairman.

"Mr. Mott, the respondent feels no need to make an opening statement at this time."

In a whisper louder than she had intended Kate protested, "I am not unqualified or dangerous to the public!"

With an air of paternal indulgence, Mott smiled and shook his head. "Mr. Van Cleve, would you care to instruct your client as to the proper conduct in a legal proceeding?"

"Yes, of course, sir. Sorry."

Scott took Kate by the hand and walked her to the door, where he whispered sternly, "I warned you. Keep your feelings under control. While you are testifying and especially when you're not. Hoskins set a trap for you. And you blundered right into it. Right now those committee members have the wrong impression of you."

"What's the use of my being here if you're going to let Hoskins get away with such outrageous charges? Why not just find me guilty and get it over with?" Kate countered.

"I don't intend to let him get away with anything. But I have to do it my way!" Scott declared, having trouble keeping his voice down to a whisper. "If you have any faith in me, trust me. I've never wanted to win a case more than I do right now. Because it's for you."

Kate realized it was more than a commitment from lawyer to client. She stared up into his gray eyes, found there the reassurance she sought.

"I'm sorry," she whispered. "We'll do it your way."

They made their way back to their places at the defense table. Scott addressed the chairman, "Mr. Mott, I can assure you that this hearing will continue in a proper manner from now on."

"Good," Mott said, turning to Hoskins, "Your first witness, sir?"

Instead of announcing the name of his witness, Hoskins strode to the door and had a brief conversation there with a guard. The guard disappeared, returning some moments later. A word passed between them, and Hoskins stepped outside, only to return with his first witness, Mrs. Claude Stuyvesant. Behind her followed her husband, Claude Stuyvesant.

Scott pressed Kate's hand. "Mrs. Stuyvesant?" he whispered. She nodded. Scott rose to his feet.

"Mr. Chairman, may I inquire if Mr. Hoskins intends to introduce this woman as his first witness?"

"I do indeed," Hoskins declared, escorting Mrs. Stuyvesant to the witness chair.

"In that case," Scott continued, "I object to her appearance on the ground that she has nothing of substance or relevance to offer this committee."

"On the contrary," Hoskins started to protest.

But Scott would not be silenced. "This woman is not a physician and therefore not competent to pass judgment on any of the events that took place during the treatment in question. It is obvious that the only purpose she can serve is to introduce an emotional element into a proceeding that would be better served by purely medical testimony."

Hoskins shook his head sadly, saying, "My worthy young colleague is not schooled in proceedings before administrative boards and committees. While this woman's testimony might not be deemed relevant in a court of law, I am sure that the members of this committee would want to hear her testimony, if only to understand the conditions surrounding the untimely and tragic death of her young daughter. I appeal to Administrative Officer Cahill for a ruling in the matter."

All eyes turned in Kevin Cahill's direction.

Fully aware of his uncle's instructions, Cahill cleared his throat before pontificating, "Mr. Chairman, beyond any question the appearance of this woman in the role of witness will bring a strong element of emotion into these proceedings."

Both Kate and Scott felt that they had scored an important point at the very outset of the proceedings, but their optimism was premature. For Cahill continued: "However, on the other hand, we must consider this. If every witness who brought into legal proceedings a degree of high emotion were disqualified, half the witnesses in any trial would be barred from testifying. What we are presented with here is an eyewitness to the events in question. Now, granted that she might not have the expertise to evaluate the events that took place, she is one of the few eyewitnesses who can tell us what happened. Let the professional members of this committee judge the correctness of those actions. If it is clearly understood at the outset that Mr. Hoskins will not ask the witness questions of a medical nature, then she is a perfectly qualified witness in this proceeding."

Scott whispered to Kate, "He could have said all that in a lot fewer words."

Chairman Mott gestured Mrs. Stuyvesant to take the witness chair. Once she was seated, the stenotypist administered the oath and asked for her name and address.

"Mrs. Nora Stuyvesant, 987 Park Avenue, New York City," she replied.

Mr. Mott took the moment to comment, "Mrs. Stuyvesant, I want you to know the members of this committee are aware of how difficult this situation must be for you. So if at any time you feel in need of a recess, please do not hesitate to ask."

"Thank you, Mr. Mott," she replied formally, as if Clarence Mott had not been a guest in her home many times.

Mott indicated that Hoskins was free to begin his examination.

"My dear woman, let me assure you that no one sympathizes with you more than I do. It must indeed be the worst nightmare of a mother's life to bring a young daughter, suffering some minor symptoms, to a supposedly excellent hospital and watch her die in less than a dozen hours."

Scott intervened. Half rising from his chair, he said, "Mr. Mott, this is exactly the emotional tone that I objected to. Can we do without these maudlin appeals of Mr. Hoskins and get to the so-called evidence he intends to introduce through this witness?"

Mott turned to Scott sharply. "Mr. Van Cleve, I find nothing offensive or detrimental in Mr. Hoskins's natural expression of sympathy. And unless Mr. Cahill overrules me, I will let the statement stand. Mr. Cahill?"

"In view of the circumstances, Mr. Hoskins's statement is quite natural and proper," young Cahill ruled.

Kate noticed that as Cahill finished his brief statement, he cast a glance in the direction of Claude Stuyvesant, who sat stone-faced at the foot of Hoskins's table. Stuyvesant was indeed an imposing presence, who, without having spoken a single word, had come to dominate the proceedings.

Cahill having ruled, Hoskins felt free to open with his first question.

"Mrs. Stuyvesant, as simply as you can, please tell us what preceded your arrival at City Hospital on that unfortunate night."

"At about eight o'clock that Saturday night my daughter, Claudia, called me. She'd been living away, on her own, for almost a year by that time. She called and asked me to come over. She hadn't been feeling well. Nausea, vomiting, slight diarrhea. Since she'd taken the usual remedies and they didn't work, I called our own doctor. But Dr. Eaves was out of town. So I decided to take her to what I considered at that time an excellent institution, City Hospital. To my great sorrow I later discovered that was not true."

"When you arrived, what happened?" Hoskins prodded.

As he had coached her to testify, Nora Stuyvesant continued. "We arrived at Emergency, were admitted after answering all those questions they ask. I suppose they have to. And we were shown to an examining room."

"And then?"

"Naturally, I asked to see a doctor. But instead they sent in a nurse. As I remember, her name was Cronin. When I again asked for a doctor, she told me one would arrive soon. But she went about taking my daughter's temperature and pulse and things. I protested, 'Don't waste time. Get my daughter a doctor!' But this nurse went about it in her own way, promising that a doctor would soon be in. But no doctor came."

"No doctor at all?" Hoskins asked.

"Not until I protested rather strongly."

"And when a doctor did arrive . . ." Hoskins urged.

"It was" — Mrs. Stuyvesant glared at the respondent's table — "it was that woman."

"And what did she do?"

"Not much more than the nurse did. She started to take Claudia's pulse and ask a few questions. Then she deserted my daughter to go off to see another patient."

"You mean she did no more than ask a few

questions and then leave?" Hoskins pretended this fact was a surprise to him.

"And when I begged her not to go, she assaulted me."

"Assaulted you?" Hoskins's feigned sense of incredulity invited more detail.

"She rudely shoved me aside and went to take care of another patient."

"You mean she laid hands on you?" Hoskins asked, pretending to be appalled at such conduct.

"Pushed me aside and just left!" Nora Stuyvesant repeated.

Kate tugged at Scott's sleeve to rebut Mrs. Stuyvesant's accusation. But he continued to make his notes.

"I trust that was the only time such a thing happened," Hoskins commented.

"No, it happened again, later, several hours later," the woman said, glaring at Kate.

"What happened after the first time Dr. Forrester assaulted you?"

Scott rose to protest. "Mr. Mott, please instruct Mr. Hoskins not to characterize my client's conduct!"

"Mr. Van Cleve," Mott responded, "if laying hands on a person and violently pushing them aside is not considered an assault, what is? Does one have to use a baseball bat, or a gun?"

"I would like the record to indicate that there is no evidence of violence and I object to such characterization," Scott insisted.

With impatient indulgence Mott addressed the stenotypist. "See that the record so signifies." He turned to Hoskins. "Sorry for the interruption. Continue."

"Mrs. Stuyvesant, please, what happened then?"

"The doctor finally came back. She asked more questions. Took some blood and sent it to the lab and said she would have to wait for the results."

"That was all?" Hoskins asked.

"She told the nurse to continue with the intravenous and to keep taking Claudia's pulse and blood pressure. I pleaded with her to at least give Claudia an antibiotic. But she refused."

"You specifically asked for an antibiotic and this doctor refused?" Hoskins asked in a tone of troubled concern.

"Yes!" Mrs. Stuyvesant declared righteously.

"Was that all that Dr. Forrester did?"

"No. After she came back several times and couldn't make up her mind what to do, she finally sent for another doctor. Which she should have done in the first place."

Before Scott could protest, Hoskins hurried

on to his next question: "Mrs. Stuyvesant, when was the first time that either doctor, Forrester or Briscoe, actually did anything for your daughter aside from the intravenous?"

"They never did do *anything* for her!" the woman protested. "The only time they were going to, Dr. Briscoe asked for a needle and was about to insert it to see if there was any bleeding. That's when . . . that's when Claudia stopped breathing."

"And then?"

"They rushed her down the hall to another room. I tried to follow, but that woman shut me out."

"When was the next time you saw either Dr. Forrester or Dr. Briscoe?"

"She" — the woman pointed at Kate — "she came out of that room. I could tell by the look on her face. I said, 'You killed her. You people killed her!' And she said — I'll never forget her words — 'Mrs. Stuyvesant, we did all we could.' All they could indeed! They did nothing! As it turned out later, they could have saved her if they'd tried!" she said accusingly. "The least they could have done was allow me in there. I would have done something . . . something." The distraught woman broke off, weeping.

"Mrs. Stuyvesant, please?" Hoskins said, trying to encourage her to continue. "Only

375

a few more questions. Do you feel able to go on, or would you like a recess?"

Scott said nothing to Kate, though inwardly he was seething. He had seen lawyers employ such shabby tactics before, using a witness for purely emotional effect. But rarely had he seen it used so shamelessly. Not only was Hoskins playing on the sympathy of the three committee members, but from time to time he glanced at Stuyvesant to make sure the tycoon would not forget him when this hearing was ended. There was no longer any doubt in Scott's mind that Hoskins's ambitions included a lucrative job in Stuyvesant's real estate enterprises or with one of the law firms he retained. To accomplish that, he was being overly generous, kind, and caring toward Mrs. Stuyvesant in order to ruthlessly destroy Kate and her career.

When Mrs. Stuyvesant had recovered sufficiently to lift her tearful face from her damp handkerchief, Hoskins asked gently, "Madam, do you feel able to continue?" She nodded. Hoskins resumed. "So they shut you out while your daughter was dying. Then this woman came to tell you — and then, Mrs. Stuyvesant?"

"Someone . . . I don't remember who . . . took me out to my limousine, in which I had arrived with a daughter who was slightly ill.

376

Now she was dead and I left alone." She broke down repeating, "Alone . . . alone."

Feeling that he had extracted the ultimate in emotional impact from this witness, Hoskins recited the comment he had prepared for exactly this moment.

"Madam, I'm sure the members of this committee understand and sympathize with your feelings at this terrible moment. I have no further questions."

Relieved of the need to testify further, Nora Stuyvesant gave way to a flood of tears of both sorrow and release from tension.

"Mr. Van Cleve?" Chairman Mott addressed him. "Do you wish to cross-examine this witness?" But by his attitude Mott was really asking, *Do you dare to cross-examine her?*

While Scott debated that challenge, Kate studied the faces of her judges.

Dr. Maurice Truscott was making copious notes while at the same time his lips twitched as if he were trying to accommodate ill-fitting dentures. In all he had the appearance of a man disturbed by what he had heard and was recording his feelings before they passed.

Dr. Gladys Ward, on the other hand, gave the impression of a woman unmoved and uninvolved. Her thoughts and reactions were totally concealed. She tried to avert her black eyes from Kate, but in the end stared at her with a look that Kate interpreted to be disapproval.

Chairman Mott shuffled the papers before him, then leaned in the direction of Administrative Officer Cahill, who left his seat to confer secretly with him. Once Cahill resumed his place, Mott turned to Scott.

"Mr. Van Cleve? We are awaiting your decision."

Chapter Twenty-seven

Fully alert to the trap that always awaited any attorney who chose to cross-examine a woman in a highly emotional state, especially a grieving mother, Scott Van Cleve said, "Mr. Mott, I am quite willing to give Mrs. Stuyvesant a brief recess before I ask the few questions I have."

Nora Stuyvesant dabbed at her eyes and sniffed. "I am ready to continue. I will do my best."

Hoskins returned to his chair, smug in the knowledge that the more strongly Van Cleve attacked Nora Stuyvesant, the more sympathy she would earn from the committee.

Equally aware of that danger, Scott approached the witness. "Mrs. Stuyvesant, please feel free to take as much time as you need before answering my questions."

"Thank you," she replied, more in resentment than in gratitude. She dabbed at her moist eyes once more.

"Now, then, when you brought your daughter to City Hospital, were her complaints slight, or moderate, or, would you say, severe?"

"I would say . . . sort of moderate," she replied, choosing what she deemed the safest estimate.

"Not alarming?" Scott sought to narrow her choices.

"Moderate," she repeated.

"Not indicating a state of crisis?" Scott continued.

"Moderate," she persisted.

"Life-threatening?" Scott tried to qualify.

Hoskins rose to his feet in his cumbersome fashion. "Mr. Chairman, Mr. Administrator, I appeal to you both in the name of reason, how is a mother like Mrs. Stuyvesant, unqualified as a medical expert, to respond to a question calling for an opinion of a patient's condition?"

"Exactly the point, Mr. Hoskins! Yet only minutes ago she said" — Scott referred to his notes — " 'I had arrived with a daughter who was slightly ill.' If her opinion was valid five minutes ago, I should think it would be valid now."

"And if that were so?" Clarence Mott interjected.

"Mrs. Stuyvesant has tried to give this committee the impression that her daughter was only slightly ill but that as a result of Dr. Forrester's actions she died. When the truth is that the patient was severely ill when brought to the hospital but, for reasons I will present later, her condition was concealed from Dr. Forrester."

Hoskins smiled condescendingly. "Mr. Van Cleve, I always assume that a physician is, *or should be,* more knowledgeable than a layperson when it comes to making a diagnosis. So that what Mrs. Stuyvesant considers moderate or slight symptoms would more readily be recognized by a competent doctor as being 'severe,' 'alarming,' and 'life threatening.'"

Kevin Cahill took the moment to intervene. "It is the ruling of the administrative officer that since the witness is not qualified as an expert, she not be asked to offer any opinions. She may testify only as to facts."

"So ruled," Mott declared, hammering the table with his gavel in a single sharp, eloquent blow. "Continue, Mr. Van Cleve, but with a new line of questioning."

Scott had no choice but to comply.

"Mrs. Stuyvesant, based on your testimony, do I understand that at the time in question your daughter was no longer residing under your roof?"

"Young people these days! All they talk about is freedom. Wanting 'their own space'! Move out. Go it on your own. Which is all very well and good as long as Daddy keeps sending big allowance checks!" Mrs. Stuyvesant replied, with due cognizance of her husband sitting at the end of the prosecutor's table.

"Until that night how long had Claudia been living away from home?" Scott asked.

"Eight months. Possibly longer," Mrs. Stuyvesant replied. Then added, "Longer. I remember Claude remarking that Claudia had been gone almost a year and had never once invited us to her place down in the Village."

"Had there been *any* contact between your daughter and you during that time?"

From his place at his table Hoskins addressed the administrator. "Mr. Cahill, we are dealing here with the competence of a physician to continue the practice of medicine. How can questions about the family life of her victim possibly be relevant?"

"Mr. Van Cleve?" Cahill demanded in his most judicial-sounding manner.

"I object to Mr. Hoskins's use of the term *victim!* But I will make the connection very shortly," Scott said. "Mrs. Stuyvesant?"

"Claudia called us, from time to time."

"Frequently?" Scott asked.

"I said, from time to time," the witness responded.

"During any of those phone calls did she ever mention a person named Rick Thomas?"

"Rick Thomas?" the woman repeated, surprised, but pretending to be confused.

"Does that name mean anything to you?"

Nora Stuyvesant paused before responding, "No. No, it does not."

"Would it surprise you to learn that your daughter and Rick Thomas were living together at the time of her —"

Before Scott could complete the question, Claude Stuyvesant was up from his chair, pointing his finger at him while shouting to the chairman, "I will not have it! I will not have such cheap shyster tricks used to defame the name of my dead daughter! I demand that you force this man to withdraw his scandalous charge."

"Mr. Stuyvesant, Mr. Stuyvesant . . ." Chairman Mott tried to interrupt the outburst. "Believe me, we are all aware of the strain you are under as the father of the victim. But in the interest of the people of this state and in your interest as well, we must conduct this proceeding in an orderly fashion."

Face still flushed, his eyes glinting in anger, Stuyvesant slowly sank back into his chair.

Mott signaled Scott to resume.

"Mrs. Stuyvesant, I was asking about a man named Rick Thomas."

Hoskins rose to object. "Mr. Mott, since Mrs. Stuyvesant has already said that she knows nothing about a person called Rick

Thomas, I do not see how she can be expected to answer any questions about him, as I am sure Mr. Cahill will agree. Please ask Mr. Van Cleve to desist. And if he has no further questions that might be helpful or enlightening to this process I ask that he conclude what is obviously a painful experience for both the witness and her husband."

Expecting that Scott would yield, Hoskins remained on his feet, ready to call his next witness.

"I have a few more questions, Mr. Mott," Scott replied.

"Proceed," Clarence Mott said, giving his permission but indicating it was against his better judgment.

"Mrs. Stuyvesant, did you have any knowledge of the fact that your daughter was a habitual user of drugs, legal and illegal?"

Again Stuyvesant was on his feet. "Damn it! I insist you force him to stop slandering my daughter!"

"Please, Mr. Stuyvesant, let me handle this in my way?" Mott interceded. "Mr. Van Cleve, is it your intention to produce the medical examiner's report, or a hospital laboratory report, to substantiate your charge?"

"Mr. Chairman, I have very substantial reason to believe that my statement is in fact true."

"Then surely the medical examiner's report would have revealed that," Hoskins argued. "Yet it contains not a single word to that effect. How do you account for that, Mr. Van Cleve?"

"As it was explained to me, once cause of death was established, the medical examiner felt no need to make such a determination," Scott replied.

"What about a hospital lab report?" Hoskins challenged. "Surely if there were such a report, Mr. Van Cleve would rush to introduce it into the record."

"My client requested a toxicological screening of the patient's blood. And one was performed. But somehow it is missing from her chart," Scott replied.

" 'Missing from her chart,' " Hoskins mimicked. "First our Mr. Van Cleve treats us to the spectacle of a mysterious and nonexistent person named Rick Thomas. Now he refers to a lab report that is 'missing' from the patient's chart. All aimed at trying to attack and besmirch the reputation of a dead woman who cannot defend herself. I challenge Mr. Van Cleve to introduce this Rick Thomas! And to bring us proof of that 'missing from the chart' lab report!"

"Mr. Van Cleve?" Chairman Mott reinforced Hoskins's demand.

"I shall do my best to comply with Mr. Hoskins's request," Scott said. Feeling that he had now set up the situation perfectly for Rick Thomas's appearance, he did not try to exploit the situation but resumed his examination of the witness.

"Mrs. Stuyvesant, earlier you described a time when you charged that Dr. Forrester 'assaulted' you."

"Yes! Because she did!" the witness replied self-righteously.

"Do you know where the doctor was going when that incident occurred?"

"I have no idea."

"Didn't you hear a nurse summon her to another emergency case?"

"Yes, there was something about another patient," Nora Stuyvesant conceded.

"Then is it fair for me to say that she wasn't 'deserting' your daughter but was momentarily leaving her to go to the aid of another patient?"

"I was only interested in my daughter's health and safety."

"Is that why you took up a position at the door to physically block Dr. Forrester from leaving?" Scott asked.

"I could not allow her to leave my daughter, who was even sicker than I thought she was," Mrs. Stuyvesant replied.

"Mrs. Stuyvesant, would you still feel the same way if you knew that Dr. Forrester was on her way to care for a man who might have been suffering a major heart attack and who might die unless he was seen by a doctor at once?" Scott asked.

"The only patient I was interested in was my daughter," Mrs. Stuyvesant said staunchly.

Encouraged, since the witness was no longer weeping but was beginning to fight back, Scott continued: "I agree with you, Mrs. Stuyvesant. A mother should be concerned first and foremost with the safety of her own child. But Dr. Forrester was responsible for many lives that night. She had to care for all of them as their needs emerged. Since you were standing in her way, she brushed by you to get on with her duties. Would you still call that an 'assault' upon your person?"

"She pushed me aside!" Mrs. Stuyvesant said accusingly. "She would probably have become more violent if I had resisted!"

"Mrs. Stuyvesant, if you can call brushing by you to go to the aid of another patient an 'assault' and if you can assume that she would have become 'more violent' if you had 'resisted,' may I suggest that there was something else at work in your mind at the time? Was there?"

The witness stared at him and did not reply.

Scott's suggestion caused Hoskins to sit up a bit more stiffly. Claude Stuyvesant's eyes narrowed in his lean, tanned face. Dr. Truscott looked up from a note he had been making. Dr. Gladys Ward, who thus far had made no notes at all, now looked on with renewed interest.

Chairman Mott seemed about to intervene. He glanced toward Kevin Cahill, but the administrator gave him no encouragement. Scott was permitted to continue.

"Mrs. Stuyvesant?" Scott prodded. When she did not respond he continued: "Mrs. Stuyvesant, when Dr. Briscoe was assisting you to your limousine, do you recall what you said?"

"I don't recall saying anything," she denied quickly.

"Strange. Because several people, Dr. Briscoe and Dr. Forrester among them, heard you say, 'He'll blame me . . . he'll blame me. . . .' Do you recall that?"

"I've already said I don't recall saying anything!" she responded sharply.

Having observed Claude Stuyvesant's intensifying anger, both Hoskins and Cahill rose quickly to interject. It was the administrator who spoke first and in ponderous fashion.

"Mr. Chairman, these unjustified tactics on

the part of Mr. Van Cleve are more aimed at distressing the witness than at aiding this committee in its function. In fact, his totally extraneous line of questioning seems calculated to obfuscate the real issue, namely the competence of Dr. Katherine Forrester to continue in medical practice."

"My question bears on the issue of what happened during those nine crucial hours, as I will make clear when I put in my defense," Scott responded.

Conscious of the fact that his words were being recorded by the stenotypist and might one day be reviewed if there were an appeal, Kevin Cahill ruled, "Subject to connection I will allow you to continue for the moment."

Scott turned back to the witness. "Mrs. Stuyvesant, did you or did you not say, 'He'll blame me . . . he'll blame me'?"

"I never said that!" she repeated more firmly.

"Then am I to believe that Dr. Briscoe, Dr. Forrester, and others who say they heard you are all lying?"

"Why not?" The woman was half up out of her chair. "They all had a part in killing my daughter! Now they are all lying to protect themselves! To protect Dr. Forrester. Doctors always conspire among themselves to protect their own little monopoly!"

On her feet now, she shouted at Kate Forrester, "You killed her! And now your lawyer is telling a pack of lies to protect you! Well, you won't get away with it! You won't! Not when you're dealing with Claude Stuyvesant!"

Her anger spent, Nora Stuyvesant slipped down into the witness chair once more.

Softly Scott Van Cleve asked, "Mrs. Stuyvesant, do you remember Dr. Forrester asking your daughter if she had been sexually active?" She did not reply at once, so Scott asked, "Mrs. Stuyvesant, do you recall that?" The woman barely nodded. Scott turned to the chairman. "Mr. Mott, can we have the stenotypist record that the witness nodded in reply to my question?"

"Yes, of course. Get on with it, Mr. Van Cleve."

"Mrs. Stuyvesant, do you recall your daughter's answer to that question?" Again Nora Stuyvesant did not respond at once. "If your memory failed you again, let me refresh your recollection. Your daughter denied that she had been sexually active. Am I correct?"

The woman nodded, but barely.

"Did the doctor also ask her if she had missed any menstrual periods?" Mrs. Stuyvesant nodded once more. "And was your daughter's response that she had not?" Once more Mrs. Stuyvesant nodded.

Scott paused before asking, "Mrs. Stuyvesant, since we now know from the medical examiner's report that both those answers were false, can you offer any reason why your daughter would have lied to the doctor who was trying to treat her?"

"No . . . no. I . . . I know no reason," Mrs. Stuyvesant said in a voice barely loud enough for the stenotypist to hear.

"Thank you, Mrs. Stuyvesant. That is all." Scott turned away, then pretended to have remembered a question he had failed to ask, "Just one more question, Mrs. Stuyvesant. When people heard you say, 'He'll blame me . . . he'll blame me,' exactly whom did you have in mind?"

"I told you, I don't remember saying any such thing!" she protested.

"Could there be any possible connection between your fear of that person and your daughter's need to give false and misleading answers to the doctor's questions?" Scott asked.

Mrs. Stuyvesant glared at him but did not respond. Hoskins sprang to her aid. "Mr. Chairman, there is no need for the witness to respond to a question that is pure conjecture."

"Of course," Scott replied. "Sorry. I have

no more questions."

"Nor do I," Hoskins said.

He approached Mrs. Stuyvesant, aided her to her feet, and escorted her toward her husband, at the same time saying consolingly, "I know this has been an ordeal. In the interest of justice and truth, I commend you for bearing up so well. I thank you. And the people of this state, whom I represent, thank you as well."

He surrendered her into the hands of her husband. "You are both free to leave now, sir."

Stuyvesant nodded grimly. He kissed his wife, a gesture that indicated that she was free to leave but that he himself had no such intention.

"I'd rather stay," she protested meekly.

"You've been through enough for one day, my dear," Stuyvesant said.

"We have to protect Claudia's name, her memory . . ." Mrs. Stuyvesant insisted.

"I will see to that, my dear. You just go on home and try to recover from this ugly business."

She lingered for a moment, until he said, "Nora, go!" Obediently she followed her husband's suggestion.

Once Mrs. Stuyvesant had left, Hoskins approached the committee table, signaling Cahill to join them. To circumvent any private agreements among them, Scott joined them quickly.

"Mr. Mott," the prosecutor said, "I would like to change the course of this proceeding."

Scott intervened: "We had agreed that after Mrs. Stuyvesant finished, I would be allowed to call Dr. Freund, who delayed his moving to Florida just to be here today." He challenged Hoskins. "Did you or didn't you agree to that?"

"Oh, yes. And I will stick by it. All I want to do is call another witness to the stand first. Which won't take long, I assure you. In fact how long it takes is in your hands, Van Cleve."

Skeptical, and intrigued, Scott asked, "My hands? Who is your new witness?"

"You!" Hoskins said.

"Are you out of your mind?" Scott shot back.

Hoskins ignored Scott to turn to the administrator for a ruling. "Mr. Cahill, it's become apparent from his last questions that Mr. Van Cleve has special knowledge that has been concealed from the rest of us. Therefore I suggest, in the interest of a full and fair hearing, that he be made to reveal what he knows."

Kevin Cahill considered the proposal for a

moment, then ruled, "Your point is well taken, Mr. Hoskins. The concentration of this committee should not be diverted from the issue before us by what may turn out to be a figment of Mr. Van Cleve's imagination." He looked to the stenotypist, "Swear in Mr. Van Cleve, please!"

Once Scott was seated in the witness chair, Hoskins began, "Mr. Van Cleve, you are a member in good standing of the bar of this state?"

"Yes."

"Then are you aware of the duty of an attorney to vouch for any witness that he produces in a courtroom or in any legal proceeding?"

"Yes."

"And is a member of the bar also responsible for the statements he himself makes in a courtroom or any legal proceeding?"

"Of course."

"When Mrs. Stuyvesant was testifying, did you question her about a person whom you called Rick Thomas?"

"I did."

"And did you also state that this Thomas person had been living with Mrs. Stuyvesant's daughter just prior to the events we are concerned with here?"

"I did."

"What was the source of those allegations, sir?"

"Rick Thomas," Scott replied.

"Don't you know, counselor, that this body has subpoena power? And that Mr. Thomas, if indeed there is such a person, could be served and forced to appear here and to testify himself?"

"Of course I know that."

"*Have* you served him with a subpoena?" Hoskins asked.

"No. I must admit I have not," Scott replied.

"Aha!" Hoskins seized on Scott's answer. "So that, as as far as we know, the accusations you made that the victim in this situation was living with the fictitious Mr. Thomas may indeed be a hoax."

"It is not a hoax," Scott insisted without raising his voice. "And I still object to your use of the word *victim!*"

"Is this Rick Thomas also the source of your accusation that Miss Stuyvesant was addicted to drugs?" Hoskins asked.

"Living with her, who would know better?" Scott countered.

"Well, Mr. Van Cleve, as for me, I prefer to draw my own conclusions. As will the members of this august committee. Rick Thomas is indeed a figment of your imagination. Conjured up by you to achieve what Mr. Stuyvesant accused you of, trying to smear his dead, defenseless daughter in an effort to take the onus off your client! That is all!"

He turned away from Scott abruptly, in so doing also glancing toward Stuyvesant for his approval. His expectations were justified.

Scott Van Cleve left the witness chair to rejoin Kate at the table. She had obviously been shaken by this last encounter.

"Why didn't you tell him? We saw Rick. We talked to him. I could testify to that," she whispered urgently.

"Oh, no! It's working perfectly. I set the trap. He fell into it. The bigger issue he makes of it, the more stunning the moment when I walk Rick Thomas into this room and say, 'Gentlemen, here is the "elusive" Mr. Thomas. Ready to testify!'

Before Dr. Freund was called to the stand, Mr. Mott declared a brief recess.

Scott Van Cleve used the opportunity to rush to the pay phone in the corridor and make one brief call. He punched in the number. Waited for two rings before he heard an answer.

"Rick? Scott Van Cleve. You okay?"

"Great, man, great."

"Stay ready. I'll let you know. And wear

that new shirt and tie I sent you."

"Got it, man, got it," Rick assured him.

Scott went back to the hearing confident and ready to resume.

Chapter Twenty-eight

As agreed in advance with Chairman Mott and Counsel Hoskins, and out of respect for a man who had served City Hospital for so many years, the hearing procedure was interrupted to allow Dr. Sol Freund to testify for the respondent so that he could depart for his retirement.

He was bald except for the slight fringe of white hair that ringed his gleaming rosy scalp, and his cheeks were concave but clean-shaven. The bony structure of Freund's face stood out almost as clearly as it would on X ray. He wore simple gold-framed glasses. Across the vest of his dark blue suit stretched a gold chain, from which hung the Phi Beta Kappa key he had been awarded more than half a century before.

After Freund had been sworn in as a witness, Chairman Mott nodded his approval to Scott Van Cleve to commence the testimony.

"Your name, sir?"

"Solomon Freund," the old man replied.

"Your profession?"

"Medical doctor."

"Sir, how many years have you trained for

and practiced that profession?"

"Fifty-two years."

"Dr. Freund, are you familiar with the general procedure and practice in large city hospitals, and in City Hospital in particular?"

"I have served as an intern, a resident, later as a member of the staff of large hospitals in this city for many years, and at City Hospital in particular for the last thirty-four."

"Are you familiar with the procedure in the Emergency Service there, sir?"

"I should be. Until my retirement some weeks ago I used to be called down there when extremely unusual cases required the possible intervention of a neurosurgeon."

Scott turned to Administrative Officer Cahill. "May I proceed on the basis that we have established that Dr. Freund is an expert witness and hence free to give opinion testimony?"

Cahill finally conceded with an unnecessarily grave nod.

Scott resumed: "Dr. Freund, several days ago I sent you a copy of the chart of a patient named Claudia Stuyvesant. Have you had time to familiarize yourself with it?"

"I studied it with great interest," Freund replied.

"Did you find it a competently written record of an Emergency case?"

"Not only competently written, quite detailed," the old man said.

"With that in mind, Doctor, and taking into account the signs, symptoms, lab reports, and other findings, was there anything you would have done differently if you had been the doctor in charge of the Stuyvesant girl on that night?"

"No. There were simply not sufficient findings on which to base a differential diagnosis. Fever, nausea, vomiting, diarrhea — who of us has not had those symptoms and had them disappear once our bodies had thrown out some irritating bit of food?"

"How would you classify those symptoms?"

"To be monitored in order to detect any marked changes. But no more significant than that."

"Alarming?"

"Oh no," Freund responded.

"Indicative of serious internal bleeding?"

"While those symptoms could be consistent with such a condition, I would expect that in such a case the symptoms would be much more pronounced. Surely the lab reports would be more startling," Freund responded.

"Since we now know that there actually was extensive internal bleeding, how would you account for the fact that the signs and the lab reports did *not* reflect that condition?" Scott asked.

"As my distinguished medical colleagues on this committee know, many factors can distort symptoms and signs. Dehydration, for one. Also the possibility that the patient's condition may have been affected by drugs of one kind or another."

Claude Stuyvesant shot up from his chair to protest, "Damn it, Clarence!" Then caught himself and continued only a little less heatedly. "Mr. Chairman, are you going to allow this witness to do what we've already said Van Cleve cannot do? I will not stand for these attacks on my daughter's reputation. I demand you make this clear to Mr. Van Cleve and to this witness!"

Not having been present at Stuyvesant's previous outbursts, Freund turned to him. "Mr. Stuyvesant . . . I assume that's who you are . . . I made no attack on your daughter. Nor did I intend to."

"You accused her of taking drugs!" Stuyvesant bellowed.

"My dear man," Freund replied, "haven't you ever awakened in the middle of the night with a pain in the belly, a heartburn, or a touch of nausea, taken something to quiet the condition, and gone back to sleep?"

"Of course. But you said *drugs!*" Stuyvesant

said accusingly.

"Ah, I see what you mean. Illegal drugs. Well, I was referring to something as simple as the kind of drugs we all have in our medicine cabinets. Some of which fizz, some do not. But they are all drugs. Even the simplest could have the effects I spoke of. Take a common one, Alka-Seltzer. We sometimes use it to replace the stomach's normal electrolytes lost in cases of severe diarrhea and dehydration.

"So, Mr. Stuyvesant, it is entirely possible that your daughter might have taken such drugs several times during the hours of discomfort before she turned up at the Emergency Service. And if she had, such simple remedies might have had some effect on the laboratory findings."

Still defiant, nevertheless Stuyvesant sat down slowly, but remained ready to defend his daughter's reputation, and, without being aware of it, his own as well.

Freund turned back toward the committee.

"I can sympathize with Mr. Stuyvesant's concern. In my specialty I have confronted too many parents with children who have suffered permanent neurological damage from illegal drugs. But the point of my being here is simply this: Without all the formality, the legal questions, the answers, it comes down to one thing. And one thing only. Based on the findings in Claudia's Stuyvesant's chart, it is my opinion that Dr. Forrester conducted herself in an efficient, professional, and exemplary manner. If she had taken any steps other than those she did take, she could have been charged with acting precipitously."

Unconsciously Freund's fingers went to his gold Phi Beta Kappa key and toyed with it as he continued: "I suggest each medical member of this committee ask himself or herself, If *you* had been there, presented by what Dr. Forrester found, what would *you* have done? I think you will respond the same as Dr. Forrester did. So put an end to this hearing and send this young woman back to the work for which she is trained and which she so deeply desires to continue."

To derive the maximum impact from Freund's words, Scott Van Cleve took a long pause before saying, "I have no further questions."

Mott looked to Hoskins, who signified that he wished to cross-examine. He began with a disarming preamble. "Dr. Freund, in deference to your desire to begin your well-deserved retirement, I will limit myself to only a few questions."

Dr. Freund made a slight gesture of appreciation. Hoskins came forward to stand between Freund and Scott's counsel table, his bulk obstructing Kate's view of the old doctor.

"Doctor, may I ask what is your personal association with the respondent in this proceeding?"

"Respondent? Do I take that to mean Dr. Forrester? I have no personal association with her. There have been two, possibly three, occasions when she has referred cases to me from other services where she served as a resident. So I may have conferred with her a few times." Then it occurred to him, "Oh, I see what you mean. You think I have come here to plead for a personal friend? Or a protégée, perhaps? No, no, no, my dear man, you are mistaken. There is nothing personal involved here. I simply hate to see young careers destroyed by baseless accusations. Unfortunately a young girl of nineteen died. But because a patient dies does not necessarily mean that the doctor was at fault. If that were true, we would all be guilty. As these doctors well know!"

His thin, yellowing, concave cheeks were now being infused with color as he became emotionally involved in the situation.

"Now, sir, what else did you want to know?" Freund asked with some irritation.

Hoskins pretended to take on a more respectful attitude as he asked, "Doctor, when was the last time you served on the Emergency Service?"

"The last time I —" Freund began. "Are you serious?"

"Quite serious."

"The last time — the last time — Forty-nine years ago, give or take —" Freund replied.

"And when was the last time you had to take the initial history of a new patient in Emergency or anywhere else, for that matter?"

"Not recently," Freund conceded.

"Not for years?"

"Not for years," the doctor agreed.

"How many years?"

Freund turned to Chairman Mott. "Sir, if you are in charge of these proceedings, please tell this man he is wasting my time, his time, and the time of these distinguished physicians with such idiotic questions. For the past thirty-one years as a neurosurgeon, by the time a case reaches my office, that patient has been seen and tested by several doctors, neurologists, possibly even psychiatrists. So the patient comes with a complete history and a chart that looks as thick as a volume from the *Encyclopaedia Britannica*. Lab reports, EEGs, CAT scans, MRIs and other tests too numerous to mention. Now, if that's what he wanted to know, why didn't he ask me?"

Unabashed, Hoskins waited out the old doctor's protest, then resumed: "Based on your last response, Doctor, is it fair to assume that it has been many years since you have had any experience similar to what happened that night in Emergency?"

"Of course. Assume!" the old doctor said with obvious irritation.

"So that your opinion of what took place that night is not based either on a knowledge of Dr. Forrester's professional capability or of the situation itself, since you have been far removed from such practice for many years," Hoskins stated.

"My opinion is based on what is written in that chart. What the doctor found. What the lab found. What modalities were instituted."

"You trust that chart completely?" Hoskins asked.

"It is a chart that appears to be written in conformity with good medical practice. I have no reason to *dis*trust it," Freund declared.

"And nothing in that record gave you reason to question Dr. Forrester's conclusions and actions?"

Freund took a moment to review what he had discovered in the chart, then replied, "No, sir, nothing gave me reason to question her competence or her actions."

Hoskins smiled indulgently. "Doctor, as a neurosurgeon and an experienced diagnostician, have you sometimes found that the *absence* of certain factors plays an important part in arriving at a diagnosis?"

"It is a given in any field of medicine. The absence of certain conditions, reactions, findings is sometimes as important, even more important, than that which is present."

"Could the same be true of a patient's chart?" Hoskins pursued.

"Sir, you will have to make your question more specific," Freund retorted.

"Allow me to show you this circled notation on the patient's chart," Hoskins said, presenting a copy to the doctor.

Freund studied certain lines that were circled in red ink. "Ah, yes. The pregnancy test. What about it?"

"What does it say there?"

"Dr. Forrester secured some urine by catheterization. She then performed one of the several immediate-result pregnancy tests generally available."

"And?"

"The result was negative," Freund replied. "As is clearly noted here."

"Have you also seen a copy of the medical examiner's report?"

"Yes, I have. Ruptured ectopic pregnancy leading to massive internal bleeding," Freund replied.

"So I ask you once more, Doctor, do you trust this chart completely?"

"Yes!" Freund repeated. "It states clearly what occurred, what the doctor did, what she found. Which is all it is supposed to do!"

"That being the case, Doctor, aren't we forced to ask ourselves, What did Dr. Forrester do, which by her own admission in this chart, resulted in that false report?"

"There is nothing in the chart that indicates she did *anything* wrong!" Freund protested.

"Of course not," Hoskins said, smiling more broadly now. "She wrote the chart. But the medical examiner's findings prove otherwise, don't they?"

"Don't be too quick to attribute that failure to the doctor," Freund grumbled. "That's the trouble in these times, blame the doctor, blame the doctor. How do we know the doctor didn't fail but the test did? No test is perfect."

It was obvious that the old man was running out of patience, either with the proceedings or with himself for failing to deal better with the prosecutor's questions.

"Only a few more questions, Doctor. Based on the chart, would you say that in your professional opinion the symptoms and signs the patient presented were consistent with an ectopic pregnancy?"

"And with fifty other possible diagnoses!" Freund replied.

"That wasn't my question. Were those signs, symptoms, lab reports, consistent with an ectopic pregnancy?" Hoskins persisted.

"Yes," Freund admitted. "They were. But as I said —"

"Please, Doctor," Mr. Mott intervened. "Let's not embroider our answers." He signaled Hoskins to continue.

"Just one more question, Doctor. If Dr. Forrester *had* come up with the correct diagnosis, would she, or some other doctor, have been able to save Claudia Stuyvesant's life?"

"No one will ever know the answer to that," Freund replied.

"Would you at least grant that if the patient's condition had been correctly diagnosed hours sooner and referred to surgery, she *might* have been saved?"

"I can't answer that," Freund replied.

"Can you *deny* the possibility?"

Impatient, Freund exploded, "I can't admit, I can't deny. No one can! All I know is that Kate Forrester acted like a well-trained, intelligent doctor, which is the only issue being considered here!"

Feeling that he had counteracted all the favorable testimony Freund had given, Hoskins was quite pleased as he concluded, "Thank you, Doctor. That will be all."

"Oh, will it?" the angered old doctor said defiantly. "Well, it is not 'all' as far as I'm concerned."

Hoskins tried to interrupt. "Doctor, please, your testimony is finished."

Freund rose from his chair to peer into the eyes of the two physicians on the committee. "We have got to be more caring about our young doctors."

Hoskins tried to interrupt. "Mr. Mott! Mr. Mott, will you please stop him?"

Freund turned on Hoskins. "You!" he accused, pointing his finger at him. "You are a lawyer! You don't have the remotest idea what I'm talking about. So stay out of it. This is a problem for doctors!"

He turned back to Dr. Ward and Dr. Truscott.

"Colleagues, in recent years, as a member of the Admissions Committee of our medical school, I have watched with great concern the applications that have crossed my desk. Until recently applications were falling off in numbers. Alarmingly so. Then in the past two years the number began to increase. While that would seem to be encouraging, we should not be fooled. Because when I examine those

410

applications closely, I discover that the quality of the students applying is not the same. The best and the brightest of our young no longer choose to become physicians and surgeons. Why? Because other fields are more attractive. The avalanche of malpractice lawsuits. The rigorous demands of our profession. The old days of teaching our young doctors by bullying them or overworking them to see how much physical and verbal abuse they can tolerate, those days are gone. Our best young men and women no longer wish to put up with all that.

"Except those few who feel a dedication, a calling, if I may say so, an almost religious calling to serve humanity. And when they do? Take this young woman. This dedicated, well-trained, conscientious woman. What is she called in the legal document? The respondent. Asked to respond to *what?* To defend herself against *what?* For acting in all respects as a good doctor should. Yet now she is put in the dock like a criminal, attacked and vilified. Called a murderer, as someone did on television."

He swung about. "Yes, by you, Mr. Stuyvesant!"

Turning back to his colleagues, Freund resumed: "This persecution, this vilification, this inquisition must cease. Else all highly intelligent, highly motivated young people like

Dr. Forrester will take their abilities elsewhere. Medicine will suffer losses it can ill afford. I warn you, put a stop to this kind of thing!"

With some disdain he glared at Hoskins. "Now, if there are no more questions, my testimony *is* finished."

Since no one objected, Freund started out, stopping on the way to say to Kate, "My dear, I tried to do you some good. But these legal games they play, I don't have the patience for them any longer. I have faith in you. And I trust all this will turn out well. I will send you my new address. Let me know how things end up here."

Kate watched the old man start for the door. He walked slowly, made an effort to stand more erect, then gave in to a slump that warned her that he might not live too long even in retirement.

Once Freund had left the hearing room, Chairman Mott asked, "Ladies, gentlemen, if there is no objection, shall we break for lunch now?"

There was general agreement except for Dr. Ward, who asked, "May I have some clarification on one point?"

"Of course," Mott agreed readily. "Mr. Hoskins, please?"

"No," she contradicted. "I want clarification from the other gentleman" — she consulted her notes — "Mr. Van Cleve."

"Yes, Doctor?" Scott replied, coming to his feet.

"I was puzzled by the introduction of Dr. Freund as a witness. This is not his field of expertise. He is far removed from gynecological practice, indeed from the usual run of cases in Emergency. I am forced to ask, Mr. Van Cleve, why?"

Several possible responses flashed through his mind, but the truthful one struck him as the most proper. "Because, Doctor, we could get no other physician to come forward and testify. There is a blackout at City Hospital; the staff are being discouraged from coming to Dr. Forrester's defense."

"And were no other doctors willing to come forward and testify on her behalf?"

"With the hostility and suspicion that doctors now harbor toward the legal system, I could find no specialist in the field who would volunteer to become involved. And I did not think the doctors on this committee would be impressed by the usual paid 'experts' whose opinions are for hire."

Kate thought she detected a sympathetic and understanding nod from Dr. Truscott. But Dr. Gladys Ward gave no outward indication of her reaction to Scott's admission.

Chapter Twenty-nine

After the interruption to accommodate the aging Dr. Freund, the hearing resumed its prescribed course. As prosecutor, Hoskins continued to build his case against Kate Forrester. His next witness was the medical examiner of the city. Though Dr. Schwartzman's written report might have sufficed, Hoskins was intent on adding dramatic emphasis to Schwartzman's findings by impressing the members of the committee with his personal testimony as well as affording them the opportunity of asking questions of their own.

In his usual brusque manner, Schwartzman's responses to Hoskins's questions were curt and economical.

From long experience in testifying, he crisply recited his education and professional background to qualify as an expert. He then proceeded to recall in detail the events surrounding the Stuyvesant case. The cadaver was sent down to the medical examiner's building with a special request that he himself perform the autopsy. Since the police and the district attorney had prior call on his services, his autopsy was delayed several days. But the result was definitive. Claudia Stuyvesant had died of an internal hemorrhage due to a ruptured ectopic pregnancy.

"Dr. Schwartzman," Hoskins continued, "did you make any other observations in the course of your autopsy?"

"Well," the medical examiner began, his attitude changing from its previous briskness to one more relaxed and conversational, "what surprised me was that, with such gross findings, I couldn't understand why her condition wasn't diagnosed."

"Do I understand you to say that in your opinion a competent doctor should have been able to make a correct diagnosis while the patient was still alive?"

"That's exactly what I am saying," Schwartzman confirmed. "I found her hemorrhage was extensive. Extensive."

"Tell us, in your opinion, if a doctor, supposedly well trained and qualified, were to have missed those indications, over some nine hours of observation . . ." Hoskins suggested.

"I would have to doubt that physician's competence to practice medicine," Schwartzman declared.

"Is there any other statement you wish to make before you conclude your testimony?"

"Just one. Aside from that condition, Claudia Stuyvesant appeared to have been in good health," Schwartzman said, casting an accusing glance in Kate's direction.

If this had been a trial and strictly limited by the rules of evidence, Scott would have objected to the last question as irrelevant. But by making many technical legal objections he risked giving the committee the impression that he was trying to minimize his client's culpability through legalistic maneuvers. However, he could not allow the medical examiner to escape without being questioned.

Scott came forward from his table to assume a position that gave him equal access to the witness and to Claude Stuyvesant, who sat at the end of the prosecutor's table.

"Dr. Schwartzman, you came here with an extensive and excellent background. I have even heard you referred to as the best-trained, most-experienced medical examiner in recent years in this city."

Schwartzman smiled faintly, a pretense at modesty.

"And I accept your findings without reservation," Scott continued. "Except for two things that trouble me."

"Whatever I can do to enlighten you, Counselor," Schwartzman volunteered. "I am here to help."

"While you were testifying, and especially

during the last phase of it, I couldn't help wondering, Doctor, when was the last time you *treated* a patient? Specifically, a young female patient, nineteen years of age?"

Schwartzman glared in resentment. "It should be obvious that once I entered the field of forensic medicine, I no longer continued to treat patients."

"And when was that, Doctor?"

"Some . . . some twenty-two or twenty-three years ago." Schwartzman replied, glancing toward Hoskins to extricate him.

Hoskins made a pretense of indulgent amusement as he called from his place at the table. "Mr. Mott, when a man appears here as medical examiner with a superb professional record in that specialty, Mr. Van Cleve's question does sound ridiculous."

Scott turned on him. "No more ridiculous, Mr. Hoskins, than asking him whether a doctor dealing with a living patient should have detected a condition that was far from obvious at the time. His peculiar professional expertise does not entitle him to venture such an opinion."

"Mr. Van Cleve, Mr. Van Cleve," Administrator Cahill intervened. "We are conducting a hearing here, not a trial."

"My client is on trial!" Scott protested.

"I am ruling, Mr. Van Cleve, that this is

417

a hearing. Counsel and witnesses are allowed some latitude in their questions and answers. Mr. Hoskins asked a question that he thought enlightening for the committee. And Dr. Schwartzman responded. Now, unless you can contradict his response, I rule his answer stands. In fact I urge you to dismiss him. He is a very busy man, to judge from the record-setting murder rate in this city."

"Mr. Cahill, I'm as interested as you are in enlightening this committee. Which is why I want them to hear from Dr. Schwartzman's mouth that he is not qualified to express an opinion as to what a doctor would find in a living patient during a hectic night in the Emergency Service, especially with a patient who was giving a false history and was, most likely, under the influence of drugs!"

At once Stuyvesant was on his feet, calling, "Mr. Mott! I thought we had agreed —"

Stuyvesant interrupted himself quite abruptly. Scott turned to stare at him, then at Mott. It had become quite clear that between them Stuyvesant had insisted, privately, and Mott had agreed, privately, that there was to be no mention of drugs during the course of the hearing.

Mott flushed slightly and addressed himself to Scott. "Mr. Van Cleve, unless and until you can present proof that drugs, legal or illegal, played any part in this case, we shall consider any mention of that subject out of order. Do I make myself clear?"

"Yes, sir," Scott replied.

"Good!" Hoskins commented. "For a minute there I was afraid he was going to resurrect his imaginary playmate Rick Thomas! Thank God we've been spared a repetition of that!"

Scott avoided Hoskins's grin to ask Mott, "May I continue with my cross-examination?"

"I thought you'd exhausted all your relevant questions," Mott remarked acerbically.

"I have one more question," Scott said. "Dr. Schwartzman, how do you account for the fact that there is no mention in your report of *any* findings relating to drugs?"

Mott struck the table with his gavel, hard and sharp. "Mr. Van Cleve, you are aware of the limitations I placed on that subject!"

"Mr. Mott, you said the mention of the *presence* of drugs was off-limits. I am now inquiring about the *absence* of same. Especially the absence from his report. I want to know if Dr. Schwartzman, too, has a little 'private' agreement with Mr. Stuyvesant on what was to be in his report!"

"This is outrageous!" Schwartzman shouted. "In all my years in forensic medicine I have never had my reputation impugned. I demand an apology!"

"As soon as you answer my question, Doctor," Scott replied. On a cue from Mott, Schwartzman addressed the stentotypist: "I wish the record to show that once I had established the cause of death, there was no need for further inquiry."

"Dr. Schwartzman, do you recall an occasion when I visited you in your office?" Scott asked.

"Yes, yes, and at that time I told you the same thing to which I just testified. Once the cause of death was established, there was no need to probe further."

"Didn't you also say that in the usual case a toxic screen was routine?"

"I might have said that," Schwartzman admitted. "I talk to so many lawyers in the course of a day, I can't remember the details of every conversation."

"Doctor, we're not talking about details, but about routine procedures!" Scott declared.

Hoskins intervened. "Mr. Cahill, he is arguing with the witness. Make him confine himself to cross-examination."

The administrator cleared his throat before admonishing, "Mr. Van Cleve, Counsel Hoskins's point is well taken. Confine yourself to proper cross-examination and forgo arguments and diatribes."

"Yes, sir. Sorry," Scott said. He turned back

to Schwartzman. "Doctor, was there anything else about this particular autopsy that failed to follow the routine?"

"Not that I'm aware of," Schwartzman replied.

"Doctor, what percentage of the autopsies performed at your institution are done by you personally?"

"What percentage . . ." Schwartzman repeated gingerly, aware of the direction in which Scott's question was leading. "Depends."

"Depends on what?" Scott asked sharply.

"Depends, young man, on my other duties. Like right now. Instead of performing an autopsy, here I am, testifying at this hearing. While down at my office three different homicides, a suspected suicide, and a body fished out of the river yesterday are all being autopsied. My assistants do most of them. But we don't think in terms of percentages, of who does what. We all pitch in and do what needs doing to keep up with the pressures of the job."

"Do I take that to mean that you either can't or won't answer my question?" Scott asked.

"Take that to mean that I *have* answered your question, young man!" Schwartzman shot back. "I do not know the exact percentage of autopsies that I personally do! Period!"

"Doctor, are there special cases that you reserve for yourself?"

"I don't understand," Schwartzman evaded.

"If a case comes along that is sexy, scandalous, notorious, so that there is bound to be heavy media interest, which will mean being interviewed extensively on television or by the press, would you be likely to reserve such a case for your own personal investigation?" Scott asked.

Schwartzman looked at Scott, shook his head slowly and smiled indulgently. "Look, kid, if you think that you are going to trap me into denying that, you're an even bigger idiot than I thought. Of course I reserve such cases for myself! For precisely the reason you mentioned. Because there *will* be media coverage. I do not want to expose some young assistant to those ravenous media hawks for fear he might make some blunder that can affect the later trial of the case. So I handle those myself. I know what to say and, more important, what not to say. So there'll be no mistrials or later reversals."

"And possibly at the same time garner a little publicity, Doctor?" Scott asked.

"Damn right!" Schwartzman insisted. "My department gets very little credit for the work we do. So when we get a chance to shine in public, why not? Good for the morale of my staff."

When Schwartzman felt that he had directed the examination away from the point Scott had been trying to establish, he made an obvious gesture of studying his wristwatch as if he were running out of the time he had allotted to this interruption in his busy schedule.

"Doctor, just a few more questions. The case of Claudia Stuyvesant, was that one of those cases you took on yourself because you felt there was great media interest?"

"There certainly has been great media interest," Schwartzman replied.

"That wasn't the question, Doctor," Scott pursued. "Is that the reason you took it on yourself to do that particular case?"

"Yes."

"The only reason?"

"Yes!" Schwartzman insisted.

"Sir, in your office didn't you admit to me that the mayor himself asked you not to reveal your findings until the funeral of Claudia Stuyvesant was over?"

"A courtesy. An act of consideration to a bereaved family. It didn't change my findings!" Schwartzman protested.

"And not doing a toxic screen, was that, too, a 'courtesy'? An act of consideration?"

"I told you, the only question was, cause

of death. Once that was determined, no further investigation was necessary," Schwartzman insisted.

"Dr. Schwartzman, with your years of forensic experience, can you tell this committee if it is possible, in the course of such an autopsy, to find residual damage resulting from extensive drug use even if one does not perform a toxic screen? Say, evidence of heart, kidney, or liver damage?"

"If one were looking for such evidence, yes," Schwartzman granted.

"Would it be readily apparent to the eye or would one have to be 'looking for such evidence'?"

"That would depend on each individual case," Schwartzman replied, responding to the question but also establishing his response to Scott's next question.

"And in the case of Claudia Stuyvesant?" Scott asked.

"That," Schwartzman responded glibly, "was one of those cases in which it was not readily apparent."

"Could such evidence be found now if her body were exhumed?"

"Young man, I told you that day, the body was cremated as soon as the autopsy was completed."

"So you did," Scott agreed. "So you did."

Then he added, "Another 'courtesy,' Doctor? Releasing the body so quickly? There must be quite a busy hot line between your office and the mayor's office."

"I resent that!" Schwartzman shouted, half rising from his chair.

"You resent the mayor calling you? Or my calling attention to the mayor calling you? First to do the autopsy yourself. Then to withhold your findings. Then to release the body for cremation so that no one . . . no one . . . could ever find evidence of drug use?"

His face red with anger and embarrassment, Schwartzman turned to the chairman. "Mr. Mott, do I have to dignify such sheer speculation with an answer?"

Hoskins was on his feet. "No, Doctor, you do not. Because the next thing you know, Van Cleve will resort once more to that figment of his imagination, Rick Thomas!"

Pretending to be defeated, Scott said, "That is all."

From her place at the table Kate Forrester studied the faces of the two medical members of the committee, wondering if Scott had succeeded in impressing them with the extent to which there had been a conspiracy to conceal Claudia's drug habits. Truscott had made continuous notes all through the exchange. Dr. Ward, who had listened with seeming detachment throughout the cross-examination, was the only one who interrupted as Schwartzman was rising from the witness chair.

"Doctor —" Gladys Ward asked so sharply that Schwartzman dropped back into his chair. "In your opinion, if Claudia Stuyvesant had been a casual or even a habitual user of drugs, how would that have changed or affected the outcome in this case?"

"You know, Doctor Ward, I've asked myself that same question," Schwartzman replied. "The way I see it, drugs could not cause her ectopic pregnancy. I've never heard of such a case."

"Nor have I," Ward agreed.

"And ectopics, undetected, *will* rupture and hemorrhage, whether the patient used drugs or not. So I do not see the relevance of all this fuss being made about drugs," Schwartzman said with finality. "Now I must go!"

Before he could move, and in direct contravention of her attorney's instructions, Kate Forrester rose in her place to demand, "Doctor! Is it possible that a patient under the influence of drugs would tend to be inexact and misleading in her answers to the physician's questions?"

"What did you expect, young woman? That when you questioned her, the patient would say, 'Doctor, I am here because I am suffering an ectopic pregnancy'? It was your job to discover that!"

"Are you also saying that drugs could not have masked symptoms and signs, could not have affected the lab findings and thus misled the doctor?" Kate persisted in an even stronger voice.

"Dr. Forrester, Dr. Forrester," Chairman Mott tried to intervene. But Kate would not be silenced.

"Doctor, could drugs mask pain and other symptoms and signs?" Kate insisted. "I demand that you answer!"

Flustered, his face growing very red, Schwartzman glared at her as he finally responded, "You really want to know what I believe? I believe that since there is no definitive evidence on this matter of drugs, you and your attorney are trying to use it as a smoke screen to divert attention from your medical blunder."

With that the medical examiner started from the room, but not without exchanging glances with Claude Stuyvesant.

Once the medical examiner was gone, Chairman Mott turned his attention to Kate Forrester.

"Young woman, we will never again tolerate a repetition of such unorthodox conduct during this hearing! Now, Mr. Hoskins, your next witness?"

"Mr. Chairman, frankly, I am so disturbed by this outlandish spectacle that I demand a recess before continuing with my next witnesses."

"Mr. Hoskins, I think we could all do with a break at this time. Fifteen minutes!" Mott rapped his gavel.

Quickly Scott took Kate by the hand and led her outside the hearing room. Before he could speak, Kate did.

"Okay, get it off your chest. I went against your orders. I intervened when I should have kept my mouth shut. And if I carry on in this way, I will be responsible for losing my case. There! I said it to save you the trouble."

"Thanks," Scott said simply.

"You're not angry? Not going to yell, shout, rant, and rave? Not going to threaten to abandon my case?"

"I would, if you hadn't unnerved Schwartzman so that he almost defeated his own testimony. I think you also registered very well with both doctors on the committee. Possibly better than I would have done."

"Oh? Really?" Kate asked, beginning to feel a bit proud of herself.

"Just one thing," Scott added.

"What?"

"Never do that again," Scott ordered. "It could be dangerous."

From the beginning of the preparation of his case against Kate Forrester, Albert Hoskins had never intended to rely solely on the testimony of the medical examiner to establish her guilt. He had carefully selected from among many specialists in obstetrics and gynecology three doctors who had no connection with City Hospital, who had no affiliation with either Dr. Gladys Ward or Dr. Maurice Truscott. He wanted expert medical testimony untainted by factors that could later lead to an appeal.

As soon as the recess was over, Hoskins presented his next witness, Dr. John Vinmont, who was on the staff of Columbia Presbyterian Hospital. With Vinmont's excellent educational and professional background it did not take Hoskins long to qualify him as an expert entitled to render opinion testimony. Slowly Hoskins led him through a recital of his knowledge of the case of Claudia Stuyvesant. Yes, he had studied the chart that Dr. Forrester had written up, had studied photocopies of orders she had written in the order book kept at the nurses' station, had carefully studied the medical examiner's report.

Hoskins now came to the hypothetical question for which all the foregoing had served as prologue.

"Dr. Vinmont, in your professional opinion, suppose a doctor had discovered all the findings noted in this chart and suppose that doctor had instituted all the modalities noted here, and suppose that as a result the patient had died of the cause reported by the medical examiner, would you say that the death of such a patient could be considered preventable and hence due to negligence and professional failure on the part of the doctor administering to such a patient?"

Though the question seemed unnecessarily long and detailed, it was in the form required for the legal expression of an expert opinion.

Vinmont's answer was as brief as the question had been long, "Yes, sir."

"Death could have been preventable?" Hoskins repeated.

"Yes, sir."

"And was due to failure on the part of the physician?"

"Yes, sir."

"One thing more, Dr. Vinmont, can you state, in your expert opinion, given the facts in this case, what would have been the outcome if a correct diagnosis had been made in the first few hours of the patient's admission and treatment by Dr. Kate Forrester?"

"Routine surgery would almost surely have had a favorable result," Vinmont replied.

"Meaning the patient could have survived?" Hoskins asked, pinning him down.

"In my opinion such surgery would have been routine and successful," Vinmont declared.

"Thank you, Doctor."

Even under Scott Van Cleve's sharp cross-examination Vinmont proved unshakable. He brushed aside questions related to Claudia Stuyvesant's untruthful answers about sexual activity and missed periods. When Scott tried to introduce questions as to the effect of drug use, Hoskins objected on the ground that no such evidence had been introduced.

"Then, Doctor," Scott continued, "let me ask it in the form of a hypothetical question: If there *had* been extensive drug use by the patient —"

But Hoskins was on his feet and objecting before Scott had even completed the question. Again Cahill sustained him, this time in an even longer opinion.

Frustrated, Scott returned to his place at the defense table.

Scott fared no better with Hoskins's next two witnesses, Dr. Florence Neary and Dr. Harold Bruno. Their expert opinions coincided with Vinmont's. When Scott cross-examined them, under the same restrictions as had been established by Cahill's rulings, their answers were the same.

Hoskins had meticulously prepared and very skillfully presented an unassailable prima facie case of medical failure on the part of the physician leading to the untimely death of a nineteen-year-old woman, which could have been prevented if a proper diagnosis had been made.

"Mr. Hoskins, may I assume this concludes the board's case against Dr. Forrester?" Scott asked.

"No, sir," Hoskins responded. "I have one more witness. But since the hour is late and this has been an exhausting day, I ask that this hearing be set over until tomorrow morning."

"Mr. Van Cleve?" Mott asked.

"I have no objection," Scott replied, since it had been an even more exhausting day for him than for Hoskins.

"Then we stand in recess until tomorrow morning at ten," Mott declared, and banged his gavel.

Chapter Thirty

Kate had hardly inserted her key into the second lock of their front door when it flew open and Rosie Chung asked anxiously, "Well? How did it go?"

"Not too well, I'm afraid," Kate admitted.

Scott contradicted her quickly. "I wouldn't say that."

Rosie led the way to the living room, insisting, "Tell me, tell me everything!"

"Mrs. Stuyvesant's testimony was bad enough," Kate started to say. "But those three doctors —"

"Three doctors?" Rosie asked, puzzled by this unexpected development.

Scott explained briefly. The legal purpose of Hoskins's introducing expert testimony was to prove the board's allegations that Kate had failed to function as a competent doctor should have.

"And you let him get away with that?" Rosie demanded.

"Okay, now! Both of you simmer down!" Scott ordered. "Let's look at things from a purely legal point of view."

"That's what I'm trying to do," Rosie said.

"Hoskins is putting in the board's case. Naturally every witness he introduces is against us. But we'll have our turn."

"Still," Kate reminded him, "you weren't able to shake those three doctors. And we didn't make much headway against Schwartzman either."

"The medical examiner?" Rosie asked.

"Yes," Kate said. "And when Dr. Ward became involved, things were even worse."

"She has a reputation for being a terror in the operating room," Rosie said.

"She's no angel in the hearing room, either, I can tell you," Kate replied.

"Kate!" Scott intervened with the severe attitude of a reproving teacher. "Let's keep things in perspective. In this situation you are the patient and I am the doctor. You are personally involved, therefore it is natural for you to react emotionally to what you saw and heard. It is my job as the doctor to remain cool. To assess all events dispassionately. To take account of what happened today and also what to expect may happen tomorrow and the day after.

"Now, did Hoskins score some telling points today? Yes. Mrs. Stuyvesant *was* a very sympathetic witness. She *had* lost a teenage daughter. But I'm sure the committee is aware that that colors her version of what happened that night."

"Not Mr. Clarence Mott, I can assure you," Kate interjected.

"Okay. He's in Stuyvesant's back pocket. But there *are* two other members of that committee," Scott pointed out. "Now, as to Schwartzman . . ."

"He had a very convincing response to every question you asked," Kate reminded him. "In fact the more questions you asked, the stronger he became."

"Is that true?" Rosie asked, even more troubled than she had been at the outset.

"Yes, it's true."

"That's what led me to question him," Kate said.

"You?" Rosie asked, astonished. "You questioned a witness? Is that allowed?"

"She got away with it this time," Scott said. "But she didn't realize I was deliberately sucking Schwartzman in. Giving him every opportunity to insist there was no evidence of Claudia's drug use. I was praying for Hoskins to intervene to emphasize the point. When he called Rick Thomas a figment of my imagination, I could have kissed him. Because when I walk that figment into the hearing room at the crucial moment, the committee will not only know we have been telling the truth, they will also realize that there is a conspiracy at work here to protect the Stuyvesant name from any further scandal by making Kate the person responsible for her death. Then I will move to bring Hoskins's three experts back and ask them the questions I was prevented from asking today."

"And when you do that, that's the ball game," Rosie concluded.

"I hope so," Scott said. "Now, Kate, I'd like a good strong drink to relax. I need it."

As soon as Kate was out of the room, Rosie adopted a low, confidential tone as she asked, "Look, Van Cleve, I appreciate you trying to put the best face on the situation to keep up Kate's morale. But you can be honest with me."

"What makes you think I've been less than honest with Kate?" Scott asked.

"You know what I mean," Rosie insisted. "Level with me. How does it look? I have to know so that I can react accordingly. If things go wrong, Kate will need someone to lean on. That someone is me. I need time to prepare. So level, Van Cleve."

"Okay. As things stand now, knowing what I can prove, and with Rick Thomas in the bullpen, so to speak, I'd say we have a pretty fair chance of clearing her completely."

" 'Fair chance'? That's all?" Rosie asked, obviously alarmed.

436

"If Kate holds up on cross-examination, yes, a fair chance. Don't forget, we have two doctors sitting in judgment. Sometimes people within a profession are tougher on their colleagues than outsiders would be. Lawyers are tough judges when it comes to deciding on disbarring other lawyers. They are quick to condemn, even quicker to appear holier than thou. If we've got one of those in Truscott or Ward, we're in big trouble."

"That Ward, she's the type," Rosie remarked grimly.

"And don't forget Ramón Gallante's series on television. That alarmed a lot of doctors in this town," Scott reminded her.

"I tried to keep Kate from going on that show," Rosie said.

"I'm not thinking of what Kate said, but of all the vicious accusations Stuyvesant made. He put the entire medical profession on trial. So Truscott and Ward might well feel they are defending their profession by condemning Kate. There's no doubt Stuyvesant owns Hoskins and Schwartzman. And Mott too. So I'd be a fool, or a liar, to make any big promises to you, or to Kate."

"Van Cleve, you simply can't lose! You don't dare lose!" Rosie Chung insisted. "I know Kate. If you lose this case, it will shatter her completely. Caring for people, healing the sick, is a religion to her."

"I know. I felt it the first time I ever interviewed her. I promise you I will do my best," Scott said.

"Have you ever considered . . ." Rosie started to ask, then stopped abruptly.

"Considered what?"

"I know how strong and independent Kate likes to feel. She doesn't want to impose on her family, so she hasn't told them how precarious things really are," Rosie said. "So I . . . Well, two nights ago I called *my* folks. Talked to my dad. Explained Kate's situation. He is willing to lend me money, enough money to let you hire added counsel."

"That would cost thousands," Scott warned. "I know," Rosie admitted. "But Dad is willing."

"What you really mean is you'd like an older, more experienced lawyer to take over," Scott interpreted.

Rosie hesitated, then nodded. Self-conscious, nevertheless she stared up at Scott with her deep black, intense almond eyes. "For Kate I'd do anything."

"I appreciate that, Rosie. But you're doing the same thing to me that Nora Stuyvesant did to Kate that night. Doubting her ability because she was young. Demanding to see another doctor, an older doctor."

438

"I'm sorry, Van Cleve, it's only Kate I'm thinking of," Rosie said. "I want the best for her."

"Believe me, no lawyer will work harder for her. Or with more devotion. This has become more than a case. Even more than a cause. That's the way I feel about Kate as a woman."

It was as close to a declaration of love as Scott Van Cleve had ever made about Kate Forrester, even to himself.

Rosie knew the truth of what he had said, saw it in his eyes. "I'm sorry for what I suggested. Please forget it if you can."

"Provided you forget this conversation. If we do lose, I wouldn't want her to know how I feel."

"Okay," Rosie agreed, then asked, "Van Cleve, I've been thinking, what if I talked to Briscoe? We've been pretty friendly. I know he likes me. Or I could have Mel talk to him. They're even better friends. Maybe Briscoe would reconsider testifying for Kate."

Scott shook his head slowly.

"How can you be sure?" Rosie asked.

"Because, Rosie, *I* went back to him. I pleaded with him. He won't take the risk. He's got that partnership waiting for him in Colorado. Visions of that big house up in the mountains. That sleek Mercedes 500 SL.

Wednesdays off for golf. Long skiing week-ends. Not you, not I, not anyone is going to shake him."

"He said that?" Rosie said doubtfully.

"He didn't have to," Scott said. "I could see it in his eyes, Rosie. There are doctors, and then there are doctors. He's one kind. Kate and you are the other."

Sadly Rosie Chung admitted, "Too bad. He's such a good surgeon. With such excellent technique."

They had dropped Rosie at the hospital to go on night duty. They picked up some sandwiches and were back at Scott's apartment, ready to continue with Kate's preparation for her turn as a witness.

Even before Scott began, Kate said, "I'm sorry."

Surprised, he looked up from his study of the questions he had listed to ask, "Sorry? About what?"

"What I said in front of Rosie. About the way you questioned Schwartzman."

"Don't give it a thought," Scott replied.

"But I did think the point you made about him having no experience with a living patient in recent years was very effective."

"Just a little maneuver. To take the sting out of his hostile testimony. To divert the committee's attention. Not particularly effective, I'm afraid. Tomorrow Hoskins will put on one last witness. Who it is almost doesn't matter. Then it's our turn. I'll lead off with Cronin and Beathard. Not that they can do much besides corroborate some of the things you will say. But I am putting them on first to get a clue as to Hoskins's plan for cross-examination. So that when I put you on, I'm prepared for what to expect.

"Because in the end this hearing eventually comes down to one thing. *You.* On the stand. Telling your story. Then being able to withstand Hoskins's cross-examination."

"And you think I won't hold up."

"In all honesty I don't know," Scott admitted.

"Well, I do!" Kate insisted.

He stared down into her face, still lovely despite the tension and strain of recent days, especially this long, taxing day. Secretly he wished, *If only we'd met in any way but this. But soon it'll be out of my hands. If she fails, we both fail. I will have let her down. And she will never forgive me.*

"Kate," he began, "we've worked on the need to give direct factual answers. On not volunteering more information than the question calls for."

"I know, don't give Hoskins any targets or

441

opportunity," Kate recalled a well-learned lesson.

"Two more things. Testifying is almost like a hypnotic experience. I have watched important men, top executives in business, in government, crack under the strain of being cross-examined by a skillful lawyer. Witnesses suddenly go blank. They forget the most obvious facts. Or they suddenly offer versions different from those they ever remembered before."

He began to pace as he said, "But the worst trap of all is when the witness tries to match wits with the lawyer, tries to outthink him. For example, Hoskins asks you a question calling for a factual response. Instead of giving him that simple answer you start thinking, 'What's he really trying to find out? What's the best way for me to answer so that he doesn't succeed?' You are no longer a witness. You have become your own lawyer. A player in a game you are not trained to play. You can't win. Because he has control. He asks the questions, so he directs the course of the examination. Do not try to outguess him."

"I know. Just answer the questions truthfully," Kate said.

"And have confidence in me," Scott said, staring down at her. "Depend on me to overcome any damage Hoskins might create."

Kate nodded. "I can do it."

"Here, now, sitting in my living room you can do it. But once you take the witness chair, everything changes."

"Try me!" Kate challenged. "Ask me the kind of questions Hoskins will ask. See how I stand up to them."

He gestured her from the couch to the armchair that had become her witness chair during their sessions. Once seated, she was ready for his attack.

"Doctor, you heard the testimony of Mrs. Stuyvesant, the mother of the deceased. That she had to insist not once but several times that you come in to take care of her daughter," Scott said.

"Yes. But I had other more urgent cases that demanded my attention."

"Kate!" Scott rebuked sharply. "Wait until you hear the question!"

"But I did," she started to protest, until she realized, "You didn't ask a question, did you?"

"I was just laying the foundation for my question. You took it to be an accusation and started to defend yourself. Don't be a lawyer! Just be the witness! Listen to the question before you answer. Then, without justifying or explaining, answer. Now, let's start again."

"Okay. Sorry."

"Doctor, is it true that one time Mrs. Stuyvesant had to track you down to get you to come in and look at her daughter?"

Kate paused, then responded as firmly as she could, "Yes, yes, sir, that's true. And it is also true that —" This time she stopped herself. "I've just answered the question. Now I should shut up."

"I wouldn't have phrased it exactly that way, but the answer is yes, shut up. Don't try to guess where Hoskins is leading."

"Got it," she said.

"Now, let's go on," he said.

For the next three hours he pounded her with questions about Mrs. Stuyvesant's testimony, about the medical examiner's testimony, about his autopsy report. Sometimes Scott's questions flowed in sequence, sometimes he posed deliberate non sequiturs, jumping from one moment in the events of that night to another, unrelated moment.

He backtracked, going over the same ground again, and then again, until she protested, "I've already answered that!" She was louder than she had wanted to be. Fatigue was beginning to take its toll.

Patiently Scott explained, "Lawyers deliberately use repetition as a weapon. Either to trip the witness up by getting her to contradict herself. Or, on the other hand, to see if she responds in exactly the same words each time. Which proves that her answers were memorized. So expect Hoskins to ask the same questions more than once. If he abuses the privilege, that's when I step in."

It was past midnight. He could see that Kate was almost exhausted. But he determined not to let up, to see if she could go the distance. Once she took that witness chair, she would be on the stand all day. If Hoskins turned out to be the pit bull Scott suspected, he might carry over Kate's testimony for a second day, even a third.

To prepare her for that, Scott decided to push Kate to the limit now.

"Doctor," he continued, "we've heard a great deal during this hearing about the pregnancy test that you say you performed —"

"I did perform it!" she responded angrily.

Taking that as a sign of her fatigue, Scott pointed out, "You're arguing again. Wait for the question. Now, let's start over. Doctor, we've heard a great deal about the pregnancy test that you say you performed. You noted it on the patient's chart. Along with the result. Negative. Can you explain to the committee why you received a false result?"

"No," she said. "I often think —" She broke off. "No. Beyond the fact that such tests have a recognized failure rate, I can't explain it."

"Doctor, you said, 'I often think —' What is it that you often think?" Scott pursued, making a point of the trap into which volunteered answers can lead.

"I'd rather not say," she replied.

"I'm afraid, Doctor, that in the process of cross-examination a witness does not have the privilege of answering only those questions she would 'rather' answer. Now, I ask you again, what is it that you 'often think'?" Scott was louder now, standing directly over her. "Mr. Cahill, I insist you instruct the witness to answer my question!" Imitating the administration law officer, Scott said rebukingly, "Dr. Forrester, unless you answer Mr. Hoskins's question, I shall have to rule out your entire testimony!"

"I often think . . . I sometimes ask myself . . . those three simple steps in the test, did I perform them correctly?"

"What do you mean?" Scott pressed.

"After so many continuous hours on duty I was so exhausted that I might have made a mistake."

"What kind of mistake?" Scott demanded quickly.

"The three reagents. Did I apply them incorrectly?"

"How?"

"Out of sequence, possibly," Kate admitted.

446

"I was so tired, doing the work of two doctors, anything could have happened."

"Anything?" Scott demanded. "Anything? Yet you made that entry in the patient's chart stating that you performed the test, did it correctly."

"That was after!" Kate fought back.

"Doctor, are you telling us that once you had a chance to calm down, you wrote things in that chart that were not true? Is that what you mean?"

"You're twisting my words," Kate protested. "I only meant when I did the test, I was sure I did it right. It was only days later, when I learned that the negative result had been wrong, that I began to think back and try to discover why." She was gripping the edges of her chair to keep from trembling.

Scott refused to let up. "So it is possible that when you wrote that note in the chart of Claudia Stuyvesant, it was wrong. Maybe *deliberately* wrong!"

"I have never in my life falsified an entry in a patient's chart!" Kate protested, rising up to confront him. "Never, do you hear? Never!" By which time she was weeping.

Scott took her in his arms and held her while her body shook with the spasms of her weeping. It took some time before she recovered. He led her to the couch and set her down.

He covered her with an afghan, said softly, "You've had a tough night. Just relax."

Minutes later, when the rhythm of her breathing changed, he realized she had fallen asleep. And why not? She had been under extreme pressure for weeks, and for the past nineteen hours on trial virtually for her life. Let her sleep.

Chapter Thirty-one

It was early the next morning. Kate Forrester came awake slowly. Her first conscious moments felt no different from those times, morning or night, when she woke from a deep sleep following a particularly exhausting tour of duty. Until she realized suddenly that she was in an unaccustomed place. She felt around her. This was not her bed. But a couch. And not even her couch. But an unfamiliar one. She heard someone bustling in another room. She smelled the strong fragrance of coffee brewing. There was the added sizzle of bacon frying. She opened her eyes. She recognized Scott's living room. She threw back the blanket to discover someone had removed her dress. She sat up, looked around. Her dress was neatly draped over what had become her witness chair.

Quickly she rose, reached for her dress, slipped into it. Hand-combed her blond hair into some semblance of order. Scott must have heard her, for he called, "Kate? You up?"

"Up," she replied.

"You'll find a fresh toothbrush and some toothpaste in the bathroom," he said.

She tried to avoid him as she went by the narrow kitchen on her way to the bathroom. But he caught sight of her, smiled. "Coffee's ready. Pancakes and bacon too."

She freshened up, combed her hair, longed for her makeup, but it was in her purse out in the living room. She decided to do without. She studied her face in the mirror of the cabinet. The ordeal of the last few weeks had not been helpful.

When she entered the kitchen, the little hinged table that was bolted to the wall had been raised into place and was already set. Fragrant steam curled up slowly from her coffee cup. Alongside was a glass of fresh-squeezed orange juice. As soon as she finished her juice, Scott whipped away the glass and replaced it with a plate of pancakes, light around the edges, brown on top, bordered by strips of crisp bacon.

He sat down opposite her.

"Good morning!" he said brightly. She smiled and started to eat. "You were so beat last night, I didn't have the heart to wake you," he explained.

"I must have been exhausted. I've never slept so soundly."

"How are the pancakes?"

"Excellent," she replied, attacking the bacon now. "You're a good cook."

"Bachelors get lots of practice."

"Are you this good with lunch and dinner, or just breakfast?" she taunted.

The import of her question came to him slowly.

"Next you'll ask how I got to be so good at removing women's dresses," he said, smiling.

"That had occurred to me."

"My mother taught me." Skeptical, Kate looked across at him, defying him to explain.

"I told you about my dad dying when I was so young. Well, my mother was a proud woman. Like you. Determined not to be dependent. Since she was pretty handy, she set up business in our house. At first doing mending and altering. Then she started making dresses. Later she developed it into a small store. Small? It became the biggest dress shop in Shenandoah, aside from the chain store. I used to help her. I trimmed the windows. Slipped the dresses on the mannequins, took them off. Very carefully. She taught me to respect the merchandise. She'd always say, 'Van, some woman is going to pay hard-earned money for this dress, so do it the least harm possible.'

"And the same about the mannequin?" Kate asked.

He was smiling again. "More coffee?"

451

"Please." They finished breakfast in silence.

"I'd better get back home, shower, change, and be ready for the hearing," Kate said.

"I'll take you," he said.

"Thanks. But no need. It's light out. And safe. Well, fairly safe," she admitted.

"There are things we have to talk about in preparation for today. This will give us the time. Let me clear the table and we can be on our way."

"I can help," she offered.

"I'm terrific at clearing dishes," he said, "especially breakfast dishes."

"You evidently associate with the wrong kind of women," Kate remarked. Then, teasing, she said, "I would think that out of sheer appreciation they would at least offer. But in this era of the liberated woman, they do as men used to. Make love and run."

"Given the chance I wouldn't run," he said, not smiling, no longer bantering.

"We'd better go," Kate said softly.

When they arrived at Kate's apartment, she found little stickup messages on the phone, on the kitchen cabinet, on the bathroom door. All from Rosie Chung. Kate's mother had called three times. Her dad was worried.

Kate rushed her shower, did her hair hurriedly, slipped into a robe, and came back to the living room.

"You look even better," Scott said.

"Cleaner, maybe, but not better. I have a mirror," Kate explained.

She called home.

"Mom?"

"Kate!" She heard her mother greet her with considerable relief. "Dad's been so worried; me too. How did it go yesterday, dear?"

"Uh . . . pretty well. Of course it was only the first day. But it was pretty good — pretty good." She tried to sound more positive than she actually felt.

Her mother must have suspected something, because she said, "Dad's been talking about going east. Maybe even bringing George Keepworth with him. George is willing."

"No need, Mom. I've got a good lawyer. A very good lawyer. And he's from a small town in Pennsylvania. So he's like home folks."

"Ah, that's nice," her mother replied, a bit more reassured. "It's those New York lawyers you have to watch out for."

"You tell Dad that everything is going along as well as can be expected. Not to worry," Kate said. "Now I have to run. Love you, Mom."

She hung up, but felt compelled to explain

to Scott, "I don't want to worry them until I have to."

"Make that 'unless.' We still have a good chance."

"Even after my disgraceful performance of last night?" Kate asked, seeking a frank answer.

"You were not disgraceful," Scott tried to encourage her. "Just inexperienced. You'll do better from now on."

All the other participants, including Claude Stuyvesant, had convened by the time Scott and Kate arrived at the hearing room. Chairman Mott accorded them a proper formal greeting, but he glanced at the gold watch before him on the table to underscore that they were six minutes late. He rapped his gavel lightly.

"Shall we begin?" He looked in Hoskins's direction.

The portly prosecutor rose from his tight-fitting chair as if disengaging from the clutch of a vise.

With a grave air he began, "Mr. Mott, I hesitate to produce my next witness without a ruling by the chair."

With corresponding gravity, Mott asked, "And what is the cause of your dilemma, Mr. Hoskins?"

"Although this is a more informal proceeding than a trial and one is granted greater latitude in the presentation of evidence and witnesses, I would like a specific ruling as to whether a person who was not a witness to the events involved might be asked to take the stand," Hoskins replied.

Mott turned in the direction of Kevin Cahill, inviting a ruling. Cahill paused a moment as if giving considerable thought to the problem and finally declared, "Mr. Hoskins, dealing as we are with matters of great moment, not only to the respondent here but to the entire medical profession, and especially the safety of the public at large, I believe that anyone who can shed light on these proceedings, anything that gives this committee a fuller grasp of the situation, is quite admissible. Produce your witness, sir."

Scott glanced at Kate, and she glanced back, indicating that they both agreed. This little drama, grave and serious as it was pretended to be for the record, was actually part of a prearranged strategy. Their suspicions were confirmed as Hoskins turned toward the end of the prosecutor's table.

"Mr. Stuyvesant? Please take the stand."

Kate tugged at Scott's sleeve. He patted her hand to reassure her, indicating, *Let's wait and see.*

After Stuyvesant was sworn in, Hoskins asked a few perfunctory questions to establish his relationship to the deceased patient and his interest in seeing justice done.

Then Hoskins zeroed in on one of the two purposes for which he had brought Stuyvesant to the stand.

"Mr. Stuyvesant, did there come a time when your daughter, Claudia, moved out of your home and into an apartment of her own?"

"Yes," Stuyvesant granted. "I guess all young people eventually get that feeling. Get out on their own. Leave the nest. Try their wings. Claudia's time came when she was eighteen." He smiled ruefully. It was a forced smile. "I guess these days: Old enough to vote, old enough to be on your own. In my day we couldn't vote until we were twenty-one, and a good deal more sensible. But Claudia wanted to leave. So I did what any father who loves his child would do. I made sure she'd have all the money she needed and I let her go. Worst decision of my life."

"While she lived away from home, did she continue to be treated by your doctor, the same doctor who had always cared for her?"

"Of course. Dr. Eaves. Wilfred Eaves. I wanted to make sure she stayed healthy," Stuyvesant explained.

"As far as you know, once she left your

home, did she visit him regularly?"

"Oh, yes," Stuyvesant replied. "I could tell from the bills. Eaves is good. But expensive."

"Did you ever discuss your daughter's condition with Dr. Eaves?"

"Several times."

"And, sir?"

"He always reported that she was in good health, excellent health."

"So that up until the time of her sudden death you had no hint that she had any health problems?"

"None!" Stuyvesant replied firmly, glancing at Kate.

"On the night in question, Mr. Stuyvesant, your daughter called your wife, complaining that she was ill. Your wife called Dr. Eaves, discovered he was out of town, and brought her to the Emergency Room at City Hospital."

"So I learned."

To defuse Scott's inevitable line of cross-examination, Hoskins asked, "Mr. Stuyvesant, why didn't your daughter call *you?*"

"She *did* call me. But I was out, entertaining a group of Japanese businessmen, at dinner at the Union Club. When I got home, I found a note from Nora, Mrs. Stuyvesant, saying she had gone down to visit Claudia. I thought that was nice. So I went off to bed."

"Then the first you knew of the tragedy

that befell your daughter was when your wife returned with the shocking news?"

"Yes."

"Now, Mr. Stuyvesant, if I may direct your attention to another topic," Hoskins resumed. "You sat here all day yesterday and heard the attorney for the respondent make a number of attempts to impute to your dead daughter such vices as living in an unmarried state with a young man, indulging in drugs; in fact he tried to give the impression that she was addicted to drugs."

Before Hoskins could put his question, Stuyvesant interrupted, "Yes, yes, I heard all those lies."

"Surely, sir, that must have been a most painful experience for any father, but especially for a man of such prominence in this city?"

"*Painful* is a small word for what I and my wife have been forced to suffer, not only during this hearing but ever since this whole outrage has been inflicted on us."

"Then, may I ask, sir, why you persist in seeing this matter through to its ultimate conclusion?"

"For the same reason we have endowed a new Emergency wing in City Hospital. Public duty, sir. If the pain we endure leads to cleansing from the ranks of medicine inefficient, dangerous doctors like Kate Forrester, then it is worth our added pain and suffering. In a word, I am here because I wish to spare other fathers and mothers the same tragedy that struck us. We suffer so that others may be spared."

Scott Van Cleve listened to Claude Stuyvesant. Kate Forrester listened. They cast glances at each other, each with the same thought: *Who wrote that nice speech for Stuyvesant, his public relations counsel?*

Scott had another and ironic thought as well: *My idea, he is using my idea about the new Emergency wing to justify his inquisition against Kate. Doesn't leave me much room to cross-examine.*

"Thank you, sir," Hoskins said. "That is all as far as I am concerned."

Under the table Scott patted Kate on the thigh to reassure her. He rose to approach Stuyvesant, who sat erect, braced to confront him.

"Sir, I assume you know that I tried to interview Dr. Eaves and to examine his case history on your daughter, but he refused."

"Of course he refused!" Stuyvesant responded. "Doctors' records are private and confidential."

"Did he refuse *before* talking to you, or only afterward?" Scott asked.

"I make no secret of it. Yes, he did call

me. I said by no means reveal those records. Bad enough my daughter's body lay there in the city morgue, naked, available to be seen by any perverted employee who wanted to stare at her. I couldn't stop that disgraceful intrusion on her privacy. But I'll be damned if I was going to let a ghoul like you prowl around in her life history trying to seize on some shred of information you can turn into more of your baseless slanders!" Stuyvesant was shouting now.

To avoid incurring the disfavor of the committee, Scott permitted the man to have his say, uninterrupted. But once Stuyvesant had finished, and in soft contrast to Stuyvesant's outburst, Scott asked, "Sir, did Dr. Eaves ever inform you that your daughter was pregnant?"

"There you go again, attacking my daughter's reputation!"

"That was not my finding but the medical examiner's," Scott pointed out respectfully.

Stuyvesant was speechless for only a moment, then managed to grumble, "Any young, inexperienced girl can make a mistake; that doesn't make her a tramp or a whore, which you are trying to do!"

"Mr. Stuyvesant, before your daughter moved out, did you ever have arguments with her about a boyfriend of whom you disapproved?"

460

"I didn't always like the young people she brought around. I don't deny it."

"Why, sir?"

"Young people these days — loud music, disgraceful attire . . ." Stuyvesant said.

"Drugs?" Scott asked. When Stuyvesant did not respond, Scott continued: "Promiscuous sex?" Stuyvesant's attitude was one of disdain, as if the question were beneath him to acknowledge.

Scott shifted his line of questioning. "Sir, you have heard the name Rick Thomas mentioned during this —"

Stuyvesant interrupted him. "My wife answered that before, young man! We do not know any Rick Thomas."

"If I assumed that your daughter left home because of your disapproval of Rick Thomas, would I be wrong?" Scott asked, to plant the thought in the minds of the committee.

"Wrong!" Stuyvesant declared vehemently. He turned to the chairman. "Mr. Mott, how long will this false and baseless questioning be allowed to continue?"

"Mr. Stuyvesant, if you'd like a break, a brief recess . . ." Mott offered.

"I don't need a recess!" Stuyvesant bellowed. "But neither do I see any purpose in going over and over the same lies. I do not know any Rick Thomas. My wife does not know any Rick Thomas. Now, either let's get on to something new or let's bring this to a halt!"

"Mr. Van Cleve?" Mott asked, referring the challenge to him.

"There *is* one subject on which Mr. Stuyvesant has not yet testified."

"In that event you may proceed," Mott was forced to permit.

"Mr. Stuyvesant, during your wife's testimony she was reminded of words she spoke when leaving the hospital. Namely, 'He'll blame me . . . he'll blame me.' "

"She denied ever saying that!" Stuyvesant shot back.

"Since there are at least two people who claim to have heard her, may we assume it is possible that she did say it?" Scott asked.

"You can assume any damn thing you want, young man!"

"If your wife *did* say that, who was the mysterious 'he' of whom she was so terrified?" Scott pursued.

"Since she never said it, I wouldn't know," Stuyvesant rebutted.

"Could that unidentified 'he' have been *you?* Did she live in such fear of your notorious temper that she was terrified?" Scott demanded.

"Mr. Mott," Stuyvesant thundered, "how

long are you going to allow this young man to subject me to these ridiculous intrusions into my family's private life?"

Kevin Cahill took the opportunity to come to Stuyvesant's rescue. "Counselor, there is a point, even in such an informal proceeding, when some questions become not only irrelevant and unnecessary but frivolous. Unless you can demonstrate some direct bearing of this line of questioning on the matter at issue, I order you to desist!"

"There is a distinct connection between this line of questioning and testimony that I intend to introduce at a later time."

"What 'distinct connection'?" Hoskins rose to challenge him.

"I will introduce a witness who will testify that Claudia Stuyvesant lived in such fear of her father that she gave false answers to Dr. Forrester's questions, misleading the doctor, thus making it impossible to arrive at an accurate diagnosis," Scott responded.

"Are we to be treated to another phantom witness like the fictitious Rick Thomas, whom we have yet to see?" Hoskins challenged. "Mr. Chairman, I urge that you rule out this entire line of testimony, as it is only the fictional invention of a very desperate young attorney."

"The chair is inclined to agree with you, Mr. Hoskins," Mott ruled. "Do you have any further questions of the witness, Mr. Van Cleve?"

"Not at the present time," Scott was forced to admit.

"And you, Mr. Hoskins?"

"No further questions of this witness, sir," Hoskins replied, then continued: "The Board of Professional Medical Conduct, having established the facts in this matter, and having presented considerable evidence of Dr. Forrester's negligent and disastrous handling of the case of Claudia Stuyvesant, thereby resulting in her death, we rest. And now, we trust that Mr. Van Cleve will respond with facts instead of charges. With credible witnesses instead of hints and innuendos. I cannot contain my curiosity as to the mystery witness to whom he alludes."

"Mr. Van Cleve?" Chairman Mott asked.

"I will need time to assemble my witnesses. May we resume the day after tomorrow?"

"We stand adjourned until then!" Mott rapped his gavel.

Scott Van Cleve went directly from the hearing room to the public phone booth at the end of the corridor. He inserted a coin, dialed the number on the top of the yellow sheet on which he had prepared the questions he intended to ask Rick Thomas. He heard three rings, four, five, but no answer. He began to experience a queasy feeling until finally, on the sixth ring, he heard the voice that allowed him to relax.

"Yeah?" came the voice of Rick Thomas.

"Rick? Scott Van Cleve."

"Oh, yeah. Hi!" Rick replied.

Scott tried to evaluate Rick's condition from his manner of speech. He did not sound spaced out. If anything, he sounded more alert than the day they had met.

"Rick, day after tomorrow will probably be the day. So you and I better spend tomorrow together. To go over what I will ask and what you will respond. And also some questions the other attorney will likely ask. Never hurts to know what to expect."

"Right. Never hurts," Rick agreed readily.

"I'll pick you up at ten tomorrow. Okay?"

"You got it, man!" Rick agreed with enthusiasm.

"Oh, one thing I want you to think about before tomorrow," Scott said. "Were there any times when Claudia said to you that she was so afraid of her father that she would lie rather than let him find out the truth?"

"*Any* times? *Every* time! She lived in fear of that old bastard," Rick replied.

"That's the idea. But when you get on the stand, don't use that particular language," Scott cautioned.

"I hear you, man," Rick agreed.

"See you tomorrow. At ten."

"Tomorrow at ten," Rick agreed, then asked, "Oh, by the way, I don't like to bring this up, but I'm tapped out again."

"I understand," Scott said. "I won't come empty-handed."

Chapter Thirty-two

It was twenty past one in the morning. Scott Van Cleve had exhausted himself, first preparing Kate for her testimony, then, after he had put her into a cab and sent her home, he had spent the next few hours mapping the precise order of his two crucial witnesses, framing his questions and his strategy for maximum impact on the committee. The presentation of a lawyer's case was as much a theatrical production as a legal one.

Which would prove more dramatic and effective? he pondered. Kate's testimony first, followed by the surprise appearance of Rick Thomas? Or Rick Thomas first, to startle Hoskins, Stuyvesant, and Mott, as well as convince the committee that he had been telling them the truth and thus predispose them more favorably to Kate's testimony?

There was no predicting how Claude Stuyvesant might react when confronted by the young man who had lived with his daughter, been her lover, caused her pregnancy, and had, in a sense, been the cause of her death. It was not impossible, Scott had to admit, that physical violence might erupt between the two men. He had to be prepared for all eventualities.

He was still debating the most effective way to present his case as he started down Charles Street. He decided to allow his strategy to depend on the condition in which he found Rick Thomas.

He arrived at Number 97. He stepped into the small, dark entryway. He scanned the bellboard until he found LENGEL, M. As agreed with Rick, he rang three short rings, pause, then one long one. He awaited the buzzer that would release the door and admit him. There was no response.

Rick was probably asleep, Scott assumed. He repeated the signal. Three short rings, pause, then one long. Again, no response. Scott began to be concerned. He repeated the signal one more time. Still no response. Scott Van Cleve could feel a light sweat breaking out on his brow.

He rang once more, this time frantically. Still no response. Sweat was coming more freely now. He rang again, deliberately, short rings, one, two, three, pause, then one long ring, so long that his finger was still on the button when the buzzer finally sounded. But it was so brief a response that he might have missed the opportunity had he not seized it at once. He raced quickly up a staircase dark enough to have benefited from some artificial light even in daytime.

He became aware of someone leaning over the bannister of the fourth-floor landing He looked up to find a young woman, just pulling on a shabby kimono. She appeared to have been suddenly awakened from deep sleep. Her hair was unruly, her eyes blinking, curious, and noticeably suspicious.

"Yeah?" she challenged.

"I'm looking for Apartment Four-C. Lengel," Scott said.

"What about?" the woman asked.

By now Scott was close enough to judge her to be in her early twenties. Her face was slightly puffy from either drink or drugs, he concluded. Otherwise, he decided, she might have been a pretty woman. He had reached the landing. They were face-to-face. She stood with her back to the partly opened door, guarding it.

"I'm looking for Marty Lengel," Scott said.

"What about?"

"Rick Thomas is crashing with him for a few days," Scott said.

"There's no 'him,' " the young woman said. "*I* am Marty Lengel."

Scott was taken aback; he had assumed Marty was a man's name.

"So Rick's bunking in with you," Scott realized. "I have a meeting with him at ten. If I'm a little early, it's because I'm eager to get on with it."

"So you have a meeting with him," Marty Lengel said. "Well, 'had' is more like it."

"I talked with him only yesterday afternoon. We arranged to meet this morning. He's set to testify tomorrow," Scott insisted.

"He's not here," Marty Lengel said.

"He must be here," Scott replied. "This is a very important matter. A doctor's career depends on it!"

"Sorry, he's not here," she repeated, moving to block Scott's entrance to her door.

"Look, Ms. Lengel, I know how it is with some witnesses. Comes time to go to court, they get stage fright. Well, there's nothing to be afraid of. And I want to tell him that."

She did not yield. Scott feinted to his right, causing her to move to cut him off, then he swiftly reversed to his left and almost made it through the door, barely colliding with her as she protested, "I told you, he's not here!"

He was past her and into the small room. It was dark, the shade down. He saw a rumpled bed in one corner. There was a small kitchenette, the sink piled with soiled dishes. A small wooden table, bare, was surrounded by three plain straight-back chairs, no two of which matched. He became aware of an odor that hinted that marijuana had been smoked here very recently.

He looked about. There was no sign of Rick Thomas. Resentful at his forcible intrusion, she gloated. "I told you, he isn't here."

"Do you realize what this means to my case? To a doctor's career, her life?"

"Look, Mister, don't bug me. Ain't my fault. In fact, he left owing me fifty-five dollars. Idiot that I am," she complained. "Never should have taken him in. But I felt sorry for him. Especially after Claudia and all."

"Do you have any idea where he went?" Scott asked.

She shook her head, at the same time trying to brush back her black hair into some semblance of order.

"He didn't say anything, didn't explain?"

"I wasn't even here," she said. "Look, I can't waste time arguing with you. I've got to get some sleep."

"Just give me a few minutes, it's important."

She surrendered with a gesture of hopelessness. "Okay, sit down."

He preferred to remain standing.

"Did Rick say anything the last time you spoke to him?"

"Not about leaving, no."

"Did he leave any message? Give you any

clue at all that he was leaving?"

"None," she replied. "All I know . . ." she started to say, but then thought better of it and became silent.

"All you know . . ." Scott insisted, "is all I want to know."

"You're the one called yesterday afternoon. That was you, wasn't it?"

"Yes."

"I heard him say he was going to meet you."

"Right."

"Then later, just before seven o'clock, he gets another call," Marty Lengel said. "Seems there was this man he knew. . . . Look, I can't get into trouble telling you this, can I? With the law, I mean?"

"I'm a lawyer. Whatever you tell me will be strictly confidential. I give you my word."

She weighed his assurance, then decided to cooperate. "He said this guy called with the promise of some very good stuff."

"Stuff?"

"Coke. But real pure," she said. "Myself I don't do coke. Mexican Gold is more my bag. But to Rick coke was like a ring in a bull's nose. You could lead him anywhere with it. So this guy calls and promises him this great coke."

"And he went for it," Scott concluded.

"Evidently. Went for it. And never came

back," Marty Lengel said. "Last I saw of him was when I went to work. I wait tables all night in this little Italian place on Fourth Street."

"Did he say anything at all that might give you a hint as to *where* he went?"

"No. Just went, that's all," she said.

"Have you any idea who the man was who called him?"

"He mentioned a name, but I didn't pay attention," she said. "I got my own troubles."

Scott nodded grimly. Half his defense, the most crucial half, had been shot out from under him. He was not only left with one witness, his own professional credibility hung in the balance. When Hoskins would challenge him to produce Rick Thomas, it would certainly appear that he had indeed invented a fictitious witness. He regretted now ever having mentioned the name Rick Thomas or even alluding to Claudia Stuyvesant's drug use.

"And he said nothing else," Scott concluded the disastrous conversation.

"Nothing," Marty Lengel confirmed, her attitude indicating she was anxious he leave so that she could go back to sleep.

He was at the landing, about to start down, when her door opened again.

"Oh, yeah, he did say one thing . . ." she began.

"Yes? What?"

"Something about getting his things back," she said. "I didn't pay too much attention."

"Getting his things back . . ." Scott considered. "The things he lost when they cleaned out Claudia's place?"

"He didn't have any other things that I know of."

"Did you know Claudia?" Scott asked.

"Sort of."

"Just sort of?" Scott pursued.

"Maybe more than sort of. Why? What are you getting at?" She was defensive again, on guard.

"Did she do drugs?" Scott asked.

"Depends."

"Depends on what?"

"There's some who do drugs and some who *really* do drugs. I mean, like Rick, into drugs all the way," Marty Lengel said.

"And Claudia?" Scott asked.

"You must be new to this scene," she observed. "Otherwise you'd know, if one of them is really into drugs, the other one is too. That's the way it goes down here."

"Tell me, Ms. Lengel, if you could do something important, help a young woman doctor defend herself against Claude Stuyvesant, save

474

her career, would you be willing to testify to what you just told me?"

"Uh-uh," she said in refusal, shaking her head stolidly. "I ain't going up against the law, not me."

"This hasn't to do with the law. It's before a committee and it's a private hearing."

"Sorry," she said. "Look, I've got to get my sleep."

"Yes, of course," Scott said. "But if you change your mind, here's my card. But I have to know in twenty-four hours."

"I can tell you now. The answer is no. I'm sorry I got mixed up with either of them. Who needs a man like Claude Stuyvesant breathing down your neck?"

"If Rick comes back —" Scott started to suggest.

"He won't," she interrupted him.

"How can you be sure?"

"I didn't like the sound of that call from the beginning. If someone wanted to get rid of Rick, the easiest way would be to . . ."

"To promise him all the pure coke he wanted," Scott concluded.

"Worse," Marty Lengel explained, "to *give* him all the pure coke he wanted. He'd go any-where, do anything for that. And one day soon end up dumped at the Emergency entrance to some hospital. In a coma. Or worse, dead of an overdose."

"Ms. Lengel, do you think it possible that Claude Stuyvesant had something to do with his disappearance?"

"Why do you ask?"

"It was Stuyvesant's man who appeared with a legal document at Claudia's place. Cleaned it out. Took Rick's things too."

"Why would Stuyvesant do that?" the young woman asked.

"To conceal from the media any of her personal possessions that could prove embarrassing," Scott suggested. "If the man who called promised to return Rick's things — there's a connection."

Though it was clear to Scott what had happened, it was even more clear that he had only one important witness left: Kate.

But how to tell her?

Her first question when they met was, "How did it go with Rick?"

Very simply, in few words, as undramatically as he could, he told her so as not to alarm her in the same way he himself had been shaken by the news.

She was stunned, breathless. "What . . . what does that do — I mean, how does it affect . . . Oh, Scott!"

She began to tremble. He put his arms around her to lend her the support and courage she needed in face of this shocking blow.

"And he was so bent on avenging himself on Stuyvesant," Scott said.

"When you've seen as many addicts as I have," Kate said, "you know that the craving can make them forgo revenge, jobs, family, anything."

"It seems Stuyvesant knows that," Scott replied.

"Rick was the strongest part of our defense," Kate said.

"Not anymore, not anymore," Scott replied, desperately trying to assess his diminished options.

Chapter Thirty-three

As he had planned, when the session opened the next morning, Scott introduced as his first witness Nurse Adelaide Cronin. Once she was sworn, Scott asked the questions that established her professional training and background and her function at City Hospital. She had been an experienced Emergency Service nurse for eleven years. She was on her regular tour of duty on that Saturday night. He then proceeded to lead her through the events of that night, asking those questions that would evoke answers in which Cronin established that Mrs. Stuyvesant was indeed a hindrance in the examining room. That based on her experience, Cronin found Kate's actions were in accord with usual practice in the Emergency Service. That when Claudia suffered her collapse, Kate and Briscoe performed all the various functions, administered the proper medications and modalities that she had seen applied in similar situations in the past by other doctors.

When Scott had finished and turned Cronin over to Hoskins for cross-examination, instead of choosing to attack her, the prosecutor said merely, "No questions."

Scott realized the prosecutor was saving his attack for Kate and had no intention of giving any hint of what that would be.

After a similar experience with Nurse Beathard, when, once again, Hoskins refused the opportunity to cross-examine, Scott was prepared to present his final witness. For the benefit of the stenotypist he announced, "I call Dr. Katherine Forrester."

"What?" Hoskins remarked. "Still no surprise witness? I thought that at long last our curiosity would be rewarded." Though phrased as an aside, it was loud enough for all to hear.

Once Kate had been sworn in, Scott's first questions concerned her early life on the family farm, her education, her medical school record, her experience as an intern, then as a resident. He aimed to present her as an intelligent, stable, well-educated, well-trained physician worthy of the committee's confidence and support. He proceeded to lead her through some of the cases she had treated on the night in question.

He came finally to the case of Claudia Stuyvesant. Slowly, with each question evoking more detail, Scott guided Kate through her first meeting with the patient. The vital signs Cronin found and that Kate confirmed.

Taking Claudia's history. Detecting insufficient signs and symptoms to produce a differential diagnosis, since Claudia Stuyvesant's symptoms were also typical of dozens of different illnesses.

As he had planned, Scott now arrived at the questions most pertinent to Claudia's eventual death.

"Dr. Forrester, did you make any inquiries of the patient concerning her private life, and if so, why?"

"With a young woman her age, it was important to know if she had been sexually active, and if so, had she missed any periods. The answers, the truthful answers to those questions, could play a large part in arriving at a definitive diagnosis," Kate explained.

"And what did the patient reply?" Scott asked.

"As I recorded on her chart, in all cases her answer was negative," Kate replied. "If the committee has copies of the chart, they will find my notes."

Both Dr. Ward and Dr. Truscott nodded, indicating they were familiar with the chart.

"Now, Doctor," Scott continued, "are there any facts about the patient and your observations that are *not* in that history?"

Hoskins raised his hand to object. "Mr. Cahill, he is leading his witness."

Cahill ruled, "The witness may answer."

"I did not think my suspicions belonged in the patient's history," Kate said.

"Suspicions? About what, Doctor?" Scott asked.

"I suspected the patient was afraid of her mother, who was rather tense and excitable. And therefore might not be telling me the truth."

"If her mother had not been there, or had been less intimidating, and you had received truthful answers, would you have been able to reach a correct diagnosis in time to intervene?"

Hoskins shot to his feet more swiftly than one would expect from a man of his bulk. "Mr. Cahill, now he is not only leading the witness, he is damn well testifying for her!"

"Mr. Van Cleve, confine yourself to questions. Let your witness testify," the administrative officer ruled.

Scott nodded in acknowledgment of the rebuke. "Sorry, sir. He turned to Kate. "Doctor?"

"Sexual activity, missed periods — all would have been crucial facts in arriving at a correct diagnosis. For that reason I feel the presence of her mother had a critical effect on —"

Claude Stuyvesant rose to his full height to

intervene. "Mr. Chairman, I object to you permitting this woman, who completely mishandled my daughter's case, who caused her death, to now put the blame on my wife! I will not stand for it!"

"Mr. Stuyvesant," Mott replied in as formal a tone as he could, in view of their relationship, "Dr. Forrester is entitled to present her defense. After which, it will be up to this committee to weigh her testimony and determine if she is worthy of belief."

Since Mott had thus predisposed the committee to rejecting Kate's version, Stuyvesant appeared mollified, though he continued to glare at Kate.

Quickly Scott led Kate through the events of that night. Taking Claudia's blood sample. Sending it off to the lab. Tending other patients until the results came back. When the lab findings were not conclusive, Kate had repeated the procedure, taking second blood samples.

He now arrived at testimony that he considered crucial as he asked, "Dr. Forrester, did you at any time decide to send for a second opinion?"

"Acting on my suspicions that the patient might be pregnant, I had performed a pelvic examination. But since an ectopic pregnancy does not present in the same way as a normal pregnancy, my findings were not conclusive. So I sent for Dr. Briscoe. Dr. Eric Briscoe."

"And what did he do?"

"Repeated the examination. With the same result."

"And what did he suggest?"

"Repeat the labs and await the results," Kate replied. "That additional set of results proved somewhat different but no more revealing."

"Doctor, did there come a time when, despite the patient's denial that she had been sexually active, you decided to perform an immediate pregnancy test?"

"Yes. Suspicious of her answers, I decided to find out for myself. To save time, I catheterized her to obtain a urine sample."

"Did anyone object to that?"

"Her mother. When she realized what I was doing, she was outraged."

"Doctor, exactly what did you do?"

"I carried out the hospital's regular three-stage urine pregnancy test."

"And the result?"

"Negative," Kate was forced to admit.

"In view of the medical examiner's later findings, how do you account for that?"

"No medical test is one hundred percent perfect."

"Doctor, when was the first time either you

or Dr. Briscoe had any warning of how serious the patient's condition had become?"

"Briscoe was about to go into her stomach cavity to see if there was occult internal bleeding when suddenly Cronin reported the patient had no pulse. We immediately commenced CPR, rushed her to the trauma room, and worked on her with all means available. Medication, infusions of blood, surgical intervention. She eventually died, due to EMD — electromechanical dissociation. As the medical members of the committe know, that is a condition in which the heart keeps pumping reflexively, but due to severe internal hemorrhages having drained the blood from the cardiovascular system into the stomach, there is no blood left for the heart to pump. And the patient dies."

"Doctor, in the presence of two of your peers, I ask you now, in your review of the chart, in your days and weeks of reliving this tragic case, have you had any second thoughts? Anything you would have done differently?" Scott asked, presenting a question he had alerted Kate that he would ask.

He was startled to hear her respond, "Second thoughts, no. But guilt? Yes."

Not only Stuyvesant but Hoskins and all three members of the committee reacted with surprise. Truscott interrupted taking his meticulous notes. Gladys Ward stared at Kate for a long moment before making her own note.

In face of such a startling admission, Scott felt forced to ask, "Why guilt, Doctor?"

"I hope I never reach a time in my practice of medicine when I will lose a nineteen-year-old patient and not feel a twinge of guilt, not only on my own behalf but on behalf of my profession. That, despite all our advances, such untimely deaths do occur."

Scott breathed only slightly more easily before he surrendered Kate Forrester to Prosecutor Hoskins for cross-examination.

Hoskins picked up his sheaf of notes, approached the witness, smiled paternally. "Doctor, I want you to know that I hold all young doctors in great esteem. The training you endure. The hours you serve. The sacrifices you make."

Silently Scott observed, *The bastard is trying to soften her up. I hope she doesn't fall for it.*

"Now," Hoskins continued, "let us see if we can help you solve the mystery of what happened that eventful night in E.R. Room C." As if reminded by a glance at his notes, he asked, "Do I understand that you were in complete charge of the Emergency Service that night?"

"Yes, sir," Kate replied. "Dr. Diaz, who

was also scheduled, came down with the flu. There was no immediate replacement."

"And so you were in sole charge?"

"Yes."

"Interesting," Hoskins remarked, not that it was, but he was trying to divert Kate's concentration to the possible significance of his remark, thus causing her to be less guarded in her other responses. "Now, you've described the variety of cases you handled that night and the generally turbulent atmosphere. Would you say that night was more hectic than an average night in Emergency?"

"It was usual, in a place where *every* night is *unusual*," Kate replied.

Hoskins smiled. "Nicely put, Doctor. May I assume that explains why you delayed for so long seeing the patient Claudia Stuyvesant?"

"You assume wrong, sir!" Kate shot back. "I did not 'delay'!"

Scott tried to flash a signal with his eyes, *Stay cool. Don't let him rile you and trap you into some admission.*

"Sorry," Hoskins pretended to apologize. "Then what was the reason it took so long for you to see her?"

"Other, more emergent cases," Kate replied.

"Doctor, is it true that even after you finally

made the time to examine Claudia Stuyvesant, you really didn't?" Hoskins asked.

"I performed a complete physical," Kate protested.

"Doctor, may I refresh your recollection? Based on testimony from a previous witness, you had no sooner started to question her than you left her to go care for another patient. Isn't that true?"

"There was another case, one with alarming symptoms, that called me away," Kate explained.

"Alarming symptoms?" Hoskins echoed.

"He had severe pain just below the sternum, was sweating profusely, and was in agony," Kate replied. "Those symptoms are classic for cardiac cases. The nurse thought he might be in immediate danger. Such a case takes precedence over all others."

"So you left Claudia Stuyvesant to attend this other 'more emergent' case. May I ask, what did you find?"

"He turned out to be passing a gallstone, among the most painful of experiences," Kate said.

"And how did you dispose of that case, Doctor?"

"Sent him up to surgery and let them determine whether surgical intervention was indicated," Kate said.

"Do you happen to know the final outcome of that case, Doctor?" Hoskins asked.

"Once the case went up to surgery, I had no further contact with the patient. That's one of the unfortunate aspects of serving in Emergency. You see patients, treat them, pass them on or send them home, and you never see them again. You rarely know the final outcome."

"Then let me inform you of what did happen to that patient. He was examined in surgery. It was decided not to operate until his situation clarified. And once he had slept off the one hundred milligrams of Demerol you had prescribed, he was sent home the next morning," Hoskins pointed out, brandishing a sheaf of records at Kate.

Distressing as that gesture might have been to Kate Forrester, it was Hoskins's last statement that was even more disturbing to Scott Van Cleve. For it revealed how meticulously and in what depth the prosecutor had researched every detail, not only of the Stuyvesant case but of all the other cases Kate had dealt with that night.

"So that, to sum up, Doctor," Hoskins resumed, "a case that you thought deserved precedence over Claudia Stuyvesant was dismissed the next morning, while Claudia Stuyvesant, who had to wait on your convenience, was dead by the next morning."

"Mr. Mott, I object!" Scott shouted. "I object vigorously to such an unwarranted conclusion! And I ask that you put the question to both doctors on this committee as to what they would have done under the circumstances!"

Unsure of what his fellow committee members might respond, Mott hesitated. But Kevin Cahill came to his rescue.

"Mr. Chairman, there is no need to submit such a question to the committee. I am sure their response will be reflected in their final opinion. Mr. Van Cleve's request must be denied."

"So ruled," Mott was relieved to agree. "Continue, Mr. Hoskins."

"Doctor, I show you now a photocopy of the chart of that gallbladder patient and ask you to identify the handwriting of the first entries." Hoskins held out a thin sheaf of papers.

Kate studied the entries and replied, "That is my handwriting.

"So that we can conclude that before you ever went back to do an examination on Claudia Stuyvesant, you took the time to write out all these entries?" Hoskins asked.

"Wrong, sir. I had no time to do that. We had enough on the history form concerning signs, symptoms, for me to make these entries when I had the time," Kate corrected.

"Aha!" Hoskins said, as if making a discovery. "So that there is often a lapse of time between treating a patient and writing up the chart?"

"Sometimes there is, sometimes there isn't. Depends on the number and frequency of cases," Kate said.

"Doctor, is there ever a time when you completely forget to write up a chart?"

"No," Kate responded at once.

"Then it seems we have a discrepancy between your testimony and what actually happened that night," Hoskins said.

Scott was half out of his chair, then forced himself to slide back down. He studied Kate's face to see what effect that strange statement had on her.

Kate Forrester pondered Hoskins's charge, urgently trying to recall if she could possibly have treated a case that night and not written up a chart. *Impossible,* she decided. *I write them all up. All.*

"I have no idea what you're referring to," she replied.

"Perhaps that will become clear a bit later on," Hoskins remarked, feeling he had created sufficient cause for concern to trouble both the witness and her attorney. "Now, when you finally found it convenient to return to Claudia Stuyvesant, what did you find?"

Resentful of Hoskins's use of the word *convenient,* Kate decided not to take the bait but answered straightforwardly, "As I testified, Nurse Cronin had already elicited her symptoms — nausea, vomiting, diarrhea — taken her vital signs, and decided she was likely dehydrated, so she had started the patient on an I.V."

"Did you approve of that?"

"Of course," Kate replied.

"Then what did you do, Doctor?"

"To get a total picture of the patient, I repeated vital signs. Began to take her history. That often tells us more than simply a recitation of symptoms."

"And did the patient respond to your questions?" Hoskins asked.

"Yes. But, unfortunately not truthfully. She denied sexual activity, missed periods, of which there likely had been at least one, based on the medical examiner's report."

Midway through Kate's responses, Hoskins began to nod, as if she were replying in exactly the way he hoped.

"Yes, yes, Doctor, I know. We are now about to witness the spectacle of transferring responsibility for the patient's death from the doctor to her mother."

Scott came to his feet, calling, "Mr. Chairman, I object!"

Before there could be a ruling, Hoskins replied, "Mr. Chairman, I withdraw the remark. But before we leave that question, may I ask Dr. Forrester another question? Doctor, did there come a time when Mrs. Stuyvesant *did* leave Room C?"

"At one point she went out to make a phone call from her limousine," Kate replied.

"Since you had the patient alone, and free of the influence of her mother, did you take the opportunity to ask her those highly personal questions?"

"Yes, yes, I did."

"And what did she answer?" Hoskins asked.

"She . . . she continued to maintain she had not been sexually active, had not missed any periods," Kate was forced to admit, adding, "I don't think she realized the danger of her denials."

"So that the presence of Mrs. Stuyvesant was not the crucial factor you have been trying to make it out to be, was it?"

"I think Claudia was terribly afraid that if she told me the truth, somehow her mother would find out. It struck me at the time that for a nineteen-year-old, who was trying to be liberated and free of parental domination, she was still very immature and frightened."

"Dr. Forrester, have you now broadened your field of expertise to include psychiatry as well?" Hoskins taunted.

"It was an observation made as a physician," Kate replied.

"Doctor, a man like me doesn't undertake such a grave proceeding asking for the revocation of a doctor's license without making sure in his own mind that he is justified. So I have long pondered the effect of Claudia Stuyvesant's untrue answers on the outcome of this case. In the end I had to ask myself, as I ask you now, let us suppose that Claudia had said, 'Yes, Doctor, I *have* been sexually active. Yes, I *have* missed my period,' what would you have done differently?"

"I would have done a pregnancy test sooner," Kate replied.

"And if you had?" Hoskins demanded. "Then what?"

Kate realized that Hoskins had led her into a trap from which she had no logical escape.

"Doctor, what leads you to believe that if you had done that test sooner, you would have come up with a different result?" Hoskins hammered away.

"I . . . I don't know . . ." Kate was forced to admit.

"Or are you telling this committee that if you had done the test an hour or two sooner, you would have been less stressed and thus more capable of doing it correctly?" Hoskins demanded.

"I was perfectly capable and in control when I performed that test!" Kate protested.

"Then how could the result have been different?" Hoskins insisted.

"I told you, I don't know," Kate was forced to admit.

He's goading her and she's taking the bait, Scott observed. He knew he had to intervene.

"Mr. Mott, my client has been on the stand for several hours. I ask for a short recess."

Hoskins greeted Scott's request with a slight smile, gratified that his opponent had acknowledged the effectiveness of his cross-examination. Confident, Hoskins decided it was a time to appear gracious. "Mr. Chairman, I have no objection. This witness obviously needs a break. A recess, I mean," As he turned away, he was rewarded by an approving nod from Claude Stuyvesant.

Mott had picked up his gavel to declare a recess when Dr. Ward raised her hand.

"Yes, Doctor?" Mott asked.

"Before we recess, may I have an opportunity to cross-examine the witness?"

At once Scott was on his feet. "Mr. Chairman, I object! A member of the committee who will later be called on to judge the respondent should not be permitted to act as prosecutor."

Mott turned to his administrative adviser for a ruling, his look inviting one that would permit him to overrule Scott's objection.

Kevin Cahill took what he considered a proper pause before ruling, "Mr. Van Cleve raises what, at first blush, appears to be an interesting procedural question. Which unfortunately is based on the misuse of one single word by Dr. Ward. I am sure she did not mean 'cross-examine' in the prosecutorial sense. But rather she meant to say 'ask' or 'examine,' and she actually meant that only in the pursuit of the truth, which is after all, why we are all here. Am I right, Dr. Ward?"

Gladys Ward responded with a precise nod of her nicely featured head.

"Mr. Mott, you may allow the doctor to continue," Cahill ruled.

"Dr. Forrester," Gladys Ward began, "let us suppose that at the outset you had received honest responses from the patient. That you had done that urine pregnancy test sooner. And the result had come up negative. Knowing the percentage of fallibility of such tests, why were you content to accept that result as final?"

"I wasn't. I ordered a sonogram," Kate replied.

495

"Then why is there no reference to the result in the patient's chart?" Gladys Ward demanded.

"Because no sonogram was ever done."

"Good God, why not?"

"Radiology informed me that sonograms for ectopic pregnancies are also rather fallible and that therefore they must be performed by an expert. That only Dr. Gladwin is authorized to do them. And she would not be on duty until the next morning. Since no sonogram was performed, I made no entry on the chart."

Satisfied as Ward appeared with Kate's explanation, she was not yet done. "Dr. Forrester, since you suspected the patient's answers from the outset, which led you to do the pregnancy test, it seems clear to me that the presence of Mrs. Stuyvesant did not actually affect, change, or alter the manner in which you treated this case."

Kate tried to reply, but her words came haltingly, "If I had not had to contend with her, things might have been different."

"Tell me, Doctor, in your experience as an intern and a resident, have you actually ever treated or assisted at a case involving an ectopic pregnancy?"

"Ectopics are actually unusual, although they are becoming less so in these times —" Kate began, but Ward interrupted.

"Doctor, have you or have you not ever treated such a case?"

"No, no, I have not," Kate was forced to admit.

"Then you were going purely on book and classroom knowledge," Ward concluded.

"Yes. But that same night I diagnosed and treated a case of Addisonian crisis without any previous firsthand experience," said Kate, fighting back.

Ward did not respond but merely made a note on her pad. From her crisp attitude and severe frown, both Kate and Scott assumed that note was not favorable and would figure importantly in Ward's final decision.

Mott banged his gavel. "Five-minute recess!"

As Kate rose from the witness chair, she found Claude Stuyvesant on his feet glaring at her with the glint of victory in his steel-gray eyes.

Chapter Thirty-four

Scott and Kate huddled outside the hearing room for a few last words of advice and caution, attorney to client.

"Remember what I said —" he began.

But Kate interrupted, "I know! Don't fight back! But I can't let Hoskins or Ward get away with snide remarks and innuendos! And nobody can stop me!"

"Now, Kate, hold on. I'm on *your* side. I'm *your* lawyer," Scott replied to calm her down. He reached for her hand. She pulled away. "Kate?" he asked softly. "Frightened?"

"Scared stiff," she admitted in a whisper, tears trembling on her eyelids. "Especially after Ward's attack."

"It's not going to get any easier. Hoskins has tasted blood. He's basking in Stuyvesant's approval. He's really going to dig in now. Just stick to the truth. It's the only chance we have."

She nodded. With a finger under her chin he lifted her face. He wiped the tears away from her eyes before they could start to flow. Then he kissed her on the lips. She drew back, stared up into his eyes as if to ask, *Did that mean what I thought?* His eyes responded, *Yes, yes it did.*

"Now, go in there and face them," he said.

Hoskins led Kate through the steps of the treatment of Claudia Stuyvesant, referring continually to the patient's chart. Try as he did, he failed to catch her in any slips of memory that would cause her testimony to differ from what she had done that night.

Hoskins then opened a new line of examination. "Doctor, how much time elapsed between the time of the events and the time you made your notes on Claudia Stuyvesant's chart?"

"I entered all orders for her treatment in the order book at once. And all observations about her condition, plan of treatment, and so forth in her chart whenever I could," Kate responded.

"Doctor, do not hospital rules require the doctor to make notes in the patient's chart each time you see her?"

"Yes."

"Yet now you tell this committee that you did it 'whenever you could,' " Hoskins taunted.

"In Emergency you do everything 'whenever' you can. There never seems enough time. But somehow it all gets done."

"So is it possible that during that passage of time a doctor would have the opportunity to reconsider what she did and then make her notes on the chart — shall we say — so they fit with what eventually happened?"

"If that's a comment, I resent it!" Kate shot back. "If it's a question, I will answer it!"

Hoskins smiled. "Let's consider it a bit of both."

"Your suggestion that I wrote up that chart to justify what I did is a lie!"

All three members of the committee stared at her in reproval. Mott was about to rebuke her, but she continued: "Everything I wrote in the chart conforms to what I observed, what I did, and why I did it."

"So that what I hold here in my hand is a copy of the complete and accurate record of the case of Claudia Stuyvesant from the time you first saw her until her disastrous and untimely end?"

"Yes," Kate replied.

"I find here a note that at one time the patient became so restless that she pulled the I.V. out of her arm," Hoskins remarked. "Did that actually happen, Doctor?"

"Yes," Kate admitted. "It sometimes happens with restless patients. Especially patients on drugs, who tend at times to become overactive."

Before Stuyvesant could interrupt the cross-examination, for Hoskins had planned it carefully and it was working well, the prosecutor remarked quickly, "Back to making unproved charges against the patient, are we? Now, if we may get on with it, what happened when the patient pulled out that I.V.?"

"I went to see her at once. I reinserted the I.V. And I taped it securely."

"And that was it? The entire episode?" Hoskins asked.

"Yes!" Kate affirmed.

Hoskins pretended to study the chart again. Without looking up at Kate, he asked, "Tell me, Doctor, do you recall how it came to your attention that the patient had pulled the I.V. out of her arm?"

"As I remember, her mother told me."

"And where were you at the time?"

"Where was I? . . ." Kate tried to recall. When the moment came clear in her memory, she realized that the truthful response would sound extremely incriminating. Nevertheless she replied, "I was at the nurses' station."

"Doing what, may I ask?" Hoskins pursued.

"I had been called to the telephone."

"By the lab? By X ray? By ICU about that cardiac patient you had referred?" Hoskins pounded away.

"It turned out to be a personal call," Kate admitted.

"In all that turmoil, doing the work of two doctors, so busy that you could barely grant a very sick Claudia Stuyvesant a few moments of your precious time, you still found time to indulge in a personal phone call?" Hoskins asked, his drooping jowls fairly trembling in simulated indignation.

Exerting every effort to retain control, Kate replied, "I was summoned to the phone by a nurse, who said it was an emergency call. When I discovered it was a personal call, I ended it at once."

"To whom were you speaking, may I ask?" Hoskins continued.

"A man I know," Kate admitted.

"You must have a very intimate relationship with this man for him to feel free to call you at the hospital at one o'clock in the morning," Hoskins remarked.

Scott was on his feet at once. "Mr. Chairman, snide innuendos are not part of proper cross-examination. Especially when they have no relevance to the issue being tried here!"

"Sorry, Counselor, but it seemed a proper inference in context. However, I withdraw the remark. Doctor, do you recall saying to this man something to the effect 'I just hope I can make it till six o'clock without cracking up'?"

Those words came back to Kate with a startling rush. She found herself unable to answer at once, but finally admitted:

"Yes, yes, I remember saying something like that."

Before Hoskins could follow up, Dr. Ward held up her forefinger to interrupt. The prosecutor yielded to her.

"Dr. Forrester," Ward asked, "did you actually feel that you were in danger of cracking up?"

"It was just a form of expression," Kate said, trying to explain. "I was tired. I'd been on continuous duty for many hours by that time."

"All doctors have been through those long, tough stretches as interns and residents. But if you really thought you were on the verge of cracking up, how could you justify continuing to treat patients?"

"I said, it was only a form of expression, an unfortunate one, as it turns out," Kate explained. "But to reply to your question, if I had felt I was incapable of rendering good medical care, I would have asked to be relieved."

While Dr. Ward made another note on her pad, Hoskins seized the opportunity provided by her question.

"Dr. Forrester, in your opinion, would you

say that if a doctor received a severe blow to the head, it might incapacitate her?"

"Depending on how severe, it might," Kate granted, puzzled by the purpose of his question.

"Suppose it *were* severe, might that render a doctor 'incapable of delivering good medical care'?"

Scott called out to object. "Mr. Chairman, such a hypothetical a question has no relevance to this hearing."

"Mr. Hoskins?" Mott demanded.

"I am sure Dr. Forrester will soon provide me with its relevance." He turned back to Kate. "Doctor, isn't it a fact that you engaged in a physical altercation with the outraged father of a patient? Which altercation resulted in you suffering a severe blow to the head?"

"Oh, that — that's easily explained," Kate said.

"Then, Doctor, please *do* explain it," Hoskins urged sarcastically.

"A mother had brought in a child who was almost comatose. I suspected child abuse and decided to keep the child in the hospital. The father appeared determined to take the child back, obviously to conceal his abuse. I refused to surrender her. He attacked me. In the struggle he hurled me against the wall. Yes, I did suffer a blow to the head."

504

"A 'severe' blow, Doctor?" Hoskins asked.

"I wouldn't characterize it beyond saying that it hurt."

"Severe enough to cause a concussion?" Hoskins pursued.

"No," Kate responded.

"Severe enough to cause dizziness?"

"A moment of dizziness perhaps," Kate admitted.

"But you didn't think that was sufficient reason to ask to be relieved?" Hoskins asked.

"My only thought was to protect that child. And I did."

"And went right on treating patients as if that had never happened," Hoskins commented.

"Yes!"

"Patients like Claudia Stuyvesant?"

"If you are trying to imply that I was not fully capable during the time I treated her, you are wrong, sir!" Kate shot back.

Undeterred, Hoskins abruptly changed the subject and the tenor of his questions.

"Doctor, are you familiar with the legal term 'a self-serving declaration'?"

"I think so," Kate conceded.

"Would I be stretching that concept if I suggested that Claudia Stuyvesant's chart is a self-serving declaration?"

"It contains a true and accurate record of

her case. Everything I found. Everything I did," Kate protested.

"According to this chart, you did everything right, gave that poor girl all the attention she needed, on time, in a highly professional manner."

"Yes!" Kate insisted.

"Yet we find nothing in here about the fact that you interrupted your attention to Claudia Stuyvesant to see another patient," Hoskins pointed out.

"I've already testified about the gall stone case," Kate responded.

"I was referring to another case, which occurred after you had finally decided to undertake Claudia Stuyvesant's case —"

"I had *many* cases," Kate interrupted to say.

"The one to which I refer involves an elderly man who did not present — what were your words? — 'alarming symptoms' of life-threatening disease that demanded immediate attention. In fact the man presented no legitimate symptoms at all. Yet you devoted considerable time to him. This, despite the fact that a nurse warned you that he was a homeless person only seeking escape from the rain."

"He was a human being in need," Kate replied.

"A doctor so burdened with cases that you

felt you might, by your own words, 'crack up,' took time away from sick patients to deal with a man who was not even sick?"

"It was raining out. Very hard. He was homeless and hungry. He had no other place to go. Once I saw him, I could tell how desperate he was from his fake symptoms."

"So, out of the goodness of your heart, you not only took the time to see him —"

"I had to make sure his symptoms were not dangerous," Kate said.

"Not only that, but you took the time to make sure he was fed." Hoskins's accusation was filled with not only sarcasm but venom.

"Coming from a small community, I can't get used to the way people are treated in this city. Allowed to fall between the cracks. Forced into a hopeless, lonely existence. Hermits in the middle of a city of millions. I happen to feel that being a physician involves more than prescribing medication and performing surgery!"

Hoskins nodded skeptically. "A very noble sentiment, I am sure. But isn't it a fact, Doctor, that you were so involved with matters aside from your assigned duties that you deprived sick patients of care to which they were entitled? And in the case of Claudia Stuyvesant, with fatal results?"

"That is a lie!" Kate Forrester fought back.

"Isn't the real reason you were so intent on removing Mrs. Stuyvesant from that room was so that she could not be witness to the improper and negligent care you visited on her daughter?"

"She should have been out in the waiting room along with family members of all other patients! Her presence impeded the treatment.

"Yes, yes, we know," Hoskins said, belittling her response. "I think Dr. Ward demolished that argument to the satisfaction of the committee. In fact I think we've all heard enough."

"Well, I don't!" Kate protested, rising from the witness chair, despite Scott's frantic gesture to silence her. But she glared at him defiantly before turning to address the committee.

"It is all well and good for you, Mr. Hoskins, and you, Dr. Ward, to sit here in the calm of a hearing room and judge my actions on a night when cases were coming faster than they could be handled.

"But it is quite another thing to have been there coping with them. Go back, as I did, and review all the cases I treated that night. Cases in which my judgment was later vindicated by the surgeons and cardiologists who took over those cases. I do not apologize for my actions that night. Did Claudia Stuyvesant receive all the time and attention that would please her mother? No. Did she receive all the time and attention that her medical condition seemed to demand? Yes!"

Kate turned now to include Claude Stuyvesant in her scope. "I should have known that night when I heard Mrs. Stuyvesant say 'He'll blame me' that it was *him* she was afraid of."

Claude Stuyvesant's face flushed in anger and indignation.

Mott tried to interrupt, banging his gavel. "Doctor! Dr. Forrester! Mr. Van Cleve, please control your client!"

But Scott made no move to intervene.

Kate continued: "It is he whom Claudia Stuyvesant was really afraid of. Not her mother, but the fact that she would tell *him*. He is the reason his daughter lied to me. If you wish to blame anyone for her death, blame him!"

Mott continued to overlap with her, "Dr. Forrester! Your remarks are out of order! You will cease at once! At once, do you hear me?"

Having said all she had intended to say, and a bit more, Kate Forrester sank down into the witness chair, trembling in anger.

Dr. Truscott shook his head gravely.

Dr. Ward remarked, "Having seen her on the television news, I am not surprised." She addressed the administrative officer, "Mr. Cahill, what is the usual procedure at this point in a hearing?"

"Since all the testimony is in, it is customary to give both counsel several days to prepare their final arguments. Once the committee hears them, they will be required to vote."

"May I assume that I can resume my regular surgery schedule next Monday morning?" Ward asked briskly.

"I'm sure that you can, Doctor," Cahill replied.

"Frankly," Ward continued, "I could vote now and save us all a great deal of time."

Mott nodded, then addressed Scott, "Counselor, is your client ready to continue?"

"In a moment, sir."

"Mr. Hoskins?" Mott asked. "Any further questions?"

"I think the respondent has shown us all we need to know. I only regret that she found it necessary to make such accusations in defense of her conduct that night. I have no more questions for her."

Hoskins left his place, approached Claude Stuyvesant to whisper, "Sorry, sir, about that unfortunate attack."

"I care about only one thing: I want that young woman forbidden to practice medicine ever again!"

"After Dr. Ward's statement a moment ago,

I have no doubt about the outcome," Hoskins assured him.

In the hearing room, then later in the elevator, Kate Forrester and her attorney exchanged no words. It was only when they were walking down the street that Kate finally spoke.

"Sorry," was all she said.

"It's okay." He tried to minimize the damage caused by her outburst.

"I undid all your hard work. But I had to say it."

"You should have told me about that altercation with that abusive father. It took me completely by surprise."

"As long as the child is okay now, and in good hands, it didn't matter."

"Everything matters now. Even that old man who came in out of the rain."

"What did you expect me to do? Ignore him? A poor old man, wet and hungry?"

"You saw how Hoskins twisted a decent impulse into an accusation. Another thing, you never told me about that phone call," Scott said accusingly.

"That was Walter. And I got rid of his call as soon as I could," Kate explained.

"*Is* it a very intimate relationship?" Scott asked.

"Walter made too much of it, far too much," Kate said evasively.

Rather than probe deeply into a subject Kate was obviously trying to avoid, Scott said, "So did Hoskins. Now, we have to put aside all the minor diversions and examine what happened today. Assess our liabilities. And our assets."

"Of which we have very few, it appears," Kate replied.

"That's why they advise young lawyers that, when the law is against you, to pound the facts. When the facts are against you, pound the law."

"And when both the law and the facts are against you?" Kate asked.

"Pound the table," Scott replied. "But I need ammunition to pound the table with."

Chapter Thirty-five

Rosie Chung already had the coffee brewing by the time Kate and Scott returned to the apartment.

"How'd it go?" Rosie sang out from the kitchen.

"Not good, I'm afraid," Kate replied.

"Not bad, either," Scott said, trying to encourage her.

Kate's blue eyes contradicted him so clearly that he was forced to admit, "No, not very good. All the way up here I kept trying to frame my summation based on all the testimony. I tried to be as tough on myself as that committee will be. Especially the two doctors. The way I figure it, Mott is like a trick you give away in a bridge game. One you know you're sure to lose. So I was banking on Truscott and Ward. But Ward showed her hand today. She is definitely not on our side. Which automatically cancels out Truscott. Because with Mott and Ward against us, Truscott doesn't even count. Therefore, our chances, Kate's chances, depend on what I can say to change Ward's mind. Now, you two are both women, both doctors. Put yourselves in

Ward's place. What would convince you?"

Rosie spoke first. "That pregnancy test."

Scott interrupted. "Ward said Kate should not have accepted that as definitive."

"But she didn't accept it," Rosie argued. "She asked for a sonogram. It wasn't available."

"Does a doctor quit there?" Scott asked as he paced between both women.

"I didn't quit there! I ordered a blood serum pregnancy test," Kate protested. "But those results take too long."

"Was there any other possible way you could have made that diagnosis?"

"Ectopics are rarely easy to detect," Rosie pointed out. "And with a patient who denied being sexually active, not having missed a period, with a negative pregnancy test, how far can a doctor pursue what is only her suspicion?"

"Are you telling me that most doctors would not have been able to make that diagnosis?" Scott asked.

"Most, if not all," Rosie insisted. "Many times they're not detectable on pelvic examination."

Frustrated, Scott thought aloud, "You can't always feel it. The tests don't always reveal it. In addition, the patient can mislead you by lying. Strikes me that instead of the patient being the victim of the doctor, the doctor is the victim of the patient. Still . . ." Scott stopped pacing to confront both women. "One thing has bothered me from the minute I heard that drugs could have masked Claudia's pain so that she could bleed to death without evidencing enough pain to warn of her condition."

"What bothered you about that?" Kate asked. "It's true."

"She was there for nine hours. Wouldn't the drugs have worn off?" Scott asked both women.

"You're assuming she took them before she went to the hospital," Kate pointed out.

"If she took them at all, she had to take them before she went to the hospital," Scott replied.

"Not necessarily," Kate disputed. When Scott turned to her, she explained, "Sometimes they bring their drugs with them."

"To the hospital?"

"Oh, yes," Rosie said. "I've caught them. So has Kate. They hide them in their pockets, their purses, their bras, their hairdos, their shoes. There is no limit to the ingenuity of a desperately hooked druggie."

"Put yourself in Claudia's situation," Kate suggested to Scott. "She's terrified enough to call her mother, whom she's been avoiding for months. Because she knows she's sick. Maybe she even senses how sick. Which only increases her need for drugs. Besides, she is going to a hospital, where she has no way of knowing if she'll be given any medication. So, to fortify herself, she takes an extra-large dose before she goes. For insurance she conceals more somewhere on her person. And she sneaks them whenever she gets the chance. Never realizing the danger it puts her in by misleading the doctor."

"Man, if there were only some way for doctors to sue patients for malpractice," Scott commented. Then he paused to consider, "Wait a minute . . ."

"I know what you're going to say: How could she take them if her mother was there?" Kate anticipated. "Her mother would never testify to seeing her take any drugs. Besides, there was at least one occasion when Cronin and I and Mrs. Stuyvesant were all out of the room at the same time."

"The time Mrs. Stuyvesant found you on the phone with Walter," Scott realized, with a touch of jealousy. "Yes. Claudia could have taken something without anyone being aware of it."

"Then that's it!" Rosie exclaimed with considerable relief.

"I'm afraid not," Scott said. "That might

be a reasonable hypothesis on which to argue. Except for one thing: We still can't prove her drug use. Whatever importance I attached to Rick's testimony before, it seems even more crucial now. Without him we can't turn Ward around — nohow."

At the mention of Rick Thomas, Kate recalled, " 'She always had a dozen prescriptions from different doctors. Valium. Darvon. Robaxen. Barbs. You name it . . .' "

" 'She had it,' " Scott supplied the rest of the quotation. "Rick said that."

"He also said, 'Which is why she didn't want me to take her to the hospital,' " Kate reminded him.

"And when I asked him why, he said, 'If they discovered —' "

" '. . . she was on something, she didn't want me to get into trouble,' " Kate responded. "There, that's it. Proof that not only was she on drugs, she may even have taken some along to the hospital."

"Why else would she think Rick might get into trouble there? Sounds perfect to me," Rosie said. "You've got your evidence!"

"There's only one thing wrong," Scott pointed out. "Kate and I can't testify."

"Why not? We both heard Rick say it," Kate insisted.

"That makes it hearsay testimony. Cahill

would never allow it. And even if he did, the committee would think we made it up between us. Just as they are now sure there was no Rick Thomas."

Scott resumed his pacing.

In her exasperation Rosie asked, "Is that what lawyers spend all their time doing, keeping out important testimony?"

"Maybe . . . maybe we don't have to testify," Kate suggested.

That puzzled Scott, but Rosie knew at once, for she blurted out, "Prescriptions!"

"What about prescriptions?" Scott asked.

"Painkillers, sedatives, barbiturates, drugs like those Claudia was taking — a doctor can only prescribe them by a special prescription form in triplicate."

"A prescription in triplicate . . ." Scott considered. "So what?"

"A copy goes to the state Department of Health in Albany," Kate explained. "So that the state can check on doctors who give out such prescriptions too freely. Or pharmacists who fill too many of them for a quick buck. And, most important, to keep a check on patients who go from doctor to doctor to support their drug habit, getting prescriptions from a number of them so that no one doctor suspects."

"Druggies like those," Rosie said, "they

know exactly how to mimic the symptoms that will convince any doctor to prescribe a pain-killer or a sedative."

"So," Scott began to fit the pieces together, "if Claudia did that, and Rick said she did, there must be a record up in Albany. Let me use your phone!"

While Kate and Rosie stood by, ready to supply any medical information he might need, Scott spent the next hour and a half on the phone to the state Board of Health in Albany. He spoke first to the Computer Section. Was transferred to the Legal Department. Then to another office. And still another office. Each time he explained in detail his position as attorney for Dr. Katherine Forrester, respondent in a state board hearing. Each of his explanations evoked the same response. "I'm sorry, Counselor, but I am not authorized to reveal such highly confidential records."

He was advised, each time, to make his request of the next highest official in the chain of command. Which he did, always with the same result. The information was so confidential that it could not be released to any outsider. Even an attorney? Even an attorney.

Working his way up the hierarchy, Scott was finally connected to the office of the Commissioner of Health himself. Scott experienced his first flicker of encouragement when the commissioner interrupted his presentation by remarking, "Counselor, spare me the details. I am quite familiar with the Forrester affair."

"Then you must be aware, Commissioner, of the vital need for this information in my defense," Scott stated with assurance of success.

"Oh, I have no doubt that it would be helpful. Unfortunately the information you seek is of such highly confidential nature that it cannot be disclosed."

"Surely there must be a way —" Scott started to protest.

But the Commissioner aborted the argument with a curt, "Counselor, it is past five o'clock. This office is closed!"

Before Scott could reply, he heard the sound of the phone being cut off. He had no need to report his failure to Kate and Rosie.

"Isn't there anything you can do?" Rosie asked.

"Yes. Think!" he said. "I need time to think!"

With that, he said good-bye and left.

It wasn't until four o'clock in the morning that Scott Van Cleve decided on his strategy. He knew it must succeed before the day appointed for his summation if Kate's career were to be preserved.

Chairman Clarence Mott was in a nasty and rebellious mood when he arrived at the New York City offices of the State Board of Professional Medical Conduct. The moment he entered Hoskins's office, he demanded, "Who the hell called this meeting? We distinctly agreed yesterday: two days off before the summation. I made plans. I have reservations for a flight to Florida."

"Van Cleve," Hoskins explained.

"What about him?"

"He demanded, no, insisted, on a meeting today."

"Does Claude know about this development?" Mott asked.

"I didn't think it advisable until we know what the hell Van Cleve is after."

"And Cahill?"

"He's on his way down from Albany right now. Should be here any minute."

"What do you suppose Van Cleve has in mind?"

"Search me. But he sounded very threatening on the phone."

"Well, we'll know soon enough," Mott consoled himself.

Within the hour Kevin Cahill arrived, breathless and sweating, having run from Grand Central Station. He was as resentful as

Clarence Mott at having to attend this un-scheduled meeting. The three of them settled down to await the noon arrival of Scott Van Cleve.

"Gentlemen," Scott addressed them, "I have an important request to make, without which I cannot do justice to my client's interests."

Mott intervened, "I can guess. You want more time to find your elusive imaginary witness."

"It's not more time I need but the cooperation of the committee."

"Cooperation?" Hoskins asked warily. "What kind of cooperation?"

"I need access to certain records," Scott announced.

"Oh, no!" Hoskins refused at once. "If you think I am going to open up the files of our investigating committee, you are wrong, Mister. Dead wrong!"

"I want more than that," Scott countered.

Mott looked at Hoskins. Hoskins glanced at Cahill. Young Cahill merely stared, unable to respond.

Finally Hoskins asked, "What 'more,' Van Cleve?"

"I want the state Board of Health to release to me their records of all prescriptions made out to Claudia Stuyvesant by any and all doctors in this state," Scott demanded.

"Aha!" Mott seized on Scott's request. "I knew it! There never was such a person as Rick Thomas. That was only a smokescreen. To set us up for this! Well, the answer is no!"

Hoskins, who was no less suspicious, no less anxious to gloat, controlled his emotional reaction better than Mott had been able to do. Very calmly he asked, "Van Cleve, are you aware that such records are of the utmost confidentiality? That the state Board of Health is forbidden to reveal them?"

"Precisely why I need your cooperation," Scott said.

"Not mine!" Mott was quick to reply.

"Or mine!" Hoskins added. "Having failed with the Rick Thomas ruse, you want us to go to the state board and ask for them? Do you think we're out of our minds?"

Prepared for such refusal, Scott now resorted to his legal argument. Ignoring Mott and Hoskins, he turned his attention to Cahill, who had said nothing up to this point.

"Cahill, as administrative officer of this hearing, it is your duty to rule on all questions of law."

"Yes," Kevin Cahill replied gingerly, awaiting Scott's next move.

"Tell me, then, in a criminal case isn't the

prosecution forced to reveal to the attorney for the defense all exculpatory evidence in its possession?"

"Of course," Cahill replied, only to point out smugly, "but what you request isn't in the board's possession. Therefore it is powerless to grant your request."

Both Mott and Hoskins smiled and nodded to reinforce Cahill's declaration.

"Oh, but it *is* in your possession," Scott shot back at Hoskins. "This board is an arm of the state Department of Health. And the Department of Health holds the records I want. So, technically they *are* in your possession. I demand that you and I, Mr. Cahill, go up to Albany and take a look at those records. If they reveal what I think, I will demand copies to present to the committee at the time of my summation."

"Now, see here, Van Cleve," Clarence Mott began to dispute him. But Kevin Cahill intervened.

"Hold on, everybody! Hold on!" Cahill declared. Assuming his judicial demeanor, he continued: "We are confronted here with a legal question of considerable gravity. It is true that a prosecutor in a criminal case is required to reveal to the defense counsel all the evidence he will use in the course of the trial, and all exculpatory evidence as well."

"Exactly!" Scott confirmed.

"However," Cahill pointed out, "this hearing is *not* a criminal proceeding."

"When a doctor's professional life is involved, I think the same rule would apply," Scott protested. "The consequences of this hearing are no less grave to the respondent than they would be to a defendant."

"No criminal trial, no disclosure requirement," Cahill ruled. "And I do not think you will find a similar case in which any judge has ruled that we are obligated to provide you with such confidential records."

"There must be —" Scott started to say.

"If you can produce such a case, I will be happy to take it into consideration. But, until then, I stand by my original decision." To appear to be less arbitrary than he was, Cahill concluded, "Of course if you can supply such records, we will admit them into evidence. That is the best we can do, Mr. Van Cleve."

Having failed to move them, Scott departed.

Once he was gone, Clarence Mott wondered, "Is that true?"

"What?" Hoskins asked.

"If he gets his hands on such records, will we be obliged to admit them?"

Cahill assured him, "We don't have to worry about that. He'll never get them. It would be nice, though, to let Mr. Stuyvesant know in some subtle way how we protected his interests here today."

Scott Van Cleve returned to his office to begin making the notes for his summation. It was late afternoon. Since he had been denied use of the secretarial staff, he was forced to do his own two-finger typing on the small computer that had not yet been removed from his office. He had never felt at ease with that electronic marvel and had not learned to take advantage of all its functions. But it would serve to produce his rough notes with all the inevitable corrections.

He began to enter phrases and key words he proposed to use in his summation: *A hearing that never should have taken place . . . unfair to punish the physician for the faults of the system . . . the physician performed as well as possible under impossible circumstances . . . blaming the physician for natural exhaustion due to unconscionable hours and stress . . . the physician in this case is being faulted for the failure of a test we all know to be imperfect. . . .*

The more times he entered the word *physician* the more strange the word looked to him on the green screen. *Physician. Physician.*

Hell, no, he thought, *not physician, Katherine Forrester. Kate.* And he knew why he was having so much trouble marshaling his thoughts.

Because these thoughts and phrases alone would not serve to clear her of the charges against her. He was merely going through the motions. Making notes that sounded hollow even to him. Notes that would surely not convince a woman as demanding as Dr. Gladys Ward. She had virtually wiped out the defense of the faulty test result. She was unimpressed by the long hours and difficult conditions under which Kate had had to treat Claudia Stuyvesant. Not even the fact that there was clear proof that Claudia had misled her by lying seemed to matter to Ward.

What it all came down to was an ectopic pregnancy concealed from the physician by lies, reinforced by the suppression of the one symptom that might have revealed the patient's dangerous condition: pain.

The more dispassionately Scott analyzed his summation, the more obvious it became that without proof of Claudia's drug addiction, it would not stand the scrutiny of the two physicians on the committee.

With that in mind, he wiped all his notes from the screen and began again.

Chapter Thirty-six

After struggling all night with a document that any legal secretary could have typed in one tenth the time, Scott was satisfied with his efforts. He watched the pages flow from the printer. When he had them all in hand, he bound them in the usual blue legal backing. He consulted his watch. It was not yet eight o'clock. Kate should be getting up, getting ready to go off to the hospital. She insisted on reporting for her assignment with Dr. Troy on the few days when the hearing was in recess.

Scott punched in her number. It rang. Four times. He feared that he had already missed her. But in the middle of the fifth ring she answered, breathless.

"Kate?"

"I was just getting out of the shower when I heard the phone. What's wrong. More bad news?" she asked.

"I want you to meet me."

"This morning? Where?" Kate asked.

"Supreme Court, New York County. Take the Independent Subway down to the Chambers Street station. Then ask anyone where the Supreme Court is. They'll direct you. And you'll recognize it. It's the building you see so often on television. With the wide stone steps leading up to the row of tall pillars at the top. And the words 'The true administration of justice is the firmest pillar of good government.' Well, this morning we're going to find out if those words mean what they say. Meet me! Before nine thirty!"

Scott Van Cleve stood on the top step of the court building scanning the street below. He spied her. He waved to attract her attention. She did not see him. He admired the way she started up the steps, firmly, resolutely. He liked that quality about her. She might seem small, disarmingly feminine, but she was a woman of purpose, reflecting the principles and habits of her family and background.

Looking up toward the top steps and the portico on which the words concerning justice were carved into the weatherworn gray stone, Kate caught sight of Scott beckoning to her. As she climbed, she admired his tall, lean frame. Much as her father looked in those long-ago photographs so carefully mounted in the family album by her mother. No amount of care had prevented those early photos from fading. Still, the resemblance was striking to

Kate. Of course in later years her father had become somewhat heavier. Never fat or self-indulgent, just more mature. She wondered, would Scott get to look that way? Before she could reach any conclusions, she was at the top step asking, "What are we doing here?"

"Going to see a judge," Scott said.

"What for?"

"You'll see," Scott said, seizing her hand and starting into the courthouse.

"Judge Wasserman is in conference," the stodgy, bespectacled secretary proclaimed firmly.

"We'll wait," Scott said.

"He has to go on the bench very soon," the woman announced, meaning he is not going to see any young lawyer this morning without an appointment.

"We'll wait," Scott insisted. "It's important."

His persistence caused the secretary to look from Scott to the very pretty young woman alongside him, then back at Scott again. Her eyes filled with a reflection of her consternation as she exclaimed, "Well, this beats all! If you two have come here to ask the judge to officiate at your wedding, you have gone about it in the wrong way. In the first place Judge Wasserman only performs marriages for the children of close friends. Or else Broadway celebrities. Never for strangers. So you are both wasting your time."

"My dear woman, we are not here to ask the judge to marry us. I am here to present an ex-parte petition for an order to examine certain state records."

"Leave it and I will show it to the judge after he comes off the bench."

"It can't wait that long," Scott informed her.

"It will have to," the secretary insisted, adjusting her heavy-framed, thick-lensed glasses, a firm and impatient gesture she often resorted to when annoyed beyond her usual ready level of annoyance, judges' secretaries being noted for a very low tolerance point, most times lower even than judges themselves.

At that moment the door to the judge's inner chambers was thrown open. Two men and two women, obviously clients and attorneys, emerged angrily after what had transpired inside. They marched toward the front door — the two women, attorney and client first; the two men, attorney and client, just behind. Before the outer door closed, from inside chambers came the angry voice of Judge Emile Wasserman.

"Freda! How many times have I told you? No matrimonial property cases first thing in the morning. Ruins my entire day!"

Freda Baumgartner turned to Scott and Kate with a look that warned, *You see, I wasn't fooling, he's not in a mood to see anyone without an appointment.* To make sure Scott and Kate heard, Freda announced loudly, "Judge, there are two people here who would like to see you with an ex-parte petition. But they have no appointment."

Before the judge could forbid them entrance, Scott was on his feet and at the open door.

"Your Honor, a doctor's career is at stake here. And time is of the essence. As you will see if you give us the chance to explain."

" 'Us'?" the judge echoed. "An ex-parte petition, no opposing counsel, and you need help to argue it? This I've got to see."

Scott beckoned Kate to join him. Together they passed disapproving Freda Baumgartner and entered Judge Wasserman's chambers.

Judge Emile Wasserman was dressed in shirtsleeves and an unbuttoned sweater vest, his usual garb before slipping into his black judicial robe. But the absence of his formal vestments did nothing to diminish his judicial impatience. "All right now, I've got no time. I'm due on the bench to charge a jury."

"Your Honor, I represent a physician who is currently facing charges before the Board of Professional Medical Conduct."

Wasserman interrupted, "Counselor, when you said 'us,' I thought you meant co-counsel. But did you have to bring your secretary with you for moral support?"

"No, Your Honor, she is the doctor in question."

"She . . ." the judge was about to ask, then stopped to stare at Kate. "Why is it these days that every policeman and every doctor I meet looks to me like a kid fresh out of high school? I must be getting old. So this is the doctor."

"And damn well trained, Your Honor," Kate broke into the proceedings. "University of Illinois. With honors! University of Iowa Medical School! Second in my graduating class!"

"Oho!" Wasserman exclaimed, "with a temper too."

Scott felt a flush of embarrassment shoot up into his craggy face. He would rather Kate had not spoken up so strongly to this man upon whose indulgence they were both so dependent.

"Sorry, Your Honor," Kate apologized to repair the damage.

Wasserman gave no sign of being mollified but turned his full attention to Scott. "Proceed, Counselor. But don't take all day."

As briefly as he could do justice to Kate's

situation, Scott explained the events leading up to the hearing, including the refusal of Hoskins and Cahill to help him secure the confidential data from the files of the state Board of Health. Then he presented for the judge's signature the order that accompanied his petition.

While Wasserman scanned the papers, he glanced beyond them at Kate, then at Scott. "You know, Counselor, one thing puzzles me. Of all the judges in this courthouse, what made you pick me?"

Scott paused to consider the most ingratiating reason he could, invent, then decided to adopt the same advice he always gave Kate, tell the truth.

"Because, Your Honor, you are a maverick."

Wasserman lowered the documents to confront Scott Van Cleve. His glowering gaze demanded an explanation.

"Since I knew of no case exactly in point where someone sought access to those particular records, I realized I needed a judge who did not restrict himself merely to applying the law but was willing to risk being overruled when he ventured beyond precedent and put justice before the law."

"A nice bit of flattery, young man," Wasserman said.

"But true," Scott replied.

"Ah, I guess so," Wasserman grudgingly admitted. "But you see what it gets me. Petitions like this. So we have to help rescue this young woman's career." He turned to Kate. "Tell me honestly, Dr. Forrester, in your own mind, in your own conscience, did you give the Stuyvesant girl the best treatment a doctor could?"

"Under the circumstances, with the information I had available to me, I did what any good doctor would have done."

"Anything else you'd like to say before I decide?"

"Yes, Your Honor," Kate replied. "This isn't merely a court order you are being asked to sign, it's my life. It's what I was born to do, practice medicine, heal the sick."

Wasserman nodded thoughtfully. He picked up his pen. Before he signed the order, he said, "Counselor, you'll never guess what convinced me. Your description of the part Claude Stuyvesant is playing in all this. He's exactly that kind of sonofabitch. It's about time someone made him face the unpleasant truths about his own life."

Having affixed his signature, Wasserman held out the document to Scott. "Here. Now, get the hell up to Albany. Get those records. And rub Stuyvesant's nose in them!"

★ ★ ★

They were racing down the steps of the courthouse when Scott said, "Did you hear what she said?"

"Who?" Kate asked.

"Wasserman's secretary, Freda. She thought we were there to get the judge to marry us."

Kate did not respond as they raced down the steps toward an empty taxi.

"Grand Central Station!" Scott ordered as they climbed in.

The tall twin towers of the Rockefeller Mall dominated the city and the countryside for miles around. Kate and Scott could see them as they emerged from the Albany station. The mall contained most of the offices of the State of New York and the office where the records they sought were stored.

They located the proper offices of the state Board of Health. Scott presented Judge Wasserman's order to the woman in charge of drug records. She glanced at the order, glanced at them, then cautiously scrutinized the order, looked at them once more with some suspicion, and said, "I'll have to see about this." She started away.

Scott and Kate waited impatiently.

"They can't refuse a judge's order, can

they?" Kate asked.

"No predicting what a bureaucrat can do," Scott said.

The woman returned, accompanied by a man who held the blue-backed order and who moved with the impatient annoyance of one whose cozy routine coffee break had been interrupted suddenly.

"You presented this?" he asked Scott.

"Yes. Now we would like to examine the records referred to in Judge Wasserman's order."

"I've never seen an order like this before," the man stated.

"Well, you've seen one now," Scott countered.

"I'd better check this with Legal."

"Look, sir, this is an order signed by a Judge of the Supreme Court. It is urgent that you comply with it at once. Time is of the essence," Scott pointed out. "We are due to resume a hearing in New York City tomorrow morning."

"Still, I think I should check this out —" the man began to say.

"Mister — what is your name?" Scott asked, taking his pen and a notepad out of his pocket.

"What does my name have to do with it?" the man demanded.

"Because," Scott said, taking a little liberty

with the facts, "Judge Wasserman authorized me to warn anyone who failed to respect his order that he will issue a contempt-of-court citation against any state employee who refuses to execute this order. And he is one tough judge," Scott said, improvising as an added pressure.

The man considered the threat for a moment, then conceded. "Come with me."

Within half an hour a printout of all the drug-related prescriptions issued to "Stuyvesant, Claudia" was in the anxious hands of Scott Van Cleve and Kate Forrester. He deferred to her medical expertise.

"Dr. Eaves is listed here. More than a few times. And doctors named Tompkins . . . Henderson . . . Goldenson . . . Fletcher . . . Davidoff . . . Crane . . . Grady . . . Fusco . . . Alberts . . ."

"Poor Claudia, she sure got around, didn't she?" Scott commented.

"Had to, considering the number and the kinds of drugs," Kate said, calling off, "Dalmane, pentobarbital . . ."

"The yellowjackets Rick referred to," Scott recalled.

"Amobarbital."

"Those the blues?" Scott asked.

"Yes. And amobarbital-secorbarbital, the

rainbows. It's all there. Everything he saw her take," Kate said. "But most significant are these," Kate said, directing Scott's attention to the last two lines of the printout. He glanced at them.

"What's so significant, or different about these?" Scott asked.

"These prescriptions, all within the last two weeks of her life. Percodan. Codeine. Benzodiazapine. That's Valium. She must have been heavily into those just before she was brought to the hospital."

"And what she likely brought with her to Emergency," Scott realized. "All enough to mask her pain?"

"When you consider the synergistic effect of those drugs taken together, with cocaine in addition, they could have masked the most intense pain," Kate explained.

"Man, she was really hooked," Scott realized with a certain sense of pity for the young woman.

"Cases like this make my flesh crawl every time I hear people refer to cocaine as a 're-creational drug.' Might as well refer to suicide as a recreational activity," Kate replied.

On the train back to Manhattan Scott spent the two hours studying Claudia's drug history, framing his legal strategy and his arguments to have the record admitted into evidence. Then he had to decide on the most effective and dramatic use of it to convince the two medical members of the committee that not the physician but the patient was at fault in the matter of Katherine Forrester, M.D., Respondent. Even with this new evidence, it might not be easy to convince Dr. Gladys Ward.

As the train passed Harmon and was making the final leg of its run toward Manhattan, Scott looked up from his study of the record to ask, "Kate, medically speaking, is there any question that one of these drugs, or a combination of them, could have suppressed Claudia's pain sufficiently to make her condition appear far less dangerous than it actually was?"

"None," Kate said. "I can testify to that."

"That won't do," Scott said, negating her. "Opinion testimony of that kind must come from an independent expert."

"There's Dr. Troy. I'm sure he'd help," Kate suggested.

"I need someone who can't be disputed on the ground that he's prejudiced in your behalf. Troy's letter of reference and character endorsement shows how he feels about you. No, this will take someone else, especially someone I won't need a lot of time to prepare."

He was silent the rest of the way, deep in

thought. Curious as she was, Kate did not intrude on his meditations. As the train plunged into the tunnel that would bring them to Grand Central in a matter of minutes, she detected from the look on his craggy face that he had decided.

As they emerged from the station onto Forty-second Street, Scott said, "Kate! I need to know everything it is possible to learn about ectopic pregnancies, about the importance of pain in making such a diagnosis, about the effect of drugs on pain, symptoms, and lab findings. And I've got to know it all by early tomorrow morning!"

For the rest of the evening and into the night, with the help of Rosie Chung, Kate instructed Scott as if he were a first-year med student. The process went on without interruption. When Rosie described pregnancies and ectopics, Kate made the coffee. When Kate looked up references in their various textbooks, Rosie made the sandwiches. Over coffee and sandwiches they both plied Scott with the details they remembered from their courses in obstetrics and their service in that wing of the hospital. For more than six hours the process went on, Scott asking, Kate and Rosie informing. Scott making notes of facts he had just learned and legal jottings on how he would use what he had just learned.

Until he leaned back exhausted, saying, "I haven't had a night like this since I studied for my bar exams. Now I've got to get home and turn all this into legal ammunition."

"If any questions occur to you while you're working, call me. No matter what the hour," Kate instructed.

"Don't worry. I will."

He took his notes, and the four textbooks Kate and Rosie had used, and left.

Once he was gone, Rosie said, "I don't know about you, Kate, but I like that man. I have great confidence in him."

"So do I."

"Like him? Or have confidence in him?" Rosie asked.

"A whole lot of both. I just hope that whatever he has in mind, it works. Almost as much for his sake as for mine. Because he feels about the law as I do about medicine."

Chapter Thirty-seven

As Kate and Scott entered the hearing room, the first person they confronted was Claude Stuyvesant, hovering over his wife, who sat at the end of Hoskins's counsel table. Obviously Nora Stuyvesant had insisted on being present for the last day.

While Scott laid out the paper and books he intended to introduce today, he noted that though Dr. Truscott was in his usual chair, armed with three fresh pads and half a dozen sharpened pencils, and Mott and Hoskins were in a corner conference with Cahill, Dr. Gladys Ward had not yet arrived. Mott was torn between nodding in response to what Hoskins was saying and studying his pocket watch, obviously distressed at Ward's failure to appear. A secretary hurried into the room, handed Mott a slip of paper. One glance and he announced, "I have just received word. Dr. Ward is on her way."

Nine minutes later Gladys Ward entered the room briskly, explaining with a curt, "Patient with post-op complications." She took her seat, set down her purse, put on her gracefully framed designer glasses, and was ready.

Mott opened the proceedings. "Since all testimony has been completed, this committee is ready to hear counsels' summations. Mr. Van Cleve, for the respondent, first."

Scott rose slowly, aware that what he was about to say would cause a furor.

"Mr. Chairman, instead of making my summation, I ask to reopen this hearing."

"Reopen?" Hoskins and Cahill both exclaimed at the same instant.

Hoskins continued: "Mr. Chairman, I object! Counsel for the respondent has had ample opportunity to present his case, and all the witnesses he chose. To reopen now would be irregular. Highly irregular. Mr. Cahill, I demand a ruling!"

Mott and Scott both looked to the administrative officer for some guidance. Cahill said in admonition, "Mr. Van Cleve, there is only one ground on which a hearing can be reopened at this stage. New evidence."

"I happen to possess new evidence," Scott said without identifying it. "In addition I wish to call a new witness."

"New evidence?" Cahill repeated. "*And* a new witness? I trust we are not back to another invisible man like Rick Thomas."

"This time the witness is readily available," Scott answered.

"This new evidence, what does it consist

of?" Mott asked.

"That will emerge in the course of the witness's testimony," Scott replied.

Perplexed and puzzled, Mott said gruffly, "One moment, Mr. Van Cleve!" With a brusque, angry gesture, he summoned Cahill to the corner of the room for a hurried conference.

"Damn it, Cahill, what the hell is Van Cleve up to now?"

"I don't know."

"This is a trick. One of the usual slimy tricks that lawyers pull." Then, aware he was talking to an attorney, he apologized. "Nothing personal, you understand. Now, rule against him and get this over with!"

"Not so fast," Cahill continued. "If this were a criminal trial and new evidence came in before the summation, no judge in this state would preclude it."

"The other day when he demanded what he called ex . . . excul . . . whatever the hell that word is —"

"Exculpatory evidence," Cahill informed him.

"Right. You ruled against him because this *isn't* a criminal trial," Mott reminded.

"That was different. Then he wanted us to provide *him* with evidence. Now he says he *has* new evidence. Unless you want this case to be appealed in court, you'd better give him permission."

Once back in his chair, Mott declared, "In line with our policy of complete fairness to the respondent, this committee will reopen this hearing to any new evidence or new witness counsel wishes to introduce. Mr. Van Cleve?"

Scott rose to his feet to announce: "Mr. Mott, respondent wishes to call Dr. Gladys Ward!"

Ward glared at Scott in stunned anger. Dr. Truscott slammed down his pencil before even making a single note. Clarence Mott glanced anxiously at Kevin Cahill, then to Prosecutor Hoskins, who could not resist furtively exchanging looks with Claude Stuyvesant before he rose to protest.

"Mr. Chairman, in all my years of prosecuting such hearings, I have never seen a member of the hearing committee called as a witness. Only a young, inexperienced lawyer, desperate for a defense, would hope to get away with such a shabby trick. I object strenuously to turning this grave proceeding into a legal circus!"

To add support to Hoskins's argument, Cahill chided, "My, my, Mr. Van Cleve, it seems only a few days ago you were objecting to Dr. Ward merely asking your witness a few questions. Yet now you wish to call her as a witness. Consistency, Mr. Van Cleve, let's have a little legal consistency."

"Exactly, Mr. Cahill," Scott challenged. "It 'seems only a few days ago' you were permitting her the privileges of a prosecutor. And justifying it, if I can recall correctly, in the name of 'pursuit of the truth, which is, after all, why we are all here.' That is all I'm asking now. Consistency!"

Scott turned to Hoskins to demand, "Sir, why was Dr. Ward chosen to sit on this particular committee?"

"It is customary to have at least one medical member of the committee be a specialist in the field under scrutiny. Because of her eminence in the field of obstetrics and gynecology, since this case involves an ectopic pregnancy with a fatal outcome, she was designated."

"Thank you, Mr. Hoskins," Scott said, "for qualifying her as an expert. Because it is in that capacity that I call her. Now, 'in pursuit of the truth' as Mr. Cahill is fond of saying, Dr. Ward, will you take the stand?"

Ward looked to Mott to exempt her from this function. Mott looked to Cahill, who, with a curt and embarrassed nod, gave his permission.

Reluctantly Dr. Gladys Ward took the witness chair and was sworn.

Scott approached her to commence the testimony on which he had been forced to risk the professional fate of Dr. Kate Forrester.

"Dr. Ward, since this committee already accepts you as an expert, there is no need to recite your distinguished professional record. So let us proceed directly to what I hope will educate the other members of the committee on the complexities of this case. To start, Doctor, would you list for them the classic symptoms of an ectopic pregnancy?"

"Counselor, I'm afraid you have been misinformed."

"Why do you say that?"

"Because there *are* no classic signs and symptoms of ectopics."

"Other conditions and illnesses present classic signs and symptoms," Scott pretended to protest.

"Ectopics unfortunately do not. For ectopics there are no signs or symptoms that are pathognomonic."

Scott made an attempt to appear puzzled. "Sorry, Doctor, that particular word is foreign to me."

"Pathognomonic," Ward explained, "means signs or symptoms specifically characteristic of a particular disease or condition, based on which a diagnosis can be made."

"Ah, I see." Scott gave every indication of grasping the definition. Then he continued: "Well, now, since ectopics present no such signs or symptoms, how *does* a doctor arrive at a diagnosis?"

Her annoyance noticeable now, Ward replied, "Really, Counselor, if you wanted a primary course in pregnancies, you should have attended one of my lectures at the medical school."

"Dr. Ward, I repeat, if there are no signs or symptoms that are pathognomonic, how does a doctor diagnose an ectopic pregnancy?"

"A combination of findings and observations may be suggestive."

" 'Suggestive,' " Scott remarked. "An intriguing word. What combination of findings and observations would be 'suggestive'?"

"There are a number of them."

"Can you name them?" Scott persevered.

Realizing that he would not relent, Ward started to enumerate impatiently, "Nausea, vomiting, cramps. Tenderness, especially on movement. Missed periods. Although in my years of practice I have seen two ectopics in which there was no missed period."

"Then, Doctor, would I be correct in concluding that very few ectopics evidence themselves in exactly the same way?"

"I would say only ten — possibly fifteen

— percent present a fairly usual picture."

"But the vast majority do not," Scott concluded.

"Correct," Ward replied, relieved to have made the point.

"Doctor, what about fever as a symptom? Claudia Stuyvesant did have a fever," Scott pointed out.

"Some ectopics present with fever, some are afebrile," Ward said.

"So fever, too, is not a reliable symptom," Scott remarked. "But you did mention nausea, vomiting, and cramps. Are they generally symptoms of an ectopic?"

"Yes," Ward replied.

"Doctor, can you name any other conditions that produce those same symptoms?"

"Oh, yes," Ward agreed quickly. "Ulcer, gastritis, stomach virus, appendix, kidney stone, threatened abortion, pelvic inflammatory disease, urinary tract disease . . ."

Scott intervened. "To save the committee time, Doctor, may I read you a statement from a recognized work on obstetrics? I quote: 'At least *fifty* pathologic conditions may be confused with extrauterine pregnancy.' Would you agree with that?"

"I would delinitely agree," Ward stated.

"Now, Doctor, if a physician *is* confronted with signs and symptoms that are 'suggestive' of an ectopic pregnancy, what should that doctor do?"

"An immediate bimanual vaginal examination," Ward replied crisply.

"And that would prove the existence of an ectopic?" Scott asked.

"Not necessarily," Ward was forced to concede.

"Why not?"

"For one thing in a normal pregnancy the cervix becomes discolored. But not necessarily in an ectopic."

"During this bimanual examination, would the physician be able to *feel* the presence of an ectopic?"

"Sometimes, but not always," Ward said.

" 'Sometimes,' Doctor?" Scott challenged. "Let me read to you from another acknowledged work on the subject. I quote: 'The findings on physical examination are frequently unremarkable or equivocal. There may or may not be pelvic or abdominal tenderness and' " — here Scott added emphasis as he continued — " *'in fifty to seventy-five percent of cases no definite adnexal or ovarian mass will be felt.'* Do you agree, Doctor?"

"Yes," Ward granted.

"So, Doctor, is it fair to say that there was no negligence on Dr. Forrester's part in not detecting a mass on pelvic examination of Claudia Stuyvesant?"

"Yes, that is a fair statement," Ward conceded.

"Was there anything else that Dr. Forrester could have done in a situation where the signs and symptoms were what you called 'suggestive'?" Scott asked.

"A urine pregnancy test."

"Which she also did, and which came up negative," Scott reminded her.

Taking that as a rebuke, Ward stiffened into her pedagogical attitude as she lectured, "Mr. Van Cleve, aware of the failure rate of such tests, Dr. Forrester should have pursued her suspicions and ordered a sonogram," Ward said, and to head off Scott's reply, she added, "which we now know was not available at the time."

"Exactly, Doctor," Scott agreed.

"However, there is always a blood serum pregnancy test available," Ward pointed out.

"Are you aware that Dr. Forrester *did* order such a test?"

"No, I am not." Ward was surprised. "What was the result?"

"We will never know. The results of that test, which were due the next day, have been lost in some unexplained way and do not appear in the patient's chart. Nor was that the only result missing. But let us continue, Doctor. I would now like to read to you from another highly regarded textbook on obstetrics and gynecology. I quote: 'Its frequently vague signs and symptoms plus the variety of other diseases it mimics, such as abdominal and pelvic diseases, makes ectopic pregnancy a puzzling diagnostic challenge.' "

For an instant Ward appeared visibly outraged, but she contained herself as Scott continued:

"The quote goes on, 'In fact we might well call tubal pregnancy "the disease of surprises." It has also been named by many clinicians "the great masquerade." ' Doctor, would you agree with those statements?"

Ward stared at Scott but did not respond beyond a slight superior smile that slowly emerged on her up-to-now stern face.

"Doctor?" Scott urged.

"If you are seeking to trap me, Mr. Van Cleve, I'm afraid you have failed," Ward replied. "I not only agree with those statements, I wrote them. You are quoting from my own text on the subject."

"Yes, Doctor," Scott admitted. "Now that we have established the great difficulty in making a diagnosis of an ectopic pregnancy, may I ask if you recall the testimony of the first witness, Mrs. Nora Stuyvesant?"

"I believe I do," Ward answered.

"Then do you recall her saying that she asked Dr. Forrester to give her daughter an antibiotic?"

"Yes, I do remember that."

"At the time, Doctor, did you attach any special significance to that?"

"Not particularly," Ward said.

"Why not?" Scott continued to probe.

"Because in time of doubt it is the first thing laypeople always think of. They regard antibiotics as magic potions that can cure anything. Which results in their prevalent misuse," Ward declared.

"Doctor, returning once more to the many difficulties in diagnosing ectopic pregnancies, are there any other factors that might complicate such a situation even further?"

"There might be," Ward conceded.

"Can you name some?"

Since she was beginning to become uneasy with the direction in which Scott was leading the examination, Ward evaded it by saying, "I would prefer that your question was more specific."

"Let me try," Scott said. "Am I correct in assuming that you served your internship and residency in a hospital in a large city?"

"Yes," Ward granted, even more puzzled now.

"During your early experience as a resident, when on Emergency Service, did you ever have occasion to treat patients who were drug addicts?"

Flashes of concern passed between Mott and Hoskins, between Hoskins and Cahill, between Hoskins and Stuyvesant. The latter caused the prosecutor to rise and protest, "Mr. Mott, such testimony is not pertinent to this hearing. It ventures into speculative fields that have no relevance to this proceeding."

Scott wheeled on him. "Mr. Hoskins, before I am done, I will prove relevance even to the satisfaction of this committee!"

Hoskins invited a ruling from Cahill. But the young administrator was considering the possibilities that confronted him. Either Van Cleve was bluffing, in which case he would destroy himself in the end. Or Van Cleve had by some means secured new and highly important evidence. If he had, Cahill could not risk appearing too arbitrary or too obvious in his motives.

"We will allow Mr. Van Cleve to continue, but only subject to connection," Cahill ruled.

Enraged, Hoskins had no choice but to slip back into his seat, ready to protest again if given a pretext.

Scott continued: "Dr. Ward, may I repeat, did you ever treat drug-addicted patients during your Emergency service?"

"Every doctor has," Ward replied. "I have even delivered babies from drug-addicted mothers. Seen some who died at birth. And others who I wished had died."

"Then the effects of drug taking on the part of a patient can have serious consequences and complications?"

"Of course."

"Have you ever detected or known of patients to take such drugs while they were *in* the hospital?" Scott asked.

"I have also seen such cases," Ward conceded.

"Doctor, if a patient were a heavy user of drugs and were deprived of all drugs for as long as seven, eight, nine hours, might they suffer withdrawal symptoms?" Scott asked.

"That many hours without a fix would be a long stretch for a real druggie," Ward replied.

"When you add to that a situation in which a patient was suffering heavy internal hemorrhaging but was experiencing only slight pain and discomfort, what conclusions would you draw from that?"

"No withdrawal symptoms and slight pain when it should have been severe, after as much as eight or nine hours having elapsed?" Ward rephrased the question.

"Yes, Doctor, what would you conclude?" Scott pressed.

"That the patient, in some way, had access to drugs *during* those nine hours," Ward said.

"Now, Doctor, I direct you back to a previous question. Did you attach any special significance to Mrs. Stuyvesant's asking Dr. Forrester for an antibiotic?"

"No, I still do not attach any special —" Ward started to reply but then stopped, thought a moment, and started afresh, "Yes, Mr. Van Cleve. If the patient were experiencing even moderate pain, a concerned mother would usually ask, 'Please, Doctor, give her something for her pain.' "

"Proving that either the patient's pain was so slight that no painkiller was called for or else that the patient's mother knew that she had already taken something for her pain?" Scott asked.

Before Ward could respond, Hoskins was shouting, "Mr. Chairman! Mr. Chairman! There is no evidence in the record to support such a question. No evidence at all as to drug use by the victim!"

Mott sought Kevin Cahill's intervention. "It seems counsel is determined to get into the record material for which he has no proof."

"The question does have a familiar echo," Cahill taunted. "Mr. Van Cleve having failed in all previous attempts, it behooves this committee not to reward him for persistence alone. Without the introduction of substantial proof as a foundation, we absolutely cannot allow such a question!"

Cahill felt sure that Claude Stuyvesant would remember that ruling with considerable gratitude.

Before Mott could bring down his gavel to close off any further discussion of the subject, Scott protested, "Mr. Chairman, since Dr. Ward has been qualified as an expert, she is permitted to answer hypothetical questions. And *I* am entitled to ask them."

"Provided," Hoskins was quick to point out, "that if counsel cannot provide a factual foundation for his questions, the entire line of testimony is thrown out!"

"Of course," Scott agreed.

On a permissive head signal from Hoskins, Mott ruled, "You may proceed, Mr. Van Cleve."

"Dr. Ward," Scott resumed, "suppose a patient had been on high doses of such drugs as Percodan, codeine, benzodiazapine, and possibly cocaine as well . . ."

"All taken concurrently within a relatively short time span?" Ward asked, betraying considerable concern.

"For the purpose of this question, yes,"

Scott confirmed.

Hoskins could not restrain himself from blurting out, "Now counsel is piling hypothesis upon hypothesis!"

But Scott perservered, "Dr. Ward, could the synergistic effect of such drugs, taken in combination, and some taken during the crucial last nine hours of a patient's life, have been sufficient to mask the pain of an ectopic pregnancy no matter how severe it would otherwise have been?"

Ward took a moment to recount, "Percodan, codeine, benzodiazapine, along with cocaine . . . there is no doubt that acting together, each heightening the effect of the others, they could easily have concealed such pain from the physician."

"Thank you, Doctor," Scott said.

As if weary and bored, Hoskins rose to his feet once more. "Mr. Chairman, now that eminent counsel has introduced his fanciful version of what might have happened but has not produced a scintilla of proof, I demand that, as agreed, this entire line of spurious questioning be thrown out!"

"Mr. Van Cleve?" Mott added his demand to that of Hoskins.

Without replying, Scott moved back to his counsel table, where Kate was ready with a sheaf of printouts. He turned back to Dr.

Ward to ask, "Doctor, would you be good enough to examine these printouts? Especially the last page containing the most recent entries?"

As the document changed hands, Hoskins objected, "I have a right to see that!"

"As soon as Dr. Ward is done with it," Scott replied.

Ward needed only a few moments to study the last page. After which, with a distressed, "Good God, no wonder . . ." she handed them back to Scott.

"Mr. Chairman, I offer into evidence this report from the state Board of Health!"

"I insist on seeing that document first!" Hoskins demanded.

"By all means, Mr. Hoskins." Scott held it out to him.

Hoskins snatched it, impatiently began to scan it. Until he slowly raised his eyes to stare at Mott, then at Cahill. Both men converged on him. Together all three studied the report of Claudia Stuyvesant's drug history.

Claude Stuyvesant started forward to join them, when his wife called out, "Claude, no!"

He dismissed his wife's outcry with a single angry, reproachful look. He reached Hoskins, Mott, and Cahill, held out his hand, asking for the document. When Hoskins hesitated, Stuyvesant insisted, "Let me see that!"

As gently as he could, Hoskins said, "Mrs. Stuyvesant is right. You don't want to see this."

Stuyvesant's open extended hand demanded the document. Hoskins had no choice but to surrender it. Stuyvesant examined it long enough for the loathsome facts to burn into his mind. The names of more than a dozen doctors. The designations of drugs, most of which he had never even heard of. Slowly, vaguely he handed the document back to anyone who would take it. He started back to his wife, who rose to comfort him.

Instead of permitting her, he said accusingly, "That night too? You saw her do it that night?"

"Yes. Even that night. So now you can stop pretending."

Ordinarily his fierce glare would have been enough to silence her. But for the first time in many years Nora Stuyvesant found the strength and the daring to defy him.

"Yes, stop denying it to the world. Because you knew too. You've always known. But instead of trying to help her, you drove her away."

"*She* left *us*," Stuyvesant protested.

"So you'd like the world to believe. Else it would mean that you had failed as a father. And Claude Stuyvesant never fails at anything.

The truth is, you were glad to be free of her. Because she was never the perfect child you always wanted. The perfect son."

"Nora! Be still!" he commanded.

This one time he could not silence her.

"You never wanted Claudia. You wanted Claude. So you shut her out. Set her adrift. You made her what she became. Once you realized that, you had to hide your ugly truth. So you blamed me. You blamed Dr. Forrester. Schemed to destroy records, to prevent testimony. Except, of course, for my carefully rehearsed testimony!"

"Damn it, Nora! Be still!"

"So the world will never know what Claude Stuyvesant has done to his only child? Well, Claudia was my child too. My daughter. And I loved her. Nights now I cry for being too weak to protect her from you. Claudie . . . Claudie . . . I did love you."

Stuyvesant's usual ruddy face, which had always been so strong, seemed ashen gray and aged. With all eyes in the room fixed on him, he stood as if stripped naked, his tyranny over his family exposed, his hostility toward Kate Forrester revealed as a shield for his own guilt.

As she watched him, mute and powerless before his wife's accusations, Kate could feel only pity for him. But even more, she felt great sorrow for Nora Stuyvesant, who had been an unwitting accomplice in her daughter's death.

Without a word Stuyvesant started for the door. His wife hurried after him, calling, "Claude . . . Claude . . . wait for me!" He did not stop to acknowledge her plea. As if to apologize for her abrupt departure, just before she slipped out of the room, she called back to them, "He'll need me . . . now, he'll need me. . . ."

And she was gone.

Once the door had closed, Mott, at a loss for words, weakly gestured Scott Van Cleve to continue.

In a subdued manner and voice, Scott asked, "Dr. Ward, considering the unusual difficulty in diagnosing an ectopic pregnancy, compounded by the patient's untruthful responses and a faulty test result, plus pain unnaturally suppressed by heavy drug usage, would you say that Dr. Forrester's treatment of Claudia Stuyvesant was in keeping with good medical practice?"

"With all the evidence now available, I would have to say her actions that night were professionally sound and beyond reproach," Ward agreed.

"And as to the charges brought against her?" Scott asked.

"I vote to exonerate her of all charges,"

Ward announced.

Hoskins protested, "A member cannot announce her vote even before the summations!"

"Highly improper," Cahill confirmed.

Though he had been quiet and reserved throughout the proceedings, Dr. Maurice Truscott now spoke up. "After hearing Dr. Ward's testimony, and she's tops in her field, I don't need to hear any summations. I say we've had too damned much legal maneuvering and too little medicine up to now. I, too, vote to dismiss all charges!"

Freed from the overbearing presence of Claude Stuyvesant, Hoskins and Cahill agreed that whatever the formalities might demand, summations now would be meaningless. The votes of Dr. Ward and Dr. Truscott would be recorded as they appeared in the stenotypist's notes. Chairman Mott was free to cast his vote by voice as well. After some moments of embarrassment he cast it in favor of vindicating Kate.

Then, with one final, sharp blow of his gavel, he officially brought to a close the hearing *In The Matter of Katherine Forrester, M.D.*

In great relief Kate exhaled slowly. Until this moment she had not been aware of how persistent had been the tense knot in her stomach for what seemed endless days. Gradually her pain began to resolve. She sat, head resting on the counsel table, now more exhausted than she had heretofore allowed herself to feel. She did not see Dr. Gladys Ward approach.

"Forrester," Ward said crisply, "you probably think me quite arbitrary and severe. But in my eyes when any woman physician fails, she brings disgrace upon all her sisters in the profession. We must prove ourselves better than any man before they will finally accept us as good enough. Having been through the fire, you measure up now. So, should you decide to specialize in female oncology, come see me!"

Brisk, professional, as was her habit, Dr. Gladys Ward strode from the room.

Hoskins approached Kate and Scott to inform them, "The vote of this committee will be transmitted to the state commissioner of health. Then through channels to the Board of Regents, which makes the final decision. But with the record of today's hearing I do not think you have anything more to fear."

"About City Hospital . . ." Kate started to ask.

"I will be in touch with Dr. Cummins within the hour. Your reinstatement to full active status should be automatic."

As Kate helped Scott gather up all his papers, she remarked, "At least we know what happened to that missing hospital tox report."

"And why the medical examiner never did one. The S-factor," Scott replied. "You realize, don't you?"

"Realize? What?" Kate asked.

"Considering the public charges he made against you, with what we know now, we have grounds for a very strong libel suit against Stuyvesant," Scott pointed out.

"No, thanks. I've had enough of the law. Too much. I just want to get on with my career and my life," Kate replied.

Kate Forrester and Scott Van Cleve came out of the claustrophobic confines of the state board office to find themselves assailed by the sounds and odors of Fortieth Street and its noisy, smelly, bumper-to-bumper traffic inching east toward Madison Avenue.

Kate looked up at what scarce patches of blue sky she could see between the towering buildings.

"In spite of the noise and the gas fumes I've never seen a brighter day! This feels like Thanksgiving, Christmas, and graduation from medical school rolled into one. It's like starting life all over again. I don't know how to thank you, Scott."

"One way is not to call me Scott."

"You mean, after all we've been through,

we're back to Dr. Forrester and Mr. Van Cleve?" Kate asked.

"I mean, people who are an important part of my life call me Van."

Kate tried it out cautiously, "Van . . . Van . . . that's not bad."

"The more you use it, the better it sounds."

She smiled up at him, fully aware of his meaning. "I've got to share my great news! There's one call I must make."

"Walter?" he asked.

"Home. Mom. Dad," Kate explained.

"Of course," Scott said with considerable relief. Then asked, "About this Walter —"

"Yes, Van?"

"I wondered . . . do you have any plans? I mean . . ."

"I know what you mean. That night when Walter called, I had refused to see him weeks before. So, no, I have no plans," Kate said frankly. She knew what he was asking. He knew what she was replying. "Look," she said, "I've got to get home and make that call." She started for a cab that was just discharging its passengers.

He called after her, "Dinner?"

"Okay," she called back.

"Tonight?"

Just before she pulled the cab door closed, she called back, "Tonight!"

Kate burst into the apartment calling, "Rosie, Rosie!" There was no reply. She remembered, Rosie was due to go on Clinic duty this week. Kate went to the phone, punched in the number. She waited impatiently for the time it took to ring through.

"Hello?" she heard her mother say.

"Mama, it's okay, it's okay!" Kate fairly shouted into the phone. "Everything turned out fine. Just fine!"

"Oh, baby, I'm so glad, so glad." Her mother began to weep in relief and celebration.

"Dad there?" Kate asked.

"I'll put him on," her mother said, calling through her tears, "Ben! Ben! It's Kate. With wonderful news!"

She heard her father clear his throat before he said, "Katie, that true, what Mother said?"

"True, Dad. Vindicated. Unanimous!" Kate was proud to announce.

"Good, darlin', good," her father said. "So that young lawyer worked out all right, did he?"

"Better than all right," Kate said.

"Well, you tell him thanks for us."

"You may get the chance to do that yourself one day soon," Kate said. "Now I've got to call the hospital and get my new assignment."

"You do that, sweetheart. Meantime I've got a call or two to make myself. Lot of folks around here'll want to know."

She hung up the phone. She called the hospital. Before asking for Administrator Cummins's office, she asked for the Pediatric Ward. Fortunately Harve Golding was on duty.

"Harve?" Kate asked.

"Kate!" he greeted her enthusiastically. "The word's already out. Congratulations! Terrific! The whole staff is elated."

"How's my little Maria?" Kate asked.

"After all the tests, physical, radiological, neurological, we held a group consult yesterday. It will be a long, slow process, but she is going to be okay."

"No residual damage?" Kate asked.

"None," Golding replied. "Well, maybe just one."

"What's that?" Kate asked with considerable alarm.

"Ever since that damned hearing started, she's been asking for you. She's afraid you've deserted her."

"I'll be there, Harve. I'll be there!" Kate promised. "I'll stop by on my way to dinner."

The employees of THORNDIKE PRESS hope you have enjoyed this Large Print book. All our Large Print titles are designed for easy reading, and all our books are made to last. Other Thorndike Large Print books are available at your library, through selected bookstores, or directly from us. For more information about current and upcoming titles, please call or mail your name and address to:

THORNDIKE PRESS
PO Box 159
Thorndike, Maine 04986
800/223-6121
207/948-2962